Michelle Smart's love of books was encouraged when she was a baby, when she would cuddle them in her cot. A voracious reader of all genres, she found her love of romance established when she stumbled across her first Mills & Boon book at the age of twelve. She's been reading (and writing) them ever since. Michelle lives in Northamptonshire with her husband and two young Smarties.

The Kalliakis Crown

MICHELLE SMART

MILLS & BOON

First Published in Great Britain 2018
by Mills & Boon, an imprint of HarperCollins*Publishers*
1 London Bridge Street, London, SE1 9GF

THE KALLIAKIS CROWN © 2018 Harlequin Books S. A.

Talos Claims His Virgin © 2015 Michelle Smart
Theseus Discovers His Heir © 2016 Michelle Smart
Helios Crowns His Mistress © 2016 Michelle Smart

ISBN: 978-0-263-27455-4

0918

MIX
Paper from
responsible sources
FSC™ C007454

This book is produced from independently certified FSC™
paper to ensure responsible forest management.

For more information visit: www.harpercollins.co.uk/green

Printed and bound in Spain
by CPI, Barcelona

TALOS CLAIMS
HIS VIRGIN

MICHELLE SMART

This book is dedicated to Amalie,
who's been on this journey with
me every step of the way. xxx

CHAPTER ONE

TALOS KALLIAKIS DIPPED his head and rubbed the nape of his neck. The consultant's words had cut through to his marrow.

Looking back up to stare at his two brothers, he read the sorrow on their faces.

Astraeus Kalliakis—the King of Agon, their grandfather—was dying.

Helios, the eldest of the three brothers and heir to the throne, folded his arms and took a visible deep breath before breaking the silence. 'We need to bring the Jubilee celebrations forward.'

The whole of Agon was gearing up to celebrate Astraeus's fifty years on the throne. Everything was planned for the end of summer, six months away. The consultant oncologist had said in no uncertain terms he wouldn't last that long.

Talos cleared his throat before speaking. His vocal cords had never felt so raw. 'I suggest we concentrate on the Jubilee Gala and cancel the rest of the celebrations—they're all superfluous. Let's make the gala a true celebration of his life.'

'Agreed,' said Theseus, the middle brother, nodding. 'We should set the date for April—three months from now. It will be a push, but between us and the courtiers we can do it and do it well.'

Any later and there was every possibility their grandfather would not be there for it. Two months of intense chemotherapy would buy him time and shrink the tumours riddling his organs. But they would not cure him. It was too late for that.

Two months later

Talos Kalliakis headed through the back of the theatre that housed the Orchestre National de Paris, noting the faded, peeling wallpaper, the threadbare carpet that had to be older than his thirty-three years, the water-stained ceiling... No wonder the building was on the verge of being condemned. Of all the orchestral homes he'd visited in the past two months, the facilities here were by far the worst.

But he wasn't here for the facilities. He'd come here on a whim, when he'd been left disappointed by the violinists from all of France's other major orchestras, as he'd been left underwhelmed by those from the major orchestras of Greece, Italy, Spain and England.

Time was running out.

What he had assumed would be a simple task had turned into a marathon of endurance.

All he wanted to find was that one special musician, someone who could stroke a bow over the bridge of their violin and make his heart soar the way his grandmother had when she'd been alive. He would never claim to have a musical ear, but he was certain that when he heard it he would know.

The chosen violinist would be rewarded with the honour of playing his grandmother's final composition, accompanied by his or her own orchestra, at his grandfather's Jubilee Gala.

At that moment approximately a dozen Orchestre National de Paris violinists were lining up, ready to audition for him.

He just wanted it to be over.

The weak, impatient part of himself told him to settle

on *anyone*. Everyone who had auditioned for him thus far had been professional, note-perfect, the sounds coming from their wooden instruments a delight to anyone's ear. But they hadn't been a delight to his heart, and for once in his life he knew he had to select the right person based on his heart, not his head.

For his grandfather's Jubilee Gala he wouldn't— couldn't—accept anything or anyone but the best. His grandfather deserved no less. His grandmother's memory deserved no less.

Flanked by the orchestra directors, an assistant and his own translator, they turned single file down a particularly narrow corridor. It was like being in an indoor, dank version of the glorious maze in the Agon palace gardens.

The violinists were lined up backstage; the rest of the musicians sat in the auditorium. He would already be seated at the front of the auditorium himself if roadworks hadn't forced his driver to detour to the back of the theatre rather than drop him at the front.

His mind filled with the dozen other things he needed to be getting on with that he'd had to let slip these past two months. A qualified lawyer, he oversaw all sales, mergers and buyouts with regard to the business empire he'd forged with his two brothers. He didn't *always* use his legal skills to get his own way.

Theseus, the middle Kalliakis brother, had identified an internet start-up seeking investment. If projections were correct, they would quadruple their investment in less than two months. Talos, though, had suspicions about the owners...

His thoughts about unscrupulous techies were cut away when a faint sound drifted out of a door to his left.

He paused, raising a hand in a request for silence.

His ears strained and he rested his head against the door.

There it was.

The only piece of classical music he knew by name.

A lump formed in his throat—a lump that grew with each passing beat.

Wanting to hear more clearly, but not wanting to disturb the violinist, he turned the handle carefully and pressed the door open.

An inch was enough to bring the solemn yet haunting music to life.

His chest filled, bittersweet memories engulfing him.

He'd been seven years old when his parents had died. The nights that had followed, before his brothers had been flown back from their English boarding school—he'd been only a year away from joining them there—had left him inconsolable.

Queen Rhea Kalliakis, the grandmother he'd adored, had soothed him the only way she knew how. She'd come into his room, sat on the edge of his bed and played the 'Méditation' from Jules Massenet's *Thaïs*.

He hadn't thought about this particular piece of music for over twenty-five years.

The tempo was different from the way his grandmother had played it, slower, but the effect was the same. Painful and yet soothing, like balm on a wound, seeping through his skin to heal him from the inside out.

This one had it—the special, elusive *it*.

'That is the one,' he said, addressing the orchestra directors collectively. His translator made the translation in French for them.

The sharp-faced woman to his left looked at him with a searching expression, as if judging whether he was serious, until her eyes lit up and, in her excitement, she flung the door open.

There, in the corner of the room, her violin still under her chin but her bow flailing in her right hand, stood a tall, lithe girl—woman. She had the distinct look of a rabbit caught in the headlights of a speeding car.

* * *

It was those eyes.

She had never seen anything like them before, nor such intensity.

The way they had fixed on her... Like lasers. Trapping her.

Amalie shivered to think of them.

She shivered again when she stepped out of the theatre exit and into the slushy car park. Keeping a firm grip on her violin case—she really needed to get the strap fixed—she tugged her red-and-grey striped beanie hat over her ears.

A long black car with darkened windows entered the car park and crunched its way through the snow to pull up beside her.

The back door opened and a giant got out.

It took a beat before her brain comprehended that it wasn't a giant but Talos Kalliakis.

Intense, striking eyes—were they brown?—fixed on her for the second time in an hour. The effect was as terrifying and giddying the second time around. More so.

When the door of the practice room had swung open and she'd seen all those faces staring at her she'd wanted to shrink into a corner. She hadn't signed up for the audition, but had been told to attend in case the orchestra as a whole was needed. She'd happily hidden away from the action in the room behind the auditorium; there, but not actually present.

Those eyes...

They had rested on her for so long she'd felt as if she'd been stuck in a time capsule. Then they had moved from her face and, without a *bonjour* or *au revoir*, he'd disappeared.

There hadn't been time for her to appreciate the sheer size of the man.

She was tall for a woman—five foot eight. But Talos

towered over her, a mass of height and muscle that not even his winter attire could hide.

Her mouth ran dry.

He wore his thick ebony hair slightly too long, messy at the front and curling over the collar of his long black trench coat. Dark stubble, also thick, abounded over his square jawline.

Despite the expensive cut of his clothing, right down to what were clearly handmade shoes, he had a feral air about him, as if he should be swinging through vines in a jungle whilst simultaneously banging his chest.

He looked dangerous. Wildly dangerous. The scar on his right eyebrow, which seemed to divide it into two, only added to this sense.

He also looked full of purpose.

He took the few steps towards her with long strides, an outstretched hand and an unsmiling face. 'Amalie Cartwright, it is a pleasure to meet you,' he said in perfect English.

How did he know she was bilingual?

God but the man was *enormous*. He had to be a good six and a half feet. Easily.

Swallowing frantically to moisten her mouth, Amalie switched her violin case to her left hand and extended her right to him. It was immediately engulfed in his strong, darkly bronzed hand. It was like being consumed by a giant paw. Even through the wool of her gloves she could feel the heat from his uncovered hand.

'Monsieur Kalliakis,' she murmured in response.

She tugged her hand free and hugged it around her violin case.

'I require your attention. Please, get in the car,' he said.

I require your attention? If she hadn't been so unsettled by him and the deepness of his voice—a low bass both throaty and rich that matched his appearance perfectly—she would have been tempted to laugh at his formality.

With a start she remembered he was a prince. Royalty. Should she curtsey or something? He'd disappeared from the practice room before they could be formally introduced.

She cleared her throat and took a tiny step back. 'My apologies, *monsieur*, but I don't believe there is anything for us to discuss.'

'I assure you there is. Get in the car. It is too cold to have this discussion out here.'

He spoke as only a man used to throwing his weight around could.

'Is this about the solo? I did explain to your assistant earlier that I have a prior engagement for the gala weekend and won't be able to attend. My apologies if the message never reached you.'

The assistant, a middle-aged man with an air of implacability about him, had been unable to hide his shock when she'd said she couldn't do it. The orchestra directors had simply stared at her with pleading eyes.

'The message did reach me—which is why I turned back from the airport and returned here, so I could discuss the matter with you directly.'

His displeasure was obvious, as if it were *her* fault his plans had been ruined.

'You will need to cancel your engagement. I wish for you to play at my grandfather's gala.'

'I wish I could as well,' she lied. A lifetime of dealing with forceful personalities had prepared her well for this moment. No personality came more forceful than her mother's. 'But, no. It is not something I can get out of.'

His brow furrowed in the manner of someone who had never had the word *no* uttered within his earshot. 'You *do* realise who my grandfather is and what a huge opportunity this is for your career?'

'Yes, he is the King of Agon—and I do understand what a great honour it is to be selected to play for him—'

'*And* the majority of the world's great statesmen who will be there—'

'But there are many other violinists in this orchestra,' she continued, speaking over him as if he had not just interrupted. 'If you audition them, as you had planned, you will find most are far more talented than me.'

Of *course* she knew what a huge event the gala was going to be. Her fellow musicians had spoken about little else for weeks. Every orchestra in Europe had been alerted to the fact that Prince Talos Kalliakis was searching for a solo violinist. When it had been confirmed yesterday that he was coming to audition the violinists at the Orchestre National de Paris there had been an immediate mass exodus as every female musician in the orchestra had headed to Paris's beauty parlours for highlights and waxing and all other manner of preening.

The three Princes of Agon were considered Europe's most eligible bachelors. *And* the most handsome.

Amalie had known she wouldn't audition, so hadn't bothered to join the exodus.

If she'd known for a second that Talos had been listening at the door to her practice she would have hit as many bum notes as she could without sounding like a screeching cat.

There was no way—*no way in the world*—she could stand on the stage at the Jubilee Gala and play for the world. No way. She couldn't. The mere thought of it was enough to bring her out in a cold sweat.

The chill of the wind was picking up. She scrunched her toes inside her cold boots, which were getting wetter by the second as the icy snow seeped through the tiny seams and spread to her socks. The back of Talos's car looked very snug and warm. Not that she would find out for herself. The chill in his eyes perfectly matched the weather whipping around them.

'Excuse me, *monsieur*, but I need to go home. We have

a concert tonight and I have to be back here in a few hours. Good luck finding your soloist.'

The hardness of his features softened by the slightest of margins, but his eyes—she'd been right, they *were* brown: a light, almost transparent brown, with the blackest of rims— remained hard.

'We will talk again on Monday, *despinis*. Until then I suggest you think hard about what you are giving up by refusing to take the solo.'

'Monday is our day off. I will be in on Tuesday, if you wish to speak to me then, but there will be nothing for us to talk about.'

He inclined his head. 'We shall see. Oh—and when we next meet you may address me by my formal title: Your Highness.'

This time her lips tugged into a smile—one she had no control over. 'But, *monsieur*, this is France. A republic. Even when we had a royal family, male heirs to the throne were addressed by the title of "Monsieur", so I am address-ing you correctly. And I feel I should remind you of what happened to those who boasted of having royal blood— they had their heads chopped off.'

Amalie took her seat on the stage, in the second row from the back, nicely encased amongst the orchestra's other sec-ond violins. Exactly where she liked to be. Hidden from the spotlight.

While she waited for Sebastien Cassel, their guest con-ductor, to make his indication for them to start she felt a prickling on her skin.

Casting her eyes out into the auditorium, she saw the projected ticket sales had been correct. She doubted they were even at half capacity.

How much longer could this go on?

Paris was a city of culture. It had accommodated and celebrated its orchestras for centuries. But the other orchestras weren't housed in a flea pit like the Théâtre de la Musique; a glorified music hall. Once, it had been full of pomp and glory. Years of neglect and underinvestment had left it teetering perilously, almost into the red.

A large figure in the stalls to her right, in the most expensive seats in the house, made her blink and look twice. Even as she squinted to focus more clearly the thumping of her heart told her who the figure was and explained the prickling sensation on her skin.

Immediately her thoughts flickered to Prince Talos. There was something about that man and the danger he exuded that made her want to run faster than if a thousand spotlights had been aimed at her. His breathtaking physical power, that gorgeous face with the scar slashing through the eyebrow, the voice that had made her blood thicken into treacle…

Juliette, the violinist she sat next to, dug a sharp elbow into her side.

Sebastien was peering at them, his baton raised.

Amalie forced her eyes to the score before her and positioned herself, praying for her fingers to work.

Being at the back of the eighty-strong number of musicians usually made her feel invisible—just another head in the crowd, with the spotlight well and truly away from her. She couldn't bear having the spotlight pointed at her, had actively avoided it since the age of twelve. More than that: she had cowered from it.

She couldn't see him clearly—indeed, she didn't even know for certain that it *was* him sitting in the stalls—but she couldn't shake the feeling that someone in the audience had their eyes fixed firmly on *her*.

Talos watched the evening unfold. The orchestra was a professional unit and played with a panache even the most musically illiterate could appreciate.

But he wasn't there to listen.

Once the concert had finished he had a meeting with the owner of this ramshackle building.

He'd originally planned to take his jet back to Agon and visit his grandfather, relieved that his two-month search for a violinist was over. Amalie Cartwright's belligerence had put paid to that.

Looking at her now, the fingers of her left hand flying over the strings of her violin, he could not believe her rudeness. Her thin, pretty face, with a sprinkling of freckles over the bridge of her straight nose, gave the illusion of someone dainty, fragile, an image compounded by a form so slender one could be forgiven for worrying about her being blown over in a breeze. She had the elegance so many Parisian women came by with seemingly no effort. He'd seen that earlier, even when her rich brown hair had been hidden under the hat she'd worn to keep the chill in the air at bay.

But looks could be deceiving.

She'd dismissed performing the solo at his grandfather's gala and, by extension, had insulted the Kalliakis name. And her jibe about the French royal family having their heads removed had been a step too far.

Amalie Cartwright *would* take the solo. He would make sure of it.

And what Talos Kalliakis wanted, he got. Always.

CHAPTER TWO

AMALIE BURIED HER HEAD under the pillow and ignored the ringing of her doorbell. She wasn't expecting any visitors or a delivery. Her French mother wouldn't dream of turning up unannounced so early in the morning—anything earlier than midday she considered to be the middle of the night—and her English father was on tour in South America. Whoever it was could come back another time.

Whoever it was clearly had no intention of coming back another time.

The ringing continued, now accompanied by the banging of fists.

Cursing in English and French, she scrambled out of bed, shrugged a thick robe over her pyjama-clad body and, still cursing, hurried down the stairs to open the front door.

'Good morning, *despinis*.'

And with those words Talos Kalliakis brushed past her and entered her home.

'What the…? Excuse me—you can't just let yourself in,' she said, rushing after him while he swept through her narrow house as if he owned it.

'I told you I would be speaking with you today.'

His tone was neutral, as if he were oblivious to her natural shock and anger.

'And I told *you* this is my day off. I would like you to leave.'

He stepped into the kitchen. 'After we have spoken.'

To reiterate his point he set his briefcase on the floor, removed his long black trench coat, which he placed on the back of a chair at her small kitchen table, and sat himself down.

'What are you doing? I didn't invite you in—if you want to speak to me you will have to wait until tomorrow.'

He waved a dismissive hand. 'I will take ten minutes of your time and then I will leave. What we need to discuss will not take long.'

Amalie bit into her cheek and forced her mind to calm. Panicked thinking would not help. 'This is my home and you are trespassing. Leave now or I will call the police.'

He didn't need to know that her mobile phone was currently atop her bedside table.

'Call them.' He shrugged his huge shoulders, the linen of his black shirt rippling with the movement. 'By the time they get here we will have concluded our conversation.'

She eyed him warily, afraid to blink, and rubbed her hands up her arms, backing away, trapping herself against the wall. What could she use as a weapon?

This man was a stranger and the most physically imposing man she had met in her life. The scar that slashed through his eyebrow only compounded the danger he oozed. If he were to...

She wouldn't be able to defend herself using her own strength. It would be like a field mouse fighting a panther.

His top lip curved with distaste. 'You have no need to worry for your safety—I am not an animal. I am here to talk, not to assault you.'

Would the panther *tell* the field mouse he intended to eat her? Of course not. He would insist it was the last thing on his mind and then, when the little field mouse got close enough...*snap!*

Staring into his striking eyes, she saw that, although cold, they contained no threat. A tiny fraction of her fear vanished.

This man would not harm her. Not physically, at any rate.

She dropped her gaze and rubbed her eyes, which had become sore from all that non-blinking.

'Okay. Ten minutes. But you should have called first. You didn't have to barge your way into my home when I was still sleeping.'

An awareness crept through her bones. While he was freshly showered, shaved—minimal stubble today—and dressed, *she* was in old cotton pyjamas and a dressing gown, and suffering from a severe case of bed hair. Talk about putting her at an immediate disadvantage.

He looked at his watch. 'It is ten a.m. A reasonable time to call on someone on a Monday morning.'

To her utter mortification, she could feel her skin heat. It might not be his problem that she'd had hardly any sleep, but it was certainly his fault.

No matter how hard she'd tried to block him from her mind, every time she'd closed her eyes his face had swum into her vision. Two nights of his arrogant face—there, right behind her eyelids. His arrogant, *handsome* face. Shockingly, devilishly handsome.

'This is my day off, *monsieur*. How I choose to spend it is my business.' Her mouth had run so dry her words came out as a croak. 'I need a coffee.'

'I take mine black.'

She didn't answer, just stepped to the other side of the kitchen and pressed the button on the coffee machine she had set before she went to bed. It kicked into action.

'Have you thought any more about the solo?' he asked as she removed two mugs from the mug tree.

'I told you—there's nothing for me to think about. I'm busy that weekend.' She heaped a spoonful of sugar into one of the mugs.

'I was afraid that would be your answer.'

His tone was akin to a teacher disappointed with his star pupil's exam results. Something about his tone made the hairs on her arms rise in warning.

Water started to drip through the filter and into the pot, drip by hot drip, the aroma of fresh coffee filling the air.

'I am going to appeal to your better nature,' Talos said, staring at Amalie, whose attention was still held by the slowly falling coffee.

She turned her head a touch. 'Oh?'

'My grandmother was a composer and musician.'

A short pause. 'Rhea Kalliakis…'

'You have heard of her?'

'I doubt there's a violinist alive who hasn't. She composed the most beautiful pieces.'

A sharp pang ran through him to know that this woman appreciated his grandmother's talents. Amalie couldn't know it, but her simple appreciation only served to harden his resolve that she was the perfect musician for the role. She was the *only* musician.

'She completed her final composition two days before her death.'

She turned from the coffee pot to face him.

Amalie Cartwright had the most beautiful almond-shaped eyes, he noted, not for the first time. The colour reminded him of the green sapphire ring his mother had worn.

That ring now lay in the Agon palace safe, where it had rested for the past twenty-six years, waiting for the day when Helios selected a suitable bride to take guardianship of it. After their grandfather's diagnosis, that day would be coming much sooner than Helios had wanted or expected. Helios needed to marry and produce an heir.

The last time Talos had seen the ring his mother had been fighting off his father. Two hours later the pair of them had been dead.

He cast his mind away from that cataclysmic night and back to the present. Back to Amalie Cartwright—the one person who could do justice to Rhea Kalliakis's final

composition and with it, bring comfort to a dying man.
A dying *king*.

'Is that the piece you wish to have played at your grand-father's gala?'

'Yes. In the five years since her death we have kept the score secure and allowed no one to play it. Now we—my brothers and I—believe it is the right time for the world to hear it. And at what better occasion than my grandfather's Jubilee Gala? I believe *you* are the person to play it.'

He deliberately made no mention of his grandfather's diagnosis. No news of his condition had been released to the public at large and nor would it be until after the gala—by decree from King Astraeus, his grandfather, himself.

Amalie poured the freshly brewed coffee into the mugs, added milk to her own, then brought them to the table and took the seat opposite him.

'I think it is a wonderful thing you are doing,' she said, speaking in measured tones. 'There isn't another violin-ist alive who wouldn't be honoured to be called upon to do it. But I am sorry, *monsieur*, that person cannot be me.'

'Why not?'

'I told you. I have a prior engagement.'

He fixed her with his stare. 'I will double the appear-ance fee. Twenty thousand euros.'

'No.'

'Fifty thousand. And that's my final offer.'

'No.'

Talos knew his stare could be intimidating, more so than his sheer physicality. He'd performed this stare numerous times in front of a mirror, looking to see what it was that others saw, but had never recognised what it might be. Whatever it was, one throw of that look was enough to en-sure he got his own way. The only people immune to it were his brothers and grandparents. Indeed, whenever his grand-mother had seen him 'pull that face', as she had referred to it, she'd clipped his ear—but only hard enough to sting.

He missed her every day.

But apart from those members of his family he had never met anyone immune to his stare. Until now.

From Amalie there was not so much as a flicker, just a shake of her head and her long hair, which was in dire need of a good brush, falling into her eyes. She swiped it away.

Talos sighed, shook his head regretfully and rubbed his chin, making a great show of disappointment.

Amalie cradled her mug and took a sip of the hot coffee, willing her nerves to stay hidden from his piercing gaze.

All her life she'd had to deal with huge personalities and even huger egos. It had taught her the importance of keeping her emotions tucked away. If the enemy—and at that very moment Talos *was* an enemy to her, she could feel it—detected any weakness then they would pounce. Never make it easy for them. Never give them the advantage.

She had never found it so hard to remain passive. *Never.* Not since she'd been twelve and the nerves she'd fought so hard to contain had taken control of her. The fear and humiliation she'd experienced on that occasion felt as strong today as they had then.

But there was something about this man that *did* things to her; to her mind, to her senses. Inside her belly, a cauldron bubbled.

Talos reached for his briefcase, and for one tiny moment she thought she had won and that he would leave. Except then he placed it on the table and opened it.

'I have tried appealing to your better nature. I have tried appealing to your greed. I have given you numerous chances to accept the easy way...' He removed a sheaf of papers and held them up for her to see. 'These are the deeds to the Théâtre de la Musique. You are welcome to read through them. You will see they confirm me as the new owner.'

Stunned into silence, all Amalie could do was shake her head.

'Would you like to read them?'

She continued shaking her head, staring from the documents in his hand to his unsmiling face.

'How is it possible?' she whispered, trying to comprehend what this could mean—for her, for the orchestra...

'I put my offer in on Saturday evening. The purchase was completed an hour ago.'

'But how is this possible?' she repeated. 'This is *France*. The home of bureaucracy and red tape.'

'Money and power talk.'

He placed the deeds back in his briefcase and leaned forward, bringing his face to within inches of hers. Any closer and she'd be able to feel his breath on her face. 'I am a prince. I have money—a lot of it—and I have power. A lot of it. You would be wise to remember that.'

Then he leant back in his chair and drank his coffee, all the while his laser eyes burned into her.

She squeezed her mug, suddenly terrified to lose her grip on it. The implications were forming an orderly queue in her brain.

'Now I am the owner of the theatre I am wondering what I will do with the building and the orchestra it houses. You see, the previous owner was so struck with greed at the amount I offered he made no stipulations for the sale...' He drained the last of his coffee and pushed his mug away so it rested against hers. 'Take the solo, *despinis*, and I will throw so much money at the theatre the crowds will come flocking back and your orchestra will be the toast of Paris. Refuse and I will turn it into a hotel.'

The jostling in her brain stopped. The implications came loud and clear, with clanging bells and ringing sirens.

'You're blackmailing me,' she said starkly. 'You're actually trying to *blackmail* me.'

He shrugged indifferently and pushed his chair back. 'Call it what you will.'

'I call it blackmail. And blackmail is illegal.'

'Tell it to the police.' He displayed his white teeth. 'However, before you call them I should advise you that I have diplomatic immunity.'

'That is *low*.'

'I can and will go even lower. You see, little songbird, I have the power to ensure you never play the violin professionally again. I can blacken your name, and the names of all those you play with, so that no orchestra—not even a provincial amateur one—would touch you.'

The bubbling cauldron moved from her belly to her head, her brain feeling as if it were boiling with poison. Never had she felt such hate towards another human.

'Get out of my house.'

'Worry not, little songbird, I am ready to leave now.' He looked at his watch. 'I will return in six hours. You can give me your considered answer then.'

Her *considered answer*?

He was threatening to destroy her career, and the careers of her friends and colleagues, and he wanted her *considered answer*?

The cauldron toppled, sending a surge of fire pulsing through her, bringing her to her feet and to his side. Even with him seated and Amalie on her feet the physical imbalance between them was all too apparent. Fear and anger collided in her and she grabbed his arm, as if the force of her will could drag him to his feet and out of her home.

'I said get out of my house!' she shouted, pulling at him, uncaring that holding his arm was akin to holding a steel boulder. 'I don't care if you're a stupid prince *or* about your stupid diplomatic immunity—get *out*!'

With reflexes that would put a cat to shame, Talos yanked her wrists together and pinned the pair of them inside one of his giant hands.

'So you *do* have fire under that pale skin,' he murmured. 'I did wonder.'

'Let go of me right now,' she demanded, panic puls-

ing through her which only increased when he twisted—
pirouetted—her around to sit on his lap, keeping a firm
hold on her wrists.

Instinct made her lift her leg and kick back at him. The
heel of her bare foot connected with his shin, the pain lancing through her immediate.

For Talos, she might as well have been a toddler doing
their worst. He gave absolutely no reaction to her kick other
than to wrap his free arm around her waist to secure her to
him, ensnaring her even more effectively.

'I feel that hurt you more than it did me,' he said, holding her trapped hands up to examine them. 'Such elegant
fingers… Now, are you going to be a good girl and behave
yourself if I let you go?'

'If you call me a good girl again I'll…'

'What? Kick me again?'

She bucked, but it was a futile gesture. It was like being
trapped in steel.

Except it wasn't steel. It was solid man. And his fingers
were digging not unpleasantly into the side of her waist.

'You're scaring me.' It was part truth. *Something* was
scaring her. Terrifying her.

'I know, and I apologise. I will let you go when you assure me that you have your emotions under control and
will not lash out at me again.'

Strangely, the deep, rough timbre of his voice had the
desired effect, calming her enough to stop her struggling
against him.

Clamping her lips together, she forced herself to breathe,
and as she did so she inhaled a darkly masculine scent.
His scent.

She swallowed the moisture that filled her mouth, suddenly aware of his breath, hot in her hair. Every one of her
senses was heightened.

She couldn't choke another breath in. Her heart was
beating so hard she could hear it echo in her ears. And in

the silence that ensued she felt Talos's huge form stiffen too, from the strong thighs she was sat upon to the giant hands holding her in their snare.

She could no longer hear or feel his breath.

The only sound in her ears was the thrumming of her blood.

And then he released her hands and pushed her to her feet.

On legs that trembled, she shot to the other side of the kitchen.

Now she could breathe, but her breaths were ragged, her chest hurting with the exertion.

For his part, Talos calmly shrugged his muscular arms into his trench coat, wrapped his navy scarf around his neck and clasped his briefcase.

'Six hours, *despinis*. I will respect your decision—but know that should your answer continue to be negative the consequences will be real and immediate.'

Amalie's phone vibrated.

She pounced on it. *'Maman?'*

'Chérie, I have found out some things.'

That was typical of her mother—getting straight to the point. There didn't exist a sliver of silence that her mother's voice couldn't fill.

'I could not reach Pierre directly.'

She sounded put out—as if Picrre Gaskin should have been holding on to his phone on the remote chance that Colette Barthez, the most famous classical singer in the world, deigned to call him.

'But I spoke to his charming assistant, who told me he arrived late to the office this morning, gave every employee five hundred euros and said he was taking the next three months off. He was last seen setting his satnav to take him to Charles de Gaulle,' she added, referring to France's largest airport.

'So it looks as if he *has* sold it, then,' Amalie murmured.

Only two weeks ago Pierre Gaskin—the owner or, as she now firmly believed, the *former* owner of the Théâtre de la Musique—had been struggling to pay the heating bill for the place.

'It looks that way, *chérie*. So tell me,' her mother went on, '*why* has Prince Talos brought the theatre? I didn't know he was a patron of the arts.'

'No idea,' she answered, her skin prickling at the mention of his name. She kneaded her brow, aware that this must be something like her tenth lie of the weekend.

What a mess.

She hadn't told her mother anything of what had happened that weekend—she didn't have the strength to handle *her* reaction on top of everything else—had only asked her to use her contacts to see if there was any truth that the theatre had been sold to Talos Kalliakis.

Now she had the answer.

Talos hadn't been bluffing. But then she hadn't really thought he had been, had turned to her mother only out of a futile sense of having to do *something* rather than any real hope.

'I knew his father, Prince Lelantos…'

Her mother's voice took on a dreamlike quality. It was a sound Amalie recognised, having been her mother's confidante of the heart since the age of twelve.

'I sang for him once. He was such a…' she scrambled for the right word '…*man*!'

'*Maman*, I need to go now.'

'Of course, *chérie*. If you meet Prince Talos again, send him my regards.'

'I will.'

Turning her phone off and placing it on the table, Amalie drew her hands down her face.

There was only one thing left that she could do. She was going to have to tell Talos Kalliakis the truth.

CHAPTER THREE

WHEN TALOS PUNCHED his finger to the bell of Amalie's front door he knew she must have been waiting for him. She pulled the door open before his hand was back by his side.

She stared at him impassively, as if what had occurred between them earlier had never happened. As if she hadn't lost her calm veneer.

Without a word being exchanged, he followed her into the kitchen.

On the table lay a tray of pastries and two plates. A pot of coffee had just finished percolating. Amalie was dressed for her part, having donned a pair of black jeans that hugged her slender frame and a silver scoop-necked top. Her straight dark hair had been brushed back into a loose bun at the nape of her slender neck. She wore no make-up, and the freckles across her nose were vivid in the harsh light beaming from above them.

It was clear to him that she had seen reason. And why on earth would she not? She was a professional musician. He shouldn't have to resort to blackmail.

Time was running out. For the gala. For his grandfather. The chemotherapy he was undergoing had weakened him badly. There were days when he couldn't leave his bed— barely had the strength to retch into a bucket. Other days Talos found him in good spirits, happy to sit outside and enjoy the Agon sunshine in the sprawling palace gardens.

Talos remembered again that he had planned to return home after the auditions on Saturday and spend the rest of the weekend with his grandfather. Instead he'd been compelled to force through—and quickly—the purchase of that awful Parisian building. And for what? Because the only professional violinist he'd found capable of doing justice to his grandmother's final composition was playing hardball.

No one played hardball with Talos Kalliakis. *No one.* To find this slender thing standing up to him...

But she had seen reason. That was all that mattered now.

He allowed himself a smile at his victory, and sat in the chair he'd vacated only six hours before.

Defeat had never crossed his mind. It was regrettable that he'd had to resort to blackmail to get his own way but time was of the essence. The Jubilee was only a month away. There was still time for her to learn the piece to performance standard and for her orchestra to learn the accompanying music. He wanted them note-perfect before they took to the palace stage.

Amalie's arm brushed against his as she placed a mug in front of him. He found his attention caught by her fingers, as it had been earlier, when he'd had them trapped in his hand. It was the nails at the end of those long, elegant fingers that had really struck him. The nails of her left hand were short and blunt. The nails of her right hand were much longer and shapely. He'd puzzled over those nails all day... over what they reminded him of.

He'd also puzzled over the reaction that had swept through him when he'd pinned her to his lap after her anger had rushed to the surface.

Talos was a man who enjoyed the company of beautiful women. And beautiful women liked *him*. Women he didn't know would catch his eye and hold it for a beat too long. When they learned who he was their gazes would stay fixed, suggestion and invitation ringing from them.

Never had he met a woman who so obviously disliked him. Never had he met anyone—man or woman—outside his immediate family who would deny him anything he wanted.

Amalie Cartwright was a pretty woman in her own unique way. The defiant attitude she'd displayed towards him infuriated and intrigued him in equal measure.

What, he wondered, would it be like to light the fire he'd glimpsed that morning in a more intimate setting?

What would it take to twist that fire and anger into passion?

He had felt the shift in her when her whole body had stilled and her breath had shortened and then stopped. The same time his own breath had stopped. One moment he'd been staring at her fingers with bemusement, the next his body had been filled with an awareness so strong it had knocked the air out of him.

He'd never experienced a reaction like it.

And now, watching her take the same seat as she had that morning, he could feel that awareness stirring within him again.

The following month held infinite possibilities...

'Monsieur,' she said once she had settled herself down and placed her green gaze on him, 'earlier you appealed to my better nature—'

'Which you disregarded,' he interjected.

She bowed her head in acknowledgement. 'I had my reasons, which I am going to share with you in the hope of appealing to *your* better nature.'

He regarded her carefully but kept silent, waiting for her to speak her mind. Surely she wasn't trying another angle to turn the solo down?

'I'm sorry but I lied to you—I do not have a prior engagement on the gala weekend.' She gnawed on her bottom lip before continuing. 'I suffer from stage fright.'

The idea was so ludicrous Talos shook his head in disbelief and laughed.

'You?' he said, not bothering to hide his incredulity. 'You—the daughter of Colette Barthez and Julian Cartwright—suffer from *stage fright*?'

'You know who I am?'

'I know exactly who you are.' He folded his arms, his brief, incredulous mirth evaporating. 'I made it my business to know.'

He caught a flash of truculence in those green eyes, the first sign that the calm façade she wore was nothing but a front.

'Your French mother is the most successful mezzo-soprano in the world. I admit I hadn't heard of your father before today, but I understand he is a famous English violinist. I also learned that your father once played at Carnegie Hall with my grandmother, when he was first establishing himself.'

He leaned forward to rest his chin on his hands.

'*You* were a noted child prodigy until the age of twelve, when your parents removed you from the spotlight so you could concentrate on your education. You became a professional musician at the age of twenty, when you joined the ranks of the Orchestre National de Paris as a second violin—a position you still hold five years on.'

She shrugged, but her face remained taut. 'What you have described is something any person with access to the internet could find out in thirty seconds. My parents didn't remove me from the spotlight because of my education—that is what my mother told the press, because she couldn't bear the shame of having a daughter unable to perform in public.'

'If you are "unable to perform in public", how do you explain the fact that you *perform in public* at least once a week with your orchestra?'

'I'm a second violin. I sit at the back of the orchestra. We have an average of eighty musicians playing at any given performance. The audience's eyes are not on me but on the collective orchestra. It's two different things. If I play at your grandfather's gala everyone's eyes will be on *me* and I will freeze. It will bring humiliation to me, to my mother—and to your grandfather. Is that what you want? To have the world's eyes witness your star performer frozen on stage, unable to play a note?'

The only person who wouldn't be ashamed of her was her father. She might have referred to it as a joint decision by her parents, but in truth it had been her father who'd gone against her mother's wishes and pulled her out of the spotlight. He'd been the one to assure her that it was okay to play just for the love of the music, even if it was only in the privacy of her own bedroom.

Talos's eyes narrowed, a shrewd expression emanating from them. 'How do I know you aren't lying to me right now?'

'I…'

'By your own admission you lied about being busy on the gala weekend.'

'It was a lie of necessity.'

'No lie is necessary. If you can't handle eyes on you when you play, how were you able to join the orchestra in the first place?'

'It was a blind audition. Everyone who applied had to play behind a screen so there could be no bias. And, before you ask, of course I practise and rehearse amongst my colleagues, But that is a world away from standing up on a stage and feeling hundreds of eyes staring at you.'

He shook his head slowly, his light brown eyes unreadable. 'I am in two minds here. Either you are speaking the truth or you are telling another lie.'

'I am speaking the truth. You need to find another soloist.'

'I think not. Nerves and stage fright are things that can be overcome, but finding another soloist who can do justice to my grandmother's final composition is a different matter.'

Never mind that time had almost run out. He could spend the rest of his life searching and not find anyone whose playing touched him the way Amalie's had in those few minutes he had listened to her.

Talos had never settled for second best in his life and he wasn't about to start now.

'What do you know about my island?' he asked her.

She looked confused at the change of direction. 'Not much. It's near Crete, isn't it?'

'Crete is our nearest neighbour. Like the Cretans, we are descended from the Minoans. Throughout the centuries Agon has been attacked by the Romans, the Ottomans and the Venetians—to name a few. We repelled them all. Only the Venetians managed to occupy us, and just for a short period. My people, under the leadership of the warrior Ares Patakis, of whom I am a direct descendent, rose against the occupiers and expelled them from our land. No other nation has occupied our shores since. History tells our story. Agonites will not be oppressed or repressed. We will fight until our last breath for our freedom.'

He paused to take a sip of his coffee. He had to hand it to her: she had excellent taste.

'You are probably wondering why I am telling you all this,' he said.

'I *am* trying to understand the relevance,' she admitted thoughtfully.

'It is to give you an awareness of the stock that I, my family and our people come from. We are fighters. There isn't an Agonite alive who would back down in the face of adversity. Stage fright? Nerves? Those are issues to be fought and conquered. And with my help you *will* conquer them.'

Amalie could imagine it only too well. Talos Kalliakis ready for battle, stripped to nothing but iron battle gear, spear in hand. He would be at the front of any fight.

It was her bad fortune that he had chosen to fight *her*.

But her stage fright *wasn't* a fight. It was just a part of her, something she had long ago accepted.

Her life was nice and cosy. Simple. No drama, no histrionics. She refused to allow the tempestuousness of her childhood seep its way into her adult life.

'I have arranged with your directors for you to come to Agon in a couple of days and to stay until the gala. Your orchestra will start rehearsals immediately and fly out a week before the gala so you can rehearse with them.'

Her pledge to be amiable evaporated. 'Excuse me, but you've done what?'

'It will give you a month in Agon to acclimatise...'

'I don't need to acclimatise. Agon is hardly the middle of a desert.'

'It will also give you a month to prepare yourself perfectly for the solo,' he continued, ignoring her interruption, although his eyes flashed another warning at her. 'No distractions.'

'But...'

'Your stage fright is something that *will* be overcome,' he said, with all the assurance of a man who had never been struck with anything as weak as nerves. 'I will see to it personally.'

He stopped speaking, leaving a pause she knew she was supposed to fill, but all she could think was how badly she wanted to throw something at him, to curse this hateful man who was attempting to destroy the comfortable, quiet life she had made for herself away from the spotlight.

'Despinis?'

She looked up to find those laser eyes striking through her again, as if he could reach right in and see what she was thinking.

'Do you accept the solo?' His voice hardened to granite. 'Or do I have to make one hundred musicians redundant? Do I have to destroy one hundred careers, including your own? Have no doubt—I will do it. I will destroy you all.'

She closed her eyes and breathed deeply, trying to extinguish the panic clawing at her throat.

She believed him. This was no idle threat. He *could* destroy her career. She had no idea how he would do it, she knew only that he could.

If she didn't loathe him so much she would wonder why he was prepared to take such dark measures to get her agreement. As it was, she couldn't give a flying viola as to his reasons.

If she didn't comply he would take away the only thing she could do.

But how could she agree to do it? The last time she'd performed solo she'd been surrounded by her parents' arty friends—musicians, actors, writers, singers. She'd humiliated herself and her mother in front of every one of them. How could she stand on a stage with dignitaries and heads of state watching her and not be shredded by the same nerves? That was if she even made it on to the stage.

The one time she'd tried after the awful incident had left her hospitalised. And what she remembered most clearly about that dreadful time was her father's fury at her mother for forcing her. He'd accused her of selfishness and of using their only child as a toy.

A lump formed in Amalie's throat as she recalled them separating mere weeks later, her father gaining primary custody of her.

She was lucky, though. If times got really hard she knew she could rely on both her parents to bail her out. She would never go hungry. She would never lose her home. Her colleagues weren't all so fortunate. Not many of them were blessed with wealthy parents.

She thought of kindly Juliette, who was seven months pregnant with her third child. Of Louis, who only last week had booked a bank-breaking holiday with his family to Australia. Grumbling Giles, who moaned every month when his mortgage payment was taken from his account…

All those musicians, all those office workers…

All unaware that their jobs, security and reputations hung in the balance.

She stared at Talos, willing him to feel every ounce of her hate.

'Yes, I'll come. But the consequences are something *you* will have to live with.'

Amalie gazed out of the window and got her first glimpse of Agon. As the plane made its descent she stared transfixed as golden beaches emerged alongside swathes of green, high mountains and built-up areas of pristine white buildings... And then they touched down, bouncing along the runway before coming to a final smooth stop.

Keeping a firm grip on her violin, she followed her fellow business-class passengers out and down the metal stairs. After the slushy iciness of Paris in March, the temperate heat was a welcome delight.

From the economy section bounded excited children and frazzled parents, there to take advantage of the sunshine Agon was blessed with, where spring and summer came earlier than to its nearest neighbour, Crete. She hadn't considered that she would be going to an island famed as a holiday destination for families and historical buffs alike. In her head she'd thought of Agon as a prison—as dark and dangerous as the man who had summoned her there.

Amalie had travelled to over thirty countries in her life, but never had she been in an airport as fresh and welcoming as the one in Agon. Going through Arrivals was quick; her luggage arriving on the conveyor belt even quicker.

A man waited in the exit lounge, holding up her name on a specially laminated board. Polite introductions out of the way, he took the trolley holding her luggage from her and led the way out to a long, black car parked in what was clearly the prime space of the whole car park.

Everything was proceeding exactly as had been stated in the clipped email Talos's private secretary had sent to her the day before. It had contained a detailed itinerary, from the time a car would be collecting her from her house all the way through to her estimated time of arrival at the villa that would be her home for the next month.

As the chauffeur navigated the roads she was able to take further stock of the island. Other than expecting it to be as dangerous as the youngest of its princes, she'd had no preconceptions. She was glad. Talos Kalliakis might be a demon sent to her from Hades, but his island was stunning.

Mementoes of Agon's early Greek heritage were everywhere, from the architecture to the road signs in the same common language. But Agon was now a sovereign island, autonomous in its rule. The thing that struck her most starkly was how clean everything was, from the well-maintained roads to the buildings and homes they drove past. When they went past a harbour she craned her neck to look more closely at the rows of white yachts stationed there—some of them as large as cruise liners.

Soon they were away from the town and winding higher into the hills and mountains. Her mouth dropped open when she caught her first glimpse of the palace, standing proudly on a hill much in the same way as the ancient Greeks had built their most sacred monuments. Enormous and sprawling, it had a Middle Eastern flavour to it, as if it had been built for a great sultan centuries ago.

But it wasn't to the palace that she was headed. No sooner had it left her sight than the chauffeur slowed down, pausing while a wrought-iron gate inched open, then drove up to a villa so large it could have been a hotel. Up the drive he took them, and then round to the back of the villa's grounds, travelling for another mile until he came to a much smaller dwelling at the edge of the extensive villa's garden—a generously sized white stone cottage.

An elderly man, with a shock of white hair flapping in the breeze above a large bald spot, came out of the front door to greet them.

'Good evening, *despinis*,' he said warmly. 'I am Kostas.'

Explaining that he ran the main villa for His Highness Prince Talos, he showed her around the cottage that would be her home for the month. The small kitchen was well stocked and a daily delivery of fresh fruit, breads and dairy products would be brought to her. If she wished to eat her meals in the main villa she only had to pick up the phone and let them know; likewise if she wished to have meals delivered to the cottage.

'The villa has a gym, a swimming pool, and spa facilities you are welcome to use whenever you wish,' he said before he left. 'There are also a number of cars you can use if you wish to travel anywhere, or we can arrange for a driver to take you.'

So Talos didn't intend to keep her prisoner in the cottage? That was handy to know.

She'd envisaged him collecting her from the airport, locking her in a cold dungeon and refusing to let her out until she was note-perfect with his grandmother's composition and all her demons had been banished.

Thinking about it sent a tremor racing up her spine.

She wondered what great psychiatrist Talos would employ to 'fix' her. She would laugh if the whole thing didn't terrify her so much. Whoever he employed had better get a move on. She had exactly four weeks and two days until she had to stand on the stage for the King of Agon's Jubilee Gala. In those thirty days she had to learn an entirely new composition, her orchestra had to learn the accompanying score, and she had to overcome the nerves that had paralysed her for over half her lifetime.

CHAPTER FOUR

THE MORNING CAME, crisp and blue. After a quick shower Amalie donned her favourite black jeans and a plum shirt, then made herself a simple breakfast, which she took out to eat on her private veranda. As she ate yogurt and honey, and sipped at strong coffee—she'd been delighted to find a brand-new state-of-the-art coffee machine, with enough pods to last her a year—she relaxed into a wicker chair and let the cool breeze brush over her. After all the bustle of Paris it felt wonderful to simply *be*.

If she closed off her mind she could forget why she was there...pretend she was on some kind of holiday.

Her tranquillity didn't last long.

After going back inside to try another of the coffee-machine pods—this time opting for the mocha—she came back onto the veranda to find Talos sitting on her vacated chair, helping himself to the cubes of melon she'd cut up.

'Good morning, little songbird,' he said with a flash of straight white teeth.

Today he was dressed casually, in baggy khaki canvas trousers, black boots and a long-sleeved V-necked grey top. He was unshaven and his hair looked as if it had been tamed with little more than the palm of a hand. As she leaned over the table to place her mug down she caught his freshly showered scent.

'Is that for me?' he asked, nodding at the mug in her shaking hand.

She shrugged, affecting nonchalance at his unexpected appearance. 'If you don't mind sharing my germs.'

'I'm sure a beautiful woman like you doesn't have anything so nasty as germs.'

She raised a suspicious eyebrow, shivering as his deep bass voice reverberated through her skin, before turning back into the cottage, glad of an excuse to escape for a moment and gather herself. Placing a new pod in the machine, she willed her racing heart to still.

He'd startled her with his presence, that was all. She'd received an email from his private secretary the evening before, while eating the light evening meal she'd prepared for herself, stating that the score would be brought to her at the cottage mid-morning. There had been nothing mentioned about the Prince himself bothering to join her. Indeed, once she'd realised she wasn't staying in the palace she'd hoped not to see him again.

When she went back outside he was cradling the mug, an expression of distaste wrinkling his face. 'What *is* this?'

'Mocha.'

'It is disgusting.'

'Don't drink it, then.'

'I won't.' He placed it on the table and gave it a shove with his fingers to move it away from him. He nodded at her fresh cup. 'What's that one?'

'Mocha—to replace the one you kidnapped. If you want something different, the coffee machine's in the kitchen.' The contract she'd signed had said nothing about making coffee for him.

That evil contract...

She dragged her thoughts away before her brain could rage anew. If she allowed herself to fume over the unfairness, her wits would be dulled, and she already knew to her bitter cost that she needed her wits about her when dealing with this man.

As she sat herself in the vacant chair, unsubtly moving it away from his side, Talos reached for an apple from the plate of fruit she'd brought out with her. Removing a stumpy metal object from his trouser pocket, he pressed a button on the side and a blade at least five inches long unfolded. The snap it made jolted her.

Talos noticed her flinch. 'Does my knife bother you?'

'Not at all. Did you get that little thing when you were a Boy Scout?'

Her dismissive tone grated on him more than it should have. *She* grated on him more than she should.

'This little thing?' He swivelled the chair, narrowed his eyes and flicked his wrist. The knife sliced through the air, landing point-first in the cherry tree standing a good ten feet from them, embedding itself in the trunk.

He didn't bother hiding his satisfaction. 'That *little thing* was a present from my grandfather when I graduated from Sandhurst.'

'I'm impressed,' she said flatly. 'I always thought Sandhurst was for gentlemen.'

Was that yet *another* insult?

'Was there a reason you came to see me other than to massacre a defenceless tree?' she asked.

He got to his feet. 'I've brought the score to you.'

He strode to the cherry tree, gripped the handle of the knife and pulled it out. This knife was a badge of honour—the mark of becoming a man, a replacement for the Swiss Army penknife each Kalliakis prince had been given on his tenth birthday. There was an apple tree in the palace gardens whose trunk still bore the scars of the three young Princes' attempts at target practice two decades before.

Back at the table, aware of wary sapphire eyes watching his every movement, he wiped the blade on his trousers, then picked up his selected apple and proceeded to peel it, as had been his intention when he'd first removed the knife from his pocket. The trick was to peel it in one single movement before the white of the inside started to brown—a relic from his childhood, when his father would peel an apple before slicing it and eating the chunks, and something he in turn had learned from *his* father. Of course Talos's father hadn't lived long enough to see any of his sons master it.

Carrying a knife was a habit all the Kalliakis men shared. Talos had no idea what had compelled him to throw it at the tree.

Had he been trying to get a rise out of her?

Never had he been in the company of anyone, let alone a woman, to whom his presence was so clearly unwelcome. People wanted his company. They sought it, they yearned to keep it. No one treated him with indifference.

And yet this woman did.

Other than that spark of fire in her home, when he'd played his trump card, she'd remained cool and poised in all their dealings, her body language giving nothing away. Only now, as he pushed the large binder that contained the solo towards her, did she show any emotion, her eyes flickering, her breath sharpening.

'Is this it?' she asked, opening the binder to peer at what lay inside.

'You look as if you're afraid to touch it.'

'I've never held anything made by a royal hand.'

He studied her, curiosity driving through him. 'You look respectfully towards a sheet of music, yet show no respect towards me, a prince of this land.'

'Respect is earned, *monsieur*, and you have done nothing to earn mine.'

Why wasn't she scared of him?

'On this island our people respect the royal family. It comes as automatically as breathing.'

'Did you use brute force to gain it? Or do you prefer simple blackmail?'

'Five hundred years ago it was considered treason to show insolence towards a member of the Agon royal family.'

'If that law were still in force now I bet your subjects' numbers would be zero.'

'The law was brought in by the senate, out of gratitude to my family for keeping this island safe from our enemies. My ancestors were the ones to abolish it.'

'I bet your subjects partied long into the night when it was abolished.'

'Do not underestimate the people of this island, *despinis*,' he said, his ire rising at her flippant attitude. 'Agonites are not and never will be subjects. This is not a dictatorship. The Kalliakis family members remain the island's figureheads by overwhelming popular consent. Our blood is their blood—their blood is our blood. They will celebrate my grandfather's Jubilee Gala with as much enthusiasm as if they were attending a party for their own grandfather.'

Her pale cheeks were tinged with a light pinkness. She swallowed. 'I didn't mean to insult your family, *monsieur*.'

He bowed his head in acceptance of her apology.

'Only you.'

'Only me?'

Her sapphire eyes sparked, but there was no light in them. 'I only meant to insult *you*.'

'If the palace dungeons hadn't been turned into a tourist attraction I would have you thrown into them.'

'And it's comments like that which make me happy to insult you. You blackmail me into coming here, you threaten my career and the careers of my friends, and you make me sign a contract including a penalty for my not performing at your grandfather's gala: the immediate disbandment of the Orchestre National de Paris... So, yes, I will happily take any opportunity I can to insult you.'

He stretched out his long legs and ran his fingers through his hair. 'It's comments like that which make me wonder...'

Her face scrunched up in a question.

'You see, little songbird, I wonder how a woman who professes to have stage fright so bad she cannot stand on a stage and play the instrument she was born to play has the nerve to show such disrespect to me. Do I not frighten you?'

She paused a beat before answering. 'You are certainly imposing.'

'That is not an answer.'

'The only thing that frightens me is the thought of standing on the stage for your grandfather's gala.' A lie, she knew, but Amalie would sooner stand on the stage naked than admit that she was *terrified* of him. Or terrified of something about him. The darkness. *His* darkness.

'Then I suggest you start learning the music for it.' He rose to his feet, his dark features set in an impenetrable mask. 'I will collect you at seven this evening and you can fill me in on your feelings for it.'

'Collect me for what?'

'Your first session in overcoming your stage fright.'

'Right.'

She bit her lip. Strangely, she'd envisaged Talos bringing an army of shrinks to *her*. That was what her mother had done during Amalie's scheduled visits after her parents' divorce. Anything would have been better than Colette Barthez's daughter being photographed at the door of a psychiatrist's office. The press wouldn't have been able to do anything with the pictures, or print any story about it, her mother had seen to that, but secrets had a way of not remaining secret once more people knew about them.

'Wear something sporty.'

'Sporty?' she asked blankly.

'I'm taking you to my gym.'

She rubbed at an eyebrow. 'I'm confused. Why would we see a shrink at your gym?'

'I never said anything about a shrink.'

'You did.'

'No, little songbird, I said *I* would help you overcome your stage fright.'

'I didn't think you meant it literally.' For the first time in her life she understood what *aghast* meant. *She* was aghast. 'You don't really mean that *you're* planning to fix me?'

He gazed down at her, unsmiling. 'Have you undertaken professional help before?'

'My mother wheeled out every psychiatrist she could get in France and England.'

'And none of them were able to help you.' It was a statement, not a question. 'You have a huge amount of spirit in your blood. It is a matter of harnessing it to your advantage. I will teach you to fight through your nerves and conquer them.'

'But…'

'Seven o'clock. Be ready.'

He strode away, his huge form relaxed. Too relaxed. So relaxed it infuriated her even more, turning her fear and anger up to a boil. Without thinking, she reached for a piece of discarded apple core and threw it at him. Unbelievably, it hit the back of his neck.

He turned around slowly, then crouched down to pick up the offending weapon, which he looked at briefly before fixing his eyes on her. Even with the distance between them the darkness in those eyes was unmistakable. As was the danger.

Amalie gulped in air, her lungs closing around it and refusing to let go.

Do I not frighten you…?

Frightened didn't even begin to describe the terror racing through her blood at that moment—a terror that increased with each long step he took back towards her.

Fighting with everything she possessed to keep herself collected, she refused to turn away from his black gaze.

It wasn't until he loomed over her, his stare piercing right through her, that she felt rather than saw the swirl flickering in it.

'You should be careful, little songbird. A lesser man than me might take the throwing of an apple core as some kind of mating ritual.'

His deep, rough voice was pitched low with an underlying playfulness that scared her almost more than anything else.

The thing that terrified her the most was the beating of her heart, so loud she was certain he must be able to hear it. Not the staccato beat of terror but the raging thrum of awareness.

He was so close she could see the individual stalks of stubble across his strong jawline, the flare of his nostrils, and the silver hue of the scar lancing his eyebrow. Her hand rose, as if a magnet had burrowed under her skin and was being drawn to reach up and touch his face...

Before she'd raised it more than a couple of inches, Talos leaned closer and whispered directly into her ear. 'I think I *do* frighten you. But not in the same way I frighten others.'

With that enigmatic comment he straightened, stepped away from her, nodded a goodbye, and then headed back to his villa.

Only when he was a good fifteen paces away did her lungs relax enough to expel the stale air, and the remnants of his woody, musky smell took its place, hitting her right in the sinuses, then spreading through her as if her body was consuming it.

If Amalie's long-sleeved white top that covered her bottom and her dark blue leggings strayed too far from the 'sporty' brief he'd given her, Talos made no mention of it when she opened her door to him at precisely seven that evening. He did, however, stare at the flat canvas shoes on her feet.

'Do you not have any proper trainers?'

'No.'

He gave a sound like a grunt.

'I'm not really into exercise,' she admitted.

'You are for the next thirty days.'

'I find it boring.'

'That's because you're not doing it right.'

It was like arguing with a plank. Except a plank would be more responsive to her argument.

But a plank wouldn't evoke such an immediate reaction within her. Or prevent her lungs from working properly.

For his part, Talos was dressed in dark grey sports pants that fitted his long, muscular legs perfectly, and a black T-shirt that stretched across his chest, showcasing his broad warrior-like athleticism.

The stubble she remembered from the morning was even thicker now...

It was like gazing at a pure shot of testosterone. The femininity right in her core responded to it, a slow ache burning in her belly, her heart racing to a thrum with one look.

He walked her to his car; a black Maserati that even in the dusk of early evening gleamed. She stepped into the passenger side, the scent of leather filling her senses.

She'd never known anyone fill the interior of a car the way Talos did. Beside him she felt strangely fragile, as if she were made of porcelain rather than flesh and blood.

She blinked the strange thought away and knotted her fingers together, silently praying the journey would be short.

'How did you find the composition?' he asked after a few minutes of silence.

'Beautiful.'

It was the only word she could summon. For five hours she had worked her way through the piece, bar by bar, section by section. She was a long way from mastering it, or understanding all its intricacies, but already the underlying melody had made itself known and had her hooked.

'You are certain you will be ready to perform it in a month's time?'

Opportunity suddenly presented itself to her gift-wrapped. 'A composition of this complexity could take me *months* to master. You would do far better to employ a soloist who can get a quicker handle on it.'

He was silent for a moment, and when he spoke there was an amused tinge to his voice. 'You don't give up, do you?'

'I don't know what you mean.'

'Oh, I think you do. I remind you, *despinis*, that you signed a contract.'

'And *you* said you would get me help.'

'I said I would help you and that is what I am doing.'

He brought the car to a stop at the front of a large cream building and faced her. Even in the dark she could see the menace on his features.

'I will accept no excuses. You *will* learn the composition and you *will* play it at the gala and you *will* do it justice. If you fail in any of those conditions then I will impose the contracted penalty.'

He didn't have to elaborate any further. The 'contracted penalty' meant turning the theatre into a hotel and causing the disbandment of the orchestra. That penalty loomed large in her mind: the threat to ruin every member of the orchestra's reputation…her own most especially.

'Understand, though,' he continued, 'that I am a man of my word. I said I would ensure that you are mentally fit to get on the stage and play, and that is what I will do. Starting now.'

He got out of the car and opened the boot, pulling out a black sports bag. 'Follow me.'

Not having any choice, she followed him into the building.

The first thing that hit her was the smell.

She'd never been in a men's locker room before, but this was *exactly* what she'd imagined it would smell like: sweat and testosterone.

The second thing to hit her was the noise.

The third thing was the sight of a man with a flat nose,

standing behind the reception desk at the entrance, spotting Talos and getting straight to his feet, a huge grin spreading over his face.

The two men greeted each other with bumped fists and a babble of Greek that ended with Talos giving the man a hearty slap on the back before indicating to Amalie to follow him. As they walked away she couldn't help but notice the blatant adoration on the flat-nosed man's face. Not a romantic adoration—she'd witnessed *that* enough times from her mother to know what it looked like—but more a look of reverence.

Past the reception area, they slipped through a door and entered the most enormous room.

Silently she took it all in: the square ring in the corner, the huge blue mats laid out in a square in another, the punching bags dangling at seemingly random places...

'Is this a *boxing* gym?'

He raised a hefty shoulder. 'I've boxed since my childhood.'

'I can't *box*!'

He gazed down at her hands. 'No. You can't. Throwing a punch at even the softest target has the danger of breaking a finger.'

She hadn't thought of that—had been too busy thinking that she'd never hit anyone or anything in her life and had always considered boxing to be the most barbaric of sports. It was fitting to learn that it was Talos's sport of choice. Her encounters with him were the closest she'd ever come to actually hitting someone.

He pointed to the corner with the blue mats. A tall, athletic blonde woman was chatting to a handful of men and women, all decked out in proper sports gear. 'That is Melina, one of the instructors here. I've signed you up for her kickboxing workout.'

Amalie sighed. 'How is enduring a kickboxing workout supposed to make me mentally fit for the stage?'

Without warning he placed his hands on her shoulders and twisted her around, so her back was to him. His thumbs pressed into the spot between her shoulder blades.

'You are rife with tension,' he said.

'Of course I am. I'm here under duress.'

She tried to duck out from his hold but his grip was too strong. *He* was too strong. His thumbs felt huge as they pressed up the nape of her neck. And warm. And surprisingly gentle, despite the strength behind them.

'The workout will help relieve tension and fire up your endorphins.' He laughed—a deep rumble that vibrated through her pores—and released his hold on her. 'All you will do is kick and punch into the air. If it helps, you can pretend I'm standing in front of you, receiving it all.'

She turned back to face him. 'That *will* help.'

The glimmer of humour left him. 'Your aggression needs an outlet.'

'I'm not aggressive!' At least she never had been before. Talos brought something out in her that, while not violent in the sense she'd always associated aggression with, made her feel as if a ferocity had been awoken within her, one that only reared up when she was with him. Or thinking about him. Or dreaming about him...

This workout might just prove to be a blessing after all.

'Maybe not, but the tension you have within you comes from somewhere...'

'That'll be from being here with you,' she grumbled.

'And once you have learned to expel it your mind will be calmer.'

'What about my body? I haven't exercised in for ever.'

His eyes swept up and down her body, taking in every part of her. It felt like a critical assessment of her physique and she squirmed under it. She waited for his verbal assessment but it never came.

'I will introduce you to Melina,' he said, striding away to the growing crowd around the instructor.

Melina's eyes gleamed when she spotted Talos, then narrowed slightly when she caught sight of Amalie, hanging back a little behind him.

Introductions were made and then Talos left them to it, heading to the ring in the corner, where a sparring bout had just started between two teenage boys. After a quick conversation with their trainer, Simeon, he left the main hall and went into the adjoining gym to start his own workout. He might spar later with Simeon, but first he wanted to warm his body up and get his muscles moving.

It felt as if it had been an age since he'd worked out, although it had only been one day.

Moving through the equipment, following the routine that had served him well since his army days, he found his concentration levels weren't as sharp as usual. Through the glass wall dividing the gym from the main hall he could see the kickboxing workout underway, and noted how Amalie had placed herself at the back of the pack, how self-conscious her movements were.

He didn't usually enjoy using the treadmill, but today he stayed on it for longer than normal, watching her. The warm-up was over and the session had begun in earnest. As the session progressed her movements went from tentative to a little less so. He could see the concentration on her face as she tried to copy what everyone around her was doing—the way she pivoted on the heel of her left foot before throwing an imaginary hook, the way she put her fists by her face, shifted her weight to her right foot, then brought her left knee up to her chest before kicking out.

She had an excellent centre of gravity, he noted. And for someone who professed to never exercise, her body was delectable, the leggings and long T-shirt she wore showing off her slender form to perfection.

She must have sensed his eyes upon her, for suddenly her gaze was on him, a scowl forming on her pretty face.

He didn't normally find a woman's anger cute, but with Amalie it was like being glared at by a harmless kitten.

Harmless kitten or not, the jabs and kicks she gave from that moment on brought to mind the image of a wildcat. She cut through the air with one particularly vicious right hook and he knew with deep certainty that it was *his* face she'd imagined her fist connecting with.

He reached for his towel and wiped his brow, inhaling deeply, trying to control the burn seeping through him. Watching Amalie work out had a strange hypnotic quality to it—as if she had magical powers pulling his attention to her.

It was time to take his attention elsewhere.

He was at the punching bags when her workout finished. He kept his focus on the bag before him, aware of her approach.

He would have been aware of her even if she hadn't cleared her throat to announce her presence by his side. Tendrils of sensation prickled his skin, and when he turned his attention from the punching bag to her, saw the dampness of her hair and the heightened colour of her cheeks, all he could think about was how she would look under the flames of passion.

'What did you think?' he asked.

Something resembling a smile spread across her face. 'Once I focused and imagined all my punches connecting with your face and all my kicks hitting your abdomen, it was great.'

He laughed. 'And how do you feel now?'

She considered the question, her lips pouting. 'I feel… *good.*'

'Is this the point where I say I told you so?'

She rolled her eyes. 'Are we going to be here much longer? Only I could really do with a shower. And something to eat.'

An image flashed into his mind of her standing naked under hot running water.

'There are showers here, with everything you need.'

'But then I'll have to change back into these sweaty things.'

'We have a selection of gym wear on sale too—I *did* say you would need suitable clothes to work out in. Choose some—and get yourself a decent pair of training shoes.'

'I haven't got any money on me.'

'Not a problem.' He looked over her head and beckoned someone.

A slight young girl of no more than sixteen appeared. Talos said something to her, then addressed Amalie again. 'This is Tessa. She will take you to our clothes store and then show you where the ladies' showers are. I'll meet you upstairs in the café when you're done.'

As soon as they'd headed off he focused back on the punching bag, trying to put aside the images of her naked that insisted on staying at the forefront of his mind.

He threw a particularly hard upper cut at the bag.

This was a singularly unique position he'd put himself in.

Amalie was incredibly desirable. He couldn't pinpoint what exactly it was, but it was as if she had some kind of aura that seeped into his skin and set a charge off inside him. Everything felt so much more heightened. He felt an awareness not only of *her* but also the chemical components that were making *him* feel off the scale. Put simply: being with her made him feel as sexy as hell.

Under any other circumstances he wouldn't hesitate to seduce her. Just imagining those long limbs wrapped around him put him on the path to arousal.

Her awareness of him was strong too—as starkly obvious as her loathing. Lust and loathing… An explosive combination.

But these were not normal circumstances. He had to get

her mentally prepared to take on the biggest solo of her life. It was the whole reason she was there. Something told him she wasn't the type of woman to go for the casual affairs he insisted on. Throwing sex into the mix could be like throwing a match into a situation that was already combustible.

He threw one last punch, then took a seat on the bench and, breathing heavily, undid the wraps around his hands, which he always put on even if only sparring with the punching bag. Experience had taught him how brittle the bones in the human hand were. The pain of breakage was negligible, but unless the hand was rested enough to allow the bones to heal it wouldn't set properly, and the boxer would be unable to punch at full power.

Resting a broken hand was as frustrating as desiring a beautiful woman, knowing she desired you too, but knowing you couldn't ever act on it.

CHAPTER FIVE

DESPITE THE LATENESS of the evening, the café upstairs was busy. Amalie had found a small table against the wall, where she could wait for Talos. Aware of the curious glances being thrown her way she pretended to examine the menu.

Testosterone abounded in the café. The vast majority of the patrons were male, all of them muscular, a fair few displaying broken noses and scarred faces. But their muscular physiques were dwarfed when Talos entered the room.

He spotted her immediately, and as he made his way over people stopped him to shake hands or bump fists.

She was glad his attention was taken, if only for a few moments. She pressed a hand to her chest and inhaled as much air into her tight lungs as she could get. The green sports pants and matching T-shirt she'd taken from the gym's sports clothing outlet suddenly felt very close against her skin. Constricting.

He'd changed into a pair of tight-fitting black jeans and a navy blue T-shirt, and had his sports bag slung over his shoulder.

He was a mountain man, and whatever he wore only emphasised his muscularity. Whether he was in a business suit, workout gear or something casual, she couldn't shake the feeling that he would be equally at home with nothing but a loin cloth wrapped around his waist.

'I thought subjects were supposed to kneel before royalty,' she said when he finally joined her.

A smirk appeared on his lips. 'If you want to get on your knees before me, I won't complain.'

She glared at him.

He settled his huge frame onto the chair opposite her. 'You have to admit your comment was an open invitation.'

'Only to someone with a dirty mind...' she said, but her voice trailed into a mumble as the imagery his comment provoked, startling and vivid, sent a pulse searing through her blood strong enough to make her entire face burn.

The fresh scent of his shower gel and the woody musk of his aftershave played under her nose, filling her senses. He still hadn't shaved, his stubble thick and covering his jawline in its entirety.

Certain she'd handed him another gold-plated open invitation, she cast her eyes down before he had a chance to read what was in them.

Instead of the expected quip, he asked in an amused tone, 'What would you like to order?'

As he spoke, he folded his arms onto the table, his biceps bulging with the motion. She should have stayed looking at his face.

Since when did blatant machismo testosterone do it for her?

The male musicians she worked with—especially her fellow violinists—were, on the whole, sensitive creatures physically *and* emotionally. There were always exceptions to the rule, such as Philippe, one of the Orchestre National de Paris's trombone players. Philippe was blond, buff and handsome, and he flirted openly with any woman who caught his eye. He was rumoured to have bedded half the female musicians in the orchestra.

But not Amalie, who found his overt masculinity a complete turn-off. The few boyfriends *she'd* had had been slight, unthreatening men, with gentle natures and a deep appreciation of music. Their evenings together had been spent discussing all things to do with music and the arts in general, with the bedroom not even an afterthought.

So why did Talos, whose physique and masculinity were ten times as potent as anything Philippe could even dream of having, make her feel all hot and squidgy just to look at him? None of her boyfriends had made her feel like he did—as if she wanted nothing more than to rip his clothes off.

'I don't read Greek,' she answered, dragging her vocal cords into working order. 'I wouldn't know what to choose.'

'We don't serve traditional Greek fare here,' he said. 'It's mostly high-carb and high-protein foods like pasta and steak.'

'Do they have burgers?'

He grinned.

'What's so funny?'

'After a hard workout I go for a burger every time.'

'With cheese?'

'It's not right without the cheese.'

'And chips?'

'It wouldn't be a complete meal without them.'

'Cheeseburger and chips for me, then, please.'

'Drink?'

'Coke?'

His sensuous lips widened into a full-blown grin that was as sinful as the food she wanted. 'Two cheeseburgers and chips, and two Cokes coming up.'

He got up from his seat, walked to the counter, fist-bumped the teenage boy working there and gave their order.

'It won't take long,' he said when he sat back at the table.

'Good. I am *starving*.'

'I'm not surprised after that workout you did.'

'It doesn't help that I forgot to have any dinner before we left.'

'How can you *forget* a meal?' He looked at her as if she'd confessed to forgetting to put her underwear on.

She shrugged. 'It happens. If I'm concentrating and lost in the music it is easy for me to forget.'

'It's no wonder you're a slip of thing.'

'I make up for it,' she said defensively. 'I might not eat at regular times, but I always eat.'

He eyed her, his look contemplative. Before he could say whatever was on his mind their food was brought over by yet another teenager.

'That *was* quick,' Amalie marvelled. Her famished belly rumbled loudly as she looked at the heaped plate. She didn't think she'd ever seen so many chips on a plate, or a burger of such epic proportions.

'We run a tight ship here.'

'That's not the first time you've said "we",' she said, picking up a thick golden chip that was so hot she dropped it back onto the plate. 'Are you involved in this place somehow?'

'This is my gym.'

She gazed at him, trying to stop her face wrinkling in puzzlement. 'But you have a gym in your villa.'

'And there's one at the palace too.' He picked up his burger and bit into it, devouring almost a quarter in one huge mouthful.

She shook her head. 'So why this place too?'

He swallowed, his light brown eyes on hers. 'This is a boxing gym. Sparring is no fun when you're on your own.'

'So you bought a gym so you could have some company?'

'There were a lot of reasons.'

'Do you run it?'

'I employ a manager. Enough questions—eat before your food gets cold.'

'Okay, but do me a favour and never tell my mother what I'm about to eat.'

His brow furrowed. 'Why? Would she disapprove?'

Amalie had already bitten into a chip, possibly the crispest and yet fluffiest chip she had ever tasted. She chewed, then swallowed it down with some Coke before answering. 'My mother is a gastronomy snob. She considers any food with English or American origin to be tantamount to eating out of a rubbish bin.'

'Yet she married an Englishman.'

'That's true,' she agreed, casting her eyes down. Her parents had been divorced for half her lifetime, yet the guilt still had the power to catch her unawares.

Talos picked up on an inflection in her tone. 'Was it a bad divorce?'

'Not at all. It was very civilised.'

'But traumatic for you?'

'It wasn't the easiest of experiences,' she conceded, before picking up her burger and taking a small bite.

It was with some satisfaction that he saw her eyes widen and her nod of approval.

'That is *good*,' she enthused when her mouth was clear.

'Maybe not the gastronomical heights your mother would approve of, but still high-quality,' he agreed.

'I think this might be the best burger I've ever had.'

'You mean you've eaten a burger *before*?' he asked, feigning surprise. 'Your mother will be shocked.'

'I hide all my convenience food when I know she's coming over.'

He grinned and took another bite of his burger. The workout had clearly done Amalie the world of good; most of her primness had been sweated out of her. She almost looked relaxed.

They ate in silence for a few minutes. It gratified him to see her eat so heartily; he had imagined from her slender frame and self-confessed lack of exercise that she would eat like a sparrow.

He tried to imagine eating with another woman here and came up blank.

In normal life this gym was his sanctuary—not somewhere he would bring a date, even if his date liked to work out. For the same reason he refused to make overtures to any of the women who worked here. Regardless of the fact that most of his female staff were, like the majority of his employees, teenagers, and so automatically off limits, he didn't want the messiness that inevitably came about when he ended a relationship to spill into his sanctuary.

Melina, his kickboxing instructor, had blatantly flirted with him when she'd first started work here and—despite her being in her mid-twenties, and attractive to boot—he'd frozen out all her innuendoes until she'd got the message.

The endorphins released during a vigorous workout always made him crave sex, but he disciplined himself with the iron will Kalliakis men were famed for. Except for his father. The Kalliakis iron will had skipped a generation with Lelantos…Lelantos had been weak and venal—a man who had allowed his strong libido and equally great temper to control him.

It *killed* Talos to know that of the three Kalliakis Princes, he was the most like their father.

The difference was that he had learned to control his appetites *and* the volatile temperament that came with it. Boxing had taught him to harness it.

Tonight, though, the endorphins seemed to have exploded within him, and the primal urge to sate himself in a willing woman's arms was stronger than ever. And not just any woman. *This* woman.

Theos, just watching Amalie eat made him feel like throwing her over his shoulder, carrying her to the nearest empty room and taking her wildly.

'Do you consider yourself French or English?' he asked, wrenching his mind away from matters carnal. He needed to concentrate on getting her mentally fit to play at his grandfather's gala, not be imagining ripping her clothes off with his teeth.

'Both. Why?'

'You speak English with a slight accent. It made me curious.'

'I suppose French is my first language. I grew up bilingual, but I've never lived full-time in England. My father's always kept a home there, but when I was a child we used it more for holidays and parties than anything else.'

'Was that because of your mother's influence?'

'I assume so. My mother definitely wore the trousers in that marriage.' A slight smile, almost sad, played at the corners of her lips.

'I have heard that she's a forceful woman.'

He'd heard many stories about Colette Barthez, not many of them complimentary. It was strange to think that the woman before him—a woman who tried desperately to fade into the background—was a child from the loins of the biggest diva on the planet. He had to assume she took after her father who, he'd learned, was regarded as a quintessential Englishman, with a dry humour and calm manner.

Amalie chewed on a chip, disliking the implication in his words and the way he'd delivered them. She, better than anyone, knew just how 'forceful' her mother could be in getting her own way, but that didn't stop her loving her and despising the people who would put her down.

'You don't become the most successful and famous mezzo-soprano in the world without having a strong will and a thick hide. If she were a man she would be celebrated.'

The scarred eyebrow rose in question.

She shook her head and pushed her plate to the side. 'She sold out Carnegie Hall and the Royal Albert Hall three nights in a row last year, but every article written about those concerts just *had* to mention her three ex-husbands, numerous lovers and so-called diva demands.'

The black scarred brow drew forward. 'That must be very hurtful for her to read,' he said, his tone careful.

'If it was the French media it would devastate her, but

in France she's revered and treated as a national icon. With the rest of the world's press, so long as they aren't criticising her voice or performance, she doesn't care—she truly does have the hide of a rhinoceros.'

But not when it came to love. When it came to affairs of the heart, her mother felt things deeply. Bored lovers had the power to shatter her.

'But they upset *you*?' he said, a shrewdness in his eyes.

'No one wants to read salacious stories about their mother,' she muttered, reaching for one more chip and popping it in her mouth before she could unloosen her tongue any further.

Her family and personal life were none of his concern, but she felt so protective when it came to her mother, who was passionate, funny, loving, predatory, egotistical and a complete one-off. She drove her up the wall, but Amalie adored her.

'That is true,' Talos agreed. 'My family also live under the spotlight. There are occasions when it can burn.'

She leaned back in her chair and stared at him through narrowed eyes. 'If you know how much the spotlight can burn, why would you push me back under it when you know it hurts me so much?'

'Because you were born to play under it,' he replied, his deep bass voice no-nonsense.

And yet she detected a whisper of warmth in those light brown eyes she hadn't seen before.

'It is my job to put you back under it without you gaining any new scars.'

'But the scars I already have haven't healed.'

There was no point in shying away from it. She'd seen enough psychologists in her early teens to know that she'd been scarred, and that it was those scars still preventing her from stepping onto a stage and performing with eyes upon her.

'Then I will heal them for you.'

A shiver ran through her as an image of his mouth drifting across her skin skittered into her mind, shockingly vivid… Talos healing her in the most erotic manner. It sent a pulse of heat deep into her abdomen.

She blinked rapidly, to dispel the unbidden image, and was grateful when another member of the gym chose that moment to come over to their table and chat with him.

Passion was something she'd always avoided. After her parents' divorce she'd spent her weekend and holiday visitations watching her mother bounce from lover to lover, marrying two of them for good measure, engulfed in desire's heady flames, trying to recapture the magic of her first marriage. Watching her get burned so many times had been pain itself. The guilt of knowing she was responsible for her mother's heartache—and her father's—had only added to it.

Her father had never brought another woman home, let alone remarried. Though he would always deny it with a sad smile, the torch he carried for her mother was too bright to extinguish.

If it hadn't been for that horrendous incident in front of her parents and their friends and its aftermath, when their child prodigy could no longer perform like the dancing seal she'd become, her parents would still be together today— she was certain of it. On the occasions when they were forced together, Amalie would watch them skirt around each other; her mother showing off her latest lover with something close to flamboyant desperation, her father accepting this behaviour with a wistful stoicism.

Amalie *liked* her quiet, orderly, passionless life. It was safe.

Talos Kalliakis made her feel anything but safe.

Talos rapped loudly on the cottage door for the second time, blowing out a breath of exasperated air. Just as he was about to try the handle and let himself in the door swung open and there Amalie stood, violin in hand and a look of startled apology on her face.

'Is it that time already?' she said, standing aside to let him through. 'Sorry, I lost track of time.'

He followed her through to the cosy living room. The baby grand piano sat in the corner, covered with sheets of paper and an old-fashioned tape recorder. Next to it stood a music stand.

She looked what could only be described as lively—as if she had springs under her feet. In the four days she'd been in Agon he'd never seen her like this.

'Would you mind if I give the workout a miss tonight?' she asked, her green sapphire eyes vibrant and shining. 'I've reached an understanding with the score and I want to solidify it in my mind before I lose the moment.'

'You are making headway?' It amused him to hear her discussing the score as if it were a living entity.

'Something has clicked today. I've made a recording of the piano accompaniment—I am so grateful your grandmother wrote an accompaniment for the piano as well as for a full orchestra—and playing along to it is making all the pieces come together.'

'Are you ready to play it for me?'

Her eyes rounded in horror. 'Absolutely *not*.'

'You're going to have to play it for me soon,' he reminded her. The countdown was on, the gala only three weeks and six days away.

'Let me master the composition before we discuss that.'

He eyed her contemplatively. 'You have until Friday.'

She'd accompanied him to his gym three nights in a row, her workouts intense and focused. Wanting her concentration to be used in figuring out the score, he'd deliberately steered any small talk between them away from the personal. Other than chauffeuring her to and from the gym, he'd left her to it.

A dart of panic shot from her eyes. 'I won't be ready by Friday.'

'Friday will give us three weeks to get you performance-ready. I know nothing of music. It makes no difference to me if you make mistakes at this early stage; I won't notice them. What concerns me is getting you used to playing solo in front of people again. We need to work on that as much as you need to work on the score itself.'

A mutinous expression flashed over her face before her features relaxed a touch and she nodded.

'You can have tonight off, but tomorrow you go back to the gym.'

'Has anyone ever told you that you're a slave-driving ogre?'

'No one has dared.'

She rolled her eyes. 'I want to get on—you can leave now.'

'And no one has ever dared tell me when I should leave before.'

'You must be getting old, because your memory is failing—I've told you to leave before, at my home in Paris when you barged your way in.'

'Ah, yes. I distinctly remember you tried using physical force to expel me.'

His loins tightened as memories of her soft, lithe body splayed on his lap while he controlled the flare of fire and passion that had exploded out of her assailed him anew. He cast a long, appreciative look up and down her body, taking in the short black skirt over sheer black tights and the short-sleeved viridian-green shirt unbuttoned to display a hint of cleavage...

'Would you like to use force to expel me now?'

She cuddled her violin to her chest as if for protection and took a step back.

'Imagine how fit all those workouts will make you,' he purred in a deliberately sensual tone, enjoying the colour heightening her cheekbones. 'Next time you choose to fight me with your body you might have a chance of overpowering me.'

'We both know I could train twenty-four hours a day, every day for a decade, and still not be strong enough to overpower you.'

'If you would like to put that theory into practice you only have to say.' He dropped his voice and stared straight into her almond eyes. *Theos*, she was temptation itself. 'I'm not averse to a beautiful woman trying to dominate me. Something tells me the results would be explosive.'

Other than the colour on her face, she showed no reaction. For the briefest of moments Talos wondered if his assumption that the attraction he felt for her was mutual was wrong—then he saw her swallow and swipe a lock of hair from her forehead.

'Enjoy your music,' he said, stepping out of the room with one last grin.

As he shut the cottage front door behind him he ruefully conceded that trying to get a rise out of the beautiful musician living in his guest house had served no purpose other than to fuel the chemistry swirling between them.

He would need an extra-long workout to expel the energy fizzing in his veins.

CHAPTER SIX

AMALIE DID SOMETHING SACRILEGIOUS. In a fit of temper, she threw the precious score onto the floor.

Immediately she felt wretched. It wasn't the poor score's fault that all the good feelings that had grown throughout the day had vanished. It was the composer's rotten grandson who had caused that with his rotten innuendoes.

Focus, Amalie, she told herself sternly.

But it was hard to focus on the sheets of wonderful music before her when all she could think about was wrestling Talos's clothes off him and seeing for herself if he was as divine naked as he was when clothed.

That body...

It would be hard. Every inch of it. But what would his skin feel like? Would it be hard too? Or would it be smooth? How would it feel against her own skin?

Focus!

It was none of her business what Talos Kalliakis's skin felt like, or how hard his body was, or to discover if it was true that the size of a man's feet was proportionate to the size of his...

Focus!

Talos had enormous feet. And enormous hands...

He also had a smile that churned her belly into soft butter.

'Stop it!' This time she shouted the words aloud and clenched her fists.

She'd woken that morning with a sense of dread that the gala was now less than four weeks away. If she didn't master the composition, then it didn't matter what tricks Talos had up his sleeve to get her performing onstage— she would be humiliated regardless. Right at that moment all that mattered was the composition.

Sitting herself on the floor, she hitched her skirt to the top of her thighs, crossed her legs and closed her eyes. There she sat for a few minutes, concentrating on nothing but her breathing—a technique taught to her by her father, who had confessed in a conspiratorial manner that it was the breathing technique her mother had learnt when she'd been in labour with Amalie. By all accounts her mother had ignored the midwife's advice and demanded more drugs.

The thought brought a smile to her face and pulled her out of the trance-like state she'd slipped into.

The edginess that had consumed her since Talos's brief visit had subsided a little, enough for her to put the sheets of music back onto her stand and press 'play' on the tape recorder.

As she waited for the backing music to begin she couldn't help thinking she *should* have gone for a work-out, which would have cleared her angst so much better than any meditation technique.

She nestled her violin under her chin and as the first notes of the accompaniment played out she counted the beats and began to play.

Soon she was immersed in the music, so much so that when a loud rap on the front door echoed through to the living room she had to physically pull herself out of it. A quick glance at her watch showed she'd been playing for two and a half hours.

She yanked the door open just as Talos raised his knuckles for another rap.

'Have you never heard the word *patience* before?' she scolded.

He grinned and held up a large cardboard box, the motion causing a warm waft of scent to emit from it. 'I'm too hungry for patience, little songbird. I bring us food.'

Us?

The divine smell triggered something in her belly, making it rumble loudly. With a start she realised she'd forgotten to eat the tray of food a member of his villa's staff had brought to the cottage for her earlier that evening.

Since their first trip to his gym, lunch and dinner had been brought to her on Talos's orders. She knew it was only the fear that she would become anaemic or something, and faint from hunger onstage, that prompted him to do it, rather than any regard for *her*, but his concern touched her nonetheless.

The tray from earlier was still on the dining table, untouched. A warm, almost fluffy feeling trickled through her blood that he'd noticed.

Hesitating for only a moment, she let him in and headed to the kitchen, grabbed a couple of plates and some cutlery, and took them through to the dining area of the living room.

What was she supposed to do? Insist that he leave when he'd gone to the trouble of bringing her food, just because she kept having erotic thoughts about him? It would be incredibly rude. He might have used blackmail to get her here, but since then he'd treated her decently. He'd treated her well. Thoughtfully. She wasn't a prisoner, as she'd feared she would be, but had his whole household staff at her disposal for whatever she wanted or needed.

More than any of that, she would be spending a *lot* more time with him in the coming weeks. She had to get used to feeling off-centre when she was with him. She *had* to. She refused to become a gibbering idiot in his presence.

Talos held aloft a bottle of rosé retsina. 'Glasses?'

Once they were settled at the table, Talos busy removing the foil lids of the dozen boxes spread out before them, she said, 'I didn't think there would be any takeaways open on a Sunday night.'

One of the chattier members of Talos's staff had warned her yesterday to get anything she needed on Saturday, as the island mostly shut down on a Sunday.

'There aren't—I got the chefs at the palace to cook for us.'

Oh, yes. He was a prince. In Paris his royalty was something she'd been acutely aware of. Here, in the relaxed atmosphere of Agon, it was an easy thing to forget.

'And they have proper takeaway boxes to hand?'

'The palace kitchens are ten times the size of this cottage and cater for all eventualities,' he answered lightly, pouring the retsina.

'Didn't you go to the gym?' He'd showered and changed into a pair of black chinos and a dark blue polo shirt since he'd turned up at the cottage earlier, so he'd clearly done his workout, but she couldn't see how he'd have had time to go the gym *and* the palace in the short time he'd been gone.

'As you weren't doing the kickboxing class I worked out at the palace gym. It gave me a chance to catch up with my brothers and my grandfather.'

That would be the King and the two other Kalliakis Princes.

'I thought you went to your gym every night?'

'I work out every night, but not always at the gym. I try and make it there a couple of times a week when I'm in the country.'

'Have you been putting yourself out for *me*, then?'

'You're my current project,' he said with a wolfish grin. 'As long as I get you on that stage for the gala I don't care if I have to be inconvenienced.'

That was right. She was his pet project. She had to remember that anything nice he did was with an ulterior motive and not for *her*.

She took a sip of retsina, expecting to grimace at the

taste, which she'd always found rather harsh. It was surprisingly mellow—like an expensive white wine but with that unmistakable resinous tang.

'You approve?' he asked.

She nodded.

'Good. It is our island's vintage.'

'Do you make it?'

'No—we rent out our land to a producer who makes it under the island's own label.'

The food looked and tasted as divine as its aroma. Amalie happily dived into *kleftiko*—the most tender slow-cooked lamb on the bone she'd ever eaten—and its accompanying *yemista*—stuffed baked tomatoes and peppers—eating as much as she could fit into her stomach. She hadn't realised how hungry she was.

As during their shared meal at his gym, Talos ate heartily. When he'd finished wolfing down every last scrap on his plate, and emptying the takeaway boxes of every last morsel, he stuck his fork into the few leftovers on her plate.

'For a prince, you don't behave in a very regal fashion,' she observed drily.

'How is a prince supposed to behave?'

She considered, before answering, 'Regally?'

He burst into laughter—a deep, booming sound that filled the small cottage. 'I leave the regal behaviour to my brothers.'

'How do you get away with that?'

'They're the heir and the spare.' He raised a hefty shoulder into a shrug. 'Helios will take over the throne when my grandfather...'

Here, his words faltered—just a light falter, that anyone who wasn't observing him closely would likely have missed. But she *was* observing him closely—was unable to tear her eyes away from him. It wasn't just the magnetic sex appeal he oozed. The more time she spent with him, the more he fascinated her. The man behind the magnetism.

'When the day comes,' he finished smoothly. 'Theseus has been groomed for the role too, for the remote eventuality that something untoward should happen to Helios.' He must have caught her shock at his unemotional analysis because he added, 'No one knows what's around the corner. Our father was heir to the throne, but life threw a curveball at him when he was only a couple of years older than I am now.'

The car crash. The tragedy that had befallen the Kalliakis family a quarter of a century before, leaving the three young Princes orphaned. Looking at the huge man sitting opposite her, she found it was almost impossible to imagine Talos as a small child. But he had been once, and had suffered the most horrendous thing that could happen to any child: the death of not one but both parents.

The sudden temptation to cover his giant hand and whisper her sympathies was smothered by the equally sudden hard warning in his eyes—a look impossible to misinterpret. *I do not want your sympathies. This subject is not open to discussion.*

Instead she said, 'Did your brothers get favourable treatment?'

He relaxed back immediately into a grin. 'Not at all. *I* got all the preferential treatment. I was the happy accident. I was raised without any expectations—a prince in a kingdom where the most that is expected of me is to protect my brothers if ever the need arises. Even my name denotes that. In ancient mythology Talos was a giant man of bronze. There are a number of differing myths about him, but the common theme is that he was a protector.'

Goosebumps broke out over her flesh.

Something told her this big brute of a man would be a fierce protector—and not simply because of his physique.

Cross him or those he loved and you would know about it.

She cleared her throat. 'Aren't older siblings supposed to protect the youngest, not the other way round?'

His smile broadened. 'Usually. But I was such a large newborn my parents knew my role would be to protect my brothers from anyone who would do harm to them or our lands.'

'And have you had to do much in the way of protection?' she asked.

'When I was a child it seemed my role was to protect them from each other,' he said with another laugh. 'They used to fight constantly. We all did.'

'Do you get on now?'

'We all still fight, but nowadays it is only verbally. We are brothers, and we get on and work well together. We protect each other. That said, they are both big enough and ugly enough to take care of themselves.'

Amalie felt a pang of envy. She would have loved a sibling of her own. Any kind of playmate would have been wonderful. Anything would have been better than a childhood spent travelling the world with her parents on their various tours, educational tutors in tow, the only child in a world full of adults.

'Even so, aren't princes supposed to travel with a retinue of protectors at all times? And have lots of flunkeys?' In Paris he'd arrived at her home alone both times. And the only staff he'd brought to the Théâtre de la Musique had been clerical.

'It would take a very brave person to take me on—don't you think, little songbird?'

She felt her cheeks turn scarlet. She wished he would stop addressing her as *little songbird*—hated the rush of warmth that flushed through her whenever he called her it. Instinct told her that to acknowledge it would be like waving a red flag to a bull.

'Helios always travels with protection—Theseus less so.' Something sparked in his eyes, as if he were asking a question of himself. 'If you would like to see me behave in a more regal fashion you can accompany me to the ball at the palace next weekend.'

'What ball?'

'It's something Helios is hosting—a private pre-gala celebration. There will be royal flunkeys and footmen everywhere, princes and princesses from around the world—and I, little songbird, will be in my most princely attire.'

'And you want me to go with you?' Was he asking her to go as his *date*?

'It will give me a chance to show you how princely I really am,' he teased.

'If it's such a formal affair, why haven't you already got someone to take with you?'

'If I took anyone else she would take it as a sign that I was serious about her and expect me to drop to one knee.'

'Do I take it that means you're not enamoured of the thought of marriage?'

Disgust crossed his face, as if she'd suggested he dunk his head into a vat of slime.

'You're a *prince*. Aren't you supposed to marry and produce heirs?'

'Helios will produce all the heirs Agon needs. Theseus will marry and produce some more as backup. Leaving me free to continue my bachelor lifestyle for eternity.'

'The eternal playboy?'

'I dislike that term,' he said, his eyes narrowing. 'It implies a certain disrespect towards women.'

She had to laugh. 'Don't tell me you're a feminist?'

'My grandmother was the strongest person I've ever known. If I was to disrespect any woman or make judgements on the basis of her gender I am certain my grandmother would hunt me down in my dreams to give me a dressing-down.'

'She sounds like a formidable woman.'

Talos nodded. Without his grandmother's loving but steely influence—especially when he'd hit his teenage years and gone completely off the rails—he knew he wouldn't be half the man he was today.

'She was a pillar of strength,' he said, raising his glass of retsina. 'And I think she would approve of you playing her final composition.'

She made a snorting sound. 'Why would you think that?'

'Because you have the same steel core she had.'

Amalie's eyes widened, and then she frowned, a V forming in the centre of her brow. 'I can't perform in front of people. *My* core is made of blancmange.'

'But, little songbird, you are the only person other than my family who dares stand up to me.'

Even now she was disagreeing with him.

For the first time he understood why Theseus had taken a two-year sabbatical after he'd completed his time at Sandhurst. The travelling part he'd always understood, but Theseus's insistence on travelling under an assumed name had been something he'd never got. Talos was proud to be a Kalliakis—proud of their family reputation as fighters, proud of his nation's people and culture. He saw himself as a protector of their proud island and had seen Theseus's insistence at disguising his identity as a snub to the Kalliakis name.

Now he understood how it must have felt for his brother to be treated as someone…*normal*. Theseus had shared many of his tales about the personal freedom he'd found in his time away, but only now did Talos understand why it had been such a special time for him.

Amalie was the first person since childhood to treat him like a normal person. She had no qualms about disagreeing with him on any subject. As he thought back over the past few days he realised that she simply didn't pander to him. He could be *anyone*.

Which meant that when she smiled at him—which, admittedly, was rarely—it was because she meant it. When those stunning green eyes became stark, their pupils enlarged, showing her desire for him—little tells she would hate to know he recognised—it was for *him*.

He'd never bedded a woman and been one hundred per cent certain whether she was in his arms out of desire for him or the aphrodisiac quality of his title. It had never bothered him—indeed, the idea that he could bed any woman he chose held an aphrodisiac quality of its own—but the mistrust had always been there, unacknowledged yet simmering away in the depths of his consciousness.

If he were to make love to Amalie there was no question that her responses would be authentic. If she made love to him it would be for *him*.

The temptation to lean over the table, cup that beautiful heart-shaped chin in his hand and taste those delectable lips was so strong he dug his toes into his boots to keep his feet grounded to the floor.

Theos, it was a temptation that grew harder to resist the more time he spent with her. His will power and control were legendary, and yet he was having to remind himself of all the reasons he had to hone them to greater strengths when with this woman.

Making love to Amalie could be disastrous. He was supposed to be getting her fit to play at his grandfather's gala, not plotting to get those lithe limbs wrapped around his waist...

He looked at his watch and got sharply to his feet. 'I need to head back. I'm flying to New York in the morning but I'll be back Thursday evening. I'll get Kostas to take you to Natalia's—she'll make a ball dress for you.'

'I haven't agreed to come,' she protested.

'I am a prince of the land, little songbird,' he answered with a grin. 'If you defy my wishes I will have you locked in the palace dungeons.'

'You've already said the dungeons are only a tourist attraction.'

He winked at her. 'It will take me two minutes to appropriate the keys for them.'

He laughed at the scowl she bestowed upon him.

'I'll see myself out. *Kali nychta*, little songbird.'

He might not have any intention of acting on the absurdly strong chemistry growing between them, but he could damn well enjoy her company for one evening of entertainment.

CHAPTER SEVEN

A LOUD RAP on the front door broke Amalie out of the spell she was under.

She froze, violin under her chin, bow bouncing lightly on the E string. There was only one person she knew who so vividly announced his presence with just a knock on the door.

The five days of peace without Talos had come to an end. He'd returned to Agon the previous evening but she'd had a lucky escape in that he hadn't bothered with her. That hadn't stopped her spending the entire evening at his gym, looking over her shoulder, waiting for him to appear. And that sinking feeling when she'd been driven back to the cottage without him having made an appearance had *not* been disappointment.

'Hello, little songbird,' he said now, with a lazy smile on his face, the mid-afternoon sun shining down on him, enveloping him in a hazy, warm aura that made her stomach flip left, right and centre. 'Have you missed me?'

'Like a migraine,' she answered with a roll of her eyes, turning back into the cottage and leaving him to shut the door and follow her in, his low laughter at her quip reverberating through her.

'Have you had a good week?' he asked, stepping into the living room.

'It's been very peaceful, thank you. And yours?'

'Incredibly boring.'

'That'll teach you to be a lawyer.'

Today he actually looked lawyerly. Well, more like Tarzan dressed up as a lawyer, the crisp white shirt, open at the neck, rippling over his muscular chest, and charcoal trousers emphasising the length and power of his thighs. No matter what he wore he would still emit enough testosterone to fill a dozen buckets.

'It's a living,' he said, deadpan.

She couldn't help it. She laughed. She doubted Talos Kalliakis had needed to work a single day in his life.

'What does a man have to do to get a coffee round here?' he asked.

'Go to the kitchen and work the coffee machine.'

'But I am royalty. I shouldn't be expected to make my own coffee.'

'I'll have a mocha while you're there,' she said, only just stopping herself throwing a wink at him.

His irreverence was contagious.

His nose wrinkled. 'I have serious doubts about your taste, knowing you drink that muck.'

She had serious doubts about her taste too. Always she'd steered herself in the direction of safe, dependable men, those with whom she could have a nice, safe, dependable life.

There was nothing *safe* about Talos.

That little fact didn't stop her thinking about him constantly.

It didn't stop her heart from hammering at a *prestissimo* pace by virtue of just being under the same roof as him.

Luckily he took himself off to the kitchen, allowing her a few minutes to compose herself. When he returned, carrying their coffees, she'd put her violin away and sat herself in an armchair.

He placed their cups on the table and sprawled onto the sofa. 'I hear you've been going to the gym every day.'

'I was under orders, remember?'

He grinned. 'Melina thinks it is a shame you can't actually fight someone in a kickboxing match.'

Likely Melina would volunteer herself for that honour. Whilst not unfriendly, there was a definite coolness in the instructor's attitude towards her.

'I enjoy it,' she admitted.

The atmosphere at Talos's gym was different from anything she'd experienced before. There was a real collective feel about it, with everyone there prepared to help everyone else. Yes, there were some big egos, but it was a different kind of egotism from the sort she was used to in the classical music world—earthier, somehow. Considering she was one of the only women there, she never felt threatened, and she didn't think it was because everyone knew she was Talos's guest. The atmosphere of the gym itself engendered respect in all its patrons.

'Good. And how are you getting on with the score?'

'Well…I think.'

He quirked his scarred brow. 'You *think*?'

'I have no way of knowing if I'm playing it as your grandmother intended.'

'How do you mean?'

'My interpretation of the tempo she played it at might be different from her interpretation.'

He shrugged. 'You played the "Méditation" from *Thaïs* at a slower tempo than she played it, but it sounded equally beautiful.'

Talos noted the colour flush over her face, the flash of embarrassed pride that darted from her eyes.

He sat forward and rested his arms on his thighs. 'It is time for you to play for me.'

Her colour faded as quickly as it had appeared. She seemed to cower in her seat.

'I did say I would listen to you play today.'

She brightened. 'I've recorded myself playing it. You can listen to that.'

He cocked his head and sighed theatrically. 'I can see

that working well at the gala—we'll introduce our star soloist and wheel on a tape recorder with a wig.'

She spluttered a sound of nervous laughter.

He softened his voice, wanting to put her at ease. 'It is only you and me. It doesn't matter how many mistakes you make—all that matters is that today you play for me.'

There were three weeks and one day until the gala.

Judging by the terror vibrating off Amalie's frame, he would need every one of them.

He'd spent the four days in New York getting as much work done as he could, organising his staff and generally ensuring that he'd need to do minimal travelling until the gala was over. The business was being neglected by all three Kalliakis princes but what alternative did they have? All of them wanted to spend as much time with their grandfather as they could, to be there when he was having a good spell and craving their company. They were fortunate that their staff were the best of the best and could run much of the business with minimum input from them.

This trip away had been different from any other. He was always impatient to spend as much time on Agon as he could, but during this trip he'd found himself thinking of home far more frequently than normal. Thinking of *her* in his little guest cottage. He'd arrived back early yesterday evening and the temptation to pay her an immediate visit had shocked him with its intensity.

He'd resisted and headed to the palace. There, he'd shared a meal with his brothers, both of whom had been in foul tempers and had declined to answer any questions about their respective bad moods. Both had excused themselves the moment they'd finished eating. Shrugging his shoulders at their odd behaviour, Talos had sought out his grandfather, spending a pleasant couple of hours playing chess with him until a sudden bout of tiredness had forced his grandfather to call a halt.

It unnerved him how quickly his grandfather could fall

into exhaustion—one minute sitting upright, laughing, holding a conversation; the next his chin drooping, his eyes struggling to stay open, his speech slurring…

Talos could feel the time ebbing away. He could see it too. He'd only been four days in New York and his grandfather had lost even more weight, the large, vital man now a shadow of his former self.

The woman before him had the power to make his grandfather's last days the sweetest they could be. She could bring his beloved Rhea's final composition to life. She was the only person in the world who could do it justice.

He watched Amalie struggle for composure, feeling a strange tugging in his chest when she visibly forced herself to her feet and over to the baby grand piano, where she'd left her violin.

Not looking at him, she removed it from its case and fiddled with the strings, tuning them as his grandmother had always done before playing for him.

Moving her music stand behind the piano, as if she were using the piano for protection, she arranged the sheets of music until she was satisfied with how they stood, then rested her violin under her chin.

About to hit the first note, she halted, bow upright, and stared at him. 'I've almost memorised it. I won't need the sheet music when I do the gala.'

It was the first time he'd heard her utter her intentions to actually perform at the gala. He wondered if she was aware of what she'd just given away—how in the nine days she had been on his island her mind-set had already altered.

He raised his hands and pulled a face to indicate his nonchalance about such matters. What did he care if she played with the music in front of her or not? All he cared was that she played it.

'I'll play without the accompaniment.'

'Stop stalling and *play*.'

She swallowed and nodded, then closed her eyes.

Her bow struck the first note.

And bounced off the string.

He watched her closely. The hand holding the violin—the hand with the short nails, which he suddenly realised were kept that length to stop them inadvertently hitting the strings when playing—was holding the instrument in a death grip. The hand holding the bow was shaking. It came to him in flash why her nails seemed so familiar. His grandmother had kept her nails in the same fashion.

'Take some deep breaths,' he instructed, hooking an ankle over his knee, making sure to keep his tone low and unthreatening.

She gave a sharp nod and, eyes still closed, inhaled deeply through her nose.

It made no difference. The bow bounced off the strings again.

She breathed in again.

The same thing happened.

'What are you thinking of right now?' he asked after a few minutes had passed, the only sound the intermittent bounce of her bow on the strings whenever she made another attempt to play. Her distress was palpable. 'What's in your head?'

'That I feel naked.'

Her eyes opened and blinked a couple of times before fixing on him. Even with Amalie at the other end of the room he could see the starkness in her stare.

'Do you ever have that dream where you go somewhere and are surrounded by people doing ordinary things, and you look down and discover you have *nothing* on?'

'I am aware of people having those dreams,' he conceded, although it wasn't one he'd personally experienced.

No, *his* dreams—nightmares—were infinitely darker, his own powerlessness represented by having to relive that last evening with his parents, when he'd jumped onto his father's back and pounded at him with his little fists.

His father had bucked him off with such force that he'd clattered to the floor and hit his head on the corner of their bed. In his dreams he had to relive his mother holding him in her arms, soothing him, kissing his sore, bleeding head and wiping away his tears which had mingled with her own.

It was the last time he'd seen them.

He hadn't been allowed to see them when they'd lain in state. The condition of their bodies had been so bad that closed caskets had been deemed the only option.

And that was the worst of his nightmares—when he would walk into the family chapel and lift the lids of their coffins to see the ravages the car crash had wreaked on them. His imagination in those nightmares was limitless...

'Try and imagine it, because it's the closest I can come to explaining how I feel right now,' she said, her voice as stark as the panic in her eyes.

For the first time he believed—*truly* believed—that her fear was genuine. He'd always believed it was real, but had assumed she'd been exaggerating for effect.

This was no exaggeration.

'You feel naked?' he asked evenly. He, more than anyone, knew how the imagination could run amok, the fear of the unknown so much worse than reality. He also knew how he could help her take the first step to overcome it.

'Yes,' she whispered.

The strange distance Amalie had seen settling over him had dissipated, and his attention on her was focused and strong.

'Then there is only one solution. You must *be* naked.'

'What...?'

But her solitary word hardly made it past her vocal cords. Talos had leant forward and was pulling his shoes and socks off.

What was he doing?

His hands went to his shirt. Before she could comprehend what she was seeing he'd deftly undone all the buttons.

'What are you doing?'

He got to his feet.

If she hadn't already pressed herself against the wall she would have taken a step back. She would have turned and run.

But there was nowhere for her to run *to*—not without getting past him first.

'The only way you're going to overcome your fear of nakedness is to *play* naked.'

His tone was calm, at complete odds with the panic careering through her.

She could not dislodge her tongue from the roof of her mouth.

He shrugged his arms out of his shirt and hung it on the back of a dining chair.

His torso was magnificent, broad and muscular, his skin a golden bronze. A light smattering of black hair covered his defined pecs, somehow tempering the muscularity.

As nonchalant as if he were undressing alone for a shower, he tugged at the belt of his trousers, then undid the button and pulled the zip down.

'Please, stop,' she beseeched him.

He fixed her with a stare that spoke no nonsense, then pulled his trousers down, taking his underwear with them. Stepping out of them, he folded and placed them over his shirt, then propped himself against the wall, his full attention back on her.

'I am not going to force you to take your clothes off,' he said, in that same deep, calm tone. 'But if you play naked for me now you will have lived out your worst fear and in the process you will have overcome it. I would not have you at the disadvantage of being naked alone so I have removed my clothes to put us on an equal footing. I will stay here, where I stand. You have my word that I will not take a step closer to you. Unless,' he added with the wolfish grin she was becoming familiar with, 'you ask me to.'

All she could do was shake her head mutely, but not with the terror he was reading in her, but because she'd been rendered speechless.

She'd known Talos naked would be a sight to behold, but she had never dreamed how magnificent he would be.

Why him? she wondered desperately.

Why did her body choose *this* man to respond to?

Why did it have to respond at all?

She knew what desire looked like, had seen her mother in its grip so many times, then seen her heart broken as her most recent lover tired of the incessant diva demands and ended things, shattering her mother's heart and fragile ego.

Passion and its companion desire were dangerous things she wanted no part of, had shied away from since early adolescence. Hearts were made to be broken, and it was desire that pulled you into its clutches.

All those protections she'd placed around her libido and sense of self were crumbling.

Talos's grin dropped. 'I said I would help you, little songbird, but you have to help yourself too. You have to take the first step.'

Her breaths were coming so hard she could feel the air expanding her lungs.

She thought frantically. She hadn't ever shown her naked body to a man before. Her few boyfriends had never put pressure on her, respecting her need to wait, the lie she'd told them in order to defer any kind of physicality. Kind men. *Safe* men.

Was it the safety she'd sought that had kept alive her fear of performing?

One of her psychiatrists—the most astute of them all—had once said he didn't believe she *wanted* to be fixed.

She'd denied it but now, looking back, she considered the possibility that he'd been partly right.

Her life was *safe*. Maybe a little boring, but she'd found her niche and she never wanted to leave it or the emotional protection it gave her.

But she had to. She couldn't stay there any longer. If she didn't step out she would lose that little niche anyway—for good. Her job would be gone. Her income would be gone. Her independence would be gone. All her friends' lives would be destroyed too.

'We are more alike than you think, you and I,' Talos said.

His voice was deeper and lower than she had ever heard it, every syllable full of meaning. He still hadn't made a move towards her.

'We have both chosen solitary pursuits. I focus on my boxing, you have your violin. No one can pull my punches for me and no one can play that violin for you. Think of the emotions you get when you're kickboxing, the adrenaline you feel through your veins. *That* is how you must imagine your fear—as something to be channelled and fought. You are on Agon, the land of warriors. We fight. And so must you. *Fight*, little songbird. Loosen your hold and *fly*.'

She gripped onto the piano for support and closed her eyes, his words resonating through her.

Was it time to confront all the fear?

If not now, then when?

If not here, then where?

'Will you turn around when I undress?'

'I will, but when you play I will watch you. I cannot guarantee I will stop my thoughts roaming to inappropriate places, but I *can* guarantee I will not act on them.'

I wish I could guarantee the same.

'If you can get through this you can get through anything. I give you my word.'

Strike her down, but she believed him.

'Right here and now it is you and me—no one else.

If you make mistakes then keep going. You can do this, Amalie.'

Whether it was the calm sincerity in his voice or the confidence emanating from him—God, he was *naked*—something worked, turning the panic inside her down low enough for her to get a grip on herself.

'Please turn around,' she said shakily.

He did as she asked, standing so his back was to her. His back was every bit as beautiful as his front, his body a mass of taut muscle and sinew. He was not professional-body-builder big, but big enough that you would trust him to pull a car off a helpless victim and then carry them over his shoulder to safety without breaking a sweat.

With fingers that fumbled she pulled off her pretty blue top and shrugged her skirt down. Her legs already bare, all that was left was her underwear. She tried to undo her bra, but what was second nature suddenly became the hardest job in the world.

'I *can't*,' she said, suddenly panic-stricken all over again.

Talos turned his head a touch before twisting his whole body round. Arms folded across his chest, he gazed at her, the look on his face something she'd never seen before. It looked as if it hurt him to breathe.

'That is enough,' he said quietly. 'Now, please—play for me.'

This time she allowed her eyes to dart down and look at what she'd tried to keep as a haze, skimming around the area as if it were pixilated.

The heat that rushed through her at one glance almost knocked her off her feet.

The knowing look that came into his eyes had the same effect.

Talos was in proportion in *every* way.

Suddenly she yanked her violin off the piano, put it under chin and began to play.

The bow swept across the strings, bouncing gently because of her less than graceful start, but then it did what it had been made to do, whilst her fingers flew up and down the strings. It was probably the worst start to a performance she'd ever given, but she wouldn't have known either way as at that moment she wasn't hearing the music, but simply relishing the fact that she was winning this fight. She was doing it. She was playing in front of someone.

God, she was virtually *naked*.

And Talos was as naked as the day he'd been born.

Somehow she settled into the music, embraced it, letting it become her. Far from closing her eyes, she kept her gaze on him, felt the heat of his returning stare.

By the time she played the last note the tension in the room had merged with the vibrato of her violin, a tangible, pulsating chemistry she felt all the way through to her core.

For long, long moments nothing was said. Not verbally.

The connection between their gazes spoke a thousand words.

'You brought my skin up in bumps,' he finally said, his voice raspy.

She gave a helpless shrug.

'You didn't play my grandmother's composition.'

She shook her head. She had played the final movement of one of Vivaldi's *Four Seasons* concertos—'Summer'. The movement that evoked a thunderstorm and perfectly fitted the storm raging beneath her skin.

'I didn't want you to hear it when I knew I wouldn't be able to do it justice. Not the first time.'

'The first time should be special, yes.'

She breathed deeply, sensing he wasn't talking about the music any more.

He made no move towards her. The look in his eyes was clear. He'd made her a promise not to get any closer to her. Not unless she invited him to.

Her blood had never felt so thick, as if she'd had hot treacle injected into her veins.

She wanted him. Desperately. Passionately…

No!

The warning shout in her head rang out loud and clear, breaking through the chemistry buffeting them, shattering it with one unsaid syllable.

Without a word she grabbed her top and pulled it back on, smoothing it over her belly as she darted a glance to see his reaction.

He inclined his head, an amused yet pained smile on his lips, then turned to his clothes and stepped back into his underwear and trousers before slipping his powerful arms into his shirt.

'You played beautifully, little songbird. And now it is time for me to leave.'

'Already?' The word escaped before she could catch it.

He dropped his stare down to his undone trousers. 'Unless you want me to break my promise?'

He cocked his head, waiting for an answer that wouldn't form.

'I thought not.' His eyes flashed. 'But we both know it's only a matter of time.'

She swallowed the moisture that had filled in her mouth, pushing it past the tightness in her throat.

'A car will collect you tomorrow at seven.'

'Seven?' she asked stupidly, her mind turning blank at his abrupt turn of conversation.

'Helios's ball,' he reminded her, fastening the last of his buttons. 'Did you receive the official invitation?'

She nodded. Her invitation had been hand delivered by a palace official, the envelope containing it a thick, creamy material, sealed with a wax insignia. Receiving it had made her feel like a princess from a bygone age.

'Keep it safe—you'll need to present it when you arrive. I'll be staying at my apartment in the palace for the weekend, so I'll send a car for you.'

She'd assumed they would travel there together, and

was unnerved by the twinge of disappointment she felt at
learning differently.

'Okay,' she answered, determined to mask the emotion.

It wasn't as if they were going on a proper date or anything, she reminded herself. She was simply his 'plus one'
for the evening.

'Are you happy with your dress?' he asked.

On Monday Amalie had been driven by a member of
Talos's staff to a pretty beachside house and introduced to
an elegant elderly woman called Natalia. Natalia had measured every inch of her, clearly seizing her up as she did
so. Then she had sat at her desk and sketched, spending
less time than it took for Amalie to finish a coffee before
she'd ripped the piece of paper off the pad and held out the
rough but strangely intricate design to her.

'This is your dress,' she had said, with calm authority.

Amalie had left the house twenty minutes later with
more excitement running through her veins than she had
ever experienced before. She'd been to plenty of high-
society parties in her lifetime, but never to a royal ball.
And she was to wear a dress like *nothing* she had worn in
her life. Natalia's vision had been so compelling and assured that she had rolled along with it, swept up in the designer's vision.

It was strange and unnerving to think she was to be the
guest of a prince. She no longer thought of Talos in that
light. Only as a man...

'Natalia is bringing it tomorrow so she can help me into
it.' The dress fastening was definitely a two-person job. If
the designer hadn't been coming to her Amalie would have
had to find someone else to help her fasten it. She might
have had to ask Talos to hook it for her...

He nodded his approval.

Dressed, Talos ran his fingers through his hair in what
looked to Amalie like a futile attempt on his behalf to
tame it.

There was nothing tameable about this man.

'Until tomorrow, little songbird,' he said, before letting himself out of the cottage.

Only when all the energy that followed him like a cloud had dissipated from the room did Amalie dare breathe properly.

With shaky legs she sat on the piano bench and pressed her face to the cool wood.

Maybe if she sat there for long enough the compulsion to chase after him and throw herself at him would dissipate too.

CHAPTER EIGHT

THE BLACK LIMOUSINE drove over a bridge and through a long archway before coming to a stop in a vast courtyard at the front of the palace.

Her heart fluttering madly beneath her ribs, Amalie stared in awe, just as she'd been gaping since she'd caught her first glimpse of it, magnificent and gleaming under the last red embers of the setting sun.

The driver opened the door for her and held out an arm, which she accepted gratefully. She had never worn heels so high. She had never felt so...*elegant*.

That's what wearing the most beautiful bespoke dress in creation does for you.

Still gaping, she stared up. The palace was so vast she had to make one-hundred-and-eighty-degree turns to see from one side to the next. Although vastly different in style, its romanticism rivalled France's beautiful Baroque palaces. Its architecture was a mixture of styles she'd seen throughout Europe and North Africa, forming its own unique and deeply beautiful style that resembled a great sultan's palace with gothic undertones.

Two dozen wide curved steps led up to a high-arched ornate entrance, where two footmen dressed in purple-and-gold livery with yellow sashes stood. She climbed the steps towards them, thinking that this was surely what Cinderella had felt like. After studiously checking her official invitation, another footman stepped forward to escort her into the palace itself.

First they entered a reception room so vast her entire

cottage would fit inside it—roof and all, with room to spare—then walked through to another room where a group of footmen were being given last-minute instructions by a man who wore a red sash over his livery.

'Am I the first to arrive?' she asked her escort, who unfortunately spoke as much French and English as she spoke Greek—none at all.

It wasn't just the footmen being given instructions or the lack of other guests that made her think she was the first. Scores of waiting staff were also being given a last-minute briefing, many straightening clothing and smoothing down hair. She could feel their eyes on her, and their muted curiosity over the strange woman who had clearly arrived too early.

As she was led into another room—narrower, but much longer than the first reception room—staff carrying trays of champagne were lining up along the walls, beneath a gallery of portraits. At the far end were three tall figures dressed in black, deep in conversation.

Amalie's heart gave a funny jump, then set off at an alarming rate that increased with every step she took towards them. Her escort by her side, she concentrated on keeping her feet moving, one in front of the other.

Suddenly Talos turned his head and met her gaze, his eyes widening with such dumbstruck appreciation that her pulse couldn't help but soar. It was a look men so often threw at her beautiful mother, but never at her. But then, Amalie had never *felt* beautiful before. Tonight, thanks to the hairstylist and beautician Natalia had brought along with her when she'd arrived at the cottage to dress her, she did. She felt like a princess.

And Talos…

Talos looked every inch the Prince.

Like the two men beside him, who matched him in height and colouring, he wore a black tuxedo with a purple bowtie and sash that matched the livery of the palace footmen, and black shoes that gleamed in the same manner as his eyes. For the first time since she'd met him she saw him freshly shaved.

She'd thought the rugged Talos, the man she was getting to know, was as sexy a man as she could ever meet. The princely Talos had lost none of his edge and the wolfish predatory air was still very much there. Not even the expensive dinner jacket could diminish his essential masculinity. He still looked like a man capable of throwing a woman over his huge shoulder and carrying her to a large nomad-style tent to pleasure her in a dozen different ways before she had time to draw breath.

Amalie drew in her own breath as molten heat pooled low inside her at the thought of Talos pleasuring *her*...

Judging from the look in his eyes, something similar was running through his mind.

He strode over to greet her, enveloping her hand in his before leaning down to kiss her on each cheek.

Suddenly she couldn't breathe, her senses completely filled with his scent and the feel of his lips against her skin.

'Little songbird, you are beautiful,' he whispered into her ear, his deep, gravelly voice sending her heart beating so fast it felt as if it would jump out of her chest. 'Let me introduce you to my brothers,' he said while she strove valiantly for composure. 'Helios, Theseus—this is my guest for the evening: Amalie Cartwright.'

Theseus nodded and smiled. 'A pleasure to meet you.'

'And you,' she murmured in reply.

Helios extended his hand to her, his dark eyes studying her. 'I understand you are playing our grandmother's composition at the gala?'

Her cheeks flushing, she nodded and accepted his hand. Suddenly she realised that this was the heir to the throne she was standing before, and bent her knees in a clumsy form of curtsy.

Helios laughed, but not unkindly, before putting his

hands on her shoulders and kissing her on each cheek. 'You are my brother's guest—please, do not stand on ceremony.'

'I'm surprised she even tried,' Talos drawled, slipping an arm around her waist and placing a giant hand on her hip.

Dear God, he was *touching* her. Even through the heavy cloqué material of her dress she could feel the weight of his touch.

'The last time Amalie and I discussed matters of ceremony she reminded me that the French chopped all their royal family's heads off.'

Mortified, she reflexively elbowed him in the stomach, only to elicit more deep laughter from the three Princes that was so contagious her nerves vanished and she found herself laughing along with them.

Although of similar height and colouring, the differences between the brothers were noticeable up close. Theseus, maybe an inch or two shorter than Talos, had a more wiry build and an edgy weariness about him. Helios was as tall as Talos and had a real air of irreverence about him; a man who enjoyed life and was comfortable in his skin.

An officious courtier appeared at their sides and addressed the Princes in Greek.

'We must take our positions,' Talos said quietly.

'Where shall I go?' she asked.

'With me…to greet our guests. Tonight you will stay by my side.'

The gleam in his eyes conveyed a multitude of meanings behind his words. A shivery thrill ran through her, and when he linked his arm through hers she accepted the warmth that followed.

'Where are your brothers' dates?' she asked in a low voice.

'That is the whole purpose of the evening,' he answered enigmatically as they stepped into a cavernous room with a medieval feel, draped with purple sashes. Long dark wood tables formed an enormous horseshoe, laid with gleaming

cutlery and crystal glasses that bounced the light from the
chandeliers.

She gasped, totally losing track of her interest in his
brothers' lack of dates. 'How many people are eating?'

'One hundred and eighty,' Talos answered, grinning.

The Banquet Room never failed to elicit a reaction. And
neither, it seemed, did Amalie ever fail to make his senses
react. One look and he wanted nothing more than to whisk
her away somewhere private and feast on *her*.

With his brothers at the main door, greeting the guests,
his role was to welcome them into the Banquet Room and
act as host until all the guests had arrived.

Scores of waiting staff were stationing themselves with
trays of champagne in hand. Talos helped himself to a glass
for them both and passed one to Amalie.

'Drink it in one,' he advised. 'It will relieve the tedium
of the next half hour.'

He laughed as she did as he suggested—with enthusiasm and without spilling a single drop.

He could not get over how ravishing she looked. If she
hadn't already been there as his guest he would have spent
the evening pursuing her, determined to learn everything
there was to know about this enchanting stranger in their
midst. He would have rearranged the table settings to be
seated next to her—would have done everything in his
power to keep her as close to him as he could.

But he didn't need to do any of that. For this evening
this stunning woman was already his.

'You look amazing,' he said. 'Natalia has outdone herself.'

Strapless, Amalie's gown showed only the slightest hint
of cleavage, cinched in at the waist before spreading out
and down to her feet, forming a train at the back. It wasn't
just the shape of the dress and the way it showcased her
slight form that made it so unique, but the heavy material
and the colour too—black, with tiny gold sequins threaded

throughout into swirling leaves, glimmering under the lights.

The dramatic effect was accentuated by a gold choker around her slender throat, and her dark hair was held in an elegant knot at the base of her neck. She wore large hooped earrings and her eyes were darkly defined, her lips the most ravishing of reds.

Her eyes, wide with obvious awe up until this point, narrowed. 'Has Natalia dressed many of your dates?'

There was a definite hint of tartness in her tone. He eyed her contemplatively. Was that tartness a sign of jealousy?

Jealousy was an emotion he had no time for. He neither cared about his lovers' past bedmates nor felt any pangs of regret when their time was over and they found someone new. If during their time together any sign of possessiveness reared its head, he would end the relationship there and then. Jealousy was dangerous—as dangerous as love itself—driving men and women to lose control of themselves with unimaginable consequences.

And yet hearing that tinge of jealousy filled his chest in a manner he didn't even want to begin contemplating. Not when he couldn't take his eyes from her...couldn't stop his imagination running wild about what lay beneath that stunning dress.

His imagination had run riot since the day before, when she'd played for him semi-naked.

In his head he'd imagined she would wear practical underwear—not the matching lacy black numbers that set off the porcelain of her skin. As slender as he'd imagined, her womanly curves were soft, her breasts high and surprisingly full. What lay beneath those pretty knickers? he'd wondered, over and over. Had she taken the route so many women seemed to favour nowadays? Or had she left herself as nature intended...?

Halfway through her playing he'd smothered a groan, thinking it would be a damn sight better if she were fully naked, as his wild imaginings were utter torture. The expression in her eyes had only added to his torment.

For the first time in his life he'd come close to breaking a promise. He'd known that if he'd taken her into his arms she would have been his. But it hadn't only been his promise that had kept him propped against the cottage wall. It had been the shyness he'd seen when she'd first stood before him wearing only her underwear—a shyness he'd not seen since his lusty teenage years. An innocence that made him certain Amalie had minimal experience with men.

That innocence had acted like an alarm. A warning. Alas, it had done nothing to diminish the ache, which hadn't abated a touch, not in his groin or in his chest. All day, helping his brothers with the evening's arrangements, his mind had been elsewhere—in the cottage, with her.

'Natalia was my grandmother's official dressmaker,' he said softly. 'She made her wedding dress and my mother's wedding dress. She's mostly retired now, but as a favour to me agreed to make your ball gown. I've never sent another woman to her.'

Dark colour stained her cheeks—almost as dark as the wide dilation of her eyes. Was that what her eyes would look like when she was in the throes of passion…?

The thought was broken when the first guests were led into the Banquet Room. Two footmen stood at the door, handing out the evening's booklets—a guide for each guest that was adorned with purple ribbon. Each booklet contained a full guest list, the menu, wine list and a seating plan, along with a list of the music to be played throughout the evening by the Agon Orchestra. The orchestra's role tonight should go some way towards mitigating any underlying resentment that a French orchestra would be playing at the official gala.

As his brothers had already given the official welcome, Talos's job was to keep the guests entertained until everyone had arrived.

He would have preferred to be at the main entrance, shaking hands. He hadn't been joking when he'd described the tedium of what was about to ensue. Almost two hundred guests filed into the Banquet Room, the majority of whom were, at the most, distant acquaintances but all of whom expected to be remembered personally and made to feel like the most important guest there.

Normally Theseus would take this role, and Talos would line up with Helios to do the official greeting. If there was one thing Talos couldn't abide, it was small talk, having to feign interest in interminably dull people. Tonight, though, he wanted to keep Amalie at his side—not wanting her to have to deal with scores of strangers alone. Palace protocol meant only members of the royal family could make the first greeting.

To his surprise, she was a natural at small talk; moving easily between people with Talos by her side, taking an interest in who they were and what they did that wasn't feigned, her smiles as warm for those from the higher echelons of society as for those much further down the social ladder.

If she was aware of all the appreciative gazes being thrown her way by men and women alike she did a good job of pretending not to be.

When the gong rang out, signalling for everyone to take their seats, Talos looked at his watch and saw over half an hour had passed since the first guests had stepped into the Banquet Room. The time had flown by.

'You mastered the room like a pro,' he said in an undertone as they found their seats on what had been designated the top table.

She cast puzzled eyes on him.

'The way you handled our welcome job,' he explained. 'Most people would be overwhelmed when faced with one hundred and eighty people wanting to make small talk.'

She shrugged with a bemused expression. 'My parents

were always throwing parties. I think I mastered the art of small talk before I learned how to walk.'

'You attended their parties?'

'I was the main party piece.'

Before he could ask what she meant another gong sounded out and a courtier bade them all into silence as Helios and Theseus strode regally into the room.

No one took a seat until Helios, the highest-ranked member of the family in attendance, had taken his.

A footman pulled Amalie's chair out for her, while Talos gathered the base of the train of her dress so she could sit down with ease. He caught a glimpse of delicate white ankle and had to resist the urge to run his fingers over it, to feel for himself the texture of her skin.

'Thank you,' she murmured, her eyes sparkling.

'You're welcome.'

Taking his own seat, he opened his booklet to peruse the menu. As Helios had directed, the four-course meal had an international flavour rather than one specifically Greek or Agonite.

White wine was poured into the appropriate glasses, the starter of dressed crab with an accompanying crab timbale, crayfish and prawns was brought out by the army of serving staff, and the banquet began.

'Is your grandfather not attending?' Amalie whispered before taking a sip of her wine.

'He is unwell.'

'Nothing serious, I hope?' she asked with concern.

He forced a smile. 'A touch of flu, that's all.'

'It must be a worry for you,' she said, clearly seeing through his brevity.

'My grandfather is eighty-seven and as tough as a horse,' he deflected artfully.

She laughed. 'My English grandfather is eighty-five and tough as a horse too. They'll outlive the lot of us!'

How he wished that was the case, he thought, his heart

turning to lead as he envisaged a life without his grand-father, a steady if often aloof presence, but someone who had always been there.

For the first time he felt the compulsion to confide, to tell the truth of his grandfather's condition. It was there, right on the tip of his tongue. And he was the man who confided in *no one*. Not even his brothers.

The thought was unsettling.

Talos had learned the art of self-containment at the age of seven. The only person able to give him enough comfort to sleep when the nightmares had become too much to bear had died five years ago.

Yet for all the solace his grandmother had given him she'd never been able to give him peace. No one could give him that. He would sit stiffly in her arms, refusing to return the physical comfort she gave him. It had been a battle of wills with himself, something he could control and that no one could ever take away.

He'd been wise not to return the affection. How much greater would his pain have been if he had? He'd loved his mother with the whole of his heart. Her death had come close to destroying him.

The pain of his grandmother's death had still hit him like one of the punches he received in the boxing ring, but it had been survivable. If he'd allowed himself to love her the way he'd loved his mother, he didn't like to think how he would have reacted. Would the control he'd spent most of his life-time perfecting have snapped? Would he have returned to those awful adolescent days when his fists had lashed out so many times he'd been on the verge of expulsion?

He was saved from having to respond by a young waiter asking if he would like his wine topped up.

If Amalie noticed his changed demeanour she gave no sign of it, craning her neck to follow their wine serv-er's progress out of the room. 'Doesn't that boy work at your gym?'

He was impressed that she'd recognised him. Workout gear was markedly different from the fitted black-and-white waiter's uniform, with the purple ribbon stitched into the sides of the trousers.

'And she's from your gym too,' Amalie whispered, nodding at a young girl in the far corner.

'Most of the kids who work at the gym are working here tonight—it's extra money for them and good experience.'

He had to admit to feeling an inordinate amount of pride, watching them performing their jobs so well. He'd fought the protocol battle a number of years ago, to allow 'his' kids to work at the palace whenever the opportunity arose.

'Do you make a point of employing teenagers?'

'It was one of the reasons I decided to build my own gym—I wanted to employ disaffected teenagers and make them feel a sense of worth in themselves. The kids who work there are free to spar and train whenever they're off duty for no charge.'

'These kids are allowed to *box*?'

'You disapprove?'

'It's one thing for a fully grown adult to choose to get into a boxing ring and have his face battered, but quite another when it's a developing teenager.'

'Teenagers are full of hormones they have to navigate their way through. It's a minefield for many of them.'

'I agree, but...'

'Agon is a wealthy island, but that doesn't mean it's problem-free,' he said, wanting her to understand. 'Our teenagers have the same problems as other Western teenagers. We give jobs and training to the ones living on the edge—the ones in danger of dropping out of society, the ones who, for whatever reason, have a problem controlling their anger. Boxing teaches them to control and channel that anger.'

Hadn't he said something similar to her just the day before, in her cottage? Amalie wondered, thinking hard about the conversation they'd shared. The problem was her own hormones and fear had played such havoc that much of their conversation was blurred in her memory.

'Is that why *you* got into boxing?'

His jaw clenched for the beat of a moment before relaxing. 'I had anger issues. My way of coping with life was using my fists.'

'Was that because of your parents?' she asked carefully, aware she was treading on dangerous ground.

He jerked a nod. 'Things came to a head when I was fourteen and punched my roommate at my English boarding school. I shattered his cheekbone. I would have been expelled if the Head of Sport hadn't intervened.'

'They wanted to expel you? But you're a *prince*.'

His eyes met hers, a troubled look in them. 'Expulsion was a rare event at my school—who wants to be the one to tell a member of a royal family or the president of a country that their child is to be permanently excluded? But it wasn't a first offence—I'd been fighting my way through school since I was eight. The incident with my roommate was the final straw.'

He couldn't read what was in her eyes, but thought he detected some kind of pity—or was it empathy?

She tilted her head, elongating the swan of her neck. 'How did your Head of Sport get them to change their mind?'

'Mr Sherman said he would personally take me under his wing and asked for three months to prove he could tame my nature.'

'He did that through boxing?' Now she thought about it, Amalie could see the sense in it. Hadn't the kickboxing workouts Talos had forced her into doing created a new equilibrium within her? Already she knew that when she returned to Paris she would join a gym that gave the same classes and carry on with it.

'At my school you had to be sixteen to join the boxing team, but he persuaded them—with the consent of my

grandparents—to allow me to join.' He laughed, his face
relaxing as he did so. 'Apart from my brothers, I was the
biggest boy in the school. There was a lot of power behind
my punches, which was what had got me into so much trouble in the first place. Mr Sherman taught me everything we
now teach the kids who use our gym—the most important
being how to channel and control my anger.'

'Did it work?'

'I haven't thrown a punch in anger since.'

'That is really something.'

Self-awareness nagged at her—an acknowledgement
that while Talos had handled his rage through using his
fists, she'd retreated from her own fears and buried them.
But while he'd confronted and tamed his demons she'd
continued hiding away, building a *faux* life for herself that
was nothing like her early childhood dreams—those early
days when she'd *wanted* to be a virtuoso on the violin, just
like her father.

She'd been five years old when she'd watched old foot-
age of him at Carnegie Hall—the same night he'd played
on stage with Talos's grandmother—and she'd said, with
all the authority of a small child, 'When I'm growed up I'll
play there with you, Papa.'

She'd let those dreams die.

CHAPTER NINE

IT TOOK A FEW beats for Amalie to regain her composure. 'Did you get to take part in proper boxing matches?'

'I was school champion for four years in a row—a record that has never been broken.' He placed a finger to the scar on his eyebrow. 'That was my most serious injury.'

She winced. 'Did you want to take it up professionally?'

'I'm a prince, so it was never an option—royal protocol.' He gave a rueful shake of his head, then flashed another grin that didn't quite meet his eyes. 'I *did* win every amateur heavyweight boxing award going, though, including an international heavyweight title.'

'No!' she gasped. 'Really?'

'It was six years ago.'

'That is incredible.'

'It was the best day of my life,' he admitted. 'Receiving the winner's belt with the Agon National Anthem playing... Yes, the best day of my life.'

She shook her head in awe, a thrill running through her as she saw a vision of Talos, standing in the centre of a boxing ring, perspiration dripping from his magnificent body, the epitome of masculinity...

'Truly, that's incredible. Do you still compete?'

'I haven't boxed in a competitive match since. I knew if I couldn't fight professionally I wanted to retire on a high.'

'You must miss it, though.'

She tried to imagine having to stop playing her violin and felt nothing but coldness. Her earliest concrete memory was receiving her first violin at the age of four. Yes, it had partly been forced on her, but she'd loved it, had adored making the same kind of music as her papa, revelled in her parents' excitement when she'd taken to it with such an affinity that they couldn't resist showing her off to the world. She'd loved pleasing her parents but before she'd reached double digits the resulting attention from the outside world had turned into her personal horror story. She might have inherited her parents' musicality, but their showmanship had skipped a generation.

He shrugged. 'I still spar regularly, but in truth I knew it was time to focus my attention on the business my brothers and I founded. Theseus had gone off on his sabbatical, so Helios was running it almost single-handedly along with dealing with his royal duties. It wasn't fair on him.'

'I don't understand why you all put so much into the business when you have so much wealth.'

He eyed her meditatively. 'How much do you think it costs to run a palace this size? The running costs, the maintenance, the staff?'

'A lot?'

'Yes. A lot. And that's just for one palace. Factor in the rest of our estates—my villa, for example—travelling costs, security...'

'I can imagine,' she cut in, feeling slightly dizzy now he was explaining it.

'My family has always had personal wealth,' Talos explained, 'but a considerable portion of our income came from taxes.'

'Came?'

He nodded. 'My brothers and I were determined to make our family self-sufficient, and three years ago we succeeded. Our islanders no longer pay a cent towards our upkeep. I might not compete any more, but I get all the intellectual stimulation I need.'

Amalie swallowed, guilt replacing the dizziness. She'd been so dismissive of his wealth.

Talos Kalliakis might be unscrupulous at getting his own way but he had a flip side—a side that was loyal, decent and thoughtful. He clearly loved his island and his people.

'What about the physical stimulation you got from competitive boxing?' she asked. 'Have you found a replacement for that?'

His eyes glistened, a lazy smile tugging at his lips. 'There is a physical pastime I partake in regularly that I find *very* stimulating...'

The breath in her lungs rushed out in a whoosh.

When he looked at her like that and spoke in that meaningful tone all her senses seemed to collide, making her tongue-tied, unable to come up with any riposte—witty or otherwise.

For the first time she asked herself why she should. Why make a joke out of something that made her blood and belly feel as warm and thick as melted chocolate? Why continue to deny herself something that could take her places she'd locked away?

Hadn't she punished herself enough?

That thought seemed to come from nowhere, making her blink sharply.

Punished herself enough?

But there was something in that. Her fear was wrapped in so many layers, with her guilt over her role in her parents' divorce bound tightly in the middle of it.

Talos had confronted his fears and mastered them. Wasn't it time she allowed herself the same? She didn't have to suppress her basic biological needs and be a virgin for ever out of fear. Or guilt.

She wasn't her mother. Allowing herself to be with Talos and experience the pleasure she just *knew* she would receive at his willing giant hands wouldn't be a prelude to falling in love. A man holding one hundred musicians' livelihoods to ransom for the sake of a *gala* could pose no risk to her heart.

She cleared her throat and dropped her voice to a murmur. 'Would you care to elucidate on this stimulation you speak of?'

She would swear his eyes darkened to match the melting chocolate in her veins.

He leaned his head forward and spoke into her exposed ear. 'I can do much better than that…'

The chocolate heated and pooled down low, right in the apex of her thighs…the feeling powerful enough to make her lips part and a silent moan escape her throat.

Just when she was certain he was going to kiss her—or, worse, *she* was going to kiss *him*—activity around them brought her to her senses.

They were in the Banquet Room of the royal palace, surrounded by almost two hundred people, the heir to the throne sitting only six seats to her right. And she was bubbling up with lust.

During the rest of the banquet she made a studious effort to speak to the gentleman on her right, a prince from the UK. Through it all, though, her mind, her senses, her *everything* were consumed by Talos, deep in conversation with the woman to his left, a duchess from Spain.

Somehow their chairs had edged closer so his thigh brushed against hers, and when their dessert of *loukoumades*—a delicious Greek doughnut, drizzled with honey, cinnamon and walnuts—was cleared away, and they were awaiting the final course of fresh fruit, a shock ran through her when his hand came to rest on her thigh.

She wished she'd tried to talk Natalia into a different material for the dress; something lighter. The heavy fabric suited the theatricality of the dress beautifully, but while she could feel the weight of Talos's hand there was none of the heat her body craved.

It wasn't enough.

She wanted to *feel* him.

Sucking in a sharp breath to tame the thundering of her heart, she casually straightened, then moved her hand under the table to rest on his. As she threaded her fingers through his he gave the gentlest of squeezes, and that one simple action sent tiny darts of sensation rippling through her abdomen.

Strong coffee and glasses of port were poured, whilst the British Prince chattered on about one of the charities he was patron of. Amalie tried hard to keep her attention fixed on him, smiling in all the right places, laughing when appropriate, all the while wishing every guest there would magically disappear and leave her alone with Talos.

She hadn't drunk much wine—a couple of glasses at most—but felt as if she'd finished a whole bottle, because at that moment she felt giddily out of control.

Talos still had hold of her thigh, his thumb making circular motions on the material so torturously barricading him from her skin.

She had no idea where her nerve came from—maybe her fingers had a life of their own, because they moved away from his hand to tentatively brush his thigh. He stiffened at her touch, his own hand tightening its hold on her.

The British Prince chattered on, clearly oblivious to the undercurrents playing out beside him.

Slowly her fingers crept over Talos's thigh until her whole hand rested on it. The fabric of his trousers felt silken to her fingers, contrasting with the taut muscularity they covered. She could *feel* him.

He sat as stiff as a statue, making no attempt to move when, with a flush of heat she realised her little finger was right at the crevice of his thigh, the line of the V that connected it to his groin…

A feeling of recklessness overtook her and she swiped the little finger up a little further—deeper into his heat, closer to the source of his masculinity.

The statue came to life.

Talos swept his hand away from her thigh to reach for his port, which he swilled down before putting the glass back on the table. Not that she saw him do any of those things, rather she felt them, her attention still, to anyone interested enough to be watching, fixed on the British Prince.

Then Talos's hand was back under the table and clasping hers, which was slowly stroking his thigh, her little finger brushing the V of his groin. Twisting it so he could hold it tightly, he entwined his fingers in hers.

'Are you okay?' the British Prince asked, pausing in his talk on water sanitation in developing countries. 'You look flushed.'

She felt her neck and cheeks flame. 'I think I need some air, that's all,' she said to the Prince, hoping she didn't sound as flustered as she felt inside.

A warm arm slipped behind her back and round her waist and Talos was there, pressing against her, ostensibly having abandoned his conversation with the Duchess to join in with theirs.

'Don't worry, little songbird,' he said, his deep voice sending reverberating thrills racing through her. 'The banquet will soon be over.'

Talos felt as if he needed air too...

If her hand had moved any higher and actually touched the hardness that was causing him such aching pain he would have come undone on the spot.

Never in his life had he been so aroused, not even yesterday in the cottage where, despite their lack of clothing, it had been a different arousal.

He sensed no fear in Amalie now.

No, this was a special kind of sweet torture and in front of all Helios's guests he was unable to do a damn thing about it.

So long as he kept her hand away from his crotch he would master it. The most sensible option would be to stop touching her altogether, but sensible didn't count for anything—not when it was Amalie Cartwright he was touching.

He let out a breath of relief when the palace quartet entered the Banquet Room, mandolins and banjos playing out the guests with the folk music beloved of all Agonites.

The Agon royal party rose first. Keeping her hand firmly clasped in his, Talos led Amalie through to the adjoining ballroom, delighting in her gasp of pleasure.

The ballroom was by far the most majestic of all the palace rooms, both in size and stature. With high ceilings and a black-and-white checked floor, even Talos experienced a thrill of stepping into a bygone age whenever he entered it.

As soon as the royal party entered, the orchestra, situated in a corner, began to play.

Most of the guests took seats at the highly decorated round tables lining the walls, free to choose where they wanted to sit. The two ornate thrones at the top of the room shone under the swooping chandeliers. Looking at them sent a pang through him. They would remain empty for the duration of the evening.

He wondered how his grandfather was, his stomach twisting at the remembrance of the vomiting episode he had witnessed just a few short hours ago. He consoled himself with the knowledge that should his grandfather take a turn for the worse he and his brothers would be notified immediately.

Talos guided Amalie to a table and poured them both a glass of wine. Theseus joined them and, as was his nature, soon had Amalie giggling as he regaled her with tales of their childhood.

A strange tightening spread across his chest to see her so clearly enthralled, and with a start he realised the cause. Jealousy. *His* jealousy. She'd never laughed so freely for him.

This was becoming dangerous.

Desire was one thing, but jealousy… That was one emotion too far and too ugly.

That was what you got for spending so much time with a beautiful woman without bedding her. If he'd bedded her from the start her allure would have vanished already and he would now be focussing on getting her performance-fit without wasting energy wondering how she looked naked or whether she moaned loudly when she came.

For all his words about 'partaking' regularly, he hadn't been with a woman in months—not since his grandfather's diagnosis. It was as if his libido had gone into stasis.

And now his libido had gone into hyperdrive.

Forget noble thoughts about not taking advantage of her position on the island, or that she was there because of his blackmail. The chemistry between them had gone off the charts. All they needed was one night to detonate it. One night. Come the morning, their chemistry would be spent. If not, they still had three weeks to expel it completely, but they would have tamed the worst of it. They would be able to concentrate on nothing but her gala performance.

At that moment the orchestra broke into a waltz, indicating the start of the evening's dancing. Talos watched Helios take a deep breath, fix a smile to his face and cross the ballroom to tap a princess from the old Greek royal family on the shoulder. She was on her feet like a shot, allowing him to lead her onto the dance floor. It was the cue for the other guests who fancied trying their hands at traditional ballroom dancing to get to their feet.

'Shouldn't you find a lady to dance with?' Talos pointedly asked his brother in Greek.

Theseus's smile dropped. He grimaced, his eyes darting around the room as if he were searching for someone. 'I'll have a drink first. But don't let me stop you—you two make a beautiful couple.'

Talos narrowed his eyes and fixed Theseus with his 'stare'. Theseus pulled a face and swigged his wine.

'Would you like to dance?' he asked Amalie. Talos might loathe dancing, but the thought of having her in his arms was a temptation not to be resisted.

'I've never waltzed,' she said dubiously.

'Most of our guests have never waltzed. I will lead you.' That was if he could remember. He hadn't waltzed since the Debutantes Ball in Vienna, which his grandfather had forced him to attend when he was twenty-one. If his brothers hadn't already been forced into attendance at the same age he would have put up more than an obligatory protest.

She allowed him to help her to her feet and guide her onto the dance floor.

Facing her, he dropped her hand, took a step back and bowed. 'You must curtsy,' he instructed.

Her luscious lips spread into a smile. 'Certainly, Your Highness.'

He returned the smile and reached for her right hand with his left and held it out to the side. 'Now, place your other hand on my bicep.'

'There's enough of it for me to hold on to,' she answered, that same smile still playing on her lips, her eyes glimmering with a private message to him—a message he understood and that made his blood pressure rise so high his heart felt in danger of thudding out of his ribs.

To hell with the traditional hold, he thought, placing his right hand on her back and resting his fingers on the bare flesh above the lining of the dress.

She felt exquisite.

Soon they were swirling around the room, the enchantment on her face making all the ridiculous ballroom-dancing lessons he and his brothers had been subjected to in their teenage years worthwhile—something he had *never* thought would happen.

Amalie felt as if she'd stepped into heaven. She'd never waltzed before but it didn't matter; Talos guided her around the dance floor with a tenderness and grace that was as unexpected as it was heavenly.

She had never felt so feminine before either, the security of his arms something she would savour and relish.

The original gap between them when they'd started dancing had closed, and suddenly she was very much aware their bodies were pressed together.

Releasing her grip on his bicep, she smoothed her hand up to clasp the nape of his neck, glad a slower waltz was now being played, one that allowed her time to do nothing but gaze up into his eyes. Her legs followed his lead with no thought.

The heels she wore elevated her enough that her breasts pressed against his chest, his abdomen against the base of her stomach, but to her intense frustration she couldn't *feel* him anywhere other than on her back, where his hand rested, his heat scorching her skin in the most wonderful way imaginable.

'Your brothers seem nice,' she said, frantic to cut through the tension between them before she was forced into something drastic—like dragging him away.

'They're good men,' he agreed, his gaze not dropping from hers.

'What did you mean earlier, when I asked if they had dates and you said that was the whole purpose of the evening?'

He laughed lightly. 'It is time for Helios to end his bachelor days. He is hoping that tonight he will meet someone suitable.'

'Someone suitable? For marriage?'

'Yes. A woman of royal blood.'

'That sounds clinical.'

'He is heir to the throne.'

His fingers were making the same circles on her back that he'd made on her thigh, but this time she could actually feel it. And it felt wonderful.

'It is traditional for the heir to marry a woman of royal descent.'

'Is there a reason why he's looking for a bride now?' She thought of their absent grandfather, the King, and wondered if there was more to his illness than Talos was letting on.

'He's of the right age.'

She felt his muscles ripple as he lifted a shoulder in a shrug.

'He wants to be young enough to enjoy his children.'

'If you marry, will it have to be someone of royal descent too?' As she asked the question a strange clenching gripped her heart.

'No.'

'So if you marry it will be for love?'

His lips twisted into a mocking grin. 'If I marry it will be because someone has placed a gun to my head.'

'Marriage is a piece of paper. It doesn't mean anything.'

Love was the state she'd always feared—not a commitment so easily broken it wasn't worth the paper it was signed on. It was passionate love that made fools of people. A piece of paper could dissolve a marriage into nothing, but a severed heart never fully healed.

'It means a lot if you're a member of the Kalliakis royal family. Divorce is forbidden.'

That's fine, she thought. *I don't want to marry you. All I want is to touch you. Everywhere.*

That was why she would be safe from the threat of a severed heart. Her passion for Talos was purely physical. When she returned to Paris her heart wouldn't feel a thing, would only skip at memories of being with him.

'Is divorce forbidden for everyone on your island?'

'Only members of the royal family,' he murmured.

'And are you allowed lovers? Before you marry?' she added, dropping her voice even lower.

His eyes were a blaze of molten lava, his strong nose

flaring, his jaw clenched. 'If I want a lover no decree is going to stop me.'

Nothing and no one could stop this man doing *anything* he wanted.

The thought should appal her, but it didn't—not when the thought of allowing him to do whatever he wanted was so strong she dug her nails into his neck to stop her fingers yanking at her dress so she could press her bare skin to him. Her desperation to feel him was matched only by her desperation for him to feel *her*.

A finger tapped her shoulder. It was the British Prince. 'May I have the next dance?'

'No,' Talos growled, not looking at him, but tightening his hold on her back and his grip on her hand.

'You can't blame a chap for trying,' the Prince said, laughing ruefully before striding off to find another dance partner.

Talos stopped dancing. The clenching of his jaw was even more pronounced. 'I have an apartment here in the palace.'

She didn't miss a beat or fake coyness. 'Is it far?'

'It's closer than my villa or your cottage.'

A spark passed between them, so real and powerful she felt it in every atom of her being.

He brought her hand to his lips. 'Follow me,' he murmured.

CHAPTER TEN

HER HAND CLASPED tightly in his, Amalie followed Talos's lead, weaving through the waltzing couples, yearning to run but keeping her pace steady, avoiding eye contact lest anyone wanted to talk.

She could see the door he was leading her to, in the left-hand corner of the great room. The closer they got, the longer his strides became, until they were nodding at the footmen posted there and then slipping out into a corridor she didn't recognise. Judging by the strong scent of food, she figured they had to be close to the palace kitchens.

They took a left into another long corridor, then another and another. Staff were everywhere, all bowing as they passed.

It wasn't until they reached a fifth corridor, this one dimly lit, that they were completely alone.

Talos had her pinned to the wall so quickly there was no chance to draw breath.

His hands clasped her cheeks and his mouth crashed onto hers with a passion her starving body responded to immediately. His tongue swept across her lips, forcing them to part, then darted into her mouth, his resulting groan stoking the heat consuming her.

She responded with fire, cradling his head, returning the kiss with all the hunger that burned inside her for him.

No sooner had it started than he broke the kiss, keeping her pinned to the wall with his strength, his thumbs running in swirls over her cheeks, his brown eyes dark with intensity.

'I have never been closer to ripping a woman's dress off and taking her in public than I was in that ballroom,' he said roughly.

A pulse ran through her, deliciously powerful. In answer, she nuzzled into his hand and kissed his palm.

He stepped back, trailing his fingers down her neck to the edge of her dress, his breathing heavy. 'We're almost at my apartment.'

They set off again to the end of the corridor, walking at a speed only a tiny rate below a run, until they came to a spiralling marble staircase with a heavy rope barrier across the base of it. Talos moved it swiftly, indicating for her to go up. At the top was a small passage with a door at the end and a small security box by the side. He punched in the code and the door swung open.

Lights came on with the motion and Amalie found herself in an enormous masculine living space, richly furnished with plump charcoal-coloured sofas against a backdrop of muted blues and creams. The room's walls were covered in huge colourful paintings.

There was no time for looking with depth. Talos threw his jacket, sash and bow tie on the floor and guided her through the living area and into a bedroom dominated by the largest bed she'd ever seen—an enormous sleigh bed with intricate carvings.

On the wall opposite the door stood a floor-length mirror, edged with the same intricately carved wood. Catching sight of her reflection, she came to a stop.

Was that woman staring back at her with the flushed cheeks and wild eyes really her? Amalie? The woman who had formed a cosy life for herself while shying away from everything this man—this gorgeous man—was offering her? The man staring at her with a hunger she had only ever seen in films.

Transfixed, she watched as he stepped behind her, not touching her other than to place his hands on the tops of her arms. A small moan escaped her throat when he dropped a kiss in the arch of her neck.

Swaying lightly, she let her eyes flutter closed and sighed as his fingers swept across her shoulder blades and down her spine to rest at the top her dress.

Bending his head to kiss her ear and brush his lips lightly against her temple, he found and unfastened the hidden hook, then pinched the concealed zipper and slowly pulled it down, all the way to the base of her spine. His hands slid back up the exposed flesh to the top of the dress, then skimmed it assuredly down to her hips, exposing her bare breasts. When he released his hold on it the dress fell in a lazy whoosh to her feet, leaving her naked bar skimpy black knickers and gold shoes.

He wrapped an arm around her middle and held her against him, so she could lift her feet one at a time and step out of the vast amount of material. Talos kicked the dress away, then met her eyes in the reflection of the mirror, a dangerous, lustful glimmer in his stare.

Her chest thrust forward, almost begging for his touch.

The hand holding her so protectively brushed over her stomach and up her side, circling round her breasts to trace along her collarbone and up her neck to the base of her head. Slowly he worked at the elegant knot of her hair until he freed it, gently pulling it down to sprawl across her shoulders.

'Have you had many lovers, little songbird?' he asked, inhaling the scent of her hair.

Speech had deserted her; all she was capable of doing was shaking her head.

'Have you had *any* lovers?'

The second shake of her head had more force behind it, but inside she reeled.

Was her virginity *that* obvious?

He must have read the question in her expression. 'I am an expert at reading between lines,' he said enigmatically, before twisting her round to face him. He ran his thumb over her bottom lip. 'Why don't we even things up and you undress me?'

With hands that trembled, she reached for the top button of his shirt, fumbled with it, then found some dexterity and undid it, then the next. Working quickly, aware of the heaviness of his breathing, she undid them all, then spread the shirt open. Not even conscious of what she was about to do, she pressed her lips to his chest and breathed him in, inhaling the muskiness that evoked thoughts of dark forests and adrenaline-filled danger.

His chest rose and swelled, his hand reaching into her hair and gathering it in his fingers.

Her fingers trailed down the thickening black hair to his abdomen and found the hook fastening his hand-stitched trousers. She swallowed as the palm of her hand felt the heat beneath. She unhooked it, but then her nerve deserted her. Suddenly a burst of sanity crashed through the lustful haze she'd been entranced in.

She'd never touched a man intimately before.

She wanted to touch Talos with a need bordering on desperation, but for the first time her virginity was something she was wholly aware of.

How could she be anything but a disappointment to him? A man as rampantly masculine as Talos would have had scores of lovers, all confident in their bodies and sexuality.

Talos felt Amalie's hesitation, felt the fear creep through her.

His suspicions about her being a virgin had been right. He would have been more surprised to learn she'd had *any* lovers.

He didn't care about her reasons for never having had a lover; cared only that at this moment she was here, with him, and that the crazy chemistry between them could be acted upon. Amalie wasn't on the hunt for a relationship any more than he was; her comment about marriage only being a piece of paper had concurred with his own thoughts entirely.

But confirmation of her virginity *did* force him to take a deep breath and try to cool his ardour. All prior thoughts of simply discarding their clothes and falling into bed were gone. He needed to take it slow. He didn't want to hurt her. By the time he made her his he wanted her so turned on but also relaxed, he could enter her without causing any pain.

Gently he twisted her back to face the mirror, placing an arm around her belly. Her eyes closed and her head rolled back to rest on his shoulder, her breath coming in tiny hitches. He could feel her heartbeat hammering with an identical rhythm to his own.

Moving quickly, he unzipped his trousers with his free hand and worked them off, deliberately keeping his boxers on so the temptation to plunge himself straight into her could be more easily denied.

Done, he pressed himself into the small of her back, felt her tremble, saw her lips part in a silent moan.

'Open your eyes,' he commanded quietly into her ear.

They fluttered open and met his gaze in the reflection of the mirror.

His fingers played on the lace of her knickers and then tugged them down, delighting to find the dark silky hair below. He dipped a finger into her heat and groaned when he found her moist and swollen.

Keeping the pressure there light and rhythmical, he splayed his other hand upwards and captured a raised breast. It fitted perfectly into his hand. He could hardly wait to taste it, to taste every part of her but before he could take her into his arms and carry her to his bed her back arched, her groin pressed hard against his finger and she stiffened. He watched in awe at their reflection. Her eyes were tightly closed, her lips parted, her cheeks flushed. Then she shuddered and became limp in his arms. If she hadn't been secure against him, he had no doubt she would have fallen to the floor.

He'd never seen or felt anything like it—such a primal, animalistic response. It filled him with something he couldn't name…could only feel, gripping his chest.

Keeping her pressed tight against him, he turned her enough to lift her into his arms.

There was no resistance; her eyes gazed into his, dazed bewilderment ringing out. When she reached a hand to press a palm to his cheek he swallowed, his heart beating so fast it had become a painful thrum.

He laid her down on the bed and shrugged his open shirt off, discarding it on the floor.

She'd covered her breasts. He took hold of her hands and carefully parted them, exposing her full nakedness to him.

To his eyes, Amalie was perfect—her arms and legs toned and smooth, her skin soft, her breasts high, ripe peaches, begging to be tasted.

Bringing his head down to hers, he captured her lips. She returned his kiss with passion, her tongue sweeping into his mouth, her hot, sweet breath flowing into his senses. Her hands reached for his head and razed through his hair.

As he deepened the kiss he stroked his fingers down her body, exploring the soft skin, delighting in the mews escaping her throat.

Breaking the kiss, he ran his lips down her throat and lower, to her breasts, capturing one in his mouth…

Theos.

For the first time since his teenage years he was on the verge of losing control already. He had never felt so constricted by his boxer shorts, the tight cotton material as tight a barrier as steel.

But she tasted so *good*, of a sweet, feminine essence his senses reacted to. Not just his senses. Every part of him reacted to it.

'Is something wrong?' she whispered, uncertainty in her voice.

'No,' he promised, dragging his mouth back up to her lips and kissing her again. 'Everything is perfect.'

Her hands grabbed at his face, her fingers kneading his cheeks before sweeping over his neck and chest and down to his abdomen. This time she didn't hesitate, pushing under the cotton to lightly touch the head of his erection.

Her kisses stopped and she sucked in a breath.

'It doesn't bite,' he teased, smoothing her hair off her forehead.

Her lips twitched into a shy smile and she burrowed her face into his neck before her tongue darted out to lick his skin. She rubbed her leg against him, all the while slowly trailing her fingers down his length, which throbbed madly under her gentle ministrations. She made no attempt to take hold of it, seemingly content simply to stroke and explore. That this only made him harder than ever—something he had not thought possible—only added to his painful ardour. If he didn't find some release soon he feared he might actually combust.

'I don't use birth control,' she whispered into his neck.

'I didn't think you did,' he assured her, moving her hand away so he could lean over to his bedside table, where he dimly remembered throwing a packet of condoms into a drawer. They were still there. He pulled one out and ripped the foil off, all the time keeping his focus on Amalie, who had sat up and was now exploring his chest with her fingers, the expression on her face something close to rapture.

Kissing her first, he got off the bed and tugged his boxers down.

She met his eyes and swallowed.

'Don't be scared,' he murmured, kneeling back on the bed and gently pushing her flat, so her head rested on the pillow and she was laid out beneath him.

Her smile was dazzling. 'I'm not.'

He kissed her again, then disentangled her arms, which had hooked around his neck at the first press of his lips.

Working swiftly, he securely rolled the condom on, then knelt between her parted thighs. He brushed his hands over her beautiful downy hair, a thrill racing through him to feel her damp heat all over again, his arousal increasing when she bucked upwards to meet his touch.

Then, moving slowly, he laid himself on top of her, taking care not to put his full weight on her. Moving even slower, he guided his erection to the welcome warmth of her opening.

Her hands gripped his shoulders, her nails digging into his flesh.

Her eyes were screwed tight shut.

'Look at me, little songbird,' he said, stroking her cheek.

She opened her eyes. That dazed look had returned to them.

He pushed forward a little more, clenching his teeth as he stopped himself from driving in any deeper. Amalie had never done this before. If he were to do what he so desperately wanted and simply plunge deep inside her he would hurt her, no matter how hot and wet she was for him.

Theos, she felt so *tight*.

He inched forward some more, giving her time to adjust before pressing a little further. Each new push forward elicited the same gasp from her lips: a hitch of surprised pleasure.

As he continued to inch slowly into her he brushed his lips against hers, relishing the short, ragged breaths she breathed back into him.

When he was fully sheathed inside her he paused to catch his own breath and closed his eyes, forcing his mind to think of something—*anything*—other than what they were doing at that moment.

But no matter how hard he tried, even with his eyes firmly shut, all he could see was Amalie.

She shifted slightly beneath him, her hands moving from his shoulders to trail down his back, causing thrills of shivers racing down his spine.

Only when he was sure he had control of himself did he withdraw—not all the way, but enough so that when he pushed back he had to grit his teeth more to retain his control.

This was *torture*. The most divine torture he had ever known.

For the first time in his life he truly wished he could make love without the barrier of a condom, to experience every single aspect of it.

He withdrew a little further, pressed back a little deeper.

Once he was certain Amalie had adjusted to this whole new experience, and that there was no discomfort for her, he allowed himself to settle into a rhythm, all the while telling himself to be gentle, to make this special for her.

He'd never experienced anything like it. Every thrust felt as if he were diving deeper into some unknown abyss, one filled with beautiful, dream-evoking colour.

There was something so *pure* about her responses. Nothing was for effect; everything—all her touches, all her kisses, all her soft moans—was an expression of how she was feeling at that moment and the pleasure she was taking from their lovemaking.

When he gripped her bottom and raised it, just enough to let him penetrate a little deeper, her cry into his mouth was the most beautiful sound he'd ever heard. Even though he was desperate for his own relief he held on, keeping the rhythm that had her tossing her head from left to right and made her breath shallow. Then he felt her thicken around him, felt her pulsing at the same moment she breathed out his name and clung to him, burying her face in his neck as her orgasm made her whole body vibrate and shudder.

He held on, waiting until her climax was spent, then raised himself onto his knees and spread her thighs further apart. He wanted to look at her, to drown in those emerald eyes. Placing one hand on her shoulder and the other on her breasts, he upped the tempo, thrusting in and out, gazing at her beautiful face, her wide eyes, her red-kissed lips, revelling in the little pulses that still came from within her, until he took one final, long thrust and his world exploded in colour.

When the jolts racketing through him finally abated his face was buried in Amalie's hair, which was sprawled over the pillow like a fan. Her arms were locked tightly round him; the only sound was the heavy thudding beat of their hearts.

Lethargy spread through him and he eased himself off her, something dim in the back of his sluggish mind reminding him he had the condom to dispose of. Dragging himself off the bed, he could feel her eyes on him as he padded to the bathroom.

He returned a few moments later, his chest tightening to see she'd slipped under the silk sheets. A shy smile played on her lips.

He hadn't thought this through. As a rule, he didn't bring women to his palace apartment, preferring to conduct his affairs in the privacy of his villa, or wherever in the world he happened to be.

It suddenly dawned on him that not only had he broken his unwritten rule of not conducting an affair within the palace walls, but he'd also run from Helios's ball. It was inconceivable that his absence would go unnoticed.

He couldn't bring himself to care. His grandfather was in bed and his brothers would understand. They'd both had their heads turned by beautiful women over the years. The ball was for Helios, and to a lesser extent for Theseus—not for him. He would never need to marry. The burden of continuing the Kalliakis dynasty was in his brothers' hands.

Now that the flush of lust had been satisfied he should

get dressed, get a chauffeur to take Amalie back to the cottage. Except…

She stretched under the covers, that smile still playing on her lips. 'Can we do that again?'

Amalie pulled Talos's shirt, discarded on the floor the evening before, closer around her, catching a wonderful whiff of his woody scent. She sighed dreamily.

That had to count as the most wonderful night of her life.

It amazed her to think she'd spent so long denying this sensual side of herself, marvelled that it had ever scared her. What had she been so frightened of? How could such pleasure be terrifying?

She gazed at Talos sleeping, from her vantage point of the bay window, where she'd settled herself earlier. She'd woken with the sun, the buzz in her blood from their passionate night still alive in her veins, zinging too loudly for her to fall back into sleep. Usually she did everything she could to eke out as much sleep as she could muster. But not today.

The view from his bedroom window was stunning, overlooking the palace maze. In the distance lay the open-air theatre the gala was to be held in—an enormous round dome, cut into the ground like something from Middle Earth. Judging by the view, and the fact that if she craned her neck she could see turrets in the distance, she figured his apartment must be in the far left tower of the palace.

The view from the window was nothing compared to the vision on the bed, curled on his side, one arm splayed out where she had been sleeping, as if he'd been seeking her. She wanted nothing more than to crawl back under the covers, but was determined to hold back and let him sleep. After all their lovemaking he would be exhausted.

She smiled. In sleep he looked curiously vulnerable.

For the first time in her life she felt complete. Like a

woman. Like she'd discovered a glorious secret. And at that moment she was happy to savour it and hold it close.

Talos stirred, his hand groping. He lifted his head.

'*Bonjour,*' she said softly, resting her chin on her knee.

He stretched onto his back and smiled lazily. '*Kalimera*, little songbird. Did you sleep well?'

She gave him a coy smile. 'No.'

'You should come back to bed, then.'

'I should,' she agreed, adopting the same mock serious tone.

He threw the sheets off him, unabashedly displaying his large erection.

Moisture filled her mouth and pooled down low. Sliding off the ledge of the bay window, she padded over to the bed. No sooner had she climbed on than Talos's huge hands were at her waist, pulling her over to straddle him.

He stared into her eyes, trailing a hand down the valley between her breasts. 'No regrets?'

She shook her head and sighed as his fingers found her nipple. 'No regrets.'

'Then make love to me, you sexy woman, and prove it.'

Sexy? *Her?* Sexy was a word she'd never associated with herself before.

Yet as she sheathed him, then sank down onto him, taking the whole of him inside her, she realised she'd never felt as sexy and as alive in her life.

And, dear heaven, it felt amazing.

CHAPTER ELEVEN

Was it truly possible to become addicted to sex?

The question played happily in Amalie's mind as she sat beside Talos in his Maserati, making polite noises as he pointed out a pile of stones he assured her had once been a monastery. Because there was no doubt about it—she was in lust. Glorious, incredible, beautifully reciprocated *desire*. It was basic biology at its finest. And it didn't frighten her in the slightest.

He'd taken her out for lunch in Resina, the main town on the island, and now they were driving back to her cottage, taking the scenic route through Agon's verdant mountains, avoiding wandering sheep and goats who seemingly had no sense of the danger posed by moving vehicles.

The view on this blue, cloudless day was spectacular, the Mediterranean was gleaming in the distance, and the temperature was sitting comfortably in the mid-twenties. She was mostly oblivious to it, too busy anticipating the moment they'd return to the privacy of the cottage to concentrate on nothing so mundane as *scenery*.

In the two weeks since the ball they hadn't spent a night apart. They'd returned to her cottage on the Sunday, leaving through Talos's private exit so at least she'd been spared the embarrassment of bumping into his brothers, and had more or less lived there since.

Amalie would work on the score during the day, while he went to his villa or the palace to do his own work. In the evening he would collect her and take her to the gym, then they would return to the cottage and make love, and would often still be awake when the sun came up.

She could now play her violin for him with hardly any nerves at all, although she still didn't feel ready to play his grandmother's piece. She wanted to be note-perfect for that. Her orchestra would arrive on Agon tomorrow morning; her first scheduled rehearsal with them was in the afternoon. They would know then if she had truly made progress.

For today, Talos had insisted on taking her out and showing her Agon, arguing that it was a Saturday and that in the three and a half weeks she'd been on his island she'd hardly seen any of it. She would have been happy to stay at the cottage and make love, but he'd brushed her arguments aside with his usual authority, claiming her lips to whisper, 'We'll only be gone a few hours.'

'What are you thinking about?' he asked now, casting a quick sideways glance at her.

Her gaze drifted to his hands, holding the steering wheel with deft assuredness in much the same manner as he handled her.

'Sex,' she answered, tingles racing through her at the thought of their imminent return to privacy and all the things they would do...

He burst into deep laughter. 'Do you ever think about anything else?'

She pretended to think about it before shaking her head. 'No.'

'I am tempted to ask *exactly* what you're thinking about in connection to sex, but if I crash the car it will take us longer to get back,' he said drily. 'You can tell me in graphic detail exactly what you're thinking later.'

'I will,' she murmured, her eyes drifting to his muscular thighs, barely contained in his chinos.

'Can I ask you a personal question?'

His voice had taken on a serious hue that made her

twist on the seat to face him properly. 'What do you want to know?'

'Why did you wait until you were twenty-five before having sex for the first time?'

It was the question she'd been waiting a fortnight for him to ask. She was still no more prepared with an answer.

She pressed her cheek to the back of the seat. If she couldn't touch him she could at least look at him.

'I never set out to stay a virgin, but I avoided relationships where lust and desire were the driving forces—I've seen my mother's heart broken too many times to have any faith in passionate *love*. The flame is too bright and burns to ashes too quickly. I didn't understand it was possible to have a passion for someone that is purely about sex.'

'Is that all this is to you?' he asked, a surprising edge to his voice. 'Sex?'

'Isn't that all it is to *you*?' she asked right back, momentarily confused.

He was quiet for a moment, before laughing. 'You're right—what we are sharing is just sex. I admit I find it disconcerting to hear that coming from a woman, and even more disconcerting to actually believe it.'

'Do all your lovers say it's just sex?'

'I set out the ground rules from the beginning. I make it clear I only want a physical relationship and they all agree.' He pulled a mocking face. 'It never takes them long to change their minds and think they can be the one to tame me.'

'I don't think anyone could tame you,' she commented idly, and swallowed away the strange acrid taste that had formed in her throat. It was no secret he'd enjoyed numerous lovers before her, and would enjoy more when she returned to Paris in little more than a week. 'You're as tameable as a fully grown wolf with territory problems.'

Now his laughter came in great booming ricochets. 'I enjoy my life. I have no wish to be tamed.'

She eyed him shrewdly, wondering why she didn't quite believe him. She believed his words, but there was a part of Talos he kept closed off. Physically, he was the most generous and giving lover she could have dreamt of, but he had demons inside him she couldn't reach—demons she caught glimpses of when he would shout out in his sleep, cries in Greek she didn't understand.

She'd asked him about it and he'd affected ignorance, saying he didn't remember his dreams. She didn't believe him but hadn't pushed the subject. If he wanted to open up to her, he would. And, really, she was hardly in a position to demand to learn all his secrets when their whole relationship was based on sex and getting her performance-ready for the gala.

'So you've never had a relationship of any kind?' he asked.

'I've had boyfriends,' she corrected him, 'Quite a few of them.'

'And they didn't try to get you into bed? Were they gay?'

She gave a bark of surprised laughter. 'I suppose it's possible, but the relationships weren't like that. It was more about a meeting of minds than physical chemistry.'

'Isn't that what normal friends are for?'

'Probably.' She swallowed. 'We would kiss... But my boyfriends were the type of men who were happier to spend an evening discussing Mozart's eccentricities and how it affected his music rather than trying to get me into bed.'

He flashed her a grin. 'I don't pretend to know anything about Mozart, but if I did I can assure you I would be happy to discuss him with you—provided I could be stripping you naked at the same time.'

'But that's what I was hiding from,' she confessed.

'You liked those men because they made you feel safe?' he asked.

For such a physically imposing man Talos was incredibly perceptive—something she was coming to understand more on a daily basis.

'I…' She stopped to gather her thoughts. 'Yes. You're right. After my parents divorced my mother fell head over heels for so many different men that I lost count, but she couldn't hold on to any of them. Her heart was broken so many times it was painful for me to watch.'

'Why couldn't she hold on to them?'

She shook her head and inhaled deeply. 'I don't know. I *think* it was because my father spoilt her during their marriage. He adored her, you see—worshipped her. He treated her like his queen for fifteen years. It was what she was used to and what she expected. And I think it's what pushed her lovers away —they would fall for her beauty and fame, but as soon as they found the needy woman inside they would run a mile. It hurt her very badly. She would smile and sing to the world, pretend nothing was wrong, but behind closed doors she would wail like a child.'

'And you witnessed this?'

She nodded.

'I can understand why that must have been painful for you,' he said quietly.

Hadn't he witnessed his own mother's pain enough times to know how damaging it could be? Especially to a child? The helplessness of being too small and insignificant to offer any protection—either an emotional or a physical sort.

'I know you must think my mother is a brat, and she *is*. But she's also funny and loving and I adore her,' she added with defiance.

'I can tell,' he said wryly, turning the car into the road marking the start of Kalliakis land. 'But you have to admit that it isn't fair of her to place all her emotional problems on *your* shoulders.'

'She can't help the way she is. And, fair or not, it's no less than I deserve.'

'What do you mean by that?'

She didn't answer, turning her face away from him to look out of the window.

'Amalie?'

She placed a hand to her throat, her words coming out in a whisper. 'Her misery is all my fault. If it wasn't for me, my father would never have divorced her.'

A lump formed in his throat at the raw emotion behind her words. 'I don't believe that for a minute.' How could a child influence its parents' marriage? 'But I am surprised to learn that your father divorced her. From what you've said, I assumed your mother had divorced *him*.'

'My father worshipped the ground she walked on but to protect me from her ego he divorced her when I was twelve.'

The pieces were coming together. 'Which was around the time you were pulled from the spotlight. I assume the two things are connected?'

'Yes,' she admitted hoarsely, before closing her mouth with a snap.

He brought the car to a stop outside her cottage and reached out to stroke the beautiful hair that felt like silk between his fingers. He wanted to gather her in his arms, not just to devour her body but to give her comfort. It was a feeling so alien to him that the lump in his throat solidified.

Giving comfort implied a form of caring, and if there was one thing Talos avoided with the zeal of a medic avoiding the plague it was caring. Sex wasn't meant to be anything but fun; it was an itch to be scratched. Nothing more.

Before he could withdraw she turned her face back to him and raised her hand to palm his cheek. Helpless to resist, he brought his mouth down to hers and breathed her in, his heart thundering as he felt her own inhalation and knew she was breathing *him* in in turn.

Being with her was like living in a fugue of desire—a constant state of arousal that needed no encouragement.

It struck him that touching her and being touched in return was becoming as necessary to him as breathing.

Theos.

He *had* to keep his mind focussed on the bigger picture.

No matter how good the sex was between them it didn't change the fact that Amalie was in Agon for the gala and that it was his job to get her on the stage and performing for his grandfather. She had come on enormously in the past fortnight, but still she wouldn't play his grandmother's composition for him, although she would perform other pieces. She swore she knew it by heart and only wanted to perfect it, and he believed her, but the clock was ticking painfully. The gala was only a week away.

Where had the time gone?

He could sense she was close to unbuttoning the secrets she clutched so tightly, and knew it was the key to unlocking what she kept hidden—the thing at the very centre of her stage fright.

A creamy envelope lay on the welcome mat of the cottage, the sight of which made him blink rapidly. It was an official royal envelope.

Amalie opened it as she walked into the living room. 'I've been invited for dinner with your grandfather,' she said, passing it to him.

His heart accelerating, he read the invitation, which was for dinner that coming Wednesday.

'Did you know about this?' she asked.

'No.'

He hadn't been told a thing. Naturally his grandfather's permission had been sought before Talos began his quest to find a soloist, his only wish concurring with Talos's—that the soloist had to be special. Other than that, his grandfather had been content to leave all the organisation for the gala in his grandsons' capable hands, his energy reserves too limited for him to want any part in it.

Talos shouldn't be surprised that he had sought out

Amalie before the gala, and made a mental note to tell his grandfather he would be attending too. Astraeus Kalliakis still grieved the love of his life, and would want to meet the woman chosen to step into her footsteps on the stage.

He knew he should take the opportunity to tell Amalie the truth about his grandfather's condition. Prepare her. But the words stuck in his throat, a cold, clammy feeling spreading through his skin as it always did whenever he thought of what the coming months would bring.

The death of the man who had raised him from the age of seven. The man who had come into Talos's bedroom and woken the small boy from his sleep, had taken him into his arms and told him in a voice filled with despair but also with an underlying strength that Talos's parents wouldn't be coming home. That they were dead—killed in a road crash on their way to an event at the Greek Embassy.

It was the only time his grandfather had ever held him in such an informal manner. He'd then left Talos in the care of his Queen, Talos's grandmother, and flown to England so he could personally tell his two other grandsons at their boarding school.

Talos thought back to how it must have been for his grandfather, having to break such tragic news while grieving the loss of his own child. His quiet strength had been something for Talos to lean on in those dark few moments when he'd learned his whole world had been turned upside down and inside out. It had been the last time Talos had ever allowed himself to lean on anyone.

And now his grandfather was nearing the end of his own life.

And there wasn't a damn thing Talos could do about it.

He could no more protect his grandfather from death than he'd been able to protect his mother from his father's fists and infidelities.

'Is something wrong?' Amalie asked, peering at him closely. 'You look a little pale.'

He swallowed and returned her stare, suddenly wishing he could throw his arms around her waist and rest his head on those soft breasts, feel her gentle fingers running through his hair, soothing all the pain away.

He wrenched his thoughts from such useless wishes.

To vocalise it…to reveal the truth about his grandfather…*Theos*, he couldn't even speak of it to his brothers. They skirted around it in conversation, none of them prepared to be the one to speak up, as if saying it would make it true.

He ignored her question, reaching out to stroke her cheek, to have one quick touch of that beautifully textured skin before he continued the conversation they'd started in the car. Except Amalie leaned in and hooked her arms around his neck, her breath on his skin as she razed his throat with her mouth before stepping onto her toes to claim his lips.

Her tongue swept into his mouth, her warm breath seeping into his senses. Wrapping his arms around her, he selfishly took the solace of her kisses, the place where all thought could be eradicated in the balm of her mouth and the softness of her willing body.

The last coherent thought to go through his mind as he carried her up the stairs to the bedroom was that he was nothing but putty in her hands.

Amalie stretched luxuriantly, then turned onto her side to run her fingers over Talos's chest, tugging gently at the dark hair that covered it, brushing the brown nipples, pressing her palm down to feel the heavy beat of his heart.

He grabbed her hand and brought it to his mouth, planting a kiss to her knuckles.

She stared into his eyes, those irresistible brown depths, and a feeling of the utmost contentment swept through her. She could stare at him and lie in his arms for ever…

His hand made circular motions in the small of her back.

She raised her leg a touch, pressing her pelvis into his thigh. It didn't matter how deep her orgasms were, still she wanted more. And more…

'You're insatiable,' he growled.

'That's your fault for being so sexy,' she protested with a grin, moving her hand lower.

His eyes gleamed, but he grabbed her hand and brought it back up to rest at his chest. '*You*, my little songbird, are the most desirable woman alive.'

My little songbird?

The possessive pronoun made her heart jolt and soar in a motion so powerful it reverberated through her whole body, right down to the tips of her toes.

My little songbird.

And in that moment came a flash of recognition of such clarity that her heart stuttered to a stop before stammering back into throbbing motion.

This wasn't about lust and desire.

She loved him.

Loved him. *Loved him.*

CHAPTER TWELVE

STRUGGLING TO COMPREHEND, Amalie detached herself from his arms and sat up, crossing her legs to stare down at the face she had, without knowing how or when, fallen in love with.

'Is something the matter?' he asked, his eyes crinkling in question. 'You look as if you've seen a ghost.'

She shook her head, partly to refute his question and partly in wonder that this could have happened to her. She waited for self-recrimination to strike, but the wonder of the moment was too great, her mind a jumble.

Shaking her head again, she said, 'You forcing me here...that horrible contract you forced me to sign...the threats you made...'

He winced and she was glad. She *wanted* him to be ashamed of his behaviour. It meant he had a conscience. And if he had a conscience that meant he was the flesh-and-blood man she'd got to know these past few weeks and not the terrifying ogre she'd first met. It meant they had a chance. A small chance, she knew. Tiny. But a chance all the same.

She rubbed her thumb over his bottom lip and said softly, 'Just because I think you're the sexiest man alive, it doesn't mean I've forgotten what you did to get me here and the abhorrent threats you made.'

But did it mean she'd forgiven him? Talos wanted to know. He opened his mouth to ask, but then closed it.

What if she said no? What if she said she could never forgive him for how he'd got her here and the threats he'd made?

Why did he even *want* her forgiveness? He'd never sought forgiveness before.

Recalling the intimidation he'd put her under to get her acquiescence made him feel tight and compressed inside, and his skin felt as if claws were digging into it. Ruthless behaviour when necessary was nothing new to him, but it had a different taste when you had spent the previous night in bed with the recipient of that behaviour. It tasted different when you knew you would maim anyone who would dare even dream of hurting a hair on the head of that person.

It suddenly struck him that he would give his life to protect this woman.

And as the shock of that revelation filtered through him she continued to speak, cross-legged beside him, naked, the sheet twisted on her lap.

'Whatever the initial circumstances, I can't help thinking coming here is the best thing that could ever have happened to me.'

'Why?' His voice sounded distant and his head was spinning, his pulse racing so hard nausea gripped the lining of his stomach.

'Because being here has given me the time and space to see things clearly.' She dipped her head and gnawed at her bottom lip before speaking again. 'One of my psychiatrists told me outright that he thought I didn't want to be fixed. He was wrong. I…' Her voice caught. When she looked at him her eyes were glassy. 'It's not that I didn't want to be fixed…it's that I didn't think I *deserved* to be fixed.'

Talos ran a hand over his jaw, at a loss as to what he could say. She was unbuttoning herself to him, ready to spill her secrets, and all he wanted to do was shout out and beg her to stop.

He didn't want to hear them. He didn't want to feel anything else for her. Not pity, not empathy. He would take his guilt like a man, but nothing more.

'Maybe you can understand the early part of my life,' she said, oblivious to the turmoil going on within him. 'You've always been public property too. Before I'd reached the age of ten I'd played for the President of France, had taken part in a celebrity-led anti-poverty concert that was beamed around the world to a billion people...'

All of these facts were things he'd learned when he'd first discovered her in that practice room and known she was 'the one'. It had made her refusal to perform at the gala all the more ridiculous to his mind.

'I was a household name, a child prodigy, and it was easy for me.' She shook her head ruefully. 'I loved performing and I loved the applause. But then I turned ten. I found the reviews my parents had kept of my performances and re-alised that people had *opinions* about my music—that they weren't just enjoying it but dissecting everything about it. They were dissecting *me*. All the joy I'd experienced on stage evaporated.'

She snapped her fingers.

'Gone. I'd never experienced fear once, and all of a sudden I was crippled by it. What if they found me wanting? What if the way I interpreted a particular piece compared unfavourably to another violinist? So many thoughts and fears, when before there had been nothing but the joy of playing. It all came to a head on my mother's birthday, when I was twelve.'

She broke away and reached for the glass of water on the bedside table.

'What happened?' he asked, once she'd placed the glass back. She'd stopped talking, clearly gathering her thoughts together.

'She had a party at our holiday home in Provence. I'd spent two years begging not to play in public any more, begging to go to school and make friends, begging for a normal life—but she wouldn't allow it. I was *special*, you see, and, in my mother's eyes I belonged on the stage, receiving the plaudits she took for granted in her own career.'

Her voice dropped.

'I love my *maman*, but she can be very manipulative. She was not ashamed to use emotional blackmail to get me to play. She'd had a stage built at the bottom of the garden. I remember standing on it and seeing all those eyes upon me—there were at least a hundred guests, most of them international household names—and I froze. And then...'

'And then?'

Her eyes were huge on his. 'I wet myself. In front of all those people. They all saw it. All of them. They stopped talking amongst themselves and stared at me—and, God, the *horror* in their eyes. The humiliation was excruciating.'

Talos's throat had closed completely. He thought back to the clip he'd found on the internet, of her at her last public performance, before she'd retreated from the limelight. It could only have been months before the party she'd described. She'd been a scrap of a girl at twelve, without any of the knowing precociousness of preadolescence, and small for her age. She'd been a *child*.

Amalie sighed and visibly gathered herself together, tucking her hair behind her ears.

'Maman was mortified, but she swore it was just a blip. I was booked to play at the Royal Albert Hall a week later, as part of a Christmas celebration, and she insisted I still play. My father tried to get her to see reason but she couldn't— really, she *couldn't*. I was her protégée; she'd created me. Minutes before I was due to go on stage I had a panic attack, bad enough that a stagehand called an ambulance. When I was released from hospital my father collected me alone. Maman had refused to listen to reason so he felt he had no choice but to leave her and take me with him for my own protection.'

She blew out a long puff of air and gave a laugh that was full of bitterness rather than humour.

'He loved her, but he knew that by staying with her he would be condoning her treatment of me. Since then I've watched my mother rebound from relationship to relationship, knowing that if I'd been stronger they would still be together—'

'No,' he cut in, finally finding his voice. 'No, it was your mother—not you. You were a child.'

Her eyes caught his and she jerked her head in a nod, relief spreading over her features that he understood.

'That's what I mean about it being good for me here in Agon,' she said. 'It's given me the space and perspective to see reason and the time to think. You see, even though my father was awarded custody of me, given sole responsibility for my welfare, I still spent holidays and weekends with her. He never stopped me seeing her. He never stopped loving her but he felt he had to put my well-being first and take any decisions about my welfare out of her hands. I watched them both suffer apart and all I could see was that it was *my* fault. I felt as if I'd destroyed their lives. I've been punishing myself because subconsciously I didn't think I deserved to have the future I'd dreamed about. I created a nice, safe life for myself and thought it was enough.'

'And now?' he asked. 'You've come so far already. You've played for me, which in itself was a huge hurdle to overcome. Your orchestra will be here tomorrow, so we will see how successful we have been, but I have faith. You can do this, my little songbird. But you need to want this for yourself, regardless of any repercussions.'

Her head tilted. 'Do those repercussions still exist?'

'I don't know,' he said honestly. 'I would prefer not to find out.'

'So would I.' A sad smile spread over her face. 'It is hard

for me to reconcile the man I'm sharing a bed with with the brute who forced his way into my home.'

'They're one and the same. I make no apologies for being the man I was raised to be. When it comes to my family and my country I fight—and when necessary I fight dirty.'

'That you certainly do,' she said with a sigh, before reaching for his hand and threading her fingers through his. 'Why is this gala so important to you? I understand a nation's pride in half a century of successful and prosperous rule by one monarch, but I can't help thinking it means more to you than that.'

'You don't think that's enough?' he deflected. 'Fifty years of rule is no easy feat. In Agon most monarchs abdicate when their heir reaches forty, allowing them to enjoy their retirement. My grandfather's heir died before he reached that age, so he was left with no choice but to carry on—which he has done with dignity and pride, for his people. Helios will be forty in four years.'

Before she could ask another question he pulled her down to him and rolled her onto her back. Devouring her mouth, he allowed the sweetness of her touch, the sweetness of *her*, to encompass him and drive away the tightness pinching his skin to his bones.

And as he moved in her, her soft moans dancing in his ear and the short nails of her left hand scratching and gripping his back and buttocks with as much need as the long nails of her right, his mind emptied of everything but the ecstasy he experienced in her arms.

Talos had dozed off. Amalie lightly traced the bow of his full top lip, resisting the urge to replace her finger with her mouth. He looked at peace, all that latent energy in hibernation.

She'd told him everything. About all the shame she carried, the shame she hadn't even known she was carrying—

not just what had occurred at her mother's birthday party but the knock-on effects. Talking about it, admitting it—not just to Talos but to herself—she'd felt cleansed. Purged. He was right. She'd been a child.

Her heart felt so full, and it was all because of him. He'd stolen her heart and it astounded her how willing she'd been in allowing him to take it. But then he'd marked her with that first look. She'd stood no chance, not once she was on his island. Not once he'd shown her his human face. Even that damnable contract didn't make her fists clench any longer. She loved that he was prepared to fight for what he believed in.

What would it be like, she thought wistfully, to have this great man's love? To be enveloped under the protection he extended to his family and his people?

She couldn't allow herself to think like that. She was not her mother. Accepting that she'd fallen in love with him did not give her any illusions that he would have fallen for her in return. Only a few hours ago he'd made it clear it was all about sex.

But hadn't she said exactly the same thing? And hadn't she meant it too?

No. She would not allow herself the futility of hope. While she was on Agon she would cherish the time she spent with him. When it was time for her to leave she would go with her head held high and slip back into her old life.

She blinked.

Did she even *want* to go back to her nice, cosy existence?

Prickles spread out over her skin as she thought about what the future could hold for her. The future she'd once dreamt about.

She'd been terrified of passion and love. With Talos she had found both and she was still standing. Not only standing, but with an energy fizzing in her veins that made her feel more alive than she'd ever known.

All the walls she'd built—in part to protect herself, in part to punish herself—had been dismantled, revealing a future that could be hers if only she had the courage to reach out and take it.

Talos was a fighter. He wore his courage in his skin. He'd forced her to fight too, had found a way to bring out her own inner warrior. Now she needed to hold that inner warrior close and never let it go.

Slipping out of the covers, she helped herself to his discarded black T-shirt and tugged it over her head as she made her way down the stairs and into the living room. There, she opened her case, tightened and slid resin over her bow, tuned her violin. Then she took one final deep breath and went back up to the bedroom.

Talos still slept, but he'd shifted position in the few minutes she'd been gone. The moment she sat on the edge of the bed he opened his eyes.

Heart thundering, she smiled shyly at him, then closed her eyes, tucked her violin under her chin and positioned the bow.

The first note rang out with a high sweetness that hit Talos like a punch in his gut, waking him fully in an instant.

She didn't need to tell him. He knew.

This was his grandmother's piece. Her final composition, never before played to a living soul.

And as he listened, watched Amalie play, the punches continued to rain down on him, throwing him back a quarter of a century to his childhood, to the time when his whole world had been ripped apart.

Whereas before he'd been eager to hear her play it, now he wanted to wrestle the violin from her hands and smash it out of the window. But he was powerless to move, to stop the music from ringing around the bedroom, to stop the memories from flooding him. He was as powerless as he'd been when he was seven years old, unable to stop his father throwing blows upon his mother.

As he was assailed by all those torrid memories something else stole through him—a balm that slowly crept through his veins to soothe his turmoil, forcing the memories from his mind and filling him with nothing but the sweet music pouring from Amalie's delicate fingers.

It was like listening to a loving ghost. If he closed his stinging eyes he could see his grandmother. But she wasn't there. It was Amalie, who had interpreted the music with love and sympathy and such raw emotion it was as if Rhea Kalliakis had pointed a finger down at her from heaven and said, *She's the one*.

To watch her play felt like a precious gift in itself—a gift to love and cherish for ever.

It wasn't until she played the final note that she opened her eyes. He read the apprehension in them, but saw something else there too—an emotion so powerful his heart seemed to explode under the weight of it.

He dragged a hand down his face and inhaled through his nostrils, trying to restore an equilibrium that was now so disjointed he couldn't find the markers to right it.

'When my parents died I suffered from terrible nightmares.' His words were hoarse from the dryness in his throat. 'My grandmother would sit on my bed, as you are now, and she would play for me until the nightmares had gone and I had fallen back to sleep.'

Amalie didn't answer; her eyes wide and brimming with emotion.

'You've brought her music to life,' he said simply.

She hugged her violin to her chest. 'It's the most beautiful piece of music I've ever been privileged enough to play, and I promise you I will fight as if I were Agon-born to play it at your grandfather's gala.'

His heart twisted to see the fierceness on her face. He knew it was directed at herself, knew the battle wasn't yet

won, but also that she would fight with everything she had
to overcome half a lifetime of fear. There was something
about the way she looked at him that made him think she
wouldn't be fighting solely for the sake of the contract and
the repercussions that would come from failure, but for *him*.

And the thought of her fighting for him made his disjointed equilibrium do a full spinning rotation.

CHAPTER THIRTEEN

TALOS GOT INTO his car and turned on the ignition. He'd barely cleared his villa before he turned the car back and turned the engine off.

He imagined her cottage, in the distance, hidden from where he sat by dense trees. He imagined her waiting by the door for him, dressed in the tight-fitting sweats that showed off her slender curves. Imagined the welcoming kiss she would give him, her enthusiasm, as if they'd been parted for weeks rather than a few hours.

Since she'd played for him in the bedroom she'd had no problem with him being around while she practised his grandmother's piece. The problem was that her orchestra had arrived a couple of days ago and proper rehearsals for the gala had begun. Amalie had taken to the stage for the first rehearsal and frozen.

Today he'd been there to witness it for himself—and this time she'd played it to the end, but only by keeping her terror-filled eyes on him. She'd visibly trembled throughout, and the notes she'd played had been tense and short—nothing like the flowing, dreamlike melody she achieved when they were alone.

Her obvious distress felt like sharpened barbs in his heart.

It was too soon for her. Maybe if the gala were in a couple of months, or even weeks, there would be time but it was only four days away. She knew her part perfectly, and the orchestra knew theirs, but what use was that when she couldn't get her fingers to work?

And he, arrogant bastard that he was, had forced this nightmare on her, believing that some fighting spirit could cure half a lifetime of severe stage fright.

There was no way to fix it in time, not without putting her through an enormous amount of distress.

Tomorrow she would dine with his grandfather. Talos had invited himself along as well and hadn't liked the look in his grandfather's eyes when he'd suggested he come. It had been far too knowing.

Amalie's solo was the one performance of the whole gala that his grandfather was looking forward to. He might have to miss large chunks of the ceremony, but he had told Talos only yesterday that he would sooner be in his coffin than miss her performance.

Swallowing the acrid bile in his throat, Talos dug his phone out of his pocket and called her. 'I'm going to have to give tonight a miss,' he said, speaking quickly. 'Something's come up.'

'Are you all right?' The concern in her voice was plain.

He didn't want her concern. He didn't deserve it. The only thing he deserved was a dozen punches to his gut for forcing this nightmare on her.

'I'm busy with work, that's all. I'll try and catch up with you later.'

He blew out a breath of stale air as he disconnected his phone and tried to clamp down on the emotions raging through him, the feeling that his whole life was converging in a tipping point over which he had no control.

Amalie stepped through the trees surrounding her cottage and gazed at the villa in the distance. The moonless night was dark, but the white building glowed brilliantly under the stars.

It took her ten minutes to cross the land and reach it, and by the time she knocked on the front door her heart was thundering at a rate of knots, her hands clammy. She'd never been inside Talos's villa before. It occurred to her that she'd never been invited. His villa was very much his private sanctuary. Kept apart from her.

All evening she'd been waiting for another call from him or a knock on the cottage door. Something was wrong, and had been for the past couple of days. There was an unbreachable distance between them.

She knew he was worried about the gala. She was too. Terrified about it. They'd both had such confidence that she was ready to play in public, but that confidence had been a deception. Her nerves were winning the war. She'd just about managed to scrape through the rehearsal earlier, when she'd had his face to focus on, but her shaking fingers had prevented any hint of musicality.

Was that the reason for his distance?

Frustration and disappointment with her?

The maid who opened the door recognised her and welcomed her in with a smile. As neither spoke the other's language, the maid beckoned Amalie to follow her.

The interior of the villa was as fresh and modern as the palace was old and medieval, but with a definite nod to Agon's Minoan ancestry; Greek sculptures and artwork adorned the walls.

After leading her down a wide flight of marble stairs and through a large door the maid stopped and pointed at another closed door, gave a quick bow, and disappeared back up the stairs, leaving Amalie on her own.

Heart in her mouth, she tapped on the door. When there was no answer she rapped again, louder, pressing her ear to it. She heard nothing. She chewed her lips before deciding to turn the handle. She pushed the door ajar and peered through the crack, pushing it wide open when she realised this was Talos's personal gym.

Weight-lifting equipment, a treadmill and a rowing machine—items she wouldn't have known one from the other a month ago—were lined up against the mirrored wall opposite the doorway. Through the same mirror she caught sight of a blur and turned to the left.

There he was, oblivious to her presence, thrashing the living daylights out of a punching bag.

She knew she should call out to him, let him know she was there, but she was captivated by what she saw.

All he wore was a pair of black shorts. His feet were bare, his hands gloveless. She winced to imagine the damage he could be doing to his fingers, her chest constricting as she realised something must be seriously wrong for him to forgo the gloves he always insisted on. Only the week before she'd seen him admonish a teenager for daring to hit a basic pad without gloves. A punching bag was a much harder target.

All the same, she was mesmerised by the energy he exuded.

This was Talos stripped back, in all his graceful, powerful glory.

Sweat dripped off him, his muscles rippled, his punches were hard and merciless—as if he were imagining the punching bag as a living target, a foe to be destroyed.

He was in pain. She knew that as surely as she knew her own name. His pain was in every one of his punches.

He must have caught sight of her in the mirror, for he suddenly stopped and spun around. Breathing heavily, he stared at her disbelievingly, his throat moving, his jaw clenched.

Her lips parted to apologise for the intrusion—and it *was* an intrusion—but the words stuck in her throat.

Not taking his eyes off her, Talos reached for a towel and wiped his face and chest, then dropped it to the floor and prowled over to stand before her.

His chest was rising and falling in rapid motion, and his nostrils flared before his mouth came crashing down on hers and she was pushed back against the wall.

His kisses were hungry, the kisses of a starving man.

His powerful strength was something she'd always been hugely aware of, but until that moment she'd never appreciated the restraint he displayed around her. Now, holding her upright against the wall with one arm, he gripped her hip with his free hand and pulled her tight against him, before loosening his grip to slide his hand down her thigh to the hem of her short skirt and rip her knickers off. Manipulating her thighs to wrap around him, he freed himself from his shorts and plunged into her with a groan that spoke as much of pain as it did of pleasure.

Amalie held him tight, breathing in his salty, woody scent, cradling his scalp, wanting only to take away his pain.

As far as lovemaking went this was fierce, primal, but she embraced every carnal thrust, felt the pulsations building in her core as she clung to him. He gave a roar and buried his face in her hair, his whole body shaking, and his final thrust pushed her over the edge as the pulsations exploded with a shocking power that took all the life from her bones and left her limp in his arms.

Time lost any meaning.

It was only when he gently placed her back on her feet, tugged her skirt down from around her waist and stepped back, that she saw the red mark on the top of his shoulder and realised she had made it with her mouth.

Talos spotted it too and gave a ragged grin. 'My first love bite,' he said, in an attempt at humour that didn't fool her for a second.

She waited for him to ask why she was there, but all he did was cup her cheeks and kiss her with something close to desperation, then pull her to him.

'I'm sorry,' he said, his voice husky. 'That was incredibly selfish of me.'

'I'm not,' she murmured, tilting her head to look up at him.

His eyes closed and he muttered an oath. 'I didn't use protection.'

That made her blink. She hadn't been in the right frame of mind to think of protection either.

'We should be okay. I'm due on tomorrow.'

'*Should* be okay?' He gave a savage shake of his head.

'I'm not an expert, but I'm certain I'm way past the ovulation stage of my cycle. And I'm always regular,' she added, trying to reassure him even while the image of a dark-haired baby wrapped in vine leaves filtered into her mind. 'I'll know within a couple of days if we have a problem.'

The pulse in his jaw was working overtime. 'Make sure to tell me the minute you know.'

'I promise.' She hesitated before asking, 'Talos, what's wrong? You've become so distant.'

He gazed back down at her, and for a moment she was certain he was about to talk. Instead, he pulled his arms away and took a step back.

'Nothing's wrong. I'm a little stressed about the gala, I have a few minor problems with work, a lack of sleep... the usual.'

'I'm sure the rehearsals tomorrow will go better,' she said, trying to inject positivity into her tone. 'At least I was able to play it today.'

Even if it *had* sounded like a cats' chorus ringing out, and even if the members of her orchestra *had* been gazing at her with something close to horror.

He raised his eyes to the ceiling and shook his head, before jerking it into a nod. 'I'm sure you're right.'

And in that moment she knew he was lying.

He wasn't merely *concerned*.

He didn't believe she could do it.

Panic took hold in her chest.

Up until that point Talos's conviction that he could fix her had taken root in her head, allowing her to believe that she could overcome her fear in time. But if her warrior prince had lost faith, what did *that* say? Where did that leave her? Where did that leave *them*?

'I need to go to Athens first thing in the morning,' he said, rubbing the back of his neck. 'I'll collect you at seven for dinner with my grandfather.'

Was this his way of dismissing her?

'Okay…' she answered uncertainly. 'Are you certain it's informal dress?'

'My grandfather insists. He wants it to be a relaxed occasion, where you can both talk without formality.'

'That sounds good,' she said. 'Are you coming back to the cottage with me?'

Instinct had already told her his answer, but she had to ask. She wouldn't presume to invite herself to stay here at the villa with him—even if it wasn't so obvious he wished her gone.

'Not tonight. I've an early start. I'll only disturb you if I stay over, and you need a good night's sleep as much as I do. I'll walk you back.'

His words made sense. That didn't stop them feeling like a knife plunging into her heart.

She forced a smile to her face and leaned up to kiss him, pretending that nothing was wrong when it was blindingly obvious that he was steeling himself to end their relationship.

Not that what they shared was a relationship, she scolded herself on their silent walk back to the cottage. It had always had an end date attached to it; she had accepted that. She just hadn't considered that he would tire of her before the end date. She hadn't considered that he would lose faith in her.

Amalie strove to hide the shock that meeting King Astraeus Kalliakis evoked.

With Talos's hand in the small of her back, they had

been escorted by a courtier to the King's private dining room—a space a fraction of the size of the Banquet Room but every bit as sumptuous.

The pictures she'd seen of the King had depicted a tall, handsome man. Even at his eightieth birthday celebrations, with his ebony hair having thinned and turned white, he'd exuded vitality. That was the man she had prepared herself to meet.

'Forgive me for not rising to greet you,' he said, his voice weak. 'If I could get up I would kiss your hand.'

She had no idea what possessed her, but when she took the unsteady hand he offered she was the one to place a kiss on the paper-thin skin, rather than giving the curtsy she'd practised earlier.

He smiled warmly, then indicated for his nurse to wheel him to the table.

Amalie tried to catch Talos's eye but he was avoiding her gaze, just as he'd avoided any conversation other than the usual pleasantries on their drive to the palace. He hadn't even mentioned her phone call early that morning confirming that her period had started.

As masochistic as she knew it to be, she'd felt a definite twinge of disappointment when she'd spotted the telltale signs of her period. She'd never even *thought* of having children before. Not once. But for less than twelve hours there had been the smallest of chances that she might have conceived and her imagination had taken root. Any initial concerns about what a disaster it would be, seeing as she was in anything *but* a loving relationship, and it would affect the career she longed to reclaim, had fallen by the wayside as she'd imagined what it would be like to have Talos's child.

It had felt almost dreamlike.

She had no idea if she would be any good as a mother, but instinct told her he would make a fantastic father. She sighed. It was something she would never know, and it was pointless to allow her thoughts to run in such wayward directions, not when there were so many other things occupying her mind.

When she'd given Talos the news his response had been a distant, 'That's one less thing to worry about.'

And now she knew why he'd been so distant. He had been thinking of his grandfather.

Why hadn't he told her his grandfather was ill? And not just ill, but clearly dying. It was there in the gauntness of his features—he must have lost half his body weight since those pictures had been taken at his eightieth. And it was there in the sallow yellow complexion of his skin, the hollowness of his eyes… It was everywhere. She could feel it.

'You must be curious as to why I wanted to meet you,' the King rasped, once their first course of tomato and basil soup had been served.

'I assumed you wanted to meet the woman who will play your wife's final composition.'

As she spoke, her skin chilled. Today's rehearsal had been a step backwards.

It had started well enough. Christophe, the orchestra's conductor for the gala, had found a screen for her to hide behind, so she could actually play in time with the orchestra. It had worked beautifully. Then the screen had been removed and she'd found herself breathing in and out of a paper bag in an effort to stem the panic attack clawing at her.

Christophe was on the verge of his own nervous breakdown, freaking out so much he'd contracted a hypnotist to fly over to Agon for her.

She'd searched in vain for Talos, waiting for him to step through the practice room's door and give her confidence with a simple smile. But he'd been in Athens. If he was by her side she would be able to get through it; they'd already proved that. With more practice, and with Talos and his calming presence, she might be able to do the score the justice she gave it when they were alone.

'Indeed.' Watery brown eyes held hers. 'Tell me about yourself, *despinis*.'

'My career?'

That would be a very short conversation.

He waved a hand. 'I want to know about *you*. The music you enjoy, the books you read, the films you watch.'

And so they fell into easy conversation, Amalie doing most of the talking and the King making the odd encouraging comment. She was thankful for her childhood spent surrounded by powerful people, otherwise she would have been completely overwhelmed to be dining with a king.

He ate very little: a few spoonfuls of soup…a couple of bites of the main course of red snapper.

Talos stayed silent, following the conversation without contributing, his gaze on his grandfather. He didn't once meet her eyes.

When the dessert was brought in—light pistachio cakes with an accompanying chocolate mousse—the King finally asked her something in connection with the violin.

'Do you find it hard, learning new music?'

She considered the question, aware that Talos was finally looking at her. 'It's like reading a book where the words are notes and all the adjectives are replaced with tempos and dynamics.'

Astraeus gave a wheezy laugh. 'I'm sure that makes sense to you.'

She couldn't help but laugh too. 'I've probably over-complicated it. I should have just said I read music the way you read a book.'

'And how did you find learning my wife's music?'

'I found it the most fulfilling experience of my entire musical life,' she answered with honesty, trying to tune out Talos's stare. 'To know I am the first person to play it publicly… Can I ask you a question?'

The King nodded.

'Did she ever play it for you?'

'No.' His eyes dimmed. 'She never spoke of her music when she was composing. When she finished a piece, only then would she tell me about it and play it for me.' His shoulders slumped. 'She contracted pneumonia shortly before she completed this one. She struggled to finish it, but my wife was a very determined woman. She died two days later.'

'I'm very sorry.'

'I still miss her. All the time.'

Forgetting protocol—not that she even knew what the protocol for an audience with the King *was*, as Talos hadn't seen fit to fill her in—she leaned over and placed her hand on his.

Shock flared in his eyes but he made no effort to relinquish her hold, tilting his frail body a little closer to her.

'What your wife created,' Amalie said gently, 'was a concerto about love. It's a tribute to *you*.'

'How do you know this?' he whispered, leaning even closer.

'It's all there in the music. I can't explain how I know, but I feel it. She wrote this score with love in her heart—not maternal love, but romantic love.'

The King's eyes closed. For a moment she allowed her glance to dart at Talos. He sat rigid, his jaw set, his eyes filled with something she couldn't comprehend.

When Astraeus opened his eyes he stared at her with great concentration, before turning his head to the courtier standing to his right and nodding at him. The courtier left the dining room, returning almost immediately with a violin case. He laid it on the table before the King.

Astraeus gestured for Amalie to open it.

Apprehensive, certain he was going to ask her to play for him, she obeyed. The gorgeous scent of wood and resin puffed out and she inhaled it greedily, as she had done since toddlerhood, when her father would open *his* violin case.

She made to lift the violin out but the King stopped her, placing his hand on the instrument and stroking it.

'This belonged to Rhea,' he said. 'It was hand-crafted for her by Massimo Cinelli. It was my wedding present to her.'

Massimo Cinelli was one of the foremost twentieth-century luthiers, a man who made string instruments of such tonal quality it was argued that they rivalled Stradivarius. His had been a life cut tragically short, and when he'd died at the age of fifty-three he had been known to have made around three hundred string instruments, a quarter of which were violins. In recent months an auction for one of his violas had fetched a value of half a million pounds.

Amalie could only imagine what a violin made for a queen would fetch—especially a queen who'd left such a huge legacy to the classical music world. It made her joyful and sad all at the same time to know this would have been the violin Rhea had used at Carnegie Hall, when she'd played with Amalie's father all those years ago.

'I am bequeathing it to you,' the King said.

'What do you mean?'

Surely he had to be talking about her using it for the gala?

'It is yours, child.'

'Mine...?'

His smile was sad. 'It's sat in darkness for five years. It needs to be played. I know you will treasure it and I know you will honour Rhea's memory. Take it, child—it's yours.'

Amalie was truly lost for words. She knew this was no joke, but all the same... The King of Agon had just given her one of his wife's most prized possessions—a gift beyond value.

'Thank you,' she said, shrugging her shoulders with helplessness at her inability to come up with anything more meaningful.

'No. Thank *you*,' he answered enigmatically, then beckoned his nurse over and spoke to her in Greek.

The nurse took hold of his wheelchair.

'And now I bid you a good night,' Astraeus said. 'It has been a pleasure meeting you, *despinis*.'

'It has been an honour, Your Majesty.'

Talos had risen to his feet, so she followed suit, only to have the King take her hand and tug her down so he could speak in her ear. 'I'm glad my grandson has found you. Please look after him for me when I'm gone.'

In another breach of protocol she kissed his cold cheek and whispered, 'I promise I'll try.'

It was the best she could do. She doubted Talos would ever give her the chance.

CHAPTER FOURTEEN

A DRIVER RETURNED them to Talos's estate. They'd been sitting in the back, the partition up, for a few minutes before he spoke.

'What did my grandfather say to you?'

That was what he was concerned about? Not that she'd been given a family heirloom? The heirloom that now sat on her lap, where she held it tightly.

'I think he whispered it to me because he didn't want you to hear,' she answered, striving for lightness.

'Don't be absurd. I'm his grandson. We have no secrets.'

She finally found the courage to look at him. '*You* hold on to your secrets extremely well. You must have inherited that from somewhere.'

'Are you deliberately talking in riddles?'

'Why didn't you tell me he was ill?'

His jaw set in the clenched fashion it had been fixed in throughout the evening. Her heart ached to see it and she wished she could breach the wall he'd erected between them. Even before they'd become lovers she'd never felt as if she couldn't touch him, but right then she was certain that if she reached out he would recoil from her.

'My grandfather's illness is not a subject for idle gossip.'

'I appreciate that.'

She took a breath. It wasn't so much his answer that had cut, but the dismissive tone in which he'd said it. As if she were no one.

'But if you'd told me the truth about his health from the beginning…'

'Then *what*?' he asked bitingly. 'You would have agreed to perform for him *without* having to be blackmailed into it?'

'I don't know.' She tightened her grip on the violin case, soothing her fingers on the velvety material. It was the only part of her she could soothe. 'I don't know if things would have been different—my point is you never gave me the chance to find out if I would have reacted differently.'

'You wouldn't have,' he said, with tight assurance.

'We'll never know.' Now she clenched her own teeth, before loosening them. 'What I don't understand is why you haven't told me since. We've shared a bed for over a fortnight.'

There had been plenty of opportunities for him to tell her. Times when she'd asked him if there was something wrong. The time she'd asked him outright if the gala held more importance to him than the reason he'd shared with her.

'Do not presume that sharing a bed means I owe you anything.'

She had never known him to be this cold. She'd never known him to be cold at all. When something angered him Talos *burned*.

This coldness chilled her to the bone.

The car came to a stop. The driver opened her door.

Not another word was exchanged as she got out and entered the cottage. Not a word of goodnight. Not a kiss. Not a touch. Not a look.

She flinched to hear the engine spark back to life and the car driving off, taking Talos to his villa.

Feeling as if lead weights had been inserted into her limbs, she kicked off her shoes and placed Rhea Kalliakis's violin on the piano. If she didn't feel so numb she would already have it out of the case and be tuning it. This was a *Cinelli*. Any other violinist in the world would likely have passed out with shock to be given it. It was the classical violinist's version of winning the lottery.

But the weight of the gift lay heavily on her. And Talos's parting words lay even heavier.

'Do not presume that sharing a bed means I owe you anything.'

He'd really said that. He'd hardly said a word all night but he'd said *that*. And as the full weight of those words filtered through her brain the numbness disappeared, pain lanced through her, and something even more powerful filled her.

Anger. Unadulterated rage.

How *dared* he talk to her as if she were nothing more than a notch on his bedpost?

Consumed with a fury she only partly understood, she flung open the front door and ran out into the night. Cutting through the trees, she saw the lights of the villa in the distance, along with the lights of the car just approaching it.

The lead in her limbs had gone. Her legs were now seemingly made of air as she flew over the fields, running faster than she'd ever known she could, the wind rippling against her face, the skirt of her blue summer dress billowing out behind her.

It seemed as if no time had passed before she set the security lights ablaze. In the time it had taken her to race there the car had dropped Talos off and begun its return journey to the palace.

As she banged on the front door with her fist, then punched the doorbell, she was assailed with memories of that morning a month before, when Talos had knocked on her own front door and turned her world on its axis.

The door was wrenched open.

Talos stood there, staring at her as if she'd just appeared from the moon.

'Sharing your bed doesn't mean I *presume* you owe me anything—let alone know what's going on in your head,' she spat from her place on the doorstep, before he could utter a word. 'But we've shared more than just a bed. Or at least *I* have.'

He looked murderous. He looked as if he wanted nothing more than to wrap his hands around her throat.

'Have you run all the way here from the cottage *in the dark*? Are you *insane*? It's the middle of the night—there could be anyone out there!'

'You didn't worry about that the other night when I walked here in the dark.'

Suddenly the exertion of her run hit her and she bent over, grabbing her knees as she fought desperately to breathe. God, but her lungs burned.

'Amalie?'

She lifted her head to look at him, puffing in air until she felt able to straighten again.

He stared at her with eyes now curiously vacant. His detachment ratcheted her fury up another notch.

She straightened. 'Do not treat me as if I'm some nothing you had sex with just because it was available. It was more than that and you know it—and you owe me more than to treat me like that.'

'I do not owe you anything. If you think your being a virgin before we became lovers means I have to treat you—'

'It's nothing to do with me being a virgin!' she yelled, punching him in the shoulder.

He didn't so much as jolt.

'This is to do with me sharing everything with you. I spilled my guts about my childhood and my life to you. I gave you *everything*! I didn't expect a marriage proposal, or declarations of love, but I *did* expect some respect.'

'It was never my intention to be disrespectful.'

'Then what *was* your intention? Tell me, damn you. Why have you closed yourself off? I thought you were frustrated because I'm still struggling to play with the orchestra, but now I'm wondering if you're just bored with me. Is that it?

Are you too gutless to tell me that you don't want me any more and rather than come out and say it you're taking the coward's way of withdrawing, hoping I'll get the hint?'

Her voice had risen to a shout. No doubt half the live-in staff had been woken.

Suddenly he jerked forward and grabbed her forearm. 'Come with me,' he said through gritted teeth, marching her through the reception room, down a wide corridor and through a door that revealed what at first glance appeared to be an office, filled with plush masculine furniture.

He slammed the door shut and loomed over her, his arms folded over his chest. His eyes had darkened to a point of blackness.

'First of all, do *not* presume to tell me what I think.'

'I have to make assumptions because you don't tell me anything!'

'What do you want me to say? Do you want me to *apologise* because my grandfather is dying?'

'No!' She clamped her teeth together and blinked back the sudden stinging tears welling in the backs of her eyes. 'Of course not. I didn't mean—'

Before she knew what was happening Talos's control shattered before her eyes.

He punched the wall, blackness seeping out of him. 'I know what you meant. You think because you have shared confidences with me that I must do the same in return.'

'No!' She shook her head over and over, terrified not for herself but for him. She'd never seen such pain before, etched on every line of his face and in every movement of his powerful body.

He seemed not to hear her, kicking the solid wood desk with such force he put a dent in it. 'Do you want me to pour my heart out about my childhood? To understand where my nightmares come from and why I went so off the rails in my adolescence? Is that what you want?'

'I—'

'Do you want to hear about the day I watched my father punch my mother not once but a dozen times in the stomach? Do you want to hear how I jumped on his back to protect her and how he threw me off with such force my head split open on their bedframe? That my lasting memory of my mother is her holding me and her tears falling on my bleeding head? Is *that* what you want? To know that I couldn't protect her then and that my vow to always protect her in the future came to nothing, because two hours later both my parents were dead? And now my grandfather is dying too. And I have to accept that as a fact of life and accept there is nothing I can do about it. You want me to share how I feel? Well, it feels as if my stomach and heart have been shredded into nothing. Is that enough for you? Is that what you wanted to hear?'

His eyes suddenly found hers, and he threw his hands in the air and stalked towards her.

'So now you know all my dirty little secrets and I know yours, is there anything else you want from me or feel I should tell you, seeing as we're having such a *wonderful* time trading confidences?'

If it hadn't been for the wildness radiating from his eyes she would have hated him for his contempt. But she couldn't. All she felt was horror.

'No?' He leaned down so his face was right against hers. 'In that case, seeing as you've got what you wanted from me, you can leave.'

Abruptly he turned away and lifted the phone on the sprawling desk, rasping words in Greek to whoever was on the receiving end.

'Talos…' she said hesitantly when he'd replaced the receiver.

She didn't know what she wanted to say. Couldn't think of anything *to* say. What she did want was to take him in her arms and hold him close, but she knew without having to be told he didn't want that. He didn't want her or the solace she yearned to give him.

'We have nothing more to say to each other.' He seemed to have regained his composure, but his focus on her was stark. 'We've enjoyed each other's company but this is as far as we go.'

A knock on the door made her start.

Talos pulled it open and indicated for her to leave. 'Kostas will take you back to the cottage. I hope for everyone's sake the hypnotist your conductor has arranged for you works, because there is nothing more *I* can do to help you.'

With as much dignity as she could summon Amalie walked past him to Kostas, who had already set off to the front door.

Talos kicked the covers off and got out of bed. A large glass of single malt should help him sleep.

He glanced out of the window. Three o'clock in the morning and all was in darkness, but in the downward sloping distance he could see the dim lights of the cottage.

Amalie was awake.

He closed his eyes. He would bet every last cent he owned that at that very minute she was playing his grandmother's violin, taking the only comfort she could. In his mind's eye he watched her fingers flying over the strings, imagined the purity of the sound she produced. Knew that to hear it would tear his soul in half. That was if any part of his soul remained. After the way he'd spoken to her the other night whatever had been left of it had been ripped out.

He'd treated her abominably. He still didn't know where all that rage had come from, knew only that she'd been getting too close. He'd been trying to protect himself. Squashing anything that resembled an emotion down into a tight little ball that could be hidden away and forgotten about.

Somehow Amalie had unpicked the edges of that ball and it had exploded back into life, making him feel more than a man could bear.

Theos, had he ever felt more wretched?

He'd been heartsick before—of course he had; the loss of his parents had devastated him. His father had been a brute, but Talos had still loved him…with the blind faith with which all small children loved their parents.

This felt different, as if the weight of a thousand bass drums had compressed inside him, beating their solemn sound through his aching bones.

He was wasted, physically and emotionally.

He closed his eyes, imagined Amalie padding into his room and settling on the corner of his bed to play for him, her music soothing him enough to drive all the demons from his head.

He hadn't known his grandfather intended to give her the violin, but he couldn't think of a better person to have it. What good would it do sitting in a glass cabinet in the Kalliakis palace museum, nothing but a tourist attraction? At least Amalie would love and care for it. When she played it she would play with her heart.

He'd spent the day deliberately avoiding anyone connected with the orchestra. But palace whispers ran more quickly than the tide, and his avoidance hadn't stopped rumours about the solo violinist having to play behind a screen for the third day in a row reaching his ears.

He imagined her standing there, shaking, her face white and pinched, terror in those beautiful green eyes, her breath coming in increasingly shallow jerks.

What was he *doing* to her?

It would be kinder to strip her naked and stand her on display. The humiliation would be less.

She'd come so far—been so incredibly brave. To force her to go ahead with the gala now would surely ensure his damnation to hell. Forget any potential ruination of the gala—forcing Amalie to go ahead would completely destroy her.

He couldn't do it to her.

He would rather rip his own heart out than let her suffer any more.

Amalie rubbed her sleep-deprived eyes, then picked up her knife and chopped the melon into small chunks, the action making her think of Talos and the knife he carried everywhere with him.

Do not think of him, she ordered herself. *Not today.*

There would be plenty of time to mourn what had happened between them when she returned to Paris, but for now she had to get through today. That was all she should focus on.

The scent of the melon was as fragrant as all the fruit she'd had since her arrival on the island, but her stomach stubbornly refused to react to it other than to gurgle with nausea.

Please, stomach, she begged, *accept some form of nourishment*.

At the rate she was going, even if she managed to get on to the outdoor stage that evening, she would likely fall into a faint when the heat of the spotlight fell upon her and her starved belly reacted to it.

Hearing movement, she cut through to the entrance hall and found a letter had been pushed through the door.

A heavy cream-coloured A4 envelope with *'Amalie Cartwright'* written on it with a penmanship that resembled a slash.

Her heart thundering erratically, it was clear her body knew who the sender was before she'd torn it open.

In the top right-hand corner was Talos's full name, including his royal title and the palace address.

Dear Mademoiselle Cartwright
    This letter is written to confirm the cancellation of the contract between us dated tenth March. All penalties stipulated in the contract are hereby revoked, and the Orchestre National de Paris shall continue in its current form.
Sincerely,
Talos Kalliakis

Her head swimming, Amalie read it a number of times before the words sank in.

Her stomach dived, nausea clutching her throat.

One hand over her mouth, the other pressed against her heavy, thundering heart, she swayed into a table, fighting to stop the deluge of misery knocking her from her feet.

He didn't believe she could do it.

He really had given up on her.

It was over.

Everything.

His belief in her.

Her reignited dreams of playing on a stage.

All gone.

But before the despair could crush her in its entirety, a thought struck her.

Why now, on the day of the gala—the day they'd spent a month preparing for…?

She rubbed her eyes, frantically trying to stem the tears pouring out of them, and read it one more time.

It didn't make any sense.

She looked at her watch. Nine a.m. The gala would be starting in six hours. She was due onstage to perform the solo and close the gala in eleven hours. The schedule had been released to the media, who were crawling all over the island in preparation for the day's events. At that moment heads of state were preparing to descend on the island.

And Talos was allowing her to leave.

No, it really did not make any sense.

Since their last encounter she'd done nothing but think of him and his words. She'd known from the beginning that her playing his grandmother's final composition was important to him—you didn't blackmail and threaten someone for something trivial. Dining with his grandfather had brought the true importance of the gala to life for her. This was King Astraeus's swansong. This was the final celebration of his life.

And now Talos was prepared to scrap what he'd fought so hard to attain.

His grandparents had raised him and his brothers since he was seven. His family meant everything to him. This piece of music meant everything to his entire family. Of all the things the gala represented, *this* was the performance that meant the most. It wasn't just the icing on the cake; it was the sponge and filling too.

She thought back to that evening three days ago, and the contempt in his voice when he'd ordered her to leave his villa. She'd thought then that the contempt was directed at *her*, but suddenly she realised it had been directed inwards, at himself.

And suddenly she realised something else.

For Talos to release her from the contract now meant he was putting her emotional well-being above *everything*.

Talos Kalliakis was a warrior. He would fight to the bitter end, even if it meant frogmarching her onto the stage and holding her upright while she played. Their time together had proved she could play when she was with him—something he would use as a weapon in his arsenal He would carry on their affair until she'd outlived her use. He wouldn't have lost faith in her because faith didn't exist in his vocabulary. For Talos it was all about spirit and belief.

She thought back to the rehearsal earlier in the week, when his presence had enabled her to play the whole piece without having to hide behind a screen. There had been pride in his brown eyes, but mingled with it had been something troubled. Now she understood what that had meant—her distress had troubled him on a *personal* level.

She scrambled for her phone and scrolled through her contacts until she found the gala coordinator's name. She pressed the call button.

'Has the schedule been changed?' Amalie asked without preamble.

'I was told an hour ago that the final orchestral piece has been changed,' the coordinator replied. 'I'm still waiting to hear what it's been changed *to*.'

'But my orchestra will still be performing the final piece?'

'Yes.'

'Thank you.'

Disconnecting the call, Amalie rubbed a hand over her mouth, then dialled Melina's number. The kickboxing instructor's *froideur* towards her had thawed over time—enough so that she'd given Amalie her number.

'Melina? I need your help...'

CHAPTER FIFTEEN

THE GALA WAS proving to be a huge success. The open-air theatre was filled; not a single seat was free. The day had started with Helios announcing his engagement to Princess Catalina of Monte Cleure, and then the guests had been treated to a variety of acts—from a children's choir to a world-famous circus troupe—and each in turn had been given rapturous applause.

Talos was too keyed up to enjoy it.

He'd sat down with his grandfather that morning and explained that Amalie would not be performing after all. He'd told him that the orchestra had rehearsed in Paris with another violinist before flying over, and how that violinist was prepared to take the role.

His grandfather had looked him straight in the eye and replied, 'An understudy won't do. We both know Amalie is the one.'

Talos had responded with a sharp nod, refusing to think of the undertone in his grandfather's words or the expression in his eyes as he'd said them.

The penultimate act was on stage now; Agon's Royal Ballet School, performing a condensed version of the *Nutcracker Suite* with the accompaniment of Agon's Royal Orchestra. Ballet bored him at the best of times, but tonight he didn't notice a single thing about it. As hard as he tried to concentrate, his mind was with Amalie.

His grandfather, sitting to his left with a blanket snug over his lap, was thoroughly enjoying it all, nodding along to the more upbeat performances and snoozing his way through those that failed to capture his attention.

If Helios and his new fiancée were enjoying it they were doing a fine job of pretending otherwise, the atmosphere between them decidedly frosty. And Theseus... He might as well not be there, for all the attention he was paying to the acts.

Finally the ballet finished and the curtains closed so that the Orchestre National de Paris could set up with privacy. Talos could not care less what piece they chose to play as a replacement. His only stipulation was that it must not be the 'Méditation' from *Thaïs*.

The compère, a famous American comedian, came on-stage and told some jokes to keep the crowd entertained. They'd been sitting in the amphitheatre for over five hours but showed no sign of restlessness.

The audience burst into a roar of laughter at a joke the compère had told but Talos hadn't heard a word of it.

Grinning hugely, the compère pressed a finger to his ear, listening to his earpiece, then raised a hand for silence.

'It is now time for the final performance,' he said, becoming solemn. 'As this is such a special occasion only the most special performance can be allowed to finish it. Ladies and gentlemen, performing the final composition of this beautiful island's Queen Rhea, I give you the Orchestre National de Paris and their celebrated violinist, Amalie Cartwright.'

What...?

Loud applause broke out, and the curtains were drawn back to reveal the orchestra already seated.

Heart thumping, Talos's first thought was that someone had forgotten to tell the compère about the change. It had been too late to alter the programmes, so they'd agreed that the compère would inform the audience that Amalie had been taken ill.

He got to his feet, ready to find out what had gone wrong.

Then he spotted the figure standing at the front left-hand side of the stage.

His heart twisted into a clenched fist. He couldn't move; his feet seemed rooted to the floor until his grandfather took hold of his wrist and gently tugged it.

Unable to move his eyes away from her, he sat back down, breathing heavily.

Amalie looked beautiful. Divine. She wore a snug-fitting mid-thigh-length dress, with a scooped neckline and short sleeves. Its red wine colour set her apart from her orchestra, who all wore black. It highlighted the paleness of her skin, and with her hair swept up in an elegant knot she looked fragile. Incredibly fragile. And scared—like the rabbit caught in the headlights he'd found in the Parisian practice room all those long weeks ago.

Her eyes searched his side of the crowd until she found the royal box. It was too dark for her to pick him out but he swore that she found him.

The conductor stood before the orchestra and silence fell. The first pluck from the string section echoed out, then the whisper of the flutes.

Amalie's teeth bit into her lip before she placed her violin under her chin and put her bow in position. She straightened, visibly strengthening. Then she closed her eyes, listened for her cue and played the first note.

Talos held his breath. Beside him, he heard his brothers and grandfather hold their breaths too. It had been an open secret around the palace that the star soloist was suffering from a severe case of stage fright.

Their worry was unfounded.

Her eyes scrunched tightly shut, Amalie began to play.

When she'd played the piece for him in the bedroom the beauty of the underlying melody had made his heart expand. Coupled with the accompanying orchestral arrangement it was taken to a whole new level of beauty, heightening the sensation he'd experienced that first time, pulling him into a swell of emotion.

Watching her, the sway of her hips as she played with the whole of her body, the marvel of her finger-work, the purity of her vibrato...

The child prodigy was reborn—a virtuoso of such melodic stature that he was certain there couldn't be a dry eye in the amphitheatre.

As she approached the climax of the piece—the part that tore his heart into shreds—her eyes flew open and found the royal box. She was crying, he realised, huge tears falling down her cheeks.

His grandfather tugged at his sleeve for attention.

Blinking away the burn at the back of his eyes, Talos felt his chest constrict to see his grandfather's face also swimming with tears.

'Surely my fighter of a grandson isn't so scared of a woman's love that he would throw away his one chance of true happiness?' he asked in a choked voice.

It was as if his grandfather had stared right into his heart and read what was there. And in that moment the truth hit him with full force.

Suddenly it was there, as if he'd always known. There in his head. In his heart.

He'd fallen in love with her.

As epiphanies went, it beat them all.

He loved her.

Gazing back at the beautiful woman who held the thousands in the audience in silent captivation, he had never felt so full; as if his heart and chest had expanded so much they could explode out of him.

Theos, she was magnificent...holding her composure right until the final note played out.

The applause was instantaneous.

Everybody got to their feet, orchestra and crowd alike.

Wiping her face with shaking hands, Amalie bowed to the royal box, then bowed again to the audience at large. The conductor strode over to her, clapping hard, then put his hands on her shoulders and kissed her cheeks, then bowed to her. She laughed and put a hand over her mouth, so clearly overwhelmed at the reaction that Talos wanted to run on to the stage and scoop her into his arms.

But this was her moment, and she needed to cherish it.

She found the royal box again, kissed her hand, then pointed it at his grandfather, more tears falling down her cheeks.

The crowd were calling for an encore.

Amalie, the rest of the Orchestre National de Paris and all the other performers were whisked back inside the palace for the after-gala do.

She took the offered champagne and drank it with gratitude, still dazed at what she had accomplished.

She had done it.

Her parents had both messaged her.

Her father's message had read: I'm very proud of you, sweetheart—maybe the old dream of playing together at Carnegie Hall might one day come true xxx, while her mother's had been much longer and more rambling, but filled with just as much pride.

On impulse, she'd messaged them both back, suggesting the two of them celebrate together. Life was too short to be miserable, and far too short to be alone. They'd been divorced from each other almost as long as they'd been married, and still neither of them was happy without the other. If there was one thing Amalie had learned during her time on Agon it was that it was time to forgive the past. They needed to forgive it too.

A gong rang out, which brought everyone in the ballroom to attention. A courtier entered the room and announced the arrival of His Majesty King Astraeus and the Princes Helios, Theseus and Talos.

Her stomach somersaulted as a different courtier approached to lead her over to the royal family. She'd been warned that she would be the first one to be addressed by them.

Taking a deep breath, she finished her champagne and followed him to where the royal family were lined up, awaiting her. The other guests were forming an orderly queue, and she was taken to the head of it.

The King, frail in his wheelchair, broke into a smile to see her and grabbed her hands with surprising strength to tug her down to him. A tear trailed down his cheek. 'Thank you, *despinis*. Thank you from the bottom of my heart.'

Her own eyes filled. Hadn't she cried enough for one evening? Having not cried in years, her life being too safe for anything emotional to pierce her, it was as if her tear ducts were now making up for it.

'It was an honour,' she whispered.

This time it was the King who breached protocol, planting a kiss to her cheek, and then he indicated for his nurse to wheel him out, leaving the queue of people behind her staring in disbelief as the King left his own party.

Theseus was next in line, and surprised her by ignoring her hand and clumsy curtsy to kiss her on both cheeks. His eyes were a darker brown than Talos's, and rang with a strong emotion he didn't have to put into words.

Helios was even more demonstrative, pulling her into his arms for a tight embrace and whispering in her ear, 'My family honours you—our island is your home for as long as you want it to be.'

And then it was Talos's turn.

Jaw clenched, he shook her hand formally—his own had a bandage wrapped tightly around its forefinger and index finger—and bowed as she made her curtsy.

She met his eyes. 'You've hurt your hand...' She thought

back to the punch he'd given the wall of his office, and to the time she'd found him thumping that punching bag without protective gloves on.

'It'll heal.' A pulse throbbed beneath his ear, the black pupils of his eyes thick and dilating as he gazed at her without speaking any further.

She didn't know what to say. She knew he cared for her, but that didn't mean anything had changed. No matter how his feelings for her had developed, it didn't change the fact that he was a lone wolf.

Did lone wolves ever pair up?

Aware of the other performers jostling next to her, eager to have their audience with him, she turned to walk away but a huge arm hooked around her waist.

'Where do you think you're going?' he said roughly, pulling her away from the line.

Joy filled her so rapidly she felt her toes lifting with the extra air it generated. 'I was letting the others have their audience with you.'

'I don't want an audience with anyone but you.' He steered her further away from the line approaching the Princes, now a good two hundred people deep.

'Shouldn't you stay with your brothers?'

His massive shoulders lifted into a nonchalant shrug. 'They can handle it.'

She couldn't prevent the smile that broadened across her face so widely she felt it pull at every muscle in her face.

Talos wanted privacy for them. This was not a conversation he wanted to have with his brothers and hundreds of guests watching.

Gripping her hand firmly, he steered her out of the ballroom and through all the corridors they'd travelled together three weeks before. He hadn't expected her to agree so readily to his request to talk. After the way he'd spoken to her the other night he hadn't expected much more from her than a possible slap around the face.

He also hadn't expected that she would hold his hand as tightly as he held hers—so tightly it was as if she didn't want to let it go...

Punching in the security code for his private apartment, he led her inside. Dropping his hold on her hand, he strode to the high window of his living area, braced himself, and then turned around to face her properly.

'Before I say anything further I need to apologise for forcing you to come here to my island. The contract I made you sign and the pressure I put you under was unforgivable.'

She smiled. 'Thank you.'

What was she smiling for? 'There is no excuse.'

'Maybe not, but I forgave you ages ago.'

'I treated you abysmally. I refused to take you or your fears seriously because I am an arrogant bastard who thinks only of himself.'

'The arrogant bit is true...' She nodded, her eyes ringing with what looked startlingly like compassion. 'But the rest of your self-assessment is wrong. If you had blackmailed me for your own needs I would never have forgiven you, but it wasn't for selfish reasons. You did it for your grandfather...because you love him.'

He sucked in a breath and swallowed. 'I must also apologise for the way I spoke to you the other night. I lashed out at you, which is also unforgivable.'

'You were in pain.' She closed the gap he'd created between them and placed her hand on his arm. 'I should never have forced the issue with you.'

How could she keep forgiving him and making excuses? He didn't deserve it. He didn't deserve *her*.

'You were right to force it. You were right that what we shared was more than sex. But I was in denial. I lashed out because I find it hard to talk about how I feel, and at the time I was struggling to understand how I felt.'

Those compassionate green eyes held steady on his. 'And how do you feel now?'

How to put into words what was in his heart? He didn't know—knew only that he must.

He took a deep breath.

'All my life I have tried to protect those I…I feel deeply for. I wanted to protect my mother from my father. The night they died I heard them argue. My mother had discovered he was having another affair. She begged him to end it.'

He took another breath.

'My father was an only child and very spoiled. He was never denied anything he wanted. Their marriage was arranged and he wanted it to be one of duty, not love and to be able to continue having his needs met by whatever woman took his eye. But my mother loved him despite all his faults and couldn't accept that. Whenever she found evidence of his affairs her jealousy would get the better of her. That night their argument escalated and he turned on her with his fists—just as I had heard him do before. This time I summoned up the courage to try and protect her, but I was too small and clumsy. I made a vow to myself that from that moment I would do everything I could to protect her, but I never got the chance.'

Talos stared at the woman he knew he had to open himself to if he had any chance of winning her love. Her eyes were tugged down into crinkles at the corners, her teeth gnawing at her lips, but she kept her silence, letting him speak of the demons in his heart.

'You're the only woman I've met who brings that same compulsion out in me. I wanted to protect you—no, I *want* to protect you. Always.'

'Is that why you released me from the contract?' she asked softly.

'Yes.'

Remembering how magnificently she'd played made him shake his head in awe. Never mind that she'd played as if she were a *Mousai*, a Muse, one of those beautiful goddesses of music and song—she'd displayed the greatest act of bravery he'd ever witnessed in his life.

'I knew you could do it—believe that—but I couldn't put you through the emotional damage it would bring. Your distress…it cuts me.' He shook his head again. 'How did you get up on that stage?'

'I got Melina to come to the palace and put me through the workout of my life. With all those endorphins racing through my blood I imagined I was an Agonite—a born warrior. I imagined your voice in my head, telling me to fight.'

'But *why*? I gave you a free pass to leave.'

'And it was that freedom which gave me the choice. Do you remember what you said to me? You told me to loosen my hold and fly, and you were right—and the only person who could cut that hold was me. I *wanted* to fly. I *wanted* to throw off the past, stand on that stage and play that beautiful score. And I wanted to do it for you and your grandfather as much as I wanted to do it for me.'

'You wanted to do it for *me*?' How he had hoped…

'I knew how much it meant to you and how much you love your grandmother.'

A painful lump formed in his throat. 'My grandmother died without ever hearing me say those words. When my parents died I became lost, out of control. I didn't want to let people get close to me—not on an emotional level. I have friends…I've had lovers…but I kept them all at an emotional distance. And then you…'

'Me?' she prompted gently, her fingers digging into his arms.

'You…' He swallowed. 'I let you in. I had no choice in it. You crept into my heart.'

Something sparked in her eyes. 'Say it,' she urged. 'Please. Even if you only say it once I won't care, once will be enough. *Say it.*'

'I…'

'Shall I say it first?' Reaching up to palm his face with her hand, she stepped flush against him. 'I love you. You're ferocious and loyal and you've taught me to fly. I will love you until I take my dying breath.'

All the air rushed from his lungs.

'Say it,' she beseeched.

'I love you.' And as he said the words more tumbled out with them. 'I love you and I want to protect and honour you until I take my dying breath.' He kissed her hard. 'I love you.'

Raining kisses all over her face and neck, he kept repeating those words, letting them sink into every part of him until he was enveloped in the love that bound them so tightly he knew it would never let them go.

'Will you let me love and worship you for ever?' he asked, his hands buried in her silky hair.

'Only if you let me love and worship *you* for ever too.'

'If we marry you'll have no choice. Divorce is forbidden for me, remember…?' He pulled back to look deep into her eyes. *'Will* you marry me?'

'It's only a piece of paper, but I'll sign my heart on it because it belongs to you now. I'm trusting you to take care of it for me.'

'I'll protect it with my life.'

And with those words his hungry mouth moulded to hers.

He felt cleansed. Whole. Loved.

He loved her. And she loved him.

He would say the words to her every day for the rest of his life.

EPILOGUE

AMALIE STEPPED ONTO the sunny balcony of the New York hotel in time to catch Talos hastily turning the page of the newspaper he was reading.

'Stop reading my reviews,' she chided him, settling herself gently onto his lap and nuzzling his neck. Even after two years of marriage she liked nothing more than to bury herself into him and smell his gorgeous, woody scent.

He laughed. 'Do you want me to tell you what it says?'

'No.'

It was a standing joke between them.

Talos trawled the media for any review and snippet about her career he could find, getting any paper versions couriered to wherever they happened to be in the world. Although his pride in her touched her deeply, she preferred to live in blissful ignorance of the critics' voices.

The past couple of years had been a whirl. It made her dizzy to think back on it. After the gala she'd been inundated with offers to perform and record all over the world. Talos had encouraged her to follow her dreams, had been by her side every step of the way. It had been hard—especially the live performing side, which she chose selectively—but the nerves she'd lived with for so long had almost been banished. *Almost.*

He placed a hand to her swollen belly. 'Did you manage to get any sleep?'

'Some.' She kissed his neck. 'Junior gave up playing football in my belly when the sun came up.'

Seven months pregnant with their first child, she already resembled a watermelon. It was a look Talos assured her suited her. She was so excited about the pregnancy she wouldn't have cared if she looked like a bus.

'And how are you feeling about tonight?'

'Sick! But excited too,' she hastened to add.

Being so heavily pregnant meant that she couldn't do the vigorous kickboxing workout that usually served her so well before a performance. And tonight would be the performance she'd spent her whole life waiting for.

Tonight she and her father would be performing onstage together at Carnegie Hall.

'As long as you're there I'll be fine.'

He rubbed a big hand over her back. 'I want you to be more than fine—I want you to enjoy it.'

'Seeing as this is likely my last performance for a very long time, I intend to make the most of every moment.'

He'd started to say something—no doubt about to offer more reassurance—when the suite's buzzer went off.

Talos groaned. 'I bet that's your mother.'

Amalie's parents, who had remarried to great fanfare six months after Amalie and Talos's own nuptials, were staying in the same hotel. Her mother was enjoying the trip enormously, dragging her husband here, there and everywhere as she threw her weight around.

'Let's pretend we're not in,' Amalie murmured.

'She has unnatural senses.'

'We'll pretend to be asleep.'

Grinning, she slipped a hand down to the waistband of his shorts and undid the button.

'Come on, my Prince, take me to bed.'

Brown eyes gleaming, he pressed a kiss to her neck. 'Nothing would give me greater pleasure.'

Smothering their laughter, in case Colette had her ear

to the door, they tiptoed into the master bedroom of their suite, sneaked under the bedcovers and pretended to be asleep for a very long time.

* * * * *

THESEUS
DISCOVERS
HIS HEIR

MICHELLE SMART

This book is dedicated to Jo aka 'Cat'.
Who has been there with me every step of the way.

CHAPTER ONE

JOANNE BROOKES COVERED her mouth to stifle a yawn and blinked rapidly to keep her eyes open. She was quite tempted to shove the thick pile of papers aside and have a nap at the small kitchen table, but she needed to read and digest as much as she could.

The floor creaked behind her and she turned to see Toby poke his head around the door of the tiny living space.

'What are you doing up, you little monkey?' she asked with a smile.

'I'm thirsty.'

'You've got water in your room.'

He gave an impish grin and padded over to her, his too-short pyjamas displaying his bare ankles. He hoisted himself up onto her lap and pressed his warm face into her neck.

'Do you *have* to go away?'

Wrapping her arms tightly around his skinny frame, Jo dropped a kiss in Toby's thick black hair. 'I wish I didn't.'

There was no point in explaining the finer details of why she had to leave for the island of Agon in the morning. Toby was four years old and any kind of rationalising normally went right over his head.

'Is ten days a long time?' he asked.

'It is to start with, but before you know it the time will have flown by and I'll be home.' She wouldn't lie to him, and could only dress her departure up into something bearable. Her stomach had been in knots all day, knitted so tightly she hadn't been able to eat a thing.

They'd only spent two nights apart since Toby's birth. Under normal circumstances she wouldn't even have considered going. It would have been a flat-out no.

'And just think what fun you'll have with Uncle Jonathan,' she added, injecting a huge dose of positivity into her voice.

'And Aunty Cathy?'

'Yes—and Aunty Cathy. And Lucy.'

Her brother and his wife lived in the local town with their year-old daughter. Toby adored them almost as much as they adored him. Even knowing that he would be in safe, loving hands, Jo hated the thought of being apart from him for such a long time.

But Giles, her boss, had been desperate. Fiona Samaras, their in-house biographer, who was working on the commemorative biography of the King of Agon, had been struck down with acute appendicitis. Jo was only a copywriter, but that didn't matter—she was the only other person who spoke Greek in the specialist publishing house she worked for. She wasn't completely fluent, but she knew enough to translate the research papers into English and make it readable.

If the biography wasn't complete by a week on Wednesday there wouldn't be time for it to be copy-edited and proofread and sent to the printers, who were waiting to print five thousand English language copies and courier them to the Agon palace in time for the gala.

The gala, exactly three weeks away, was to be a huge affair, celebrating fifty years of King Astraeus's reign. If they messed up the commemorative biography they would lose all the custom they'd gained from Agon's palace museum over the decades. Their reputation as a publisher of biographies and historical tomes would take a battering. Possibly a fatal one.

Jo loved her job—loved the work, loved the people. It might not be the exact career she'd dreamed of, but the support she'd received throughout the years had made up for it.

Giles had been so desperate for her to take on the job that he'd promised her a bonus and an extra fortnight's paid leave. How could she have said no? When everything was factored in, she hadn't been able to.

She'd been through the emotional mill enough to know she would survive this separation. It would rip her apart but she would get through it—and Toby would too. The past five years had taught her to be a survivor. And the money would be welcome. She would finally have enough to take Toby to Greece and begin the task of tracking down his father.

She wondered if she would have any time to begin her search whilst she was on Agon. Although Agon wasn't technically a Greek island, its closest neighbour was Crete and its people spoke Greek—which was why Jo had been the person her boss had turned to.

'We'll speak every day on the computer while I'm gone,' she said now, reiterating what she'd already told him a dozen times that day.

'And you'll get me a present?'

'I'll get you an *enormous* present,' she promised with a smile.

'The biggest present in the world?'

She tickled his sides. 'The biggest present I can stick in my suitcase.'

Toby giggled and tickled her neck. 'Can I see where you're going?'

'Sure.' She manoeuvred him around so that he faced her desk, pulled her laptop closer to them and clicked a button to bring it out of hibernation.

Having had only a day to prepare for the trip, she'd spent hours making arrangements for herself and Toby while trying to familiarise herself with the biography she needed to finish. She hadn't yet had the time to do any research on the island she was travelling to.

Keeping an arm around her son's waist to secure him on her lap, she typed *'Agon Royal Palace'* into the search bar and selected images.

Toby gasped when he saw what appeared and pressed a finger to the screen. 'You're going *there*?'

Jo was just as taken with the images, which showed an enormous sprawling palace that evoked romantic thoughts of hot Arabian nights.

'Yes, I am.'

'Will you have your own room?'

'I'll get an apartment in the palace.'

Until that moment she hadn't had time to consider the fact that she would be staying in a royal palace for ten nights. She moved her cursor down the screen slowly, looking for a better picture.

'Will you meet the King?'

She smiled at the eagerness in Toby's voice. She wondered how he would react if she were to tell him that she and Toby were distantly—*very* distantly—related to the British royal family. He'd probably spring to the ceiling with excitement.

'I'll be working for the King's grandson, who's a prince, but I might meet the King too. Shall I find a picture of him?'

She typed in *'King of Agon'* and hit the search button.

She supposed she should send Toby back to bed, but she really didn't want to—not when he was so warm and snuggly on her lap, and especially not when she knew he wouldn't be warm and snuggly on her lap again for another ten days.

The search revealed hundreds, if not thousands of pictures of the King. Scrolling through them, she thought how distinguished he looked. There were pictures of him with his late wife, Queen Rhea, who had died five years ago, others with his eldest grandson and heir, Helios, and one of King Astraeus standing with all three of his grandsons—one of whom must be Theseus, the Prince she would be directly reporting to…

She stared hard at the picture of the King and his grandsons and felt the hairs on her arms lifting. With a hand that suddenly seemed to be filled with lead, she enlarged the photo to fill the screen.

It couldn't be.

Making sure not to squash her son, she leaned forward and adjusted the screen so she could peer at it more closely. The picture was too grainy for her to see with any certainty.

It couldn't be…

'Are those men kings too?' Toby asked.

She couldn't speak, could only manage a quick shake of her head before she clicked on to another picture of the King with his grandsons.

This photo was of a much higher quality and had been taken from less distance.

Her head buzzed and burned, every pulse in her body hammering.

Working frantically, she clicked through dozens of pictures until she found one that showed him alone. She enlarged it.

It was him.

For an age she did nothing but hold her son so tightly she could feel the thrum of his little heart vibrating through his back.

How was it possible?

Two hours later she was still there on her laptop, searching through everything the internet had to offer about Prince Theseus Kalliakis. Somehow she'd managed to pull herself out of the cold stupor she'd slipped into at seeing Theo's face on the screen for long enough to tuck Toby back into bed and kiss him goodnight.

All that ran through her head now was crystal clarity.

No wonder her years of searching for Theo had been fruitless. She'd assumed that living in the age of social media would have made it an easy task, but she had been foiled at every turn. It hadn't stopped her looking. She'd never given up hope of finding him.

But she might have searched for a thousand years and would still never have found him. Because the man she'd been seeking didn't exist.

It had all been a big lie.

Toby's father wasn't Theo Patakis, an engineer from Athens. He was Theseus Kalliakis. A prince.

Prince Theseus Kalliakis stepped out of his office and into his private apartment just as his phone vibrated in his pocket. He dug it out and put it to his ear.

'She's on her way,' said Dimitris, his private secretary, without any preamble.

Theseus killed the call, strode into his bedroom and put the phone on his bureau.

He'd spent most of the day sleeping off the after-effects of the Royal Ball his older brother, Helios had hosted the night before, and catching up on reports relating to the various businesses he and his two brothers invested in under the Kalliakis Investment Company name. Now it was time to change out of his jeans and T-shirt.

He would greet Miss Brookes, then spend some time with his grandfather while she settled in. His grandfather's nurse had messaged him to say the King was having a good spell and Theseus was loath to miss spending private time with him when he was lucid.

Nikos, his right-hand man, had laid out a freshly pressed

suit for him. Theseus had heard tales of royalty from other nations actually being dressed by their personal staff, something that had always struck him as slightly ludicrous. He was a man. He dressed himself. His lips curved in amusement as he imagined Nikos's reaction should he request that the man do his shirt buttons up for him. All Nikos's respect would be gone in an instant. He would think Theseus had lost his testosterone.

Once dressed, he rubbed a little wax between his hands and worked it quickly into his hair, then added a splash of cologne. He was done.

Exiting his apartment, he headed down a flight of stairs and walked briskly along a long, narrow corridor lit up by tiny ceiling lights. After walking through three more corridors he cut through the palace kitchens, then through four more corridors, until he arrived at the stateroom where he would meet Fiona Samaras's replacement.

Murmured voices sounded from behind the open door. The replacement had clearly arrived—something that relieved him greatly.

His grandfather's illness had forced the brothers to bring the Jubilee Gala forward by three months. That had meant that the deadline for completing a biography of his grandfather—which Theseus had tasked himself with producing—had been brought forward too.

His relationship with his grandfather had never been easy. Theseus freely admitted he'd been a nightmare to raise. He'd thoroughly enjoyed the outdoor pursuits which had come with being a young Agon prince, but had openly despised the rest of it—the boundaries, the stuffy protocol and all the other constraints that came with his title.

His demand for a sabbatical and the consequences of his absence had caused a further rift between him and his grandfather that had never fully healed. He hoped the biography would go some way to mending that rift before his grandfather's frail body succumbed to the cancer eating at it.

Five years of exemplary behaviour did not make up for almost three decades of errant behaviour. This was his last chance to prove to his grandfather that the Kalliakis name *did* mean something to him.

But first the damn thing needed to be completed. The deadline was tight enough without Fiona's appendicitis derailing the project further.

Her replacement had better be up for the task. Giles had sworn she was perfect for it… Theseus had no choice but to trust his judgement.

Dimitris stood with his back to the door, talking to the woman Theseus assumed to be Despinis Brookes.

'You got back from the airport quickly,' he said as he stepped into the stateroom.

Dimitris turned around and straightened. 'Traffic was light, Your Highness.'

The woman behind him stepped forward. He moved towards her, his hand outstretched. 'It is a pleasure to meet you, Miss Brookes,' he said in English. 'Thank you for coming at such short notice.'

He would keep his doubts to himself. She would be under enough pressure to deliver without him adding to it. His job, from this point onwards, was as support vehicle. He would treat her as if she were one of the young men and women whose start-up businesses he and his brothers invested in.

His role in their company was officially finance director. Unofficially he saw himself as chief cheerleader—good cop to his younger brother Talos's bad cop—there to give encouragement and help those people realise their dreams in a way he could never realise his own. But woe betide them if they should lie to him or cheat him. The few who'd been foolish enough to do that had been taught a lesson they would never forget.

He wasn't a Kalliakis for nothing.

He waited for Miss Brookes to take his hand. Possibly she would curtsey. Many non-islanders did, although protocol did not insist on it unless it was an official function.

She didn't take his offered hand. Just stared at him with an expression he didn't quite understand but which made the hairs on his nape shoot up.

'Despinis?'

Possibly she was overwhelmed at meeting a prince? It happened…

In the hanging silence he looked at her properly, seeing things that he'd failed to notice in his hurry to be introduced and get down to business. The colour of her hair was familiar, a deep russet-red, like the colour of the autumn leaves he'd used to crunch through when he'd been at boarding school in England. It fell like an undulating wave over her shoulders and down her back, framing a pretty face with an English rose complexion, high cheekbones and generous bee-stung lips. Blue-grey eyes pierced him with a look of intense concentration…

He *knew* those eyes. He *knew* that hair. It wasn't a common colour, more like something from the artistic imagination of the old masters of the Renaissance than anything real. But it was those eyes that really cut him short. They too were an unusual shade—impossible to define, but evocative of early-morning skies before the sun had fully risen.

And as all these thoughts rushed through his mind she finally advanced her hand into his and spoke two words. The final two little syllables were delivered with a compacted tightness that sliced through him upon impact.

'Hello, *Theo*.'

He didn't recognise her.

Jo didn't know what she'd expected. A hundred scenarios had played out in her mind over the past twenty hours.

Not one of those scenarios had involved him not remembering her.

It was like rubbing salt in an open, festering wound.

Something flickered in his dark eyes, and then she caught the flare of recognition.

'*Jo?*'

As he spoke her name, the question strongly inflected in a rich, accented voice that sounded just as she imagined a creamy chocolate mousse would sound if it could talk, his long fingers wrapped around hers.

She nodded and bit into her bottom lip, which had gone decidedly wobbly. Her whole body suddenly felt very wobbly, as if her bones had turned into overcooked noodles.

His hand felt so *warm*.

It shouldn't feel warm. It should feel as cold as his lying heart.

And she shouldn't feel an overwhelming urge to burst into tears.

She wouldn't give him the satisfaction.

Straightening her spine, Jo tugged her hand out of his warm hold and resisted the impulse to wipe it on her skirt, to rid herself of a touch she had once yearned for.

'It's been a long time,' she said, deliberately keeping her tone cool, trying to turn her lips upwards into the semblance of a smile.

But how could you smile when your one and only lover, the man you'd spent five years searching for, the father of your child, didn't remember your face?

How could you force a smile when you'd spent five years searching for a lie?

Dimitris, the man who'd collected her from the airport and introduced himself as His Highness's private secretary, was watching their interaction with interest.

'Do you two know each other?'

'Despinis Brookes is an old acquaintance of mine,' said

Theo—or Theseus—or whatever his name was. 'We met when I was on my sabbatical.'

Oh, was *that* what he'd been doing on Illya? He'd been on a *sabbatical*?

And she was an *acquaintance*?

She supposed it was better than being described as one of his one-night stands.

And at least he hadn't had the temerity to call her an old friend.

'I saw a picture of you on the internet last night when I was researching your island,' she said, injecting brightness into her tone, giving no hint that she'd even *thought* of him during the intervening years. 'I thought it looked like you.'

She might not have much pride left after spending the last four years as a single mother, but she still had enough to be wounded and not to want to show it, especially as they had an audience. One thing motherhood had taught her was resilience. In fact it had taught her a lot of things, all of which had made her infinitely stronger than she'd been before.

Theseus appraised her openly, his dark brown eyes sweeping over her body. 'You look different to how I remember you.'

She knew she was physically memorable—it had been the bane of her childhood. Red hair and a weight problem had made her an easy target for bullies. Having Toby had been the kick she'd needed to shift the weight and keep it off. She would never be a stick-thin model but she'd grown to accept her curves.

She might be a few stone lighter, and her hair a few inches longer, but there was nothing else different about her.

'Your hair's shorter than I remember,' she said in return.

Five years ago Theseus's hair—so dark it appeared black—had been long, skimming his shoulders. Now it was short at the back, with the front sweeping across his forehead. On Illya she'd only ever seen him in shorts and the occasional T-shirt. Half the time he hadn't bothered with footwear. Now he wore a blue suit that looked as if it had cost more than her annual food bill, and shoes that shone so brightly he could probably see his reflection in them.

'You're looking good, though,' she added, nodding her head to add extra sincerity to her words.

What a shame that it was the truth.

Theo—or Theseus—or His Highness—wasn't the most handsome man she'd ever met, but there was something about him that captured the eye and kept you looking. A magnetism. He had a nose too bumpy to be considered ideal, deep-set dark brown eyes, a wide mouth that smiled easily and a strong jawline. This combined with his olive colouring, his height—which had to be a good foot over her own five foot four inches—and the wiry athleticism of his physique, gave the immediate impression of an un-reconstructed 'man's man'.

Her awareness of him had been instant, from the second he'd stepped into Marin's Bar on Illya with a crowd of Scandinavian travellers hanging onto his every word. She'd taken one look at him and her heart had flipped over.

It had been a mad infatuation. Totally crazy. Irrational. All the things she'd reached the age of twenty-one without having once experienced had hit her with the force of a tsunami.

But now she was five years older, five years wiser, and she had a child to protect. Any infatuation had long gone.

Or so she'd thought.

But when he'd strode through the door of the stateroom the effect had been the same; as if the past five years had been erased.

'Different to all those years ago,' Theseus agreed, look-ing at his watch. 'I appreciate you've had a long day, but time is against us to get the biography complete. Let's take a walk to your apartment so you can freshen up and settle in. We can talk en route.'

He set off with Dimitris at his side.

Staring at his retreating back, it took Jo a few beats before she pulled herself together and scrambled after them.

Dull thuds pounded in her brain, bruising it, as the magnitude of her situation hit her.

For all these years she'd sworn to herself that she would find Toby's father and tell Theo about their son. She'd had no expectations of what would happen afterwards, but had known that at the very least she owed it to Toby to find him. She'd also thought she owed it to Theo to tell him he had a child.

But Theo didn't exist.

Whoever this man was, he was not the Theo Patakis she had once fallen in love with.

Theseus wasn't the father of her son; he was a stranger dressed in his skin.

CHAPTER TWO

'Visitors to the palace often get lost, so I've arranged for a map to be left in your apartment,' Theseus said as they climbed a narrow set of stairs.

'A map? Seriously?' She would remain civil if it killed her. Which it probably would.

So many emotions were running through her she didn't know where one began and another ended.

He nodded, still steaming ahead. Her legs were working at a quick march to keep up with him as he turned into a dark corridor lit by tiny round ceiling lights.

'The palace has five hundred and seventy-three rooms.'

'Then I guess a map could come in handy,' she conceded, for want of anything else to say.

'There will not be time for you to explore the palace as you might like,' he said. 'However, we will do everything in our power to make your stay here as comfortable as it can be.'

'That's very kind of you,' she said, trying not to choke on her words.

'Are you up to speed with the project?'

'I read a good chunk of it on the plane,' she confirmed tightly.

As the deadline for the biography's completion was so tight, Fiona had been emailing each chapter as she'd finished it so they could be immediately edited. The editor working on it had spent the past six weeks or so with a distinctly frazzled look about her.

'Fiona has completed the bulk of the biography, but there is still another twenty-five years of my grandfather's life to be written about. I appreciate this must sound daunting, but you will find when you read through the research papers that there is much less complexity there than in his early years. Are you confident you can do this within the time constraints?'

'I wouldn't have accepted the job if I wasn't.' Fiona's editor, who Jo was now working with, had assured her that the last three decades of King Astraeus's life had been comparatively quiet after his early years.

But Jo had accepted the job before discovering who she would be working for and exactly who he was.

As she clung to the gold banister that lined the wall above a wide, cantilevered staircase that plunged them into another warren of passageways and corridors Jo remembered a trip to Buckingham Palace a few years back, and recalled how bright and airy it had seemed. The Agon Royal Palace matched Buckingham Palace for size, but it had a much darker, far greater gothic quality to it. It was a palace of secrets and intrigue.

Or was that just her rioting emotions making her read more into things? Her body had never felt so tight with nerves, while her brain had become a fog of hurt, anger, bewilderment and confusion.

'I don't remember you speaking Greek when we were on Illya,' he said, casting her a curious, almost suspicious glance that made her heart shudder.

'Everyone spoke English there,' she replied in faultless Greek, staring pointedly ahead and praying the dim light bouncing off the dark hardwood flooring would hide the burn suddenly ravaging her skin.

'That is true.' He came to a halt by a door at the beginning of another wide corridor. He turned the handle and pushed it open. 'This is your apartment for the duration of your stay. I'm going to visit my grandfather while you settle in—a maid will be with you shortly to unpack. Dimitris will come for you in an hour, and then we can sit down and discuss the project properly.'

And just like that he walked back down the corridor, leaving Jo staring at his retreating figure with a mixture of fury and incredibly lancing pain raging through her.

Was that *it*?

Was that all she was worth?

A woman he's once been intimate with suddenly reappears in his life and he doesn't even ask how she's been? Not the slightest hint of curiosity?

The only real reference to their past had been a comment about her speaking his language.

He'd sought *her* out back then. It had been *her* comfort he'd needed that night. And now she wasn't worth even a simple, *How are you?* or *How have you been?*

But then, she thought bitterly, it had all been a lie.

This man *wasn't* Theo.

A soft cough behind her reminded her that Dimitris was still there. He handed her a set of keys, wished her a pleasant stay and left her alone to explore her apartment.

Theseus blew air out of his mouth, nodding an automatic greeting to a passing servant.

Joanne Brookes.

Or, as he'd known her five years ago, Jo.

Now, *this* was a complication he hadn't anticipated. A most unwelcome complication.

Hers was a face from his past he'd never expected to see again, and certainly not in the palace, where a twist of fate had decreed she would spend ten days working closely with him.

She'd been there for him during the second worst night of his life, when he'd been forced to wait until the morning before he could leave the island of Illya and be taken to his seriously ill grandmother.

Jo had taken care of him. In more ways than one.

He remembered his surprise when he'd learned her age—twenty-one and fresh out of university. She'd looked much younger. She'd seemed younger than her years too.

He supposed that would now make her twenty-six. Strangely, she now seemed *older* than her years—not in her appearance, but in the way she held herself.

He experienced an awful sinking feeling as he remembered taking her number and making promises to call.

That sinking feeling deepened as he recalled his certainty after they'd had sex that she'd been a virgin.

She couldn't have been. She would have told you. Who would give her virginity to a man who was effectively a stranger?

Irrelevant, he told himself sharply.

Illya and his entire sabbatical had been a different life, and it was one he could never return to.

He was Prince Theseus Kalliakis, second in line to the Agon throne. *This* was his life. The fact that the new biographer was a face from the best time of his life meant nothing.

Theo Patakis was dead and all his memories had gone with him.

'*This* is where I'll be working?' Jo asked, hoping against hope that she was wrong.

She'd spent the past hour giving herself a good talking-to, reminding herself that anger didn't achieve anything. Whatever the next ten days had in store, holding on to her fury would do nothing but give her an ulcer. But then Dimitris had collected her from the small but well-appointed apartment she'd been given and taken her to Theseus's private offices, just across the corridor, and the fury had surged anew.

Her office was inside his private apartment and connected to his own office without so much as a doorway to separate them.

'This is the office Fiona used.' Theseus waved a hand at the sprawling fitted desks set against two walls to make an L shape. 'Nobody has touched it since she was admitted into hospital.'

'There's a spare room in my apartment that will make a perfectly functional office.'

'Fiona used that room when she first came here, but it proved problematic. The research papers I collated and my own notes only give the facts about my grandfather's life. I want this biography to show the man behind the throne. As I know you're aware, this project is going to be a surprise for my grandfather so any questions need to be directed to me. With the time constraints we're working under it is better for me to be on hand for whatever you need.'

'Whatever you feel is for the best.'

A black eyebrow rose at her tone but he nodded. 'Are you happy with your apartment?'

'It's perfectly adequate.'

Apart from being in the same wing as his.

How was she going to be able to concentrate on anything whilst being in such close proximity to him? Her stomach was a tangle of knots, her heart was all twisted and aching…and her head burned as her son's gorgeous little face swam before her eyes.

Toby deserved better than to have been conceived from a lie.

She knew nothing of this man other than the fact that he was a prince in a nation that revered its monarchy.

He was descended from warriors. He and his brothers had forged a reputation for being savvy businessmen. They'd also forged a reputation as ruthless. It didn't pay to cross any of them.

Theseus was powerful.

Until she got to know this man she couldn't even consider telling him about Toby. Not until she knew in her heart that he posed no threat to either of them.

'Only "adequate"?' he asked. 'If there is anything you feel is lacking, or anything you want, you need only say. I want your head free of trivia so you can concentrate on getting the biography completed on time.'

'I'll be sure to remember that.'

'Make sure you do. I have lived and breathed this project for many months. I will not have it derailed at the last hurdle.'

The threat in his voice was implicit.

Now she believed what Giles had told her when he'd begged her to take the job—if she failed Hamlin & Associates would lose their best client and likely their reputation in the process.

'I have ten days to complete it,' she replied tightly. 'I will make the deadline.'

'So long as we have an understanding, I suggest we don't waste another minute.'

Where was the charmer she remembered from Illya? The man who had made every woman's IQ plummet by just being in his presence?

She'd spent five years thinking about this man, four years living with a miniature version of him, and his presence in her life had been so great she'd been incapable of meeting anyone else. Once Toby had been born the secret dream she'd held of Theo—*Theseus*—calling her out of the blue with apologies that he'd lost his phone had died. As had the fantasy that she would tell him of their son and he would want to be involved in their lives.

Motherhood had brought out a pragmatism she hadn't known existed inside her. Until precisely one day ago she hadn't given up on her dream of finding him, but that wish had been purely for Toby's sake. All she'd wanted for herself was to find the courage to move on. She'd accepted she'd been nothing but a one-night stand for him and had found peace with that idea. Or so she'd thought.

Because somehow that was the worst part of it. Her body still reacted to him in exactly the way it had on Illya, with a sick, almost helpless longing. If he looked closely enough he'd be able to see her heart beating beneath the smart black top she wore.

His indifference towards her cut like a scalpel slicing through flesh.

He couldn't give a damn about her.

A swell of nausea rose in her and she knew she had to say something.

She couldn't spend the next ten days with such an enormous elephant in the room, even if she was the only one who could see it.

Heart hammering, she plunged in. 'Before I start work there's something we need to talk about.'

He contemplated her with narrowed eyes that showed nothing but indifference.

'I'm sorry,' she continued, swallowing back the fear, 'but if you want me focused I need to know why you let me and everyone else on Illya believe you were an engineer from Athens, travelling the world on the fruits of an inheritance, when you were really a prince from Agon.'

'It hardly matters—it was five years ago,' he said sardonically.

'You lied to me and every person you met on Illya.'

You lied to him too, her conscience reminded her, and she felt her cheeks flame as she recalled how her one lie had been the most grievous of all, a remembrance that knocked back a little of her fury and allowed her to gain a touch of perspective.

Her lie had been the catalyst for everything.

He contemplated her a little longer before leaning back against the wall and folding his arms across his chest.

'Let me tell you about life here on Agon,' he said thoughtfully. 'Outsiders struggle to understand but Agonites revere my family and have done so for over eight hundred years, ever since my ancestor Ares Patakis led a successful rebellion against the Venetian invaders.'

'Patakis?' she repeated. 'Is that where you got your assumed surname from?'

He nodded. 'My family have held the throne since then by overwhelming popular consent. With my family at the helm we've repelled any other nation foolish enough to think it can invade us. To prevent any despotic behaviour down the years my ancestors introduced a senate, for the people to have a voice, but still they look to us—their royal family—for leadership.'

Theseus's mind filtered to his father; the man who would have been king if a tragic car crash hadn't killed him prematurely along with his wife, Theseus's mother. Lelantos Kalliakis had been exactly the kind of man his ancestors had feared taking the throne and having absolute power. Yet, regardless of how debauched and narcissistic the man had been, the Agonites had mourned him as if a member of their own family had been killed. His sons, however, had only truly mourned their mother.

'We live in a goldfish bowl. The people here look up to my family. They revere us. Children on this island learn to read with picture books depicting tales of my ancestors. I wanted to meet *real* people and explore the world as a normal person would. I was curious as to how people would react to *me*—the man, not the Prince. So, yes, I lied to you about my true identity, just as I lied to everyone else. And if I had my time again I would tell the same lies, because they gave me a freedom I hadn't experienced before and will never experience again.'

The majority of this speech was one he had spouted numerous times, first to his grandfather, when he'd announced his intention to see the world, and then to his brothers, who'd seen his actions as a snub to the family name. After a lifetime of bad behaviour, when he'd effectively turned his back on protocol, taking off and renouncing the family name had been his most heinous crime of all. Even now he was still trying to make amends.

'If I hurt your feelings I apologise,' he added when she gave no response.

He didn't owe Jo anything, but neither did he want working with her to be a trial. There wasn't time to bring in anyone else to complete the biography and they'd already lost three precious days.

If getting her to soften towards him meant he had to eat a little humble pie, then so be it. He would accept it as penance for the greater good.

And, if he was being honest with himself, apologising went a little way towards easing the guilt that had been nibbling at his guts.

The only change in her demeanour was a deep breath and the clenching of her jaw. When she did speak it was through gritted teeth. 'I don't even know what to call you. Are you Theo or Theseus? Do I address you as Your Highness or Your Grace? Am I expected to curtsey to you?'

In the hazy realms of his memory lay the whisper of her shy smile and the memory of how her cheeks would turn as red as her hair whenever he spoke to her.

It was on the tip of his tongue to tell her to call him Theo. Being Theo had been the best time of his life…

No. He would not let those memories spring free. He'd locked them away for a reason and they could damn well stay there.

'You can call me Theseus. And no curtseying.'

Having people bow and scrape to him turned his stomach. All his life people had treated him with a reverence he'd done nothing to earn other than be born.

She nodded, biting her bottom lip. And what a gorgeous lip it was, he thought. How eminently kissable. He'd kissed that delectable mouth once…

'I ask you to put your bad feelings towards me to one side so we can work together effectively. Can you do that?'

After a long pause she inclined her head and her long red hair fell forward. She brushed it back and tucked it behind her ears.

'Do you remember the night those American travellers came into Marin's Bar?' she asked, in a voice that was definitely milder than the tone she'd used so far. 'You were with the Scandinavians on the big round table…'

He raised a shoulder in a shrug, unsure of what day she was speaking of. He'd hit it off with a group of Scandinavian travellers on the ferry from Split to Illya and had spent the majority of his fortnight on the unspoilt island in their company. Marin's Bar, which was two steps from the beach, had been the only place to go, but with its excellent beer, good food and a juke box that had pumped out classic tracks, it had engendered an easy, relaxed atmosphere.

Jo and her friends, whose names he didn't think he'd ever known, had always been on the periphery—there but in the background, rather like wallpaper.

'They were touching us up,' she reminded him.

'Ah.'

Now he remembered. The Americans—college graduates taking time out before joining the corporate world—had drunk far too much of the local liquor and had started harassing Jo and her friends. He remembered there had been something nasty about it, well beyond the usual banter one might expect in such an environment. He'd taken exception to it and had personally thrown the men out, then he had insisted Jo and her friends join him and his friends at their table.

And now her face did soften. Not completely—her cheeks were still clenched—but enough that her lips regained their plumpness. They almost curled into a smile.

'You stepped in to help us,' she said. 'Whether you were there as a lie or not, in that one aspect it doesn't matter. You did a good thing. I'll try to hold on to that whenever I feel like stabbing you. How does that sound?'

A bubble of laughter was propelled up his throat, startling him. He quickly recovered.

'I think that sounds like an excellent start.'

She rocked her head forward. 'Good.'

'But just in case you ever do feel like stabbing me I'll be sure to hide all the sharp objects.'

The plump lips finally formed into a smile and something dark flickered in her eyes, but was gone before he could analyse it.

'It's a deal. Now, if you'll excuse me, I believe this is the perfect cue for me to go back to my apartment and carry on reading Fiona's work.'

'Will you be ready to start writing in the morning?'

'That's very unlikely—I'm only two-thirds through and I still need to familiarise myself with the research papers. What I *can* promise is that I will have this biography completed by the deadline even if I have to kill myself doing it.'

She stepped out of the door, giving him a full view of her round bottom, perfectly displayed in the smart navy blue skirt she wore. What kind of underwear lay beneath…?

He blinked away the inappropriate thought.

Her underwear was none of his business.

But there was no denying the gauche young girl he'd known before had gone; in her place was a confident and, yes, a sexy woman.

It had been a long time since he'd considered a woman sexy or pondered over her underwear.

There was nothing wrong with admitting she had an allure about her. Thoughts and actions were different things. The days when he would already have been plotting her seduction were long gone. The Theseus who had put pleasure above duty had been banished.

The next woman he shared a bed with would be his wife.

CHAPTER THREE

Jo GAZED AT the picture Toby proudly held up. Apparently it was a drawing of the two of them. It resembled a pair of colourful ants, one of which had been given long purple hair as his red felt-tip pen had run out.

'That's amazing,' she said, trying not to laugh, and inordinately proud of his attempt at a family portrait.

'Uncle Jon says he'll scab it for you.'

She stifled another giggle at his word for scan. At some point she knew she would have to tell him when he mangled words and mixed them up—like using alligator for escalator and Camilla for vanilla—but for the moment it was too cute. She'd start correcting him properly when he started school in five months' time.

She was dreading it—her baby growing up. They'd only been apart for one night so far, and this was already the second time they'd spoken via video-link. Thank God for technology.

She wondered how parents had handled time away from their children before video conferencing had been invented. A voice on the end of a phone was no substitute to seeing their faces as they spoke. Not that she would count her own parents in that equation.

She remembered going on a week-long school trip when she'd been eleven and calling home after three days only to have her mother say, 'Is there an emergency?'

'No, I—'

'Then I don't have the time to talk. It's feeding time.'

And that had been the end of *that* conversation. In the Brookes household the animals came first, Jonathan came second, with Jo and her father vying for last place.

'Sorry, sweet pea, but I have to go to work now,' Jo said, infusing her words with all the love her own mother had denied her.

He pulled a face. 'Already?'

'We'll talk again later.' Theseus would be expecting her at any minute.

'After lunch?'

'Tell Aunty Cathy we'll speak before you go to bed,' she promised, knowing full well that Cathy would be listening to their conversation and would make sure Toby was ready for her.

'Have you brought me a present yet, Mummy?' Toby asked, clearly doing everything he could to keep her talking for a little longer.

'I haven't been anywhere to get you one yet, you little monkey. Now, blow me a kiss and shoo before you're late for preschool.'

Toby did better than blow her a kiss. He put his face to the screen, puckered his lips and kissed it.

With her heart feeling as if it were about to expand out of her body, she pressed her fingers to her lips and then extended them to touch her screen. 'Love you.'

Before he could respond the connection was lost. No doubt he'd leaned on something he shouldn't have pressed when he'd leaned forward to kiss her.

Laughing whilst simultaneously wiping away a tear, Jo turned off her laptop.

She took three deep breaths to compose herself, then left her apartment, took four paces to the door opposite and entered her office, yawning widely.

'Late night?'

Theseus's voice startled her.

He stood in the archway that separated their offices, dressed in a navy suit and white shirt, without a tie.

She would never have imagined Theo in a suit, much less that he would look so unutterably gorgeous in it. On Illya he had lived in shorts, his golden chest with those defined muscles and that fine hair dusting over his pecs unashamedly on display.

But this man wasn't Theo, she reminded herself sharply. He was *nothing* like him. *This* man's lips seemed not to know how to smile. *This* man carried none of the warmth Theo had had in spades.

The only thing the two had in common was that same vivid masculinity. That vital presence. Her eyes would have been drawn to him even if she'd never known him as Theo.

'I stayed up to finish reading what Fiona had written,' she answered.

'Was that necessary?'

'I needed to find the rhythm of her work,' she explained evenly. 'I'll need to replicate it if I'm to make the transition seamless for the reader.'

'And are you ready to start writing now?'

'Not yet. I need to read through the research papers for the period of your grandfather's life I'm covering.'

He inclined his head and straightened. 'I shall leave you to it. I'll be back later if you find you have any questions for me.'

She forced a smile in acknowledgement, but the second she was alone she dropped her head onto the desk and closed her eyes.

Barely five minutes in his company and now not a single part of her felt right, as if being with him had caused her entire body to turn itself inside out.

She would have to find a way to manage it.

With grim determination she forced her attention to the piles of research papers before her.

The work Fiona had done on the biography had made for compelling reading.

King Astraeus had led a fascinating life, one filled with glory and honour. While many men of his nation had fought for the allies in the war—his brother among them—the then Prince Astraeus had led the defence of his own island. When a battalion of naval ships had approached the island with the intention to occupy it, Astraeus had led the counterattack. The fleet had been obliterated before it had reached the shore.

No other enemy ship had attempted to land on Agon since.

That would have been impressive on its own, but only the day before Astraeus had been given the news that his only brother had been killed in action.

This was Jo's son's heritage—a family that led from the front and who were all prepared to put their lives on the line to defend their home and their people.

A powerful family. And in it fitted Theseus—the father of her son.

The chapter Fiona had finished just before being taken ill detailed the death of Astraeus's only son and daughter-in-law in a tragic car crash twenty-six years ago. Theseus's parents. He'd been nine years old. So very young.

Her heart cracked a little to imagine what he must have gone through.

But that had been a long time ago, she reminded herself. Theseus the child had no bearing on Theseus the adult. She could not allow sympathy to lower her guard. Until she knew the real Theseus she couldn't afford to lower it for one second.

Theseus put his phone down. He could hear the soft rustle of papers being turned in the adjoining office.

When Fiona had worked on the biography he'd hardly

been aware of her. Other than the times when she would ask him questions, she might not have existed. Fiona using that office hadn't interrupted the flow of his own work.

As the financial figurehead of the Kalliakis Investment Company, and with his newer role of overseeing the palace accounts, which his grandfather had finally agreed to a year ago, he had plenty to keep his brain occupied.

In his childhood he'd dreamed of being an astronaut, of flying through the universe exploring new planets and solar systems. Astronauts had to be good with numbers, and he'd practised his arithmetic with a zeal that had astounded his tutor.

He could still remember one of the rare occasions when his father had come into Theseus's bedroom, mere months before he'd died. He'd looked at the star charts and pictures of rockets that had filled the walls and told him to rid his mind of such nonsense. A Kalliakis prince could *never* be an astronaut.

Even now Theseus would stare up at the night sky and be filled with longing.

He could have done it. He had the talent and the enthusiasm. He was fit, healthy and active.

But it could never be.

Now he used his talents, if not his enthusiasm, for financial reports. At least when he was going through the accounts he didn't have to put on a face and make small talk; didn't have to remember he was an ambassador for his family and his island.

So he kept himself busy. Too much time on his hands left his mind free to wander, to dream, to imagine *what if...?*

Today, though, the woman next door with hair like autumn leaves kept intruding. And she hadn't made so much as a peep of noise.

He couldn't get over how damned sexy she'd become. Even now, wearing nothing but charcoal three-quarter-length leggings, and a plain long-sleeved tunic-style black top that made her hair appear even more vibrant, she exuded a beguiling allure.

It had been a long time since he'd experienced such a primitive reaction to a woman.

Five years, to be exact.

His return to Agon from his sabbatical had been a turning point for him. Battling grief for his grandmother and ugly home truths from his grandfather, he'd known it was time to stop fighting. He would never be free. Sitting on the summit of Aconcagua in Argentina, the highest point in the Southern Hemisphere, was the closest he would ever get to the stars.

It had been time to accept his destiny.

He had decided he would curb his pleasure-seeking and throw himself into palace life. His grandfather had already been an old man. Helios had taken on many of his duties. It had been time for Theseus to take his share of them and relieve the burden.

He had been determined to prove to his grandfather that the Kalliakis name *did* mean something to him and had spent the years since his sabbatical doing exactly that—throwing himself into palace life and royal duties. In that time his appetite for sex had diminished to nothing, which suited him perfectly. Women who would usually turn his head had elicited minimal reaction. Neither his heart not his libido had been in it.

Now, for the first time in years, he felt the thrill of the chase coiling in his veins and cursed that such feelings should be unleashed.

Jo might be walking temptation, but there was no place in his life for desire. His next relationship would be with the woman he made his wife, even if he did intend on putting off the moment for as long as he could.

He stepped away from his desk and crossed the threshold into the adjoining office.

'How are you getting on?'

She didn't respond.

He was about to repeat his question but then saw she had earphones in.

She must have sensed his presence, for she turned her head and pulled them out.

'I will be leaving the palace shortly. Is there anything you need to talk to me about?'

'Not yet. I'm still going through the research papers and making notes on anything I feel could be relevant. As so many aspects are connected I think it will be best if we sit down and discuss it all when I'm done.'

'Will that not eat into your writing time?'

'It will make it easier—it means it will be solid in my head and I'll be in a position to work through it all without having to stop and interrupt you every five minutes. I'll probably still have further questions, but they will be far fewer this way.'

'I'm hosting a function for a delegation of French businessmen today, and I have a dinner at the US Embassy to attend this evening, but I can clear most of my diary for the next few days so I'll be available when you're ready.'

'That would be good, thank you,' she answered with a brief smile, her brilliant blue-grey eyes meeting his. She looked away, casting her gaze to her desk, then back up to him. 'Can I ask you something?'

'Of course.' So long as it wasn't about Illya. He refused to give headspace to memories from that time.

'Your grandfather's ill, isn't he?'

'How do you know that?' he asked, taken aback.

No one outside of the family circle and some select palace staff were supposed to know of his grandfather's cancer—which naturally meant the whole palace knew. However,

Theseus knew none of them would discuss it with anyone on the outside. Working in the Agon Royal Palace was considered an honour. To share confidential matters would be deemed treasonous.

'The publishing deadline was brought forward by three months and it was a tight enough deadline to begin with.' She shrugged, as if ashamed of her conclusion.

But it *was* the right conclusion.

It had occurred to Theseus, when the Jubilee Gala plans were first being discussed, that his grandfather had never seen his legacy in print. Usually Agon biographies were written after the reigning monarch had abdicated, then another would be written upon their death. As his grandfather had never abdicated that first book had never been written. He'd spent fifty years on the throne—the longest reign in three hundred years.

Suddenly he'd stumbled upon a tangible way to prove to his grandfather that he was proud of his heritage, proud to be a Kalliakis and, more than any of that, proud to call Astraeus his grandfather.

The more he'd immersed himself in his grandfather's life, the greater his pride had become. Astraeus Kalliakis was a true king. A man of honour. A man Theseus knew he should have emulated, not turned his back on for all those years.

This biography would be his personal tribute to him.

But then fate had stepped in. No sooner had he finished his research, and Fiona had flown over to the island to start writing it, than his grandfather had been given his diagnosis and everything had been brought forward by three months.

The Gala, the biography…everything was being rushed. Because now there lay the real danger that his grandfather wouldn't live long enough to see any of it.

The day drew nearer when he would have to say goodbye for the last time to the man who had raised him from the age of nine.

Theos, he would give his soul for a miracle.

Jo watched Theseus carefully. For a man usually so full of vitality he had a sudden stillness about him that she found unnerving.

Then his lips curved into a pensive smile and he nodded. 'Your intuition is right. My grandfather has cancer.'

'I'm sorry.'

'He's eighty-seven,' he said philosophically, but his eyes had dimmed.

'That doesn't make it any easier.' Jo had only known one of her grandparents: her paternal grandfather. She'd never seen much of him when she'd been growing up but she remembered how she'd always looked forward to his visits. When Granddad Bill came over her mother would bake even more cakes than usual and her father would drag himself out of the study where he spent his days drinking cheap whisky.

His death had saddened her but the distance between their lives had meant it had caused a dull ache rather than an acute pain.

It would be a thousand times harder for Theseus. The King was like a father to him.

He must be going through hell.

She remembered his despondency five years ago, when he'd learned his grandmother was dying. Whatever regrets Jo might have over that night, she would never regret being there for him.

Who amongst this palace of courtiers did he turn to for solace now? Who wrapped their arms around his neck and stroked his hair? Who tried to absorb his pain and give him comfort?

Because surely—*surely*—his pain that night had been real. Even if everything else had been a lie, that had been true.

Somewhere beneath the brooding façade Theseus was in agony. She would bet every penny she owned on it.

He tugged at his shirt collar as if it constricted him. 'The hardest thing to understand is why he didn't say anything sooner. He's known for a number of years that something was wrong but didn't say a word until the pain became intolerable. If he'd spoken sooner they might have been able to cure him, but…' He shrugged and closed his eyes. 'He left it too late. He's riddled with it.'

'Is he having any treatment?'

'Against the doctor's advice, yes.'

'They don't think it's a good idea?'

'His age and frailty are factors against it, but my grandfather is a stubborn old man who has never had to bow to the opinions of those he disagrees with—he is a king. He wants to live long enough to celebrate his jubilee and see Helios married. He has tasked the doctors with making that happen.'

Silence hung, forming a strangely intimate atmosphere that was broken by a knock on the door.

Theseus's eyes held hers for a beat longer before he called out, 'Come,' and a courtier entered with news that the delegation he was expecting had arrived.

Excusing himself, he disappeared, leaving Jo with nothing but her own confused thoughts for company.

She doubled over and laid her cheek on the desk, gazing at the closed door with unfocused eyes, trying to control the savage beat of her heart.

The King—her son's great-grandfather—was dying.

It brought it home as nothing else had that this family, however great and powerful they might be, were Toby's kin.

She gripped her head, felt a cramping pain catching in her belly. Her emotions were riding an unpredictable roller coaster. She might as well be blindfolded for all she knew of what the immediate future would bring.

But her conscience spoke loud and clear. Toby would start school in five months and the innocence with which he looked at the world would change. He knew he had a daddy who lived in Greece, but so far that was the extent of his knowledge and his curiosity. Soon the notion of a father wouldn't be some abstract thing but something concrete that all the other kids had and he would want too.

And didn't Theseus deserve to know that he was a father and be given the choice to be in Toby's life?

If only she had a crystal ball.

But no matter how much guilt she carried she could not forget that her overriding priority was her son. She would do *anything* to keep him safe, and if that meant keeping Theseus in the dark until she was certain his knowing could bring no harm to Toby, then that was what she must do.

Dictaphone and notepad in hand, Jo slipped through the archway into Theseus's office. After almost two days of going through the research papers she was ready for him.

He was on the phone. His desk—which, like her own, curved to cover two walls but was twice the size—was heaped with neat piles of files and folders. His three desktop computers were all switched on.

He nodded briefly in acknowledgement and raised a hand to indicate that he wouldn't be long.

While he continued his conversation she felt his eyes follow her as she stepped over to the window.

She loved gazing out over the palace grounds. No matter which window she looked out from the vista was always spectacular, with sprawling gardens that ran as far as the eye could see, lush with colourful spring flowers and verdant lawn, and the palace maze rising high in the distance.

When she looked back he was unabashedly studying her.

Prickles of self-consciousness swept through her. Flustered, she smoothed her sweater down over her stomach and forced her gaze back outside, scolding herself for reading anything into his contemplative study of her. Her thin cream sweater and faded blue jeans were hardly the height of fashion.

'What can I help you with?' he asked once he'd finished his call.

'I'm ready with my questions for you.'

'Ask away.'

'It'll probably take a couple of hours to go through them all,' she warned him, conscious of how busy he must be.

'My diary is clear. I'm at your disposal. Please, take a seat.' He pointed to the armchair in the corner of his office and put his computers into sleep mode.

Sinking into the armchair's cosy softness, she resisted the urge to tuck her feet under her bottom.

'Before we discuss anything, I want to say how sorry I was to read about your parents' accident.'

Their tragic car crash had changed the course of Agon's history. It was something Jo knew would reverberate through the rest of her work, and as much as she would have liked to steer away from it, knowing that to talk about it would bring back painful memories for him, it wasn't something she could avoid.

His gaze held hers before he brushed away a lock of hair that had fallen into his eyes.

'See,' he said quietly, emotion swirling in his brown eyes, 'I didn't lie to you about everything.'

She didn't answer, keeping her gaze on his and then wrenching her eyes away to look at her notebook, trying to keep her thoughts coherent.

When they'd sat in his cabin on Illya he'd swigged at his bottle of gin and told her how much his grandmother meant to him, that she'd been the one to whom he'd turned after the death of his parents. Jo's heart had broken when she'd known he would be returning home to say his final goodbye.

'Did you know when you left Illya that that would be it for Theo Patakis?' she asked.

'Yes.'

'And are you happy with your real life or were you happier as Theo?'

His demeanour didn't change but his eyes became steely. 'I don't think these questions have any relevance to my grandfather's biography.'

'I know.'

'I am a prince of Agon. My duty is to my family and my island.'

'But does it make you *happy*?' she persisted.

'Happiness is not quantifiable,' he answered shortly, looking away to press a button on one of the four landline telephones on his desk. 'I'll order refreshments.'

With the thread of their conversation dismissed, Jo pulled out a small table tucked next to her so it sat between them, and put her Dictaphone on it.

'Do you mind if I record our conversation rather than take notes?' she asked once he'd ordered coffee and cake.

'If that's what works for you, then by all means.'

She pressed 'record' and glanced again at her notes.

'Am I right in thinking your grandfather would have abdicated when your father reached the age of forty?'

'That is correct. Agon monarchs traditionally step down when their heir turns forty. When my parents died Helios became heir.'

'And Helios was ten at the time?'

'Yes.'

'So any thoughts of abdication and retirement had to be put to one side?'

'My father was an only child. My grandfather's only sibling died fighting in the war, so there was no one suitable to act as regent until Helios came of age.'

'What plans did your grandfather have for his retirement?'

A shadow crossed his face, lines forming on his forehead. 'He was going to take a back seat for my grandmother.'

'She was a violinist?'

'Yes. When they married she was already world-famous. My grandfather's coronation limited the scope of when and where she could perform, so she concentrated on composing music rather than performing, which was her first love.'

'So that was their plan? For her to start performing again?'

'She still performed, but only a couple of times a year at carefully arranged events. His abdication would have freed her and enabled her to tour the world—something my grandfather was fully behind. He was looking forward to travelling with her.'

'He'd travelled much of the world as a monarch,' she pointed out.

'Travelling as monarch is different. He was an ambassador for our island.' He smiled grimly. 'When a member of my family travels on royal business he has a retinue of staff and an itinerary that leaves no room for spontaneity. Every minute is accounted for.'

Jo tried to imagine the Theo she'd met five years ago, the carefree adrenaline addict with the infectious smile and an impulsive zest for life, living under such restrictions.

An image flashed into her mind of a fully mature lion trapped in a small cage.

'Is that why your grandfather agreed you could take a sabbatical from your duties at the palace and travel the world?'

'It wasn't a question of agreement,' he replied shortly.

When Theseus had decided to leave he'd discussed it with his grandfather as a matter of courtesy. He'd wanted his blessing but it hadn't been imperative. He would have gone anyway. He'd graduated from Sandhurst and, loving military life, had stayed on in the army for a few more years. But then he'd turned twenty-eight and his family's eyes had turned to him. He'd been expected to take his place in the palace, as a good prince was supposed to do...

It had felt as if a hook had been placed around his neck, tightening as the day had loomed ever closer.

He'd known that once he was in the palace permanently, any hope of freedom would be gone for ever. His childhood dream of becoming an astronaut had long been buried, but that yearning for freedom, the wish to see new horizons and control his own destiny without thinking of the impact on the palace, had still been so vivid he'd been able to taste it on his tongue.

He'd thought of his parents, dead at an age not much older than he was now, their lives snuffed out in the blink of an eye. Would they have lived that final day in the same way if they'd known it would be their last?

And so he'd made up his mind to leave before protocol engulfed him and to live his life as if each day really was his last.

He'd become Theo Patakis: the man he might have been if fate hadn't made him a prince.

CHAPTER FOUR

A STRANGE DISQUIET slipped through him. Theseus shrugged it off, and was thankful when a maid came into the office with their refreshments, placing a tray down on the table where Jo had put her Dictaphone.

He saw her gaze flitter to the *karidopita*, a walnut and spice cake.

'Have a slice.' He lifted the plate for her.

'No, thank you.' While she poured the coffee her gaze lingered on the cake.

'Are you sure?'

She pulled a face. 'I put on weight just looking at it.'

'One slice won't hurt.'

'If I have one slice I'll want the rest of it, and before we know it I'll be running to the kitchen and holding the chef to ransom until he's made me a fresh one.' She said it with laughter in her voice, but there was no disguising the longing on her face.

He was about to encourage her again—to his mind a little bit of everything never hurt anyone—when he remembered her as she'd been on Illya. She still had her luscious curves now, but there was no denying that she'd lost weight—perhaps a couple of stone if he were any judge. It seemed her weight loss was an ongoing battle.

Moving the plate to his desk and out of her eyeline, he settled back in his chair, cradling his coffee cup in his hands.

He didn't miss the quick smile of gratitude she threw his

way. It was a smile that made his stomach pull and a wave of something he couldn't distinguish race through him.

'We were discussing my grandfather's plans for abdication,' he prompted her, keen to steer them back to their conversation and focus his mind on the job at hand rather than on *her*.

She threw him another grateful smile and leaned forward to press 'record' on her Dictaphone again. The movement pulled her sweater down enough to give him the tiniest glimpse of her milky cleavage.

A stab of lust pierced him. Thoughts he'd done his damnedest to keep at bay pushed through.

She had skin like satin. Breasts that...

With resolve like steel he pushed the unbidden memory away.

He was not that man who put his own pleasure above everything else any more.

Holding on to his steely resolve and keeping his head together, he answered her many questions, one leading directly to another, all the while stopping his thoughts from straying any further into forbidden territory.

It was a hard thing to do when the mouth posing the questions was so sinfully kissable.

By the time she'd asked her last question Jo's lower back ached from sitting in the same position for so long—three hours, according to her watch. She got up to stretch her legs and went to stand at the window.

Discussing his grandfather's life had felt strangely intimate and she was relieved that it was over. The way Theseus had stared at her throughout...

His dark eyes had never left her face. And she hadn't been able to wrench her gaze from his.

'There's a load of schoolchildren in your garden,' she said, saying the first thing that popped into her mind as she tried desperately to break through the weird atmosphere that had shrunk the spacious office into a tight, claustrophobic room.

'They'll be here for the tour,' he murmured, coming to stand by her side. 'The palace museum and grounds only open at weekends in the off season, but we arrange private midweek tours for schools and other groups. From the first of May until the first of September the grounds, museum and some parts of the palace are open every day. You can't walk anywhere without tripping over a tourist.'

'Is it hard, opening your home to strangers?'

He gave a tight smile. 'This is a palace—not a home.'

'It's *your* home.'

'Our private quarters are off-limits to visitors, but look around you. Where can I go if I want to enjoy the sun in privacy? As soon as I step out of my apartment there are courtiers by my side—' He broke off and muttered what sounded like an oath.

Jo would have pressed him further, but her throat had closed up. Theseus's nearness, his heat and the warm, oaky scent she remembered so well were all there, igniting her senses... She clenched her fists, fighting her body and its yearning to press closer, to actually touch him.

A heavily fortified black four-by-four pulled to a stop below them.

A tall man, very similar in looks to Theseus, stepped out of the back, followed by a rake-thin woman with raven-black hair and enormous sunglasses.

'Is that Helios?' she asked, grabbing at the distraction.

'Yes. And that's Princess Catalina from the principality of Monte Cleure.' Theseus placed his enormous hands on the windowsill. 'Between you and me, he'll be announcing their engagement at the Gala.'

'That's quick. Didn't they only meet at the ball last Saturday?'

'Our families have been friends for decades. Catalina's brother went to boarding school with us.'

'They don't look like a couple in love.'

Jo wasn't an expert in body language, but the way they walked together—past the schoolchildren who had all stopped what they were doing to gape at them—reminded her of her parents, who walked as if even brushing against each other might give them a disease.

And as she thought this, Theseus's arm brushed lightly against hers.

Her lungs tightened.

She could *feel* him.

'Heirs to the Agon throne marry for duty, not love,' he said, his voice unusually hard.

She looked at him. He was gazing intently out of the window, his jaw set.

'It's the twenty-first century.'

'And protocol has been adapted. Helios is the first Agon heir free to choose his own bride.'

'Can he choose anyone?'

'Anyone of royal blood.'

'Freedom with caveats? How sad.'

'It is the way things work here. Change takes time.'

'I hope they at least like and respect each other.'

She wondered if her parents' marriage would have been different if her mother had ever respected her father. Would her father have resorted to the demon drink if her mother hadn't been so disparaging towards him?

'My brother would never have married someone he didn't respect.' A marriage without respect had to be just as bad as a marriage without love, if not worse.

'When will they marry?'

'As soon as it can be arranged. Hopefully before...'

He didn't need to finish his sentence. Jo knew what he meant.

Before his grandfather died.

The mood shifted, the atmosphere becoming even heavier.

'It will be a full state wedding,' he explained curtly. 'That usually takes a good six months to organise. Helios wants this one to be arranged in a maximum of two months.'

'That's asking a lot.'

He shrugged. 'Our staff are the best. It will be done.'

'Are you expected to marry too?'

'The spare to the heir must produce more spares,' he said scathingly. 'Once Helios is married I will have to find a suitable royal bride of my own.'

'And what do you consider "suitable"?' she asked.

Of course it was only the fact that Theseus marrying meant Toby would have a stepmother, and eventually half-siblings to contend with, that made it feel as if a knife had been plunged into her heart.

Theseus was a prince. Princes needed their princesses.

'Someone who understands that it will be a union within which to make children.'

She strove to keep her voice casual. 'Don't you want love?'

The look he cast her could have curdled milk. 'Absolutely not. Only fools marry for love.'

'That's very cynical.'

'You think? Well, my mother loved my father, and all she got for her trouble was endless infidelity. My grandparents loved each other, but when my grandmother died my grandfather aged a decade overnight. It's not the cancer that's killing him; it's his broken heart. Love causes misery and I want no part of it. I want a bride who understands what palace life entails and who I can respect. Nothing more.'

Jo swallowed the bile rising in her throat.

Her memories of this man were filled with such warmth that this coldness chilled her.

Where had that man gone?

She wanted to argue with him, to tell him that surely the sweetness of love overrode anything else, but what would she know about it? The only person who'd ever truly loved her was her son, and in all honesty he had no choice in the matter, just as she had no choice but to love her own cold mother. In Jo's experience filial love was as automatic as breathing. Parental love was not.

What if Theseus's disdain for love extended to his children? There was a cynicism to him that scared her.

She couldn't bring herself to ask. Instead she took a quick breath and said, 'Will Helios's children be sent to boarding school, like you and your brothers were?'

This was a question that had played on her mind since she'd realised all the Princes had been packed off to boarding school. If she told Theseus about Toby, and if he recognised him as his son, would he expect him to be sent away too?

That was *if* he recognised him as his son.

What if he demanded a DNA test? The thought made her shudder.

So many 'what ifs'.

If only she could see what the future held.

'Of course. It is the Kalliakis tradition.'

'Is it traditional to be sent away at *eight*?'

'Yes.'

'That's such a young age.' She thought again of Toby, who still struggled to put his own socks on. To imagine being separated from him for months on end... No, she couldn't do it. Being apart from him while she was here on Agon was hard enough.

'I agree. Too young.'

She swallowed back her relief. 'Did you find it hard, leaving your home and family?'

'You have no idea,' he said, his tone harsher than she'd ever heard it.

'Was it easier for you, having Helios there already when you went?'

He looked at her and paused for a moment. 'Harder. I was always being compared to him. I wanted to be judged in my own right.'

'So were you always rivals?'

'What makes you ask that?' The intensity of his stare grew.

She pulled a rueful face, knowing she was reaching dangerous territory. 'I've been putting two and two together again. I saw a press cutting about your grandparents' wedding anniversary party, where you punched him in the face.'

To her amazement he shook his head and burst into laughter.

The transformation took her breath away.

It was the first time she'd heard him laugh since she'd arrived at the palace, and the sound dived straight through her skin.

Almost lazily he reached out and pressed a finger to her lips. 'You are a very astute woman.'

It was the lightest of touches, but enough for all the breath in her lungs to rush out in a whoosh and for her heart, which was already hammering, to accelerate.

'Yes, we were rivals,' he murmured. 'Helios was always destined to be King. My destiny was to be the perfect Prince, tucked in his shadow. It was a destiny I fought against. I didn't want to be in his shadow. I wanted to be in the sun.'

His finger drifted away from her mouth and slid across her cheek, leaving flickers of heat following his trail. If he moved any closer he'd be able to feel the thundering of her heart...

He stepped closer. 'My childhood was a battle for attention and freedom.'

He was going to kiss her.

Her senses were filled with him; his scent, his heat, the masculine essence he carried so effortlessly and that every part of her sang to.

She mustn't give in to it. She mustn't.

She cleared her throat. 'Is that why you're the perfect Prince now? Are you making up for your behaviour then?' Judging by the press cuttings, his behaviour over these past few years had been exemplary.

He stiffened. The hazy mist that had appeared in his eyes cleared. He pulled his hand away from her face and stepped back, his regal skin slipping into place effortlessly.

Breathing heavily, Jo tried to collect her scattered thoughts, tried dispelling the tingles racing through her.

He'd been about to kiss her.

And she'd been about to kiss him right back.

She still wanted to. Her mouth *ached* to feel his warm, firm lips upon hers again.

She could feel the invisible mark his finger had left on her lips, had to clench her hands into fists to stop them tracing it.

'Yes, you *are* an astute woman.' Theseus had regained his composure. 'Now, unless you have further questions about my grandfather, I have work to do.'

'I'm done,' she said quietly, edging away from him, side-stepping into her own office, glad of the dismissal.

Only when she was completely alone did she place her fingers to her lips and trace the mark he'd made on her mouth.

Theseus stood in the adjoining archway and looked into Joanne's office, as he'd done numerous times since she'd arrived on his island.

There she sat, hunched over her computer, earphones in, seemingly oblivious to his pursuing eyes.

Any doubts he'd had about Hamlin & Associates sending a relative novice to take Fiona's place had gone. Unashamed of asking for help with translation when needed, Jo had finished four chapters in three days, passing them to him for approval before sending them to the Oxford office for editing. At the rate she was going she would beat the Wednesday deadline by a comfortable margin.

It wasn't only her speed and work ethic that impressed him, but also the quality of the chapters she'd produced. He was certain the reader wouldn't be able to spot the transition between the two biographers.

His grandfather was coming to life on the page in a way he'd never anticipated. He'd enjoyed Fiona's chapters, and had read them almost like a history lesson. But Jo had taken up the story from Theseus's own childhood. Reading her chapters was like seeing his own life through his grandfather's eyes, with events he'd lived through taking on greater significance.

His grandparents' fortieth wedding anniversary celebrations were vivid on the page. He could taste the food that had been served, hear the music of the Agon orchestra, see the dancing couples on the ballroom floor... And, although she'd wisely left it unwritten, he could see his fourteen-year-old self launching at fifteen-year-old Helios in full view of all the distinguished guests, breaking his nose.

He could see his brother's blood soaking into the royal purple sash, see his grandmother's horror and his grandfather's fury. He could still taste his own blood as Helios—never one to shy away from a fight like any good Agonite—had launched himself right back at him.

What he couldn't remember was *why* he'd done it.

He remembered hating the stupid penguin suits he and his brothers had been forced to wear, hating the forced small talk with boring old people, hating it that a president's daughter he'd taken a liking to had made a beeline for his older brother.

Everyone had made a beeline for Helios.

Helios lived under even greater restrictions than he did, but his brother had always taken it in his stride, acting as if going on a date with three burly men with guns accompanying him was natural and not something to resent.

Their rivalry had been immense.

He smiled as he recalled their younger brother, Talos, then only twelve, pulling them apart.

Theseus had been in disgrace for months and confined to the five-hundred-and-seventy-three-roomed palace over the long hot summer.

And then his smile dropped.

He'd ruined his grandparents' special day. He'd shamed them.

He had shamed them many times with his selfish behaviour. Royal military parades, state banquets—all the events the three young Princes had attended Theseus had treated with an indifference bordering on disdain. He'd wanted to be somewhere, *anywhere* else, and he hadn't cared who'd known it.

Reading about these events in the book, even with his churlish behaviour omitted, had brought it all back to him—everything he was fighting to atone for. It was the humanity Jo brought to both his grandparents on the page that made it all seem so vivid again.

Yes. His doubts about her ability had truly been expelled. He enjoyed working with her, their back and forth conversations, the flashes of shared humour. He especially liked the way she blushed when she caught him looking at her. She made his veins bubble and his skin tingle, long-dead sensations blazing back to life.

He found it fascinating to watch her work; her face scrunched with intensity, her fingers flying over the keys of her computer, completely in the zone. Sometimes she sensed his presence and would turn her head, colour creeping over her cheeks when she saw him…

She drove him crazy. It had become a constant battle to keep his hands to himself. He'd been so close to kissing her. *So close.* He'd breathed in her scent and every part of him had reacted.

And that was dangerous.

He was about to turn away and return to the safety of his own desk when her phone vibrated loudly next to her.

With her earphones still in, she grabbed it with her right hand and swiped the screen in an absent manner. Whoever had messaged her must have been deemed worthy, for she straightened, brought the phone close to her face and pressed the screen.

She gazed at whatever she'd received, brushing her fingers gently over it, before lifting the phone to her mouth and kissing it gently.

His stomach roiled.

He'd assumed she didn't have a lover. It was easy to tell if a woman was in love—there was a certain glow she carried. Jo didn't have that glow. But the way she'd pressed her lips to that phone…as if she'd been trying to breathe in the essence of whoever had sent that message to her…

It was a gesture that made his skin feel as if needles were being pricked into it.

He remembered the way those lips had once felt under his own mouth, the clumsy eagerness he'd found there. The innocence.

'Who was that?' he asked loudly, stepping into the room, his curiosity burning.

But of course she didn't hear him. By the time he'd tapped on her shoulder, making her almost jump out of her seat, the screen on her phone had gone black.

'Who was that?' he repeated, when she'd tugged the earphones out with trembling hands.

Dark colour stained her cheeks, her teeth bit into her full lips and her eyes were wide...*fearful*?

What on earth did she have to be frightened of?

Her throat moved before she answered. 'It's private.'

'Private?'

'Private,' she repeated more decisively. 'Did you want me for anything?'

'Yes.' He folded his arms across his chest and without even considering his words said, 'I'm taking you out for dinner tonight.'

If there had been fear in her eyes before, all that rang out of them now was confusion. 'Why?'

'You need a break. You haven't seen anything of my island.'

'I'm here to work—not sightsee.'

'You'll burn out if you don't take a break.' He needed a break too, time away from the palace and the reams of courtiers if only for a few hours.

He knew next to nothing of this woman who had once been a beacon of light for him on a long, cold night.

An evening out would do them both good.

Her brows furrowed. 'I thought Agon was closed on Sundays.'

He fixed her with the stare his brother Talos used to such great effect. 'Let me worry about finding somewhere to go. You need a break from this office. I want you ready for a night out by seven o'clock—and no arguments or I'll have you taken to the dungeons.'

Her eyes widened in surprise before she let out a bark of laughter.

He felt his own bubble of mirth rise up too, but smothered it. 'Seven o'clock,' he said, his voice brooking no argument.

'I haven't got anything to wear,' she said matter-of-factly, as if that clinched it. As if that would let her off the hook.

On impulse, he leaned down to place his face before hers, taking in the ringing blue-grey eyes. He caught a hint of a light, feminine scent and inhaled.

'Dress casually. And if suitable clothing is an issue I would suggest not wearing anything at all.'

Her cheeks turned so red they nearly matched the colour of her hair.

Pulling back, feeling lighter than he'd felt in years, he sauntered through to his office, pausing at the threshold to add, 'If you're not finished by five o'clock Nikos will escort you out of here. The office door will be locked until the morning. See you at seven.'

He walked into his apartment, his pulse thundering in his ears, and closed the door behind him.

What the *hell* was he playing at? A night out was one thing—but suggesting she go *naked*? That was inviting trouble. It was the kind of comment Theo would have made.

For five years his physical desires had been dormant. Being around beautiful women was a regular occurrence in his life, but not one of them had tempted him. None of them made him feel as if his veins had been injected with red-hot treacle the way being with Jo did.

None of them had propelled him to make an impulsive offer of a date. Well, give an *order* for a date.

No, *not* a date. Merely an evening away from the confines of the palace for them both.

Now his senses were straining to remember what she had looked like naked, but their night together was still a blur; a ghost that couldn't be seen.

Something told him it would be best for that memory to remain a ghost.

CHAPTER FIVE

A LOUD KNOCK on her apartment door announced Theseus's arrival.

Jo took a deep breath through her nose and pulled open the door, her heart thundering erratically.

And there he stood.

Tonight he'd forsaken the business attire he usually wore and donned a pair of slim-fitting dark blue jeans that hugged his long, muscular thighs, a light grey shirt unbuttoned at the neck and a fitted brown leather jacket that showed off the breadth of his chest to perfection.

All of that, coupled with his deep olive features and thick dark hair... He looked sexy. And dangerous. So dangerous she should close the door in his face and plead a headache.

He looked...

He looked like *Theo*.

He stepped over the threshold and stood before her, gazing down with a slow shake of his head. The look in his eyes threatened to send her pulses racing out of her skin.

She tried to swallow but her throat had dried up. Only once had she seen that look. Five years ago.

She'd thought he was beautiful. She hadn't been stupid; had known she'd had no chance with him. He'd been as unobtainable as the film stars she'd loved to watch so much. Even then he'd been a man surrounded by a legion of admirers, men and women who all hung on to his every word and laughed at his every joke. Men like him didn't notice girls like her apart from to make fun of them.

The last thing she'd expected—the very last thing—was for him to stand up for her. To protect her. That one action had turned her crush into something more, making her heart swell and attach itself to him.

Even then she hadn't been naïve enough to think her adoration would be reciprocated. The world didn't work like that. Gorgeous, fit Greeks didn't fall for plump, shy English girls. He could befriend her, but desire her? Impossible.

And then he'd turned up at the chalet she'd shared with her friends, bottle of gin in hand, hair in disarray and wildness in his eyes...

That look in his eyes when he'd first kissed her... That same look was in his eyes now. It was a look that pierced her skin and made her recall for the thousandth time their one night together.

That night...

Losing her virginity to a drunk, melancholic man had been something she could never have expected, but it was something she would never regret, and not just because that one time had created Toby.

Theseus had needed her that night. That hadn't been a lie. He'd lain on the bed with the back of his head resting against her breasts, swigging from the bottle of gin. She'd run her fingers through his hair and listened to him talk.

He'd told her about his brothers and their fierce competitiveness, the penknives they'd each been given at the age of ten by their grandfather and how they would spend hours finding inanimate objects to throw them at as target practice, how the loser would be subjected to knuckle-rubs.

And then—she had never figured out how or why—the atmosphere had changed and he'd stopped talking. His eyes had gazed into hers with an expression she had never seen before but which had acted like a magnet, pulling her to him.

The stars might not have shone and fireworks might

not have exploded but she hadn't needed them to. For a few precious moments she had belonged to him and he had belonged to her.

For one solitary night she had been needed and loved and wanted, and it had filled her romantic heart with hope and tenderness.

She couldn't bear to think it had *all* been a lie.

She'd stood in the shower an hour ago with anticipation thrumming through her and had known she had to tell him about Toby. She could not in all good conscience keep it from him any longer.

Theseus was arrogant, and often curt, but he was also generous and thoughtful. He was a powerful man, but she'd seen no sign of him abusing that power. He wasn't Theo, but there had been a couple of times when she'd sworn she'd glimpsed the man she'd fallen in love with five years before.

She would wait until the biography was complete. It meant everything to him. For all his talk about disavowing love, she knew he loved his grandfather just as he'd loved his grandmother.

A few more days—that was all it would take. Two days at the most. Then her job would be done and she could turn his life upside down with the truth.

All she had to do was smother the awful feeling of deception she carried everywhere.

She felt such guilt. Every minute with him was clouded by her total awareness of him and the knowledge that she was hiding something so monumental. She'd thought her heart might jump out of her ribcage earlier, when he had almost caught her looking at another picture Toby had drawn which Jonathan had scanned and emailed over to her.

And now her heart was beating just as frantically, but with a hugely different rhythm. Flames licked through her veins at the look in Theseus's eyes. It was as if he wanted nothing more than to eat her whole. As if her knee-length mint crêpe dress with its flared sleeves and her flat black sandals made up the sexiest outfit he'd ever seen on a woman.

The nervous excitement that had built in her stomach almost skipped up and out of her throat when he dived a hand around her neck and gathered her hair in a bunch.

Without breaking stride, he kicked the door shut behind him, moved his other hand to her cheek and brought his mouth down on hers.

If a body could spontaneously combust, then Jo's did. The lit flames became a blaze—a dark, fiery ache which deepened in her pelvis as his lips moved over hers, firm but gentle, seductive but checked. Firmly controlled. His tongue darted out, prising her lips apart so it could slide slowly inside and dance against her own. His fingers were making gentle kneading motions against her cheek.

Everything was pushed out of her mind, clearing it to only him; his hot, lightly coffee-scented breath, his warm strong fingers, the heat unfurling from him and moving through her aching body. Sensation threaded everywhere... right through to the soles of her feet and the delicate skin of her eyelids.

She gripped his jacket, then reached up to wind her arms around his neck, the tips of her fingers skimming the smooth skin and rubbing against the soft bristles running up from his nape.

Deepening the kiss, he dropped his hand from her cheek to snake it around her waist, breaching that final physical distance between them so she stood flush against him, lost to everything but the rush of his deeply sensuous assault.

And then he jerked away and the kiss was broken.

Ramming his hands into his jeans pockets, he closed his eyes and swore. 'I apologise,' he said, his jaw clenched, his breathing heavy. 'I never meant for that to happen.'

'Neither did I,' she said quietly. She looked away, not wanting him to see the enormous dollop of guilt she knew must be reflected in her eyes.

'You're driving me crazy,' he said, with such starkness her gaze flew back to him.

Hunger. That was what she saw. His hunger for her.

She was slipping into dangerous waters and had no idea how to navigate her way out, a task made harder by the fact that her body throbbed from head to toe. She knew if he were to touch her again she would respond with the same wantonness.

How could she have allowed him to kiss her when she was keeping such a huge secret from him? Even if he knew about Toby it would be madness to think anything could happen between them. In a few months he would be searching for a bride. A *royal* bride.

She was as far removed from his ideal of the perfect royal bride as possible.

He held her gaze a beat longer before striding to the door and yanking it open.

His eyes flashed as he said, 'I suggest we leave now, because if you keep looking at me like that, I will not be responsible for the consequences.'

Jo paused for far too long, desire waging war with common sense.

Common sense clinched the victory.

She held her breath as she slipped past him, then followed him in silence out into the clear spring evening.

Her lips still burned from his kiss.

When he'd made love to her on Illya he'd been drunk.

This time he'd kissed her when he was sober. He desired her.

It shouldn't have made a difference.

It made all the difference in the world.

* * *

That had been the journey from hell, Theseus thought as Nikos brought the car to a stop.

What had he been *thinking*, kissing her like that?

He *hadn't* been thinking. At least not with his brain.

It had been that expression in her eyes that had done it for him, that open, wide-eyed desire.

Theos, how could *any* man look into those eyes and not want to drown in them?

Sitting in the back of the car for twenty minutes with her so close had been tantamount to torture. They hadn't exchanged a word.

He ran through all the reasons why he couldn't allow anything to happen between them. Or he tried to.

He couldn't think of one good reason why he shouldn't make love to her when every ounce of his being burned for her touch...

Because Jo wants more than you can ever give.

His spine stiffened as he recalled the promise he'd made to her on Illya. The promise he'd broken. Try as he might to ignore it, the guilt ate at him.

Jo wasn't the type of woman to go in for casual flings. She just wasn't. He'd known that five years ago but had allowed his desire and the emotions that had racked him that dark night to take over.

He would not do it again, would not take advantage of a woman who needed more from a lover than a solitary night. He could never offer her anything more, especially not now, when marriage loomed ever closer.

He might desire her, but he would control it.

Whatever the night might bring.

Club Giroud was one of the best kept secrets on Agon, open twenty-four-seven and located in a deceptively shabby secluded stone building near the top of Agon's highest mountain. No casual passer-by would guess that inside, at any one time, were dozens of the world's richest people and a fleet of parked cars collectively worth millions of dollars.

The interior was an entirely different matter.

They were met at the door by the concierge, who'd been watching out for them. Puffed up with importance at one of the royal Princes paying the establishment a visit, the man led them through a cavernous golden-hued dining hall, filled with beautiful, thin, chic women and men of varying shapes and sizes, all of whom turned their heads to stare at them. The concierge took them past the sweeping staircase that led up to the club itself, and outside to the sprawling terrace.

'I am totally underdressed,' Jo hissed the moment the fawning concierge had left them alone. 'All those women look as if they've just come off a catwalk.'

'You look beautiful,' he said simply, his eyes taking in every inch of her. Again.

There was nothing wrong with looking. Nothing at all.

'And don't forget I'm a prince of this island. I could wear a sack and my guest a binliner and I'd still be treated like royalty.'

'You *are* royalty,' she said with a mock scowl, although her cheeks heightened with colour at his compliment.

'Exactly. My presence gives the place a certain cache. It's a secret club for the filthy rich—playboys and billionaires who moor their yachts in our harbour and like to dine and play somewhere elusive and exclusive.'

'You like to come here?' she asked doubtfully, as if she knew of his disdain for these people whose lives were consumed with money: how to make it and how to spend it.

'If I were to take you anywhere else our picture would be all over the press by morning.' He gave a rueful shrug.

'I can always take you to Talos's boxing gym, if you would prefer?'

She raised her pretty red-brown eyebrows.

'And here you get to see my island.'

'Do I?'

'If you look, you'll see this is the best view in the whole of Agon.'

He'd ensured she had the best seat at the table—one that looked out from the mountain over the villages and towns dotted in the distance, towards the palace in the thickets of trees on the adjacent mountain and the dark blue of the Mediterranean, where the sun blinked its last goodnight. In a couple of hours the moon would be high enough to illuminate the whole island. It was a sight he wanted her to see.

It gave him enormous satisfaction to see she hadn't paid the blindest bit of attention to the view. Since they'd been seated she'd only had eyes for *him*.

He pointed. 'Do you see that high, rocky mountain in the distance?'

She nodded.

'When we were teenagers, my brothers and I would have races to the top.'

'You were allowed?'

'Of course. Within the palace walls we were expected to behave like princes, but outside we were expected to be fighting fit.'

'And who would win?'

'Normally Talos. Helios and I were so intent on beating each other we always forgot what a mountain Talos was himself. We'd get to the top and find him already there.' He smiled at the memories.

Jo squinted as she took it all in, her features softening. She nodded in the direction of the palace. 'Is that the maze all lit up?'

'It is,' he confirmed. 'There must be a group doing

an evening tour—there are night lights embedded in the hedges to light the way for them.'

She gave a sigh of wonder. 'I bet that's a fabulous experience. Your maze is huge—much bigger than the one at Hampton Court Palace. I got lost in that on a school trip when I was twelve.'

Her delight at the recollection of being lost in a maze made her whole face light up, whilst the mention of the British palace sparked a memory of his own. 'Aren't you distantly related to *your* royal family?'

Surprise ringed her blue-grey eyes. 'How can you remember that?'

'I have an excellent memory.'

The truth was his memories of those last few days on Illya were becoming clearer. The hazy details were crystallising.

The night after he'd evicted those Americans from Marin's Bar for their ill-treatment of her, he'd gone back there with his Scandinavian friends and invited Jo and her friends to join them again. Conversation had turned to everyone having to say one interesting fact about themselves. Jo's had been that she was distantly related to the British royal family. She'd found it so amusing that she'd burst into laughter.

It had been the first time he'd heard or seen her laugh—usually she was so shy. Her whole face had lit up, just as it was doing now. It had been the first time he'd noticed what a pretty face she had. It had been such a transformation that his interest had been well and truly piqued. He'd spent the rest of the evening talking to her, enchanted by this shy young woman who, once she got going, became witty and talkative.

Talking to her had been like bathing in a clear, sun-drenched lake after months of soaking in the salty sea. He remembered how torn she'd looked when her friends had said they wanted to return to their chalet. How disappointed he'd been when she'd got up from the table and wished him goodnight.

The next day he'd tried to convince her to go surfing on the north side of the island with them all. Her friends had jumped at the chance but Jo had politely refused. She'd happily tagged along to watch, however, sitting on the beach and refusing to acknowledge his cajoling to come into the water.

Shortly after that he'd gone with his Scandinavian friends to a nearby uninhabited island for a couple of days of mountain climbing.

When they'd returned, the first thing he'd heard when he'd charged his phone had been Helios's message telling him to come home. Their grandmother had been taken seriously ill and wasn't expected to survive.

For the second time in his life he'd been lost. The first time had been the night their grandfather had flown to their English boarding school to tell him and Helios that their parents had been killed. Nothing could ever touch that night for pain, but he'd had his brother there, and for that one night his grandfather—who in that moment had been a true grandfather to them—had held his two grandsons close.

On Illya he'd been alone, and far from his family. He'd been on an island in the middle of the Adriatic Sea where the only means of transport had been the daily ferry.

He'd finished half a bottle of gin in his chalet alone, waiting until he'd figured everyone would be in bed before staggering outside, intending to sit on the beach.

There had been a light on in Jo's chalet.

Thinking back, he was surprised he'd known which chalet had been hers.

'According to my mother, her side of the family has a direct link to Queen Victoria via many marriages,' she said now, in that same amused tone he remembered from five years ago. 'I think I'm something like six-hundred-and-thirty-ninth in line to the throne.'

'Being that far up the chain you must have grown up in your own palace,' he teased, playing along with her irreverence.

'I grew up in an Oxfordshire manor house so old and draughty it would have been warmer sleeping in an igloo.'

'Rather like sleeping in a palace, then,' he observed with a grin.

She laughed, her eyes meeting his. 'Your palace is wonderful and has hot running water. My parents' house has a boiler so old my mother passes it off as an original feature. Saying that, the kennels and the stables always have decent heating.'

'Did you have a lot of pets?' He could just see her fussing over a small army of dogs.

She pulled a face. 'Not quite. My mother turned the old outhouses into an animal sanctuary. She'll take any animal in: cats, dogs, hedgehogs, horses—donkeys, even. Those she can't rehome, she keeps.'

'How many animals does she have?'

Her lips pursed as she thought. 'Anything up to fifty of them. If she runs out of space she brings them into the house.'

'That must have been magical for you as a child.'

She gave a shrug, her answer delayed by the waiter coming over with a jug of water and taking their order.

'So your mother runs an animal sanctuary—what does your father do?' he asked once they were alone again.

'He drinks.'

His hand paused on his glass.

'He's an alcoholic.'

'I'm sorry. Is he violent?' He thought again of the drunken American college students who'd been so abusive to Jo and her friends. Drink had a habit of making some people cruel.

'God, no. He's actually very placid. He just sits in his study all day, working his way through his whisky.'

'How does your mother cope?'

'By ignoring him.'

'Really?'

'She despises him,' Jo said flatly. 'As far as she's concerned, Dad spending his days pickling his liver is the best thing for him.'

His brow furrowed. 'That's harsh.'

'It's the truth. She thinks he's weak and foolish. Maybe she's right. He was a stockbroker, but he lost his job to the drink when I was a baby.'

'So how do they survive?' He couldn't imagine an animal sanctuary made much money.

'Mum's got a tiny trust fund, and she makes a little from donations to the sanctuary. She bakes a lot of cakes and sells them for high prices which our rich neighbours are happy to pay because they are utterly gorgeous.'

Not as gorgeous as the mouth doing the talking now, Theseus thought, noticing the faraway look in her eyes as she spoke of the cakes and remembering the longing she'd shown towards the *karidopita*.

'She sounds like a formidable woman,' he observed. His own mother had been the opposite of formidable.

Jo met his eyes. 'That's one way of describing her. She's very blunt with her opinions, and has no time for people she considers to be fools. Most people are scared of her and she knows it—she leaves the cakes in the front room with price tags on and no one has ever tried to short-change her or steal the money box.' She sighed. 'I'll say this much for her, though—she's dotty about the animals. It's only creatures who *don't* walk on four legs she has no interest in.'

The waiter returned with their wine and poured them each a glass.

'Do you still live with your parents?' Theseus asked after taking a sip of the mellow red liquid.

'I'm in Oxford itself now. It's easier to commute to work.'

That reminded him of something else she'd once told him. 'I thought you were moving to London?'

Her eyes widened. 'Gosh, your memory is on fire to-night.'

He flashed her a grin, wondering if he'd imagined the flicker of fright that had crossed over her face.

'So what happened to London?' he asked, watching as she reached for her glass of wine and noting the tremor in her hands. She reminded him of a jumpy cat walking on freshly tossed hot coals.

She looked out over the mountains. 'Life. But never mind about me—tell me about the business you run with your brothers. You invest in young start-up companies?'

He eyed her contemplatively. Yes. The jumpy cat analogy perfectly described her at this moment. Her discomfort had come on so suddenly it made him suspicious—until he reminded himself that he had no right to her secrets.

Jo was in his employ. The fact that they had once made love half a decade ago didn't mean he had the right to know everything about her.

Yet the more he was with her, the more he wanted to peel back every secret until she was stripped bare before him.

Did she have a lover? Instinct told him no—she wasn't the kind of woman to kiss a man if she was involved with someone else—but there was something going on with her…something she had no intention of sharing with him.

He took another sip of wine and pulled his errant thoughts back under control.

No more intimacies. This was *not* a seduction.

There would be no peeling back of anything; not secrets nor clothes.

So he told her about the business, keeping the conversation throughout their meal light and easy. By the time they'd finished their starters and main course—the pair of them having shared a generous *souvlaki* platter filled with marinated pork and chicken skewers, roasted vegetables, hot pitta, salads and tzatziki—and ordered coffee, she was as relaxed as he'd seen her on his island. So relaxed that when she declined dessert he held himself back from asking if her refusal of sweet foods was related to her mother's cakes.

And he'd relaxed too. With each sip of wine and every bite of food he'd felt the weight he lived with lift until it was just them. Two people who couldn't keep their eyes off each other.

Jo truly was glorious, with her autumn leaf hair thick around her shoulders, a lock falling around her cleavage. It would take no effort to lean across the table and slowly sweep it away, to trace his fingers over her satin skin...

'What?' she asked, one brow raised.

She must have read something in his expression, for her eyes suddenly widened and she grabbed her glass, holding it up like a shield.

Another memory flashed through his mind, of lying on his bed with her, his head cushioned on those wonderful breasts...

She'd been awake, book in hand, when he'd knocked on her chalet door. Her friends had been fast asleep.

When he'd swigged from his bottle of gin, shrugged his shoulders helplessly and said, 'I think I need a friend,' she'd stared at him, taking in his disarrayed state, then giving the most loving, sympathetic smile he'd ever been on the receiving end of.

'Come on,' she'd said, putting her book down and taking his hand to lead him back to his own chalet.

The bed being the only place to sit, she'd climbed on and sat against the headboard. He'd leaned into her. She'd laced her fingers through his hair and let him talk.

He still couldn't pinpoint when the mood had changed. He'd been drunk, but there had come a moment when he'd suddenly become aware of the erratic thud of her heart. He'd tilted his head to look at her and realised that while he'd been talking so self-indulgently his head had been resting on her comforting breasts. Breasts separated from him by nothing but a thin white T-shirt.

She'd worn no bra.

She'd smiled with those stunning blue-grey eyes and suddenly he'd known he could lose himself in them.

And just like that he'd been in a full state of arousal.

Forget comforting. She wasn't *comforting*. She was the sexiest creature on the planet and his desire for her in that moment had been the most concentrated, intense desire he'd ever experienced.

By the time he'd pulled her T-shirt off and wriggled out of his shorts he'd been ready to devour her. And he had done just that.

He'd fallen asleep as soon as it was over and had slept until she'd gently woken him to say that the ferry was approaching the island.

'That night in Illya,' he asked quietly, 'was I your first?'

'My first?'

'Lover.'

Understanding flashed over her and she covered her mouth with her hand.

'I was, wasn't I?'

She gave the barest of nods. 'I'm surprised you remember anything.'

Her face was suffused with colour. Abruptly she got to her feet, knocking into the table as she did so, spilling water from her glass.

'I need to use the ladies',' she said starkly.

He captured her wrist and stared at her, concerned. 'Are you okay?'

She nodded, but her eyes were wild. She tugged her hand free. 'I won't be long.'

Puzzled, he watched her flee inside.

No sooner had the door shut behind her than her phone began to vibrate and dance on the table.

CHAPTER SIX

JOANNE STARED AT her reflection in the lavish ladies' restroom—which was mercifully empty—and prayed for courage. Her hands were clammy, her skin burned and a heavy beat played in her head.

She had to tell him. Tonight. Forget waiting until the biography was finished. Things had gone too far to keep it hidden from him any longer. He was seducing her with his every word and every look.

She hadn't tasted a morsel of her food; could hardly remember what she'd had. Her senses had been too busy relishing the taste of his earlier kisses, the whispers of which still lay on her tongue and lips. She could still feel his huge hand warm on her wrist.

She inhaled deeply a couple of times before smoothing her hair and straightening her dress. She would drink her coffee, Nikos would drive them back to the palace and then, as soon as they were alone, she would tell Theseus the truth.

She slipped back into the club's restaurant and weaved her way through the tables of beautiful people, all looking at her with unabashed curiosity. She heard their whispers as she passed: this stranger in their midst was the guest of one of Agon's most eligible bachelors.

Avoiding Theseus's eyes, she took her seat and reached for her coffee, which had been brought in her absence.

Before she could plead a headache and ask if they could return to the palace, Theseus said, 'Jonathan called.'

Startled, she looked at him.

Impassively he handed over her phone. 'He called when you were in the bathroom.'

In her rush to escape from him and in the haze she'd fallen into she'd left her phone exposed on the table.

She swallowed, her heart immediately starting to hammer. 'Did you answer it?'

'Yes. I thought it might be important.' Curiosity rang from his dark eyes. And something else…something darker.

'What did he say?' she croaked, fighting the cold paralysis sweeping through her.

'Only that he was calling for a chat and that his scanner's broken, so he'll give you Toby's pictures when you get home.'

Jo felt the colour drain from her face at hearing him vocalise their son's name, the blood abandoning her head and leaving a cold fog in its place.

She hadn't told Jonathan or Cathy about finding Toby's father. She hadn't told anyone.

This was it. This was where the truth came out.

A pulse flickered in Theseus's jaw. 'So who are they?'

'Jonathan's my brother.'

'And Toby? Is he your nephew?'

It was a struggle to breathe. Her body didn't know what it was doing. She was hot and cold, thrumming and paralysed all at once.

Hot. Cold. Hot. Cold.

Fat tears welled in her eyes and spilled over before she had the chance to feel them form.

She took the biggest, most painful breath of her life.

'Toby is my son.'

The shock on his face was so stark it was clear that hadn't been the answer he'd expected. 'You have a *child*?'

She nodded and swiped the tears away, only to find them replaced with more.

He rubbed a hand through his hair and shook his head

in disbelief. 'I had no idea. You have a child...? How old is he?'

She wrapped her arms around herself and whispered, 'Four.'

His hand froze on his head. Slowly his gaze drifted to fix on her, then stilled, his expression like those on the statues of the fierce Minoan gods that lined the palace corridors.

Her stomach churned as she watched him make the connection.

An age passed before he showed any sign of movement other than the narrowing of his unblinking eyes. Slowly he brought his hand down from his head to grip his glass, which still had a little red wine in it. Without taking his eyes from her face he knocked it back, emptied the remnants of the bottle into the glass and knocked that back too.

He wiped his mouth with the back of his hand and got to his feet.

When he spoke, his words were laced with a snarl. 'Get up. We leave *now*.'

He was a father.

Those four words were all Theseus could focus on.

He'd known there was something in her life that was putting her on edge, but the truth was nothing like he'd imagined.

Jo had a child.

And *he* was the father.

He'd been on the brink of tossing away his vow of celibacy for a lying, deceptive...

Theos. He had a four-year-old boy out there—a child of his blood.

He hadn't needed to do more than rudimentary maths to know the child was his. One look at Jo's terrified, tearful face had confirmed the truth.

She'd denied him their son's existence.

She was sitting in the back of the stretch Mercedes alone while he rode in front with Nikos, who wisely hadn't uttered a word since they'd come out of Club Giroud. The partition was up. He couldn't bring himself to look at her.

His control hung by the tiniest of threads. There were so many emotions playing through him it was as if a tsunami had been set loose in his chest.

When they arrived back at the palace he got straight out of the car and yanked open the back door. 'Get out.'

Not looking at her, or waiting to see if she obeyed, Theseus unlocked the door to his private apartment and held it open for her.

As she walked past him he caught a whiff of that feminine scent that had been driving him crazy all week and his loathing ratcheted up another notch.

When they were alone in his apartment he slammed the door shut behind him and faced her.

'I was going to tell you,' she said, jumping in before he could say anything. She stood in the middle of the living area, her arms folded across her chest, her face as white as a freshly laundered sheet. 'I swear.'

'I'm sure you were,' he said with deliberate silkiness. 'Tell me, when *were* you planning on telling me? When my son was ten? When I was on my deathbed?'

'When the biography was finished.'

'You should have told me the minute you landed on Agon.' He gritted his teeth. 'You've had a whole week to tell me the truth. A whole week during which you have lied to me—so *many* lies. You sicken me.'

She blanched under the assault of his words, but straightened and kept her composure. 'I didn't know who you were until a week ago. I spent *five years* searching for an engineer called Theo, not a prince called Theseus. I thought *Theo* was Toby's father. When I realised, I had to do what was right for Toby. I had to protect him.'

He stopped his voice turning into a roar by the skin of his teeth. 'Protect him from me? His own father?'

'*Yes!* Look at you! You're a prince from a hugely powerful family with a reputation for ferocity. I didn't know *you*—I still don't. When I arrived here you were a stranger in Theo's skin. I had to be sure you posed no risk. To be honest, I'm still not sure. But I knew today that I had to tell you.'

'You *would* say that,' he said, fighting to hold on to his temper before it exploded out of him.

'It's the truth!' she cried. 'I know how much the biography means to you and I knew that to tell you before we'd finished it would derail you. I swear I was going to tell you as soon as it was done. I *swear.*'

'Stop with the swearing. Right now I don't know if I even care to believe your lies.' Something else occurred to him—something so profound he couldn't believe it had taken him so long to consider it. 'You said you were on the pill.'

She winced and gazed down at the floor. 'I lied,' she whispered. 'I'm so very sorry.'

'What?' He grabbed at his hair, then grazed his fingers down his face. 'How could you lie about such a thing?'

'I didn't mean to. I'm sorry. I wasn't thinking of the consequences,' she said, her voice muffled by her hair. 'I...'

But he didn't want to hear her excuses. There was only one thing he wanted from her, and that—*he*—was thousands of miles away.

'Where is my son?'

'At my brother's house.'

'*Where?*'

'In Oxford.'

'Where in Oxford?'

'At...' She stopped talking and raised her head to look at him. 'Why?'

'I'm going to send Nikos to collect him.'

She shook her head. 'He hasn't got a passport.'

'That is not a problem. The address?'

'You can't conjure a passport out of thin air,' she said with an air of desperation. 'There's a form that needs to be filled in, photos to be taken—it doesn't happen overnight.'

'I can make it happen overnight.'

'He's a British citizen. Only *I* can complete those forms because only *my* name is on his birth certificate.'

That cut him short.

Jo gave a hollow laugh. 'Yes, Theseus, your son has *my* name. Because his father promised he would be in touch, then probably deleted my number before the ferry had lost sight of Illya. You can condemn me for lying about being on the pill, but if you'd kept your promise I would have told you the minute the pregnancy test came back positive. You could have had your name put on that birth certificate alongside mine. If you'd told me the truth about who you were you would already *know* your son.'

That her words were mostly true did nothing to placate him. Did she really expect him to believe she would have told him? He didn't believe a word that came out of her pretty, lying mouth.

All he could think was that his son and heir had some sort of version of *'father unknown'* on his birth certificate. It was like another iced dagger being pushed through his frozen heart.

'Trust me,' he said coldly, 'I have ways of getting things done. My son will have my name and an Agon passport by morning.'

'You can't bring him here yet. He doesn't know you...'

'And it's past time that he did. Now, for the last time, give me the address.'

'I won't.' Jo refused to back down. However guilty she felt, and however understandably furious Theseus was, her first priority was her son. She would not have him frightened.

The pulse in his jaw throbbed. Her heart was beating to match it. He stalked over, crouched before her on his haunches and cupped her cheek.

'I want to see my son and you *will* facilitate this.'

He spoke the words with such quiet menace that acrid bile surged up her throat. She had never seen such naked rage before.

'Toby is not a toy,' she said, with as much steely control as she could muster, refusing to quail under the weight of his power and loathing. Strangely, his hold on her cheek, although firm, was surprisingly soothing. 'Your wish to see him does not trump his need to be and feel safe. I am not having a complete stranger whisk him away from everything he knows and loves. He's a *little boy.*'

His thumb brushed her cheekbone. 'A little boy who is my son. He belongs here in Agon.'

'Right now he belongs in England. You're a stranger to him—he needs time to get to know you before we even *think* about bringing him here.'

Was this really happening? Were they really having this discussion? She'd prepared herself for anger, or rejection, or if she was lucky faint promises of future contact—but not *this*.

'I have a four-year-old son I have never met. He *will* be brought here.'

She clamped her jaw together and forced air into her lungs. All she succeeded in doing was filling herself with his scent. She almost wished he would shout or throw something. Anything had to be better than this cool yet venomous reasoning.

'*I'm* his legal parent. I *want* you to be a part of his life, for Toby's sake, but I will not allow you to rush things.'

'How little you understand the workings of my country,'

he said, with what almost sounded like a purr—although there was nothing kitten-like about his tone. Its timbre and his stance were reminiscent of an alpha lion, getting ready to pounce. He stood up to his full height and headed to the apartment's front door. 'I have the means to bring him here and I *will* use them.'

Fresh panic clawed at her.

Where was he going?

'You *will* meet Toby, I promise. I know learning about him has come as a complete shock to you. You need time to process it—'

'Save me the psychobabble,' he cut in icily. 'All you need to think about is this: you will not be allowed to leave Agon until my son is brought here.'

Something cold and sharp pierced her chest.

'What are you talking about?' she whispered.

'I will put out an order that you're not to leave the palace without my express permission.' His lips curved but his brown eyes fired bullets at her. 'Even if you manage to escape you'll find yourself unable to leave the island. The minute you turn up at the airport or the harbour you'll be arrested.'

'You can't do that.' But the needles crawling over her skin reminded her that he could.

'You know the history of Agon as well as I do. My family may not rule the island alone any more but we do hold power. A lot of it. One phone call is all it will take.'

'Please, Theseus, think about what you're saying. I promise you will meet your son—but not like *this*.'

He turned the handle of the door. 'Do you think I will trust a single word you say when you have proved yourself to be a remorseless liar? I want my son here in his rightful home and I don't trust you to bring this about. If that means keeping you locked up until you come round to my way of thinking, then so be it.'

* * *

The clock's hands had barely turned to one a.m. when the apartment door was thrown open. Theseus strode in, a sheaf of papers in his hand.

After his threat to keep her locked up he'd left, disappearing into the maze that was the Agon Royal Palace.

She'd felt it best to let him go, hoping a little distance would give him time to calm down and see reason. She'd stayed where she was on his sofa, clutching at her hair, alternating between feeling frozen to her core one minute and burning hot the next.

And now, judging by the grim, dishevelled look on his handsome face and the wild, dangerous glint in his eye, she saw the past hour hadn't calmed him down at all.

Their time apart hadn't worked to restore her own equilibrium either, leaving her stuck in a strange form of paralysed limbo. It was almost a relief to have him charge back in.

'Fill this out and sign where the cross is,' he said without preamble, placing the papers on the bureau in the corner and stabbing the one on top with a finger.

'What is it?'

'A form acknowledging me as Toby's natural father. I need the relevant birth details from you. From this I will produce an Agon birth certificate. When you've completed this form I need you to sign this one for his passport.' He held up a pink sheet of paper. 'Nikos will fly to England and meet up with Agon's Ambassador. They will collect Toby, take his photo and produce the passport, then fly him here. Tell your brother to have Toby ready for midday.'

'Be reasonable,' she pleaded, knowing she was being backed into a corner she couldn't fight her way out of, but knowing that she *had* to fight—for Toby's sake if not her own. 'Toby will be *terrified* when two strangers turn up to spirit him away.'

'Not if he's properly prepared. You can call him first thing and tell him that two nice men are coming to bring him to you. Tell him to think of it as a great adventure.'

'If having Toby here means so much to you, then why aren't you going to get him yourself?' she asked, a sudden burst of bitterness running through her.

'Because my absence will be noted. I can't afford for anyone to know about him yet.'

'So you're going to bring him here and hide him away—is that what you're saying?'

'Only until after the Gala. That will give me almost a fortnight to get things organised and time to prepare my family—especially my grandfather—for the shock Toby's appearance will bring.'

'What are you going to do?' she demanded, spreading out her hands. 'Hide him in the dungeons? He looks *exactly* like you. Anyone will take one look at him and know he's of Kalliakis blood.'

Theseus felt his heart jolt at that information. He'd been so full of fire and fury that he hadn't yet considered what his son looked like. Or what his personality was like. *Theos*, did four-year-old boys even *have* personalities?

'I have a private villa on the outskirts of Resina,' he said, referring to Agon's capital. 'Toby will be taken there until after the Gala.'

'And what about me?' Her voice was high with anxiety. 'You can't keep him away from me. That would be beyond cruel.'

His lips curved into a sneer but he shook his head. 'Do not hold me to your own low standards. You will be taken there in the morning to wait for him.'

Not even in the darkest recess of his mind had he entertained the thought of keeping them apart—not even before he'd spoken to Dimitris and been given the hard facts about what having a child here would mean...not just for him but for Jo too.

For a moment his throat thickened as he saw the despair in her eyes.

She'd lied to him about being on the pill, he reminded himself angrily, whilst images of leaving Illya rained down in his mind.

He'd stood at the back of the ferry, staring at the woman who had helped him through one of the worst nights of his life. Jo had sat on the beach, hugging her legs and watching him leave. He'd kissed her goodbye before boarding, had tasted her sweetness for what he had thought would be the last time.

Why had he strung her along as he had? He'd never made false promises to a woman before. He'd known even as he'd stored her number in his phone that he would never call her. He'd never done that to a woman before. If he had no intention of calling, he never pretended that he would.

But she had *really* lied to him. He might have broken a minor promise to call but she had lied about being on the pill. If she hadn't told such a wicked lie...

He wouldn't have a son.

She'd hit a nerve when she'd asked why he wasn't going to collect him personally. *Theos*, he wanted to. If he had superhuman powers he would have already flown to him. And yet...

Trepidation had taken root.

He wasn't ready for this—wasn't ready to be an instant father. These few hours while his son was being brought to him would allow him to prepare himself and get his villa made suitable for a small boy.

'I'll give you twenty minutes to get the paperwork complete,' he said.

He'd left Dimitris in the palace library, researching constitutional matters, and he needed to check in with him. He could also do without Jo's accusatory stare following his every move. She had no right to look at him as if *he* were the bad guy.

If she thought things were bad for her now, she was in for a nasty shock when he told her the rest of it.

CHAPTER SEVEN

Jo HAD LONG given up trying to sleep.

It had been three hours since she'd completed those forms. She'd left them on Theseus's bureau and returned to her own apartment, locking the door behind her.

She wanted to be alone, was too mentally exhausted to cope with anything else.

Padding over to the kitchen, she poured herself a glass of water and then rummaged in her handbag for some headache tablets. Just as she popped them into her mouth there was a soft rap on the door, followed by the sound of the handle being turned.

She swallowed the tablets down, more pathetic tears swimming in her eyes. It could only be Theseus.

She didn't want to see him. Not right now, when she was so angry and heartsick that she could punch him in the face. She ignored the knock.

Her numb shock had gone…had been replaced with a burning anger that he could be so cruel. Whatever wrong she'd done—and she'd always known what a terrible wrong it was—this was infinitely worse.

All those years of searching, all those years of raising her child as a single parent, and he thought he could sweep in and turn it all upside down with no consideration for Toby's emotional state.

And there was nothing she could do about it.

Every scratch of the pen on those forms had felt like a scratch on her heart.

But what choice had she had but to sign them? Theseus was fully prepared to keep her a prisoner until Toby was brought to him. She'd seen the threat in his eyes.

What this meant for her future she didn't know. His power was too much for her to fight—more than she could ever have appreciated. She was fighting from a power base of zero.

Her head pounded. And her eyes… They'd never felt so gritty—not even when she'd spent a whole day sobbing in fear over how her mother would react to her unexpected pregnancy. The fact that her mother's only comment had been, 'For God's sake, girl, I thought you had more sense than that,' had been rather anticlimactic after all the angst she'd put herself through.

She should have known her mother wouldn't be angry. For her to be angry would mean she cared, and if there was one thing Joanne had grown up knowing it was that her mother didn't care. Harriet Brookes had done her duty. She had fed her and clothed her. But that was the extent of any mothering she'd extended towards her daughter.

Even when Jo had spent a month in hospital whilst pregnant her mother had paid only one visit, and that had been to drive her back to the frigid shell she called a home.

At least her father had shown some kindness—but she'd had to catch him at the right time if she'd wanted any coherence from him, considering he started drinking in the morning and was generally comatose in the chair in his study by mid-afternoon.

Her poor father… That weak-willed, spineless man, who'd realised too late that the pretty young woman he'd impregnated and been forced to marry was far too strong for him. He'd once said, intoxicated over Sunday dinner, that she'd emasculated him. Her mother had replied in her usual no-nonsense manner that one needed balls to begin with in order to be emasculated.

Jo had not understood why they stayed together—and had *never* understood how they'd come to make *her*.

She knew she must get some sleep. Even if she only managed a couple of hours that would be better than nothing at all.

As she was about to climb back into the huge four-poster bed she froze when she heard the click of a door being unlocked, followed by a creak.

Slowly she turned her head to look at the door adjacent to her dressing room. She'd never been able to open it and had wondered a couple of times what lay on the other side. Now she stared as it opened, too frozen with fear to move.

Fight or flight? At that moment she wasn't capable of either option.

And then Theseus stepped over the threshold, allowing her to expel the breath she'd been holding.

He looked haggard, as if the events of the night had caused him to unravel.

'You scared the life out of me!' she said, on the verge of tears with shock. Her heart had been kick-started and was now pumping at the rate of knots. 'Where did you come from?'

'You didn't answer my knock so I came through the hidden passageway connecting your apartment with mine.' He pushed the door shut with his back and folded his arms. 'We need to talk.'

'It's four o'clock in the morning.' And she was wearing nothing but an old T-shirt that only just skimmed her fortunately covered bottom.

'And you're managing to sleep as well as I am.' His eyes flickered over her, taking in her attire. 'Nikos is on his way to England. There's a helicopter on standby to fly him and the ambassador to Oxford,' he added.

Jo gnawed at her lip and tried to fight the fresh tide of panic she felt as she did the maths. With the time difference between Agon and the UK, Nikos and the ambassador would easily make it to Toby by midday—just as Theseus had promised.

'I think it would be best if I meet him at the airport.' She mentally prepared herself for another fight she knew she was in no position to win.

To her surprise he gave a sharp nod of agreement. 'I'll get that arranged.'

'And we'll go straight to your villa?' she clarified.

'Yes.'

She chose her next words with care. Theseus might have calmed down, but she was aware that his temper was currently as flammable as dry kindling. 'I know you want us to stay until the Gala, and then introduce Toby to your family, but I need to know how long you'll want us to stay afterwards so I can make arrangements with work.'

At that moment she couldn't think about the biography and the work that still needed to be done to finish it.

When Theseus didn't answer, and simply stared at her with an unfathomable expression on his handsome face, alarm bells began to chime softly, reverberating through her stomach.

'How long do you envisage us staying on Agon for?' she asked again, more forcefully.

He rubbed the back of his neck. 'Dimitris and I have been refreshing our memories of Agon laws…'

'What's that got to do with how long Toby and I stay?'

'Everything.'

The alarm bells in her stomach upped their tempo, clanging loudly enough that they seemed to echo through her skin.

The silence thickened, closing in.

'You'll be staying on Agon indefinitely.'

'What are you talking about?'

'The only way Toby can be my heir is if we marry.'

Jo felt her jaw go slack. 'You have *got* to be joking.'

'I wish I was.' Theseus closed his eyes, then snapped them open to focus on her. 'Agon law states clearly that only legitimate heirs of the royal family can be recognised and allowed to inherit.'

'I don't understand…' she whispered, although the implications were already rushing through her.

'The law was created two hundred years ago, when the eldest of King Helios the Second's illegitimate children fought with his lawful heir for the right to take the throne. To prevent such a situation happening again it was explicitly spelt out in the constitution that only legitimate heirs can be recognised.'

'But Toby wasn't born in wedlock, so he'll be illegitimate regardless.'

'Our marriage will legitimise him. There is nothing in the constitution that states that the child must have been conceived or born in wedlock—only that they must be a child of a lawful marriage.'

Her hands fluttered to her throat. Her head shook slowly from left to right as she tried to take in exactly what he was saying. 'We can't marry. The idea is just…stupid.'

'Do you think I *want* to marry you?' he said harshly. 'It's the only way I can claim Toby as my own and give him the protection of the Kalliakis name.'

'He doesn't need protection. We live in Middle England—not a war zone.'

'The minute it's made public that I have a son he'll be a target for kidnappers the world over. But that's missing the point, which is that Toby is my son and deserves to be recognised as such. He deserves to be allowed to inherit my personal wealth.'

'What would you do if you were already married?' she challenged. 'Because you surely couldn't marry me then? Unless bigamy is legal on Agon?'

'We are not in that situation, so that's irrelevant. Let me put this in simple terms for you. You and I will marry as soon as we can. If you refuse you will be escorted—alone—off Agon and never allowed to return.'

'You wouldn't...' She shook her head, swallowing back her fury and distress as the full weight of his threat hit her like a brick.

His nostrils flared and he eased himself away from the door. 'Try me. If you refuse to marry me Toby will be raised on Agon without you. He will know the reason he's not recognised as a member of his own family and is unable to be my heir is because of his mother's selfishness.'

The room swam. 'Would you really stoop so low as to keep us apart and twist his mind against me?'

He raised a strong shoulder and sauntered to stand before her, where she still stood rooted to the spot beside the bed. 'Whatever I tell him would be nothing compared to the conclusions he would draw on his own. Now, do I have your agreement?'

She backed away lest she give in to her fingers' need to slap him. She wasn't being selfish. *She wasn't.* What Theseus demanded of her was unconscionable.

A thought raced through her, which she grasped and clung on to. 'You *can't* marry me—you have to marry a princess. Remember? You told me that yourself.'

'No, I have to marry someone with royal blood—which you have.'

'But my blood is so diluted it's weaker than supermarket own-brand blackcurrant squash!' She clung on to the thought desperately, too scared to let go of this last glimmer of hope. 'My family don't have titles or acres of land. There's not a lord or a viscount in sight!'

'It's enough to satisfy the constitution. It would be different if Helios was in my position—*he* is expected to marry a princess, or someone of equal heritage. Now, for the last time, do I have your agreement?'

With her stomach curdling and her skin feeling so tight she could feel her bones pushing through the flesh, Jo blinked frantically to keep her focus, to maintain some measure of control.

There was no way out. No other avenue to take. Theseus had thought of everything and had an answer to everything.

But she wouldn't let him have it all his own way.

'Seeing as I have no choice, I'll marry you. But only for long enough to satisfy whatever draconian law your ridiculous island insists on before we can divorce.'

He shook his head, his mouth twisting into a rueful grimace. 'It is illegal for members of the Agon royal family to divorce.'

'That's not possible.' Coldness like nothing she'd experienced before crept through her bones.

'The constitution—'

But she cut him off before he could say another word. All the fear and anger that had been brewing within her converged to the point of explosion and she launched herself at him, pushing him onto the bed, her fists striking his chest.

'Your constitution can take a running jump, for all I care, and so can you,' she raged. 'I'm *not* giving up my entire life for you.'

Theseus had her hands pinned and her body trapped beneath him before she could take another breath.

'You're not sacrificing your life for me but for Toby,' he snarled, his breath hot on her face.

She could sense his fury, matching hers in its strength. Her blood was pumping so fast it heated her veins to boiling point.

She bucked beneath him, kicking her legs out wildly. 'Toby is the happiest child in the world! I've sacrificed *everything* to love and care for him and now you want me to throw our lives away just so you can lay claim to him, as if he's some possession and not a flesh and blood boy.'

'He's a prince of Agon and he deserves the protection and everything else that comes with the title.'

Theseus trapped her kicking legs with a thigh. *Theos*, the shy wallflower he'd met in Illya had more fight in her than he'd ever imagined. Even though his emotions were as intense as he'd ever known them, his body could not help but react to her.

'If *you're* a reflection of the way a prince of Agon turns out then I'd much rather he stays a commoner,' she spat back.

He gazed down at her, fully pinned beneath him, and took in the fire shooting at him from her beautiful eyes, the heightened colour of her cheeks.

'No amount of insults will change anything,' he said roughly. 'Accept it, *agapi mou*. You and I are going to marry.'

After all the lies she'd told, she should repulse him. Yet he was far from being repelled.

He'd spent a whole week with this woman's scent playing to his senses like an orchestra. A whole week fighting his fantasies, fighting his baser instincts.

Now, with her hair fanned out on the sheets like an autumnal cloud, it was like gazing down at the *Venus de Milo*. And as he stared the fire blazing from her eyes suddenly burned in a wholly different manner, her look turning from hate to confusion to desire.

She stilled, her body's only movement her heaving chest.

He *ached* for her.

They were going to marry. There was nothing to stop them acting on their desires. There was no need to fight any longer.

He brought his mouth down at the same moment she

raised her face to his, bringing them together in a mesh of lips and tongues and merging breath.

Their kisses were hard, almost cruel, all pleasure and pain at once. Everything rushed out of him, leaving behind only the desire that had held him in its tightening grip since she'd walked into the palace.

He had no recollection of releasing her hands, but a groan ripped through him when her fingers found his scalp and dug into it, her nails grazing through his hair and scratching down his neck.

There was no slow burn. Every inch of flesh she touched became scorched, and his hunger for her accelerated in a rush of blood that burned. *Everything* burned.

He pulled away to stare at her, taking in the dilation of her pupils and the heightened colour of her cheeks.

He wanted to drown in her.

Touching her, holding her... Whatever deceptions there had been between them, this hunger couldn't be faked.

He straddled her thighs and pulled his shirt over his head, too impatient to bother with the buttons. No sooner had he thrown it to the floor than her hands were flat on his chest, spreading all over him, her touch penetrating through to his veins.

It had been like this on Illya; his desire for her so instantaneous and combustible that one touch had blinded him to everything else. It had turned from nothing to the deepest desire he had ever known.

And that had been nothing compared to the way he felt at this moment.

Had he been naked he would already be buried deep inside her.

From the darkness in Jo's eyes, her short ragged breaths, the way her hands roamed his chest as if she *needed* to touch him, he could tell this desire was just as flammable for her too.

Wordlessly she lifted herself, enough for him to bunch her T-shirt up to her waist and slide it off, just as he'd done once before. As he pulled it free her russet hair fell down with the motion, sprawling over her naked shoulders and spilling out over the breasts he'd spent the past week wishing he could remember with the same clarity he remembered everything else. They were better than anything his imagination could have conjured, the nipples a dark, tempting pink.

She lay down, her smouldering eyes never leaving his face. He swooped in to kiss her again, needing to feel the sweetness of her lips merging with his own. Her arms wrapped tightly around him and her legs bucked, this time not to throw him off but in an attempt to part and wrap around him.

He shifted so the weight of his thighs was no longer trapping her and propped himself up on an elbow to gaze at her.

He couldn't stop himself from staring at her.

He'd never known his heart to beat so hard or so fast.

He ran a hand over the buttery skin of her thigh, which had risen to jut against him, and traced his fingers up over her soft stomach. He spread his hands to cover her breasts, a huge jolt of need coursing through him as he felt the joyous weight of them.

Save for her knickers, she was naked. Her curvaceous figure was every bit as enticing and womanly as the last time he'd lain with her, exuding a soft ripeness begging to be touched and tasted.

Bending his head, he caught a taut nipple in his mouth, felt more jolts bursting through him when he tasted her for himself.

Massaging her with his mouth and fingers, he used his free hand to unbuckle his belt and work off his trousers and underwear. The relief at being released from the confines of their material was immense. All that lay between them now was the cotton of her underwear.

She might not be clad in expensive silky lingerie, but he had never seen a more tempting, beautiful sight.

Joanne…a glorious *Venus de Milo* that only he knew about…

'Have there been many others?' He hauled himself up, the words falling from his tongue too quickly for him to stop them.

Her throat moved, hate suddenly flashing in her eyes. 'You have no right to ask.'

'You're going to be my wife. I have every right.' The thought of another man's eyes seeing her like this, another man's hands touching her…

'And I have every right not to answer.'

Her hand brushed down his stomach to his freed erection, encircling it. Her breaths deepened.

Theseus closed his eyes and counted to three. All thoughts of her with other men disappeared as he gritted his teeth at the delight of her gentle touch. The pressure was light—too light. Torturously light.

He swooped down to claim her mouth for his own. Whatever men there might have been in the intervening years, he would drive them from her mind. He would mark her. He would make her understand with more than words that from this moment on she would be his and only his.

For the rest of her life.

In a swarm of kisses and touches he explored her, trailing his lips over her breasts and stomach, finding a strawberry birthmark as he tugged her underwear down and threw it onto the heap of clothes piled on the floor beside them, discovering a small mole at the top of her thigh… It was all for him. All for his eyes only.

Jo thrashed beneath him, her own hands reaching out and grasping, her nails digging into his back, her hips bucking upwards, inviting his possession. She gasped and cried out when he dipped his head between her legs.

He shuddered with need.

Five years without a woman...

Was it any wonder he felt so desperately on the edge?

But he had felt like this before. Once. With Jo...

He drove the thought from his mind.

He pressed his tongue against her.

Theos, she tasted divine.

She pushed her pelvis into him, her back arching. Her little moans of pleasure were like music to his ears and he increased the friction just a little, enough so that when she grabbed at his head she caught his hair in her hands and clasped it tightly. She was on the brink.

But he didn't want her to come yet. Not this time. He wanted to read her eyes as she cried out with the pleasure of him being inside her. Selfishly, he wanted it all, and he wanted it now, before the craven need in him burst.

Trailing his tongue all the way back up her body, helpless to resist nuzzling into her gorgeous breasts once more, he lay between her parted legs and kissed her, possessing her with his mouth before guiding his erection to the heart of her and sliding into the tight, welcoming heat.

She cried out and stiffened.

'Okay?' he asked, only just able to get the word out.

Her answer was to nip at his cheek with her teeth and wrap her legs around him.

He thrust as deep as he could go, the sensations spreading through him at being fully sheathed inside her making him groan out loud.

Forget savouring the moment—he was long past that point. If he'd ever been there. All he wanted was to lose himself in the incredible feelings rushing through him, to listen to the wanton moans escaping her delicious mouth, and to find the release clamouring inside him.

As he pushed feverishly into her all he knew was that she must have some magical quality he reacted to. That she cast a spell that turned his body into a slave for pleasure.

Her response was as fevered as his own, her arms clasping him so tightly that he lay fully locked inside her, on her, fused with her into one being. Nothing mattered but this heady hunger that had to be satisfied or else they would both fall off the precipice.

Then she broke away from his kisses, pressing her cheek tightly to his own, and her moans deepened as her nails dug painfully—but oh, so pleasurably—into his back. He felt her climax swell within her, thickening around him and then pulling him into the headiness of release. Of surrender.

CHAPTER EIGHT

Jo's eyes flew open. Instant wakefulness.

The room was dusky, the early-morning sun making its first peeks through the heavy drapes. The only sound to be heard was the deep, heavy breathing of Theseus in sleep.

She'd awoken to the same sounds on Illya. To the same weight of his arm slung around her waist, the same body pressed into her back, encircling her almost protectively.

It had been nothing but an illusion. However protectively he'd behaved in his sleep he'd sailed away the next morning and never given her another thought...

Everything came back in a flood.

Theseus learning about Toby. His demands of marriage. Making love.

Oh, Lord, what had possessed her?

Where was her pride? Her self-control?

The only crumb of comfort she could take was that whatever mad fever she'd fallen into, Theseus had fallen into it as well.

Flames licked her cheeks as she remembered how willingly she had given herself to him. His caresses and kisses had lit the touch-paper to her desperate, emotion-ridden body.

A tear trickled down her cheek and landed on her pillow. Blinking furiously, she tried her hardest to stop any more from forming but they fell through her lashes, soaking the fabric.

Helpless to stop them, she let the tears fall, wishing with

all her heart that she could turn the clock back a week and tell him about Toby the minute they'd been alone in his office for the first time. The outcome wouldn't be any different—Theseus would still be insisting on marriage, of that she was certain—but *they* would be different. This loathing wouldn't be there.

Making love wouldn't have felt like waging war with their bodies.

She'd never imagined sex could be like that—angry, yet tender, with shining highlights of bliss that had taken her to a place she'd never known existed.

It had been beautiful.

But how could she do it? How could she spend her life with a man who despised her?

Lust was transient. When desire was spent, and without a deeper bond to glue them together, hate and resentment would fill the space, and there was already enough loathing between them to fill a room.

Her parents had once lusted after each other. Her brother Jonathan had been the result of their passion and the reason they had been forced to marry. A decade later, when Jo had been born, their marriage had deteriorated into a union as cold and barren as Siberia. It was a surprise they'd thawed enough to make *her*.

For Jo, having a father who spent his days in an alcoholic stupor and a mother who treated flea-ridden hedgehogs with more compassion than she extended to her husband or daughter had been normal.

As she'd grown up and seen how other families interacted she'd slowly realised it *wasn't* normal.

And so she'd vowed never to be like them, to never treat her husband or any children she might have that way.

Her very worst nightmare was being trapped in a cold, loveless marriage like her parents.

She choked in a breath.

All her dreams were over. The nightmare had come to life.

She would never find love. And love would never find her.

Theseus would never love her. All he wanted was their son. She was the unwanted appendage that came with Toby.

She was trapped.

With fresh tears falling, she shuffled out from under Theseus's arm and rooted around until she found her T-shirt, slipped it back on and stole into the bathroom. She blew her nose, trying desperately to get a grip on herself.

She couldn't fall to pieces. All she could do was try and salvage something from this mess. If she could survive pregnancy and motherhood alone, she could survive anything.

When she stepped back into the bedroom her eyes were drawn straight to him. The dusky light solidified his sleeping form. A lock of black hair had fallen over his cheek. The lines that had etched his face since their return from the club had been smoothed away.

Her heart stuck in her throat. He looked so peaceful.

Hate was an alien emotion to her. Even throughout all the years of her mother's cold indifference she'd never hated her. Neither had she hated her father for his weakness and failure to stand up for her, nor hated her brother for being treated as if he mattered.

She didn't want to hate Theseus. He was the father of her son.

She'd loved him once. To hate him would be to turn all those memories into dust.

As she climbed back into bed, trying hard to keep her movements smooth so as not to wake him, she realised his breathing had quietened.

Pinching the bridge of her nose to stop another batch of tears from falling, she slid under the covers and held herself tightly.

After long minutes of silence, during which she became certain that he was as awake as she was, the words playing in her head finally came out. 'I want to tell you the story of a young woman who graduated from university with her virginity intact.'

She spoke quietly, keeping her eyes trained on the ceiling. She could feel his gaze upon her. If she said it as if she were talking about someone else, maybe she could tell it all without any more tears.

'That young woman had spent her life as the butt of her schoolmates' jokes—mostly on account of the size of her actual butt.'

She laughed quietly, but there was nothing funny about the memory. Jo's only truly happy memories were of that magical time on Illya and the birth of her son.

'She thought university would be different but it wasn't. She made a couple of good friends, but socially she was never accepted. She graduated with her virginity because the only men who had wanted to sleep with her had only tried it on for a bet.'

Theseus jerked, as if recoiling, but she didn't look at him. She had to stay dispassionate or she would fall to pieces, and that was the last thing she wanted. Theseus had enough power over her as it was.

'She had her life mapped out. She was finally leaving the home she'd never felt wanted in and moving to London with her friends. She even had a job lined up. And before she moved into her new life she took her first trip abroad, as a goodbye to her old life. There she met a man—a Greek engineer.'

She laughed again at her naivety.

'One night some men came into the bar and started harassing her. Her Greek crush stepped in and… Well, you know the rest.'

She swallowed and finally turned onto her side to face him. His expression in the half-light was unreadable.

'You were good to me like no one had ever been before. You *included* me. You were *nice* to me. And do you remember when you turned up at my chalet? You were a mess.'

She caught the briefest of flickers in his eyes.

'I'd never been in love before,' she whispered, staring intently at him.

His face was inches from her own, close enough for her to feel the warmth of his breath.

'I hero-worshipped you like you were a sun-kissed idol. And you needed me that night. You made me feel...*necessary*. When you kissed me...it was like a dream. You *wanted* me. That was the best moment of my life. So my lie about being on the pill came out without any thought or regard for the consequences. I didn't want that moment to end so I was stupid and reckless, and I deserve your contempt. I hate that I lied to you, and I will live with it on my conscience for the rest of my life. But even if you never believe anything else, please believe that I was going to tell you about our son and that I'm more sorry than I can ever say.'

He was silent for a long time before he hoisted himself onto an elbow to stare down at her. His eyes were penetrating, as if he were trying to read her.

Jo held her breath as she waited for him to speak.

Instead of saying anything, he turned away and threw off the covers, then swung his legs over to sit on the edge of the bed.

'That night on Illya, I behaved very badly towards you,' he said, his back to her.

'No...'

'I knew you had feelings for me. I took advantage of that.' Now he turned his head. His jaw clenched and he looked at her with hard eyes. 'But those feelings you once had for me...keep them locked away. Never let them return. You know what I expect from a marriage and there will be no place in ours for love. You need to get that in your head *now*.'

He rubbed his palm over his face, then slid his underwear on.

'Any romantic notions you may have—kill them. I will try to be a good husband to you but I will never love you. Protect your heart. Because if you don't it will not only be you who suffers for it but our son.'

She stared at him, the heart he wanted her to protect against him beating so hard that pain shuddered against her ribcage.

He pulled his trousers on, slung his shirt over his shoulder and faced her.

'My parents' marriage was a disaster. If they hadn't died so young they would have likely killed each other anyway. She loved him too much to share him; he loved himself too much and was too spoiled and pampered to deny himself anything he wanted—and that included other women. He would hit my mother for questioning his infidelities and yet, still she loved him. It was a lethal combination and not the kind of marriage I would wish on anyone. I will not have our son exposed to the horrors I witnessed. I will not have him used as a pawn in a game between two adults who should know better.'

He reached the door to the secret passage which led to his apartment and looked at her one last time.

'Just think—you will be a princess, *agapi mou*. That must go some way to mitigating the restrictions you will now face.'

'Like being a prince has in any way mitigated the restrictions *you* live with?' she countered pointedly, a tremor in her voice.

Eyes narrowed, he slowly inclined his head. 'I learned,

and you will learn too—fighting destiny is pointless. Embrace your new life. It's the only way to survive it.'

Knowing there was no chance of falling back to sleep, Theseus took a long shower, hoping the steaming water would do something to soothe the darkness that had dragged him under after his dawn-lit talk with Jo.

He hoped she'd take his warnings to heart.

She was a dreamer like his mother. He'd seen it in her eyes when he'd told her not to fall in love with him and bluntly spelt out that he would never love her.

He had done it the way a cruel child might pick the wings off an injured fly. Except he'd taken no enjoyment in destroying her dreams.

Yes, she'd told him a lie, but listening to her explain how it had been for her had released more memories and he'd found himself feeling sickened. At himself.

He'd *known* she'd had feelings for him and had taken advantage of that because he hadn't been able to cope with his grief alone. He had turned to the one person on the island he'd instinctively known would be able to give him comfort.

But he couldn't forgive her for not telling him of his son sooner. They'd spent a week working closely together and all that time she'd been keeping something life-changing from him. No, that was a deception he would struggle ever to forgive.

Yet he would try. The only way they were going to endure spending the rest of their lives together would be through mutual respect. He needed to find a way to let the anger go, otherwise his bitterness towards her would nullify any respect.

At least making love to her and those few hours of snatched sleep had driven out much of the anger, allowing him to look at the situation with a fresh perspective.

He laughed bitterly. A fresh perspective? In less than

twelve hours his whole life had changed. He'd learned he was a father. And soon—very soon—he would be a husband: a role he'd known was looming but which he had hoped to avoid a little longer…at least until after Helios had married Princess Catalina.

After years of silent dread at the thought of marrying and starting a family it turned out he had a ready-made one. He would laugh at the irony, but his humour had dried up over the past twenty-four hours.

After drying himself and dressing, he splashed cologne on his face and caught sight of his reflection in the mirror. He looked exactly like a man who had managed only two hours' sleep.

He was surprised he'd managed even those. So many thoughts in his head had clamoured for attention, the loudest of which was trying to ensure the news of his son was kept secret for another two weeks. He had a good body of personal staff in his employ, whom he trusted implicitly, but, short of keeping Jo and Toby locked up there was nothing he could do to remove the danger that someone would see them and put two and two together.

God alone knew how his grandfather would react. Would the fact that his most wayward grandson had fathered a child out of wedlock and intended to marry a woman with minimal royal blood be another disappointment to add to the long list?

He closed his eyes, his brain burning as he recalled his grandfather's words when Theseus had finally arrived back on Agon.

He'd gone straight to his grandmother's room, knowing this would be his last goodbye. His grandfather had been alone with her, holding her hand.

He'd looked at him with eyes swimming with tears. 'You're too late.'

Too late?

He'd inched closer to the bed and, his heart in his mouth, had seen the essence which made life had gone.

He'd staggered back, reeling, while his grandfather had pulled himself to his feet and faced him. The King had aged a decade since he'd last seen him.

'How could you not be here for her? She asked for you—many times—but you let her down again. And this time right at the moment she needed you the most. You disappointed her. I'm ashamed to call you my blood.'

It had been five years and still the words were as fresh to Theseus's ears as they'd been back then.

He *wanted* them fresh.

He *needed* to remember how low he'd felt and how sickened he'd been with himself. It was what kept him focused when the walls of the palace threatened to close in on him and the urge in his heart for freedom beat too hard.

A quiet knock on the door that connected his apartment with Jo's brought him out of his painful reverie.

Opening it, he found her standing there, shielding her stomach with her laptop, her eyes wary.

She'd donned a pair of black jeans and a pale blue sweater that hugged her generous curves. Her hair was damp.

'I thought you'd like to be there when I call Toby,' she said, making no move to enter the room.

His pulse raced and a lump formed in his throat.

'I've spoken to my brother and told him what's going on,' she added, pulling a wry face. 'They're expecting me to connect in the next five minutes so I can prepare Toby.'

A blast of dread shot through him.

Theseus had no experience whatsoever with children. How was he supposed to talk to his son? He didn't know the language of four-year-olds.

'I think it's best if you stay off-camera.' She looked unashamedly around his bedroom. 'Let me talk to him.'

He gave a curt nod and led her through to the living area.

'How did your brother take the news?' he asked.

'He was shocked. I don't think any of my family ever expected me to find you.' She shook her head, then flashed him a sly grin. 'I should warn you he's liable to punch you in the face for lying about your identity.'

'He's protective of you?'

'He discovered his protective gene when I had Toby.'

So at least there was one member of her family who acted as they should towards her. In Theseus's world blood looked out for blood, even if someone was in the process of spilling another's blood. That had been what had made his desertion and subsequent failure to be there during his grandmother's final hours so unforgivable.

'What about when you were growing up?' he asked, determined to keep his mind focused and far away from his own past.

'I was the nuisance kid sister, ten years younger than him. He had zero interest in me.'

'There's *ten years* between you?' Theseus thought of the tiny age gaps between him and his brothers, who had all been born in quick succession. It had led to much fighting and sibling rivalry, but it had also given them ready-made playmates—something he felt was an important aspect of a child's life, especially for children unable to form other friendships in their homeland.

'I was an accident,' she said matter-of-factly.

'Talos was a happy accident too,' he mused. 'My parents bred their heir and their spare and then two years later he came along.'

Her eyes flashed with something dark, but her lips moved into a smile. 'I don't think my mother has ever regarded me as a happy accident.'

'Surely you don't mean that?' But then he recalled how

she'd described her parents' marriage and her mother's coldness and knew that she did mean it.

'She never wanted more children. She especially didn't want a girl.'

She must have felt his shock, for she raised a shoulder in a half-shrug.

'My mother is one of four girls. Her sisters are all very girly, which she's very contemptuous of. She has no time for what she considers "frills and fancy". I don't think she actually sees herself as a woman.'

'How does she treat you?'

'My mother is difficult—my relationship with her even more so. Maybe she would have treated me differently if I'd been a boy. Who knows? Still, that's all ancient history. Let's concentrate on Toby and not on my mother.'

Jo took a long, steadying breath and brought her son's face to the front of her mind as a reminder to stay calm. Talking of her mother's contempt towards her did nothing to induce serenity.

Now that she had semi-recovered from the distress she'd felt at Theseus's reaction last night she could appreciate the charms of his apartment, which was a shop of wonders.

While his offices were functional spaces, created for maximum efficiency, his private rooms were a masculine yet homely delight. The huge living space with its high ceilings had dark wood flooring and enormous arched windows, the walls filled with vibrant paintings, ceramics and wooden carvings that had a strong South American vibe— no doubt objects collected on his travels. She remembered him telling her he'd scaled the highest peaks of the Andes and remembered how impressed she'd been. *She* had trouble scaling an anthill.

She placed her laptop on the bureau where only hours before she had been forced into signing the forms which recognised Toby as Theseus's son.

For all his fury towards her, not once had he questioned Toby's paternity. He hadn't even asked to see a photograph as evidence. But then, he'd been too busy laying down the law over his rights as a father to bother with anything so trivial as what his son actually looked like.

Stop it, she chided herself. *You can't judge him for his reaction. You don't walk in his shoes. You knew it wouldn't be easy.*

Whatever Theseus might think of her—and she knew it would be a long time before he forgave her—it seemed not to have crossed his mind that someone else might be the father, and from that she took comfort.

It was the only comfort she *could* take.

She had no idea what the future held, and that terrified her.

How could she keep her heart away from him when they would be sharing a bed and a life together? Making love…

His words of warning against loving him had come at the right time. She'd loved him once. Desperately. She couldn't take that pain again. Especially not now, when he'd categorically told her he would never love her.

She would build on the strength she had gathered over these past few years and make her heart as impenetrable to love as his.

Even if it *did* mean saying goodbye to all her dreams.

Most little girls dreamed of being princesses, but for her it had never been about that. All she'd wanted was someone to love her for who she was.

Had that really been such a big thing to want?

Shaking off the melancholy, she opened her laptop and turned it on. She took a seat and adjusted the screen.

'Do you know what you're going to say?' he asked, standing behind her, close enough for her to smell his freshly showered scent and that gorgeous cologne she could never get enough of.

She jerked her head in a nod and did a test run of the camera. 'You need to stand to my left a bit more to keep out of shot.'

His heart thumping erratically, the palms of his hands damp, Theseus watched as the call rang out from the computer.

It connected almost immediately. The screen went blue, and then suddenly a little face appeared.

'I'm eating my breakfast!' the face said, in a high, chirpy voice.

'Good morning to you too!' Jo laughed.

The face grinned and laughed as a pudgy hand pushed away a lock of black hair that had fallen over his eyes.

Theseus couldn't move. His body was frozen as he gazed at the happy little boy dressed in cartoon pyjamas.

Jo had been right.

No one looking at this child could ever doubt he was a Kalliakis. It was like looking at a living version of his own childhood photographs.

CHAPTER NINE

'I'VE DRAWN YOU another picture,' the boy—Toby—his son—was saying. 'I'll go and get it.'

The screen emptied, then seconds later he reappeared, waving a piece of paper.

'Keep still so I can see it,' Jo chided lightly.

Toby pressed the paper right to the screen.

'Wow, that's an *amazing* dinosaur,' she said.

The picture was dropped and Toby was back. 'Silly Mummy—is not a 'saur,' he said crossly. 'Is a *plane*.'

Theseus covered his mouth to stop the sudden burst of laughter that wanted to escape.

'It's good that you've drawn an aeroplane,' Jo said, clearly holding back her own amusement, 'because guess what?'

'What?'

'*You're* going on an aeroplane.'

'Wow! Am I? When?'

'Today! Two nice men are coming to collect you and you're going to get on an aeroplane with them and come and see Mummy on Agon.'

'What—now? Right now?'

'Lunchtime.'

Toby's eyebrows drew in. Theseus almost laughed again. It was the same face Talos pulled when he was unamused about something.

'Aunty Cathy is making meatballs for lunch,' he said,

as if missing that would be the biggest disappointment of his short life.

'I'm sure they'll let you eat the meatballs before you leave.'

That cheered him up. 'Can I bring my cars?'

'Of course you can.'

'And can I meet the King?'

Finally her voice faltered. 'Let's get you here first, and then we can see about meeting the King.'

'Can I meet your Prince?'

The knuckles of her fists whitened. 'Yes, sweet pea, you can definitely meet the Prince.'

'Have you got me a present yet?'

'Enough with the questions! Finish your breakfast and then go and help Aunty Cathy pack.'

The cute, mischievous face pressed right against the screen, a pair of lips kissed the monitor with a slapping noise and then the screen went blank.

Jo's shoulders rose in a laugh, then she fell quiet.

'*Have* you got him a present?' Theseus asked, breaking the heavy silence that had come over the room.

She shook her head, keeping her gaze fixed on the computer screen. 'I was going to get him something from the museum gift shop when I'd finished the biography.'

Suddenly she seemed to crumple before him, her head sinking into her hands.

'God, what are we going to do about the biography?'

With all that had been going on the biography had completely slipped from his mind.

Theos. Right then all he could see was that little face, so like his own—the child he had helped create.

So many emotions were driving through him, filling him so completely that he felt as if his heart might explode out of his chest.

She staggered to her feet. 'I need to get back to work.'

Her face was white. He could see how much keeping her composure in front of their son had cost her.

'Now?'

'Yes. Now. I need to do something.' Her hands had balled back into fists. 'We're turning his life upside down, ripping him away from everything and everyone he knows—'

'No,' he cut in. 'You can't think of it like that. We're building him a new, *better* life.'

'I *am* trying to think of it like that. I'm trying not to be selfish and not to think of the personal cost. I'm trying not to think that I'm throwing away my future happiness just so you can secure your heir when your heir is happy exactly as he is!'

The colour on her face had risen to match the raising of her voice.

'He will be happy *here*,' he said with authority. He would ensure it. Whatever it took.

But would she…?

'We will work together to make him happy,' he added in a softer tone.

She breathed heavily, then unfurled her fists and gave a long sigh. She nodded almost absently.

He watched her closely to see if she had herself under control.

'The book needs to be finished. Are you sure you can carry on with it?'

Her face twitched and she looked away, biting into her lip. Then she seemed to shake herself and met his gaze. 'Your grandfather is our son's great-grandfather. He is a remarkable man and deserves to have his story told. I will do it for him.'

Those blue-grey eyes held his, and understanding flew between them.

Jo understood.

'But *you'll* need to do the bulk of the childcare when

Toby gets here,' she added, after a beat in which the tension between them had grown thick enough to swim through.

'I know nothing about childcare.'

She laughed, but there was no humour in the sound. 'You're the one insisting on being an instant father. I'll work until he arrives—the distraction will be good for me—but when he gets here… Trust me, there is nothing like an energetic four-year-old to put the brakes on whatever you're supposed to be doing.'

'How much longer do you think you'll need to get it finished?'

'I can make the deadline, but I will need help with Toby for the next few days.'

'I have excellent staff at my home who will happily entertain a child.' He began to think who amongst them would be best placed for the job.

Jo's eyes hardened, then sent him a look he was already starting to recognise—it was the mother tiger preparing to appear.

'You are not turning his life upside down only to palm him off on *staff*,' she said steadily. 'Being a father requires a lot more than marrying the child's mother, giving him a title and writing him into your will.'

His temperature rose at her implied rebuke, but he spoke coolly. 'I know exactly what being a father entails, but it is impossible for me to put all my work and duties to one side without prior planning.'

'Don't lie to me.' Her eyes flashed a warning. 'There have been enough lies between us. Now we draw a line in the sand and tell no more. From now on we speak only the truth. You want Toby here and in your life, so it's up to you to forge a relationship with him. You're the adult, so it must come from you. He's a sociable, gregarious boy and I know that the second he learns you're his father he'll be stuck to your side like glue.'

That was what scared him.

Theseus remembered being a small boy and wanting nothing more than his father's attention. But his father's attention had been wrapped up entirely in his eldest son and heir, Helios. As the spare, Theseus had never been deemed worthy of his father's time, had always been left trailing in Helios's wake.

The favouritism had been blatant, and with only a year between them Theseus had felt the rift deeply. His mother had tried to make up for it, lavishing him with love, but it hadn't been enough. It had been his father's respect and love he had so desired.

What if Toby found him lacking? What if he was as great a disappointment as a father as he had been as a son and a grandson?

He needed time.

His overriding priority was to get his son safely to the island and under his protection. Anything after that…

'I will make the necessary arrangements after I have spoken to Helios,' he said, ignoring her swift intake of breath. 'There is much to arrange, *agapi mou*,' he continued smoothly. 'A prince's wedding on this island is usually a state affair, but I am not prepared to wait for the months of planning that will take. I am going to tell Helios of our plans—I want my ring on your finger as soon as it can be arranged.'

'I thought you were going to keep things a secret until after the Gala?' This time there was no hiding her bitterness. He knew he was railroading her into this marriage, but he also knew it was the best course of action for all of them—especially for Toby.

'Only from my grandfather. Since we've known of his illness Helios has been running things in preparation for when…' He shook his head. She knew when. 'Helios's staff can work with mine to get the preparations up and running.'

'You don't hang around, do you?'

'Not when it comes to important matters, no.'

She rubbed her eyes, then sighed. 'Will Helios want to meet me?'

'For sure. But don't worry about it—he's a good guy.'

'And what about Talos? Will you tell him too?'

'If I can get him to myself for more than a minute. He's working closely with the Gala's solo violinist, and if the rumours are to be believed—which they probably are, as palace gossip here is generally reliable—she's playing more than just her violin for him.'

Jo gave a bark of surprised laughter at his innuendo.

He grinned as the sound lightened his heart. That was better. Seeing Jo laugh was a whole lot better than seeing her cry.

He might not be anywhere near a place of forgiveness, but he was no sadist.

He swallowed down the notion that seeing Jo cry felt like a knife being stabbed in his heart.

The sun had long gone down over Theseus's Mediterranean beachside villa when the driver pulled to a stop outside. Toby had fallen asleep in the car, curled up in her arms. According to Nikos he'd spent the entire flight talking. No wonder he was so exhausted.

But, other than being worn out with all the travel and excitement of the day, Toby had been his usual happy self and overjoyed to be with his mummy.

The butler, a man who looked as if he should be surfing in Hawaii rather than running a prince's household, was there to greet them. Nikos took Toby's suitcase inside, leaving Jo, at her insistence, to carry Toby inside.

She'd packed her clothes and then worked on the biography until the call had come through that the plane was circling above the island. Dimitris had accompanied her to the airport. She'd had no idea where Theseus was; she hadn't seen him since the morning.

Her blood had boiled. She had been totally unable to believe that the man who was turning three lives inside out was failing to meet his own son.

Now, as she followed the butler inside, treading over the cool marble tiles, she wondered if all her work stuff had been brought over as Dimitris had promised. She hoped they'd remembered to bring her suitcase. There were so many things to think of her head was full enough to overspill.

Although not as grand as the palace—how could *any* dwelling possibly compare with that?—Theseus's villa had an eclectic majesty all of its own. The façade a dusky yellow, the interiors were wide and spacious; filled with more of the South American vibe she'd felt in his palace apartment. Bold colours, stunning canvases and statuettes—homely, yet rich. A place she felt immediately at ease in.

It was the kind of vibe she'd always imagined Theo's home would have.

Shivers coiled up her spine.

For all of Theseus's talk that Theo didn't exist, this house proved that he did.

She and Toby had been given rooms opposite each other on the second floor. Toby's was large and airy, with a double bed. His sleepy eyes widened to see it.

'Is that mine?' he asked, yawning.

'While we're here, yes.' Placing him on the bed, she rooted through his suitcase until she found a pair of pyjamas.

'How long are we staying for, Mummy?'

What could she say? He'd only just arrived. Did she have to tell him so soon that their stay here would be for ever and that the life he knew and loved was gone?

She was saved from having to answer by a soft tap on the door. A young woman, no older than twenty, stood at the doorway almost bouncing with excitement. She introduced herself as her maid, Elektra.

'My maid?' Jo asked, puzzled.

'Yes, *despinis*. I am excited to meet you and your son.'

Elektra stepped into the room. When she looked at Toby her eyes widened. 'He has—'

'I need to get Toby settled down for the night,' Jo interrupted, certain the maid was about to make a reference to Toby's likeness to Theseus. 'If you give me ten minutes, then you can show me what's what.'

Understanding flashed in Elektra's eyes. 'I'll unpack your cases. Nice to meet you, Toby.'

When she was alone with her son, Jo got him washed, teeth brushed and into his pyjamas. He was already falling asleep when she kissed him goodnight and slipped from his room, going across the corridor into her own.

She stepped inside on weary feet, but still had enough energy to sigh with pleasure at the room's graceful simplicity and creamy palette. Looking at the four-poster bed, with its inviting plump pillows, she knew she at least had a sanctuary that was all her own. This room was entirely feminine.

Her chest squeezed and she shut her eyes tight, fighting back a sudden batch of tears.

Shouldn't she be happy? She was going to be a princess! Her son would never want for anything ever again. There would be no more juggling money or eking out her salary, no more shame at sending Toby to preschool with trousers an inch too short. As Theseus's son he would have the best of everything, from clothing to education. And so would she, as his wife.

She would never have to struggle again.

She should be as happy as one of her mother's pampered animals.

So why did she feel so heartsick?

* * *

The villa sat in silence when Nikos dropped Theseus off outside the main door.

Philippe, his young, energetic butler, greeted him. After exchanging a few words about the two new members of the household, Theseus dismissed him for the night.

At the palace there were always staff members on shift. If he wanted a three-course meal at three o'clock in the morning, a three-course meal would appear. Always somewhere there would be activity.

Here, in his personal domain, away from stuffy protocol, he liked a more relaxed, informal atmosphere. If he wanted a three-course meal at three o'clock in the morning he would damn well make it himself. Not that he could cook anything other than cheese on toast—a hangover from his English boarding school days and still his favourite evening snack.

Tonight he was too tired to eat.

Dragging himself up the stairs on legs that felt as if they had weights in them, he reached the room his son slept in. He stood at the partly open door for an age before stepping inside.

A night light in the shape of a train had been placed by the bed, giving the room a soft, warm glow. On the bed itself he could see nothing but a tiny bundle, swamped by the outsized proportions of the sheets, fast asleep.

He trod forward silently and reached Toby's side. All that was visible of him in the pile of sheets was a shock of black hair. He stood there for a long time, doing nothing but watching the little bundle's frame rise and fall.

He waited for a feeling of triumph to hit him.

His son was here, sleeping in his home, safe under his protection. But there was no triumph he could discern in the assortment of emotions raging through him, just a swelling of his chest and a tightness in his gut.

He went to lean over and kiss him but stopped. If he woke him it would scare him. In his son's eyes Theseus was a stranger.

Jo's bedroom door opposite was also ajar. A light, fruity scent pervaded the air. He went in and stuck his head around the open en-suite bathroom door.

Jo lay in the sunken bath, her russet hair piled on top of her head, her eyes shut.

She must have sensed his presence for she turned her head, jolted, and sat up quickly, sloshing water everywhere. She folded her arms to cover her breasts and glared at him.

'Sorry—I didn't mean to scare you,' he said, his mood lifting. After feeling as if he could fall asleep standing up, he now felt a burst of energy zing through him at seeing her in all her delicious nakedness. Not that he could see much of her; the bath was filled with so many bubbles he suspected she'd poured in half the bottle of bubble bath.

'Have you never heard of knocking?' she asked crossly.

'The door was open,' he said with a shrug.

She lay down again, still keeping her arms across her breasts. She raised her left thigh and twisted slightly away from him, to keep her modesty. 'I kept the door open so I could hear if Toby woke up.'

He perched on the edge of the bath. 'Does he normally wake?'

'No, but he's been flown here from England to this strange place with hardly any warning—that's got to be unsettling.' Her accusatory glare dared him to contradict her.

'He's fast asleep now,' he pointed out reasonably. He studied her face, taking in the dark shadows under her eyes. 'You look as if you'll be fast asleep soon too.'

'I'm shattered.' Thus saying, she smothered a yawn, although still taking care to cover as much of her breasts as she could.

'It's been a long day,' he agreed, unable to tear his eyes

away from her. Every inch of her was perfect, from the autumn-leaf-coloured hair to the softly curved stomach and shapely legs. She was a treasure trove of womanly delights he was certain had not been shared by many others.

Her cheeks coloured under the weight of his stare. 'Did you speak to Helios?'

'Yes.'

'How did he react?' She looked as if she hoped his brother had put the brakes on their marriage.

'He was shocked.'

An understatement. Helios had looked as if he'd walked into a door. But after he'd got over the shock he'd given his full, enthusiastic backing. Thinking back, there had been something in his brother's manner which had made Theseus think Helios was relieved, but he couldn't for the life of him fathom why.

'He was also in agreement that we should keep it from our grandfather until after the Gala.'

Her eyes narrowed. '*It*? Do you mean *Toby*?'

'I mean the whole situation—Toby and our forthcoming marriage.'

He leaned forward and traced a thumb over her cheekbone. 'The date has been set for a fortnight after the Gala. We marry in four weeks.'

CHAPTER TEN

WITH TINGLES CREEPING along her skin at his touch, Jo swallowed. 'Four weeks? That soon?'

'Yes, *agapi mou*. Helios agrees the sooner the better.'

'But he has his own wedding to arrange. Shouldn't his take precedence?'

His thumb brushed over to dance around her ear. 'His will be a large state affair and will take months to arrange.' His voice thickened. 'Ours will be more intimate. There will have to be some pomp to it, as that is expected, but nothing like his.'

Jo closed her eyes, thinking her head might just spin off. Four weeks... *Four weeks?*

Who the hell could organise a royal wedding in four weeks? She knew he wanted to get his ring on her finger quickly, but this...

Her eyes flew open as she felt his fingertips trail down her neck to her chest, then dip lower to run gently along the top of her cleavage. He took hold of her arms, still stubbornly covering her breasts, and gently prised them apart, exposing her to him.

'You're beautiful,' he murmured. 'Don't hide yourself from me.'

She sucked in air, willing herself not to respond.

'You're going to be my wife,' he continued, a finger now encircling a nipple. 'And you might already have the cells of a new life growing within you,' he added, reminding her of their failure to use contraception the night before, something that hadn't yet been spoken of.

His hand flattened over her stomach and continued to move lower.

'Think of how much fun we can have while we make another spare for the throne.'

'What a crass thing to… *Ohhh*…' Her head fell back as he reached under the bubbles to rub a finger against her, the pleasure like salve on a wound.

She should tell him to stop. She should be outraged that he would behave so proprietorially, as if her body were his to do with as he liked…

But his touch felt so good, somehow driving out all the angst she'd been carrying. The gentle friction increased and sensation built inside her.

'You're getting wet,' she whispered, struggling to find her voice under this assault on her senses.

His eyes gleamed and dilated, and he increased the pressure a touch. 'So are you.'

His free hand cradled her head, pulling her up to meet his mouth and begin a fresh assault with his lips.

'You are remarkably responsive,' he murmured, moving his mouth across her cheek and burying his face in her neck, then moving down to taste her breast, all the while keeping the pressure of his hand firm.

It was as if he knew her body better than she did—as if he knew exactly what she needed—bringing her to a peak until the pleasure exploded out of her, making her clamp her thighs around his hand and cry out as she gripped his scalp and clung to him.

He kissed her again, riding the shudders rippling through her body, murmuring words that deepened the sensations, until she felt weak and depleted and utterly dazed.

Where had *that* come from?

How was it possible to go from nothing to total bliss in seconds?

Theseus brought her to life, made all the atoms that created her fuse together into a bright ball of ecstasy that stopped her thinking and left her only feeling.

He kissed her one more time. 'On your feet.'

Beyond caring that she was naked, Jo held his hand for support and stood, water and foamy bubbles dripping off her. Immediately she was enveloped in his arms and pressed against his hard chest, his fresh, deeply passionate kisses preventing her legs from falling from under her.

She knew Theseus was strong, but his lifting her out of the bath took away what little was left of her breath. When he stood her on her feet she gazed up at him in wonderment, her heart swelling as she took in the defined angles of his face and the dark, dizzying desire ringing from his eyes.

One touch and she melted like butter for him.

Was it possible that one touch and he melted for her too…?

His white shirt had become transparent with the soaking her wet body had just given it, leaving the dark hairs of his chest vivid, emphasising his deep, potent masculinity.

Theseus caught her look. 'Do you want to take it off?'

She didn't answer, simply flattened her hands over his pecs, delighting in the feel of him.

She worked on his buttons, tugging the shirt open and sliding the sleeves off his muscular arms, gazing greedily at his magnificent torso, the smooth olive skin, the dark hair…

'Damn, you are so sexy,' he muttered, breathing into her hair and pulling her close. His hands raced up and down her back, then moved lower to cup her bottom.

She believed him. She could sense it in the urgency of his words and the rapid beat of his heart reverberating in her ear.

And then she was back in his arms, with his hot mouth

devouring hers, pressing her backwards to the chair in the corner of the room.

Holding her tight, he sat her down, then sank to his knees before her, unfastening the buttons and zipper of his trousers.

'You have no idea what you do to me,' he growled, biting gently into her neck.

Emboldened, she cupped his chin and stared into his liquid eyes. 'It's nothing that you don't do to me.'

Their mouths connected again in a kiss that blew away the last of her coherence. All she could do was feel…and it all felt incredible, every touch scalding her, every kiss marking her. She was losing herself in him.

His arms tightened and pulled her to the edge of the chair, then he guided himself to her and pushed inside her with one long thrust.

She stilled in his arms, closing her eyes as she savoured the feel of him inside her, filling her. When she opened them again he was staring right at her, as if trying to peer into the innermost reaches of her mind.

Their lips came together in the lightest of touches. With his arm still around her, Theseus began to move. Hesitantly at first she moved with him, but soon the last of her inhibitions vanished and she found his rhythm, holding on to him as tightly as she could.

As the speed of his thrusts increased she clung to him, her lips still pressed to his, their breaths merging into one. Dark heat swirled and built between them, until the sensations he'd released in her such a short time ago spilled over again—yet somehow deeper and *fuller*—and she was crying out his name.

She managed to hold on to it, riding the climax until his hands gripped her and he thrust into her one final time.

When the shudders coursing through his great body finally subsided he enveloped her in his arms. With her face buried in his neck, his hands stroking her hair, the strong thud of his heart reverberating through him to her, the moment was as close to bliss as Jo had ever known.

She wanted to cry when he finally disentangled himself. She couldn't speak. She could hardly think.

What was he *doing* to her?

'You're cold,' he chided, his voice hoarse.

So she was. After the warmth of the bath and the heat of Theseus's body the chill felt particularly acute.

He pulled a large fluffy white towel from the heated towel rack and gently wrapped it around her.

It was such a touching gesture that her heart doubled over, aching with a need she knew could never be fulfilled no matter what beautiful things he did to her body.

'I need to get some sleep,' she muttered, no longer able to look at him.

'We both do,' he agreed. 'But first I need a shower. I'll join you in a few minutes.'

Anxiety fluttered through her. 'You can't sleep *here*,' she said, ignoring the fact that this was Theseus's home and he could sleep wherever he liked.

His eyes narrowed.

'If Toby wakes up and sees you in my bed it will confuse him.'

'He's not used to seeing you with men?' Theseus's question was delivered evenly, but with an undertone she couldn't distinguish.

'No. Never.'

His lips clamped into a tight line before he nodded. 'We're going to spend the rest of our lives together. He will have to get used to us sleeping together.'

'You mean we'll share a bed?'

'It's the only upside of marriage,' he said sardonically, pulling his trousers up. 'We'll have our own separate rooms, but I have no intention of sleeping in a cold bed alone when we can keep each other warm.'

'It's too soon. Toby will need time.'

I'll need time, she almost added. Night after night of being held in his arms, made love to… Where would that leave her already frazzled emotions?

Theseus slipped his shirt back on and fixed her with a hard stare.

'I will allow you to sleep alone for the next couple of nights, so Toby isn't upset in the morning, but from then on we will sleep together. For the avoidance of any doubt: our marriage might not be a love match but it *will* be a real marriage.'

She nodded, her chin jutting up. 'Fine. But just so you know, I snore.'

He shook his head and laughed, killing the dark atmosphere that had been brewing between them. 'I thought you said you didn't want there to be any more lies between us?'

Theseus slept long and deep, but when he awoke he didn't feel refreshed. On the contrary—he felt as if he'd slept through a battle.

Apprehension lay heavily on him. He debated with himself whether to have his breakfast brought to his room but then dismissed the idea. He'd never been scared of anything in his life. Why should he be frightened of a four-year-old boy?

Making his way downstairs, he headed towards the dining room, where voices could be heard.

Swallowing to try and rid himself of the lump in his throat, he entered to find Jo and Toby seated at the table.

They fell silent. Toby's spoon hovered between his cereal bowl and his mouth, his dark brown eyes widening.

Jo placed a hand on his back and shuffled her chair closer to him. 'Toby, this is Theseus.'

'Are you the Prince?' Toby asked, his eyes still as wide as an owl's.

Theseus nodded. That damn lump in his throat was still there.

One of the maids came into the dining room to take his breakfast order. He used the time to collect his thoughts and sit opposite his family.

After his coffee was poured for him the maid bustled off, leaving the three of them alone in the most awkward silence he had ever experienced.

Toby gawped at him as if he'd been taking lessons from a goldfish. 'Do you have a crown?'

'No.' Theseus could not take his eyes off him. He hadn't known children could be so perfectly formed and so damnably cute. 'My grandfather does, though.'

'Is he the King?'

'He is.'

Toby's face screwed up. 'Does he have a flying carpet?'

'I'm sure he would like one,' he said, and laughed, feeling the tension slowly lessen.

'Do *you* have a flying carpet?'

'No, but I *do* have some really fast sports cars I can take you for a drive in.'

Toby pulled a face Theseus recognised as the one which Jo made when she was unimpressed about something.

'If I ever get a flying carpet you'll be the first person I take on it,' Theseus said, ignoring Jo's raised eyebrows.

Now Toby beamed. *'Yes!'*

And just like that his son came to life, peppering him with questions about being a prince, demanding to know if they still kept 'naughty men' in the dungeons and asking if there were any dinosaurs at the palace.

This was *much* easier than Theseus had envisaged.

The knots in his stomach loosened and he relaxed, enjoying the moment for what it was: the first of many meals

he would share with his son over the course of the rest of
his life.

'Has your mother told you who I am?' he asked when
they'd all finished eating and Toby had finally paused for
breath.

Jo's eyebrows rose again and she straightened.

'You're a prince!'

'Would *you* like to be a prince?'

Toby contemplated the question, twiddling with the buttons of his pyjamas. 'Would I have to kiss girls?'

Theseus's eyes flickered to Jo. 'Not if you didn't want to.'

'Would I have a flying carpet?'

'No, but you could have horses, and when you're old
enough sports cars like mine.'

'I *would* like to be a prince,' Toby said, as if confiding
something important. 'But when I'm growed up I want to
clean windows on a ladder.'

'You could do both,' Theseus said gravely, fighting to
stop his lips from twitching in laughter. 'You see, Toby,
you *are* a prince.'

'Mummy says I'm a cheeky monkey.'

'My mummy used to say the same thing to my brother
Talos. He was a cheeky monkey when he was a little boy—
just like you.'

'I'm not little,' Toby said indignantly, lifting his arm and
flexing it to show off his non-existent muscles. 'I'm a big
boy. I'm going to big school in September.'

As she relaxed from her previously ramrod-straight position it was obvious Jo was fighting her own laughter. Finally she took pity and stepped in to save him.

'Remember what Mummy told you about having a Greek
daddy who was lost?'

Toby nodded.

'Well, Mummy's found him. Theseus is your daddy.'

A look of utmost suspicion crossed his tiny face. 'My daddy's name is Theo—not Theseus.'

'Theo's his nickname,' she said smoothly, although her eyes darted to Theseus with an expression that sliced through his guts.

She really *had* spoken of him to their son...

'Theseus is his real name.'

Toby contemplated him some more. 'You're my daddy?'

'Yes. And because I'm a prince, that means you're a prince too.'

The suspicion vanished, a beaming smile replacing it. 'Does that mean Mummy is a princess?'

'Kind of,' Jo said, taking control again. 'How would you like to spend the day with Theseus? He can tell you all about being a prince. Ask him anything you like—he just *loves* answering questions. And you can explore this brilliant house with him.'

Toby nodded really hard, his eyes like an owl's again.

Theseus felt his own eyes widen too, at the underhand stunt Jo had just pulled, but knew he couldn't say anything to the contrary—not unless he wanted to disappoint his son on their first meeting.

She kissed Toby's cheek and threw Theseus a beatific smile. 'He's not a fussy eater, so ignore him if he tells you he doesn't like carrots. Have fun!'

And with that she left the dining room, leaving Theseus with the miniature version of himself.

Jo turned her head in time to see Theseus step into the room that had been converted into an office for her. He closed the door behind him and folded his arms.

'What?' she asked innocently.

'You are a cruel woman.'

'It was for the greater good. Have you had a good day?'

A half-smile played on his lips. 'It's been something. I've

left Toby in the kitchen with Elektra and the kitchen staff—he's already got them eating out of his hands. They're baking flapjacks for him.'

'Flapjacks are his favourite.'

'He made a point of telling all of us that.'

She sniggered. 'You must be exhausted.'

He nodded. 'Does he ever stop?'

'Stop what? Talking? Or wanting to do things?'

'Both.'

'Nope. I swear he's got rocket fuel in his veins. Still, he sleeps really well—that must be when he recharges his batteries.'

'And he eats so *much*!' He shook his head with incredulity.

'Tell me about it,' she said drily. 'He costs a fortune to feed.' She stretched her back, which had gone stiff after hours hunched over the laptop. 'Other than being worn out, how did you get on?'

'I think he had a nice time.'

'Sorry for coercing you into it,' she said, without an ounce of penitence in her tone.

Theseus brushed a stray lock of hair from his eyes. 'I'm glad you did. I admit I was a little nervous. All I know of children is what I remember from my own childhood, and that was hardly normal.'

'No, I suppose it wasn't,' she said softly, wondering how anyone could have a normal childhood after losing both parents at the age of nine as well as being something akin to a deity in his own country. 'I know being an instant father is going to be hard, but this is what you wanted. All you can do is try your hardest and make the best of it.'

'Is that what you're doing?' he asked, a strange expression on his face.

'That's all I've done since I found out I was pregnant. I will try my hardest to make our marriage work but only because it's best for Toby, and not because you've black-mailed me into it.'

He winced, then nodded sharply. 'That's all I can ask from you.'

'But first we need to get this biography finished. Right now I can't think of anything else.' Well, she could. She just didn't want to...

The words she'd spouted about parenthood had come from the same store of pragmatism that had driven her to move out of her family home when Toby had been three months old and she'd realised that her mother's indifference to her only daughter had extended to her only grandson.

It had been a particularly chilly day, and the manor had been even more draughty than usual. She'd put the heating on. Her mother had promptly turned it off, overriding Jo's protests with a sharp, 'If the child's cold, put another blanket on him.'

In the snap of two fingers Jo had known she had to leave. She'd gone straight into action, borrowing money from her brother to rent a tiny flat from a sympathetic landlady.

She'd refused to dwell on it. Whatever the future held for them, she'd reasoned at the time, it would be better for Toby than living with her parents.

She didn't want her son running up to his grandmother and being met with cold indifference, or thinking that drinking a bottle of whisky a day was normal.

Jo had spent her childhood devouring her mother's cakes, getting fatter and fatter in the process, all in the vain hope of gaining attention—even if only a reprimand for eating too much. She hadn't been worth even that...not even when the school nurse had sent a letter home warning that Jo was dangerously overweight. Her mother had carried on letting her eat as much as she liked. She simply hadn't cared.

Jo would rather have put her head in a vice than put Toby through that.

Much like the time she'd left home, to think of her future now was to feel a weight sink in her stomach and drag her to the floor. Finishing the biography had turned into a godsend. If she kept her mind active and distracted she would survive.

'How have you done today?'

'I'm nearly there. I emailed you an hour ago with the latest chapters.'

'I'll read them after dinner,' he promised. 'We'll be eating at six—does that suit you?'

'That's early for you.'

'I didn't think Toby would last much longer than that. He's been saying he's starving since half an hour after lunch.'

She smiled, unable to believe how deeply that touched her. 'I'll stop now and do some more tonight. If I fuel myself with caffeine there's a good chance I'll get it finished before the sun comes up.'

'Don't kill yourself.'

'It's what I signed up for.'

He inclined his head, his chest rising. 'I'm going to catch up on some work. I'll see you at dinner.'

Dinner itself was a relaxed affair. Toby happily wolfed down the spaghetti bolognaise the chef had made especially for him, but with the threat that tomorrow he would have to learn to eat 'proper' Agon fare.

'Are chicken nuggets from Agon?' he'd asked with total solemnity, to many smothered smiles.

All things considered, however, his son's first day on the island had gone much better than Theseus could have hoped. He'd enjoyed being with him, which he hadn't expected.

Maybe he *could* do this fatherhood thing.

'I have to go to the palace in the morning. I thought I'd borrow my brother's dog and bring him back. We could take him for a walk on the beach,' he said to Toby, who had insisted on sitting next to him, which had filled him with pride.

'Can I go to the palace with you?' he asked hopefully. His face and T-shirt were covered in tomato sauce.

'Not yet. It's too busy there at the moment. I'll take you in a week or two.'

Toby thought about this answer, then darted panicked eyes to his mother. 'Am I still going to Ellie's party on Saturday?'

Now Jo was the one to look panic-stricken. 'I'm sorry, but we're going to have to miss that.'

'But Aunty Cathy's got me a Waspman outfit.'

'I know... I know.'

She inhaled deeply through her nose and smiled at their son, a smile that looked forced to Theseus's eyes.

'We'll do something fun on Saturday to make up for missing it.'

'But I want to go to Ellie's party. You *promised*.'

To Theseus's distress, huge tears pooled in Toby's eyes and rolled down his cheeks, landing on his plate.

He placed a tentative hand on his son's thin shoulder, wanting to give comfort, but Toby shrugged it away and slipped off his chair to run around the table to Jo and throw himself into her arms.

She shoved her chair back and scooped him up, sitting him on her lap so he could bury himself in her softness.

'I want to go home!' Toby sobbed, his tiny frame shaking.

'I know... I know,' she soothed again, stroking his hair.

She met Theseus's gaze. He'd expected to see recrimination in her stare, but all he could see was anguish. She dropped a kiss on Toby's head, saying nothing more, just letting him cry it out.

Only when he'd stopped sobbing and blown his nose did she say, 'How about we ask the chef for some ice cream?'

Toby nodded bravely, but still clung to her.

Theseus remembered the cold days that had followed his return to the palace from his sabbatical. Night after night he'd lain in his bed, in the moonless dark, and had found his thoughts returning over and over to the woman he'd met on Illya. To Jo.

He would have given anything—all his wealth, his royal title, everything he had—to be enfolded in her arms once again and to feel her gentle hands stroke his pain away... just as they were doing now to their son.

The image of her sitting on the beach watching him sail away had haunted him until he'd blotted her from his mind.

'I'll see to it,' he said, getting to his feet and making no mention of the bell that he could ring if he required service. Suddenly he was desperate to get out of the dining room.

He did not want the look of gratitude Jo threw at him. He didn't deserve it. Toby's distress was *his* fault.

As soon as he was out of the room and out of their sight he rubbed at his temples and blew out a breath of air.

He couldn't explain even to himself how agonising he'd found that scene.

CHAPTER ELEVEN

Jo HIT 'SEND' and threw her head back to gaze at the ceiling.

She'd done it. She'd finished the biography.

Theseus had given her the green light on the chapters she'd completed earlier and she'd forwarded them to her editor in Oxford. All that was left was for Theseus to approve the last two.

Once she'd imagined that she would want to celebrate. Now she felt that any celebration would be more like a wake.

Her work hadn't just opened up the King's life for her, but the lives of his family too. *Theseus's* life. This was a family bound by blood and duty.

When she'd arrived on Agon she'd been too angry at Theseus's deception to understand why he'd lied about his identity. Now she understood.

He'd spent his entire life being scrutinised, having his every waking hour planned for him—whether at home in the palace, at boarding school, or in the armed forces. His life had never been his own to do as he wanted. He really *had* been like a trapped grown lion in a tiny cage.

No wonder he had kicked back. Who could blame him for wanting to experience what most people took for granted?

But now he was a model prince—a model Kalliakis.

She admired him for the way he handled his role, but wondered what it had cost him.

He'd been happy on Illya. Here, it was clear he did his duty but she saw no joy in it for him.

Stretching her back, she listened carefully. Unlike in the palace, where there was always the undercurrent of movement even if it couldn't be heard, the villa lay in silence. If she strained her ears she could hear Toby snoring lightly in his bedroom next door to her makeshift office. After his earlier meltdown she'd worried he would struggle to sleep, but he'd been out for the count within minutes of his head hitting the pillow.

She'd felt so bad for Theseus, who had watched the unfolding scene with something akin to horror. She wished she could ask him what he'd been thinking, but no sooner had their dessert been cleared away than he'd excused himself. Other than his email confirming approval for the earlier chapters she hadn't heard from him.

She'd bathed Toby and put him to bed alone. Theseus hadn't even come to give him a goodnight kiss.

Had that been the moment when the reality of parenthood had hit home and he'd decided that keeping his distance was the way forward? Not having to deal with any of the literal or figurative messy stuff?

Inexplicably, hot tears welled up, gushing out of her in a torrent. She didn't try to hold them back.

She didn't have a clue what she was crying about.

When Theseus returned to the villa from the palace the next day, the beaming smile Toby gave him lightened the weight bearing down on his shoulders.

Toby even jumped down from his seat at the garden table where he and Jo were sitting and ran to him.

It was only when he got close that Theseus realised all of Toby's joy was bound up in Theseus's companion—Helios's black Labrador. It didn't matter. It was good to see him smile after his misery the night before.

'What's his name?' Toby asked, flinging his arms around the dog's neck.

'Benedict.'

Luckily Benedict was the softest dog in the world, and happy to have a four-year-old hurtle into him. His only response was to give Toby a great big lick on the cheek. If Benedict had been a human he would have been a slur on the Kalliakis name, but because he was a dog everyone could love him and fuss over him unimpeded.

'That's a silly name for a dog.'

'I'll be sure to tell my brother that,' he answered drily, not adding that his brother was in fact Toby's uncle. He didn't want to upset him any more, and had no idea what the triggers might be.

'Can we take him for a walk on the beach?'

'Sure. Give me five minutes to change and we can go.'

Throughout this exchange Jo didn't say a word as she leaned over the table, putting in the pieces of what he saw to be a jigsaw.

'Are you going to join us?' he called, certain that she'd been listening.

'I would love to.'

'Five minutes.'

He strolled inside and headed up to his room, changing out of his trousers and shirt into a pair of his favourite cargo shorts and a white T-shirt. When he got back Jo and Toby were waiting for him, bottles of water in hand.

Jo looked pointedly at his feet. 'No shoes?'

'I like to feel the sand on my feet.'

The strangest expression crossed her face. But if she meant to say anything the moment was lost when Toby tugged at her hand.

'Come *on*,' he urged impatiently.

Together they walked out of the garden and down a

rocky trail, with Jo holding Toby's hand tightly until they reached Theseus's private beach.

As soon as his feet hit the sand Toby pulled his socks and trainers off and went chasing after Benedict.

'He seems happier now,' Theseus observed nonchalantly.

His attempt at indifference was met with a wry smile. 'Don't beat yourself up about last night. He was tired.'

'He was also very upset.'

'Tiredness always affects his mood. Don't forget he's in a strange place, with strange people, and a man claiming to be his father...'

'I *am* his father.'

She looked at him. 'He's only ever had a mother. Stories of his father have been, in his head, the same as stories about the tooth fairy. He'll be okay. Children accept change and adapt to it far more easily than we do, but it's unrealistic to expect that to happen immediately. He needs time, that's all. Be patient. He'll come to accept you *and* our new life.'

He wasn't convinced. Did he really want his son to be just *okay*? Childhood was a time of innocence and magic. Break the innocence and the magic evaporated.

Even before his parents' deaths he'd had little innocence left. Having a father who'd made no attempt to disguise his irritation with his second son had had an insidious effect on him. His mother had tried her hardest to make up for it and he'd worshipped her in return. When she'd died it had been as if his whole world had ended. Yet he'd mourned his father too. Loving him and hating him had lived side by side within him. For his mother, though, he had felt only love, and it had been the hole left in his heart by her loss that had cut the most. If not for his grandparents he would have been completely lost. They'd always been there for him.

As he'd read through the final chapters of his grandfather's biography that morning, before heading to the palace, it had played on his mind how much his grandparents had given up for him and his brothers to ensure they had stability. It wasn't just that his grandfather had kept the monarch's crown, but the way his grandparents had enfolded their grandsons in their care.

Given that Helios was heir, it was hardly surprising that Astraeus had taken him under his wing more than he had Theseus or Talos. But Theseus had never felt excluded by it, in the way his father had made him feel excluded. His grandfather was often remote—he was the King after all—and he'd been strict with them all, but growing up Theseus had never doubted his love. And his remoteness had been countered by their grandmother; a loving, generous woman with all the time in the world for him.

Theos, he missed her as much as he missed his mother.

After reading the biography in its entirety, with all the pieces of his research stitched together to create the final picture, he'd understood just how much they'd given up for their grandchildren and for duty. The death of their son and heir had meant the death of their dreams, but they'd risen to the challenge with a grace that left him humbled and aching with regret. It was too late to tell his grandmother how much he loved her and to thank her for all she'd done and all she'd given up.

Toby bounded back to them, waving an enormous stick in his hand. Theseus marvelled at the freedom that came with simply being a child.

Did he really want to take that freedom away from him?

And could he do it to Jo too?

'I've found a stick,' Toby said, coming right up to him and holding it out like an offering.

'Throw it to Benedict and see if he'll catch it.'

''Kay. How will he know what to do?'

'He'll know,' he said, smiling down at him. 'You can always yell *ferto* to him when you throw it—that's the Greek word for fetch.'

'*Ferto,*' Toby repeated, then ran off, shouting, '*Sas efcharisto,*' over his shoulder.

'Did he just say thank you to me?' he asked, staring at Jo in astonishment, certain that his ears must be blocked with water from his morning swim.

'I've taught him a few words and phrases in Greek,' she conceded.

The admission caught him right in the throat.

He'd become so accustomed to speaking to her in both their languages that he'd taken her fluency in his language for granted. It was a joke amongst Greeks, Cretans and Agonites alike how dismally the British spoke their tongue.

Fate did indeed work in strange ways.

If Jo hadn't been fluent in his language and the only credible person to take over the workings of the biography—

Suddenly he was certain that she hadn't spoken Greek when he'd known her on Illya. Her speech now was practised, but not flawless. She could read the language well, but struggled with the more obscure words. He'd never seen her attempt to write it, but he was sure it would be an area she would have trouble with.

This wasn't a woman who'd been taught his language from a young age.

'When did you learn Greek?'

'When I couldn't find you.' She looked briefly at him, then shifted her focus back to the light pink sand before them, following in Toby's little footsteps. 'I bought some of those audio lessons and spent every night listening to them, and I got Fiona to give me lessons too. She helped me with context and pronunciation.'

'You did all that in five years?'

'Four,' she corrected. 'And now I'm trying to teach Toby too.'

'But why?' His head spun to think of all the hours she must have spent studying, the determination it must have taken...

'I told you before—I wanted to find you. I even started a savings account to pay for me and Toby to go to Athens.'

'How did you think you would find me?' he asked, more harshly than he'd intended. 'Athens is a huge city. It would have been like looking for a specific tile in a mosaic.'

She shrugged. 'I knew it was a long shot, but I'd have tried for Toby's sake.'

'And what did you think would happen if you'd found me?'

'I stopped thinking about that. All the potential consequences were too scary.'

'But you were still going to try?'

Her smile was wan. 'It was the right thing to do. If I hadn't have found you I still could have shown Toby your culture. Or what I *thought* was your culture.'

She cast her eyes a few metres into the distance, to where Toby was splashing at the shoreline.

'No further!' she called to him, before adding to Theseus, 'He can't swim.'

As she joined their son Theseus hung back, watching them.

They were the tightest of units. Seeing them together, he could appreciate how hard it must have been for her to leave Toby behind and come to Agon.

It seemed she'd accepted the job because of the large bonus she'd been offered, which would have meant she'd have been able to take Toby to Greece to find *him*.

If he hadn't believed her before, he did now. With all his heart.

She really had searched for him.

She really had wanted him to be a part of Toby's life.

If fate hadn't brought her to the palace she would never have found him. He would have spent the rest of his life unaware of the miracle that had occurred and he would have had no one to blame but himself.

Jo followed the squeals of delight echoing from the swimming pool with a smile playing on her face.

The sun was bright, the sky was blue—in all it was a glorious day. She'd caught a snippet of the English weather forecast and had given a sly snigger to see her country was expecting torrential downpours and heavy gales.

There could certainly be worse places to be a forced wife than on Agon, she thought wryly.

Toby spotted her first, and waved cheerfully from Theseus's arms.

For his part, Theseus's eyes gleamed to see her, and a knowing look spread over his face when she removed her sarong to reveal the modest bikini she'd bought the day before on a shopping trip with Elektra.

'Sexy,' he growled, for her ears only, when she slipped tentatively down the steps and into the cool water.

She stopped with the water at mid-thigh. 'Inappropriate,' she whispered.

'He's not listening.'

That was true enough. Toby had paddled off in his armbands to the shallow end, to play with the array of water guns, lilos and balls Theseus had bought for him.

'I've never seen you in a bikini before.' Theseus grinned, sitting on the step beside her.

'I was so fat I never dared wear one,' she admitted wistfully. 'Everyone else on Illya had such fabulous figures.'

She still wasn't fully confident displaying her body, but after spending her nights sharing a bed with Theseus and having him revel in her curves, her confidence was increasing by the day.

He tilted his head and stared at her, then reached out a hand to tuck a lock of her hair behind her ear. 'Never feel you aren't good enough, *agapi mou*. Those women on Illya couldn't hold a light to you, whatever size you were. You're beautiful.'

Everything in her contracted—from her toes to her pelvis to the hairs on her head. She couldn't think of a reply; was too stunned that this glorious, gorgeous man could call her beautiful. If she could float she would be sky-high by now...

Theseus didn't care how thin she was. No matter what, he would still desire her.

She giggled.

'What?' he asked, his eyes puzzled.

She clamped a hand over her mouth.

'What?' he demanded to know, playfully pulling her hand away. 'Why are you laughing? Share the joke. I command it!'

But she couldn't. How could she say that his compliment was the most wonderful she'd ever heard?

'Tell me or I'll get you wet,' he threatened, clearly remembering her aversion to water from their time on Illya.

But she could no more stop the laughter that erupted than she could have grown wings.

Theseus was as good as his word.

He got to his feet, scooped her up in his arms, then threw her into the middle of the pool.

She was still laughing when she came up for air.

Preparations for the Gala meant Theseus was caught up at the palace more than he would have liked over the next few days. He made sure always to eat breakfast with his new family, and spent snatches of time with them, but he knew it wasn't enough. Not for him. He wanted them...*close*.

He brushed away the strange word.

Things would change after the Gala, when he would be able to announce their existence to his grandfather and the rest of the world. Jo and Toby would move into the palace then.

Living in his villa was like a holiday for them. The sun shone whilst they played in the pool and built sandcastles on the beach. The magic of it all had caught him too. The memory of last night lay fresh in his mind; taking a moonlit walk with Jo down to the cove, making love to her on the sand and then, when they were replete and naked in each other's arms, gazing up at the stars in peaceable silence.

For the first time he'd stared up at the night sky and not felt the pull to be up there in space. The only pull he'd felt was to the woman in his arms, and he'd rolled her onto her back and made love to her again.

More and more it played on his mind... How was she going to cope with palace life? She'd lived there briefly, but that had been there for a specific purpose, not as a member of the household. She would need time to settle in and then, once they were married in a few weeks, her royal duties would begin.

His good memories from the beach evaporated as he recalled her startled face that morning, when they'd lingered over breakfast. Toby had disappeared into the kitchen to badger the chef into making more flapjacks for him and he'd given her the résumés of the staff he was recommending she interview after the Gala.

She'd looked at him blankly.

'Your private staff,' he'd explained. 'You'll need staff to manage your diary, to do research for you for when we meet with ambassadors and business people. You'll need someone to help with your wardrobe—my grandmother and my mother both had a personal seamstress to make their clothes—and you'll need a private secretary to manage all of them…'

By the time he'd stopped talking she'd looked quite faint. The reality of palace life was clearly not something she was prepared for.

He threw his pen at the wall and swore.

How much guilt could one man carry?

It was late when he returned to the villa. A few members of staff were still up, but Jo and Toby had both gone to bed.

He found Toby fast asleep, lying spread out like a starfish. Theseus padded quietly to him and pulled the covers which had been thrown off back over him, before placing a kiss on his forehead.

With his guts playing havoc inside him, he went into Jo's room, closing the door behind him.

She was sitting up in bed, reading.

'I thought you'd be asleep,' he said.

'So did I.'

He sat on the edge of the bed and reached out to bury a hand in her hair. She shuffled closer and wrapped her arms around him.

'How are things going with the Gala?' she asked softly.

'Like a well-oiled machine. Apart from the soloist Talos found to play our grandmother's final composition…'

'What's wrong with her?'

'Turns out she suffers from severe stage fright.'

'Ah—is *that* why they've been spending so much time together?'

The suggestive tone in her voice made him laugh. He raised one eyebrow. 'Talos says he's *helping* her…'

With that, they both rolled back onto the bed, smothering their sniggers so as not to wake Toby across the hall. Their laughter quickly turned into passion as Jo's hungry lips found his and her robe fell open to showcase her unashamed nakedness...

Time sped away in whirl of sunshine until suddenly it was the eve of the Gala.

Where had the time gone? Jo wondered in amazement.

Theseus had spent the day at the palace and arrived back so late she was dozing off when he slipped into the dark bedroom.

'All done?' she asked, raising her head.

He turned the light on at a low setting. 'All done. The books are en route as we speak.'

A problem with the printers had kept him at the palace long into the night. All week he'd had to work late. The pace had been relentless. She'd found herself missing him, constantly checking her watch and waiting for the time when he would come back to the villa.

'Have you slept?' he asked, unbuttoning his shirt.

'A little.' She sat up, hugging the sheets to her. 'I think there's too much going on in my brain for me to switch off properly.'

'Nervous?'

'Terrified.'

Tomorrow she would meet the King. When the Gala was all over he would be informed about Toby. Their lives would change irrevocably.

'Don't be.'

She sighed. That was easy for *him* to say.

'I spoke to Giles earlier.'

'How was he?'

'Busy.' He slid his trousers off. 'He said to pass on his congratulations for your part in the book.'

She smiled wistfully.

'You never told me you got the job with him by working for free.'

She shrugged. 'I was desperate. I'd had to give up the job I'd originally had lined up in London…'

'Why?'

'I suffered from a condition commonly known as acute morning sickness. I was sick pretty much all the time. I could hardly get out of bed, never mind move to London and start a new job. I ended up being hospitalised for a month. By the time I'd recovered, when I was just over four months pregnant, the job had been given to someone else.'

Stark, stunned silence greeted her news.

'It wasn't all bad,' she said, trying to reassure him. 'I lost a load of weight, and Toby didn't suffer for it.'

'It must have been hell,' he refuted flatly.

'At the time, yes—but Toby was worth it. And I turned into slimline Jo, so that was a bonus.'

'With the way you always refuse cake I assumed you'd dieted.'

'Not initially. Once I got better the temptation was still there, but I stopped myself. I knew things had to change— for my health *and* my emotional wellbeing.' She shook her head and sighed. 'I fell in love with Toby long before he was born, and that was what made me see that I could eat as many of my mother's cakes as possible and she'd *still* never love me. Not as a mother should.'

At his shocked stare, she went on.

'When I was little I was allowed to eat as much cake as I liked. I thought that was how mums showed their love. Looking back, I can see that it was just her way of keeping me quiet. Carrying Toby, feeling him grow inside me… it changed me. I knew I couldn't let her have that kind of power over me any more.'

'And what's your relationship with her like now?'

'Challenging… I pop in every month or so, to make sure Dad's okay. If he's not comatose he's happy to see me.'

'How does Toby get on with them?'

'I never take him. Maybe when he's older…' Her voice trailed off.

'So what *were* you going to do in London?' he asked quietly.

Theseus hadn't intended to open a Pandora's box with his innocuous comment about Giles, but now it was open he needed to know it all.

'I was going to work at a children's book publishing company.' She pushed a lock of hair from her face. 'I loved reading as a child. Anything was possible in the books I read. Good overcame evil. The ugly ducklings became beautiful swans. Anyone could find love. I wanted to work with those books and be a part of the magic.'

And instead she'd ended up working on historical tomes and museum pieces. He could just see her, sitting in her bedroom, forgetting her mother's cruel indifference and her father's love affair with the bottle by burying her head in dreams.

'When I recovered from the morning sickness I went to every publisher I could find in Oxford and offered my services for free until the baby was born—the deal being that if I proved myself they had to consider me when a suitable job came up. Giles took me up on it.'

Theseus shook his head to imagine that he'd once dismissed this woman as 'wallpaper'. She had more tenacity than anyone he'd ever met.

'They say fortune favours the brave,' she continued, 'and it really does. A week after I'd decided I couldn't raise Toby in the toxic atmosphere of Brookes Manor and we'd moved into our own flat, Giles called with the offer of a job as copywriter. It came at just the right time too—I was hours away from starting my first shift as a waitress.'

He smiled, although he felt anything but amused. 'And you were happy there?'

'Gosh, yes. Very happy. The staff are wonderful. I grew to love it.'

Of course she had. She could have wallowed in self-pity at the destruction of her dreams, but instead she had embraced the cards she'd been dealt, just as she would put on a brave smile when she married into his family and became royalty.

He thought of his grandmother, who'd curtailed her performing career when she'd married his grandfather. The difference was his grandmother had been born a princess and been promised to his grandfather from birth. She'd always known that marriage would mean a limit to what she could do with her career.

He thought of his mother. Had *she* ever dreamed of being anything other than Lelantos Kalliakis's wife?

Yes, he thought, remembering the wistful look that had used to come into her eyes when he'd spoken of his naïve childhood plan to become an astronaut. She'd had dreams of something different too. It was the greatest tragedy of his life that he would never know what they had been.

CHAPTER TWELVE

'DO I LOOK all right?' Jo asked, the second Theseus stepped into the room.

The appreciative gleam that came into his eyes gave her the answer.

When he pulled her into his arms and made to kiss her, she turned her cheek. 'You'll smudge my lipstick!' she chided.

'I don't care.'

'Well, *I* do. I've spent over two hours getting ready.'

'And you look spectacular.'

She felt her cheeks flame at his heartfelt compliment and couldn't resist one more glance in the mirror.

Another shopping trip with Elektra had resulted in Jo picking an ivory crêpe dress that dipped in a V at the front and fell to mid-calf. She'd finished the outfit with a wide tan leather belt across her middle and pair of high, braided white leather sandals.

A fortnight ago she wouldn't have dreamed of wearing something that put so much emphasis on her buxom figure—although the height of the sandals elongated her nicely—but Theseus's genuine delight in her curves had given her real confidence. She'd never shown so much cleavage in her life!

Elektra had twisted her hair into an elegant knot and gone to work on her face. The result was a dream. Her eyes had never looked so blue, her lips so…kissable. Yes, the lips she'd always hated for being as plump as her bottom looked *kissable*. She even had defined cheekbones!

Today she was going to meet the King and dozens of other dignitaries as Theseus's guest at a select pre-Gala lunch.

Boxes of the biography had arrived in the early hours, and a dozen members of the palace staff were already organising them for distribution amongst the five thousand Gala attendees.

But first Theseus wanted to present his grandfather with his own copy.

He hadn't said anything but she knew he was apprehensive about his grandfather's reaction, so she was trying hard to smother her terror at the thought of all the important people she would be forced to converse with as an equal and to be bright and cheerful for Theseus, in the hope that it might settle his own silent nerves.

Once the lunch was over they would go to the amphitheatre. Theseus would sit with his family in the royal box and Jo would sit with Toby and Elektra, who was caring for him in the meantime.

After kissing Toby goodbye—and his, 'Wow, Mummy, you look like a princess!' had made her feel ten feet tall— she and Theseus got into the car and were driven to the palace.

It felt strange, coming back to it.

Barely a fortnight had passed since she'd moved into Theseus's villa but it felt like so much longer. It felt as if she was looking at the palace with fresh eyes.

The sun shone high above, its rays beaming down and soaking the palace in glorious sunlight, making the different coloured roofs brighter and all the ornate gothic and mythological statues and frescoes come to life.

When they arrived, entering through Theseus's private entrance, they passed the door of her old apartment. She looked at it with a touch of wistfulness, wondering who the next person to inhabit it would be.

Climbing the stairs, she watched as the carefree man who had slowly re-emerged during her time in his villa put his princely skin back on. She wished with all her heart that she could pull it off him.

Theseus felt no joy as a prince, spending his days at official functions with stuffy dignitaries and being sent abroad to protect and advance his island's interests. There was no time to climb the peaks or stare at the stars.

He needed to be out in the air. He needed to be free.

The man she'd met five years ago had been free and happy. Joy had radiated from him.

Courtiers appeared at their side and Dimitris was with them. In his hand was a hardback book, with a portrait of the King on the cover... It was the biography...

'He's ready for you,' Dimitris murmured.

He had to mean King Astraeus.

This was the moment when he would learn what his grandson had done in his honour. She hoped he'd recognise the incredible effort Theseus had put into it. She hoped the King would be proud.

Theseus turned to Jo. 'A courtier will take you to the stateroom where the guests are meeting for lunch. Wait for me there.'

The strain was huge in his eyes.

'Are you okay?' she asked softly.

He met her gaze. Understanding passed between them.

Theseus brushed a thumb along her cheekbone, resisting the urge to kiss her. Instead he gave a curt nod and left for his grandfather's quarters.

He found him sat in his wheelchair, looking out of a high window, dressed in full regalia, with his dark purple sash tied from shoulder to hip in the same way as Theseus's own. Only his nurse was in attendance.

'You wanted to see me?' his grandfather said, interest on his wizened face.

Taking a deep breath, Theseus crossed the threshold.

He'd prepared a speech for this moment; words which might explain the regret he carried for all the shame and worry he'd put on this great man's shoulders and how this book had been created to honour him.

But the words stuck.

He held the book out to him.

With curiosity on his face, his grandfather took it from him. Wordlessly he placed it on his lap, and with hands that shook he opened it.

After several long minutes during which the only sound in the room was the King's wheezy breathing, his grandfather raised misty eyes to him.

'You did this?'

Theseus bowed his head.

'It is incredible.' His grandfather shook his head, turning the pages slowly. 'When did you do this…? How…? I knew nothing of it.'

'I wanted it to be a surprise.'

'It's not often a secret is kept in this palace,' his grandfather observed, a tremble in his aged voice.

'Loss of limbs may have been threatened…'

Astraeus's laugh turned into a cough, and then the amusement faded. 'This is a wonderful thing you have done for me, and I thank you with all my heart.'

Theseus took a breath. 'I wanted to create something that would show how much you mean to me. I used to be disrespectful, and I brought much dishonour upon you, but I truly am proud to be your grandson.'

His words were met with a shake of the old King's head. 'Theseus, you weren't a bad boy. Rhea always said you were a lost soul.'

At the mention of his grandmother's name Theseus felt his throat close.

'She adored you.'

'I know. I will never forgive myself for not being there—' His voice cracked, guilt filling him all over again.

Astraeus gripped his wrist and tugged him down so they were at eye level. 'The past is over. What you have created here for me...' A tear ran down his cheek. 'Your grandmother would be very proud of you—for this and for how you've turned your life around. You are a credit to the Kalliakis name and I'm proud to call you my grandson.'

The backs of his retinas burning, Theseus closed his eyes, then leaned forward to place a kiss on his grandfather's cheek. But before he could absorb the moment, and his grandfather's words, a knock on the door preceded his brothers strolling into the room.

'Is there a lovefest going on that we weren't invited to?' Helios asked.

Talos snatched the book out of their grandfather's hands and soon all four of them were going through the pictures within, reminiscing with sad amusement, until the King's private secretary announced that it was time for them to greet their guests.

An army of staff bustled around, handing out champagne and fresh juices as the stateroom filled. On an antique table to the left of the door sat a pile of hardback copies of the biography.

'May I?' Jo asked, dazzled.

'Of course.' A courtier handed one to her.

She studied the cover and the back, then flipped through the pages, inhaling the lovely papery scent only a new book emitted.

At the bottom of the front cover were the words *Fiona Samaras & Joanne Brookes*.

She traced her finger over her name, then carefully turned some pages. Pride filled her to know that this was something *she'd* helped create, but with it came a tinge of sadness that Fiona couldn't be there to revel in their accomplishment too. After four years of working together, and all Fiona's Greek tuition, they'd become good friends. Jo knew how much she would have loved to be there today.

While she waited for Theseus to join her she studied the photographs in the biography, which dated back a century, to the King's own parents' marriage. What a family she was moving into...

Where before she'd felt terror at the mere thought of becoming a Kalliakis, she now felt an immense pride and a determination to play her part. She'd grown to love the island, and the fierce but passionate people who inhabited it.

And what a man she was pledging the rest of her life to...

An image floated in her mind of when she had watched him teach Toby to swim in the villa's outdoor pool the day before. She could still hear their laughter. He'd come back from the palace especially. She'd watched them with a heart so full she had wanted to burst. All her fears for Toby had gone. Seeing them together had been like watching two peas in a pod.

Toby loved his father. And Theseus loved him. She could see it in his tenderness towards him. And sometimes when he looked at her she thought she saw the same tenderness directed at *her*.

It gave her hope. Maybe love really *could* grow between them...

Activity at the entrance of the stateroom caught her attention.

An old wizened man in a wheelchair, who nonetheless had the most incredible aura about him, had entered the room. Theseus was at his side, Helios and another man who had to be Talos were with them.

The four of them together looked majestic. But it was only Theseus she had eyes for.

It came to her then in a burst of crystal clear clarity.

She was head over heels in love with him.

She had belonged to him since he'd stood up for her on Illya, and no matter how hard she'd tried to dislodge him from her heart—had convinced herself for years that she'd succeeded—he was nestled in too deep.

She stared at him as if she'd never seen him before, her heart as swollen as the highest river.

She *loved* him.

He came straight to her and took her hand. 'My grandfather wishes to meet you before we go in to lunch.'

There was a lightness to him and his eyes were brighter than she had seen them since her arrival on Agon.

She cleared her throat, almost dumbstruck at what she had finally admitted to herself. 'Do I curtsey?'

'As it's an official function, yes—but only to my grandfather.'

And then she was there before him, this wonderful man who'd sacrificed so much for his glorious island and his magnificent grandsons.

It was with enormous pride that Theseus made the introductions. Jo, pale and shaking, was obviously overcome by the occasion, but she curtseyed gracefully.

His grandfather reached for her hand. 'Thank you,' he rasped, clasping her hand in both his own. 'My book... I will treasure it.'

'It was an honour to be involved,' she said with feeling. 'But Fiona wrote most of it.'

'My grandson tells me you came at short notice and have barely slept?'

'It was all down to Theseus.' She stepped closer to meet his grandfather's gaze properly. 'However many hours

Fiona and I have put into this book, it's nothing compared to the time Theseus spent on the research.'

His grandfather turned his face to him, his eyes brimming. 'Yes. I am a lucky man. I have three fine grandsons—my island is in safe hands.'

Theseus's chest had grown so tight during this exchange it felt bruised. *She was championing him.*

A footman came into the room to announce that lunch was ready to be served. Before they could file out Astraeus caught hold of Theseus's wrist and beckoned him down.

'I am guessing she is the mother of your son?'

His mouth dropped open.

His grandfather gave a laugh. 'Did you think you could keep such a secret from me? A biography is one thing but a child…? I might be on my way to my deathbed, but I am still King.'

'I was going to tell you…'

'I know—after the Gala.' There was no sign of irritation. 'I am disappointed to have heard the news from a third party, but I do understand your reasons. How *is* the boy?'

'Settling in well.'

'I am very much looking forward to meeting him.'

'He is looking forward to meeting you too.'

'Have him brought to me when lunch is finished.'

'He would like that,' Theseus said, imagining Toby's delight at meeting a real-life king. 'Be warned: he's hoping you have a flying carpet.'

Astraeus gave a laugh, which quickly turned into a cough that made Theseus flinch, although he took pains not to show it. His grandfather despised pity.

'I hear he looks like you?' he said, when he'd recovered from his coughing fit.

'Your spies are very reliable,' Theseus said drily.

'That is why they're my spies. You can inherit them when I'm dead.'

Theseus wasn't quick enough to hide his wince. Here was his grandfather, welcoming death with open arms and a smile, and here was Theseus, who would give the flesh from his bones to keep him alive for ever.

'You are planning to marry the mother in a few weeks, I believe?'

'Yes. I apologise for not asking your permission.'

Astraeus waved a frail dismissive hand. 'You have never asked for my permission for anything—why should this be any different?'

'I've *always* asked your blessing.'

'Having already made up your mind,' his grandfather countered, with a twinkle in his eye that made them both laugh. 'Does the mother *want* to marry you?'

'She knows it's the best thing for our son.'

'Don't evade the question, Theseus. Does she want to marry you or not?'

There was a moment when his vocal cords stuck together.

'Do I take your silence as a negative?'

'What alternative do we have? The law forbids Toby from being a part of our family or inheriting my wealth unless we marry.'

The dismissive hand rose again. 'Do you think you are the first member of our family to impregnate a woman out of wedlock? You're wealthy in your own right. There are means, if the will is strong enough.'

'Are you suggesting that I *shouldn't* marry her?' Now he really *was* shocked. He knew how much importance his grandfather placed on matrimony, and how important it was to him to see the family line secured.

'I am suggesting you think in more depth about it before you tie yourself into a marriage neither of you can back away from.' His lined face softened. 'Whatever you choose…know that I will support you. Now, let us meet our guests and enjoy the day.'

Theseus dragged himself off the sofa in his palace apartment, clutching his head with one hand. From the look of the sunlight filtering through the shutters he hadn't closed properly it seemed that the sun had long beaten him awake.

He hadn't intended to stay the night. His plan had been to return to the villa once the official after-Gala party in the palace had finished. But with Talos long gone—chasing after the fabulous violinist who'd brought the entire audience to tears—and their grandfather having already retired, it had been left to him and Helios to play hosts to their distinguished guests.

When the last of the crowds had gone, all abuzz with the news of Helios's engagement to Princess Catalina, which had been announced during the gala, the Princess had flown home with her father and Helios had muttered that he needed a 'proper' drink.

Armed with a bottle of gin and two glasses, they'd hidden away in Helios's apartment and drunk until the small hours. He didn't know which of them had needed it the most. It was the first time Theseus had drunk so much in years.

They should have been celebrating.

Theseus had achieved the one thing he'd set out to do all those years ago, when he'd turned his back on being Theo and embraced who he truly was: he'd made his grandfather proud. The biography had been completed on time and it was a true celebration of the King's life—exactly as Theseus had wanted it to be.

And Helios had just got engaged to be married, so he should have been celebrating too.

Instead, the pair of them had drowned their sorrows.

All Theseus had been able to think about was Jo, and

how animated her face had been when she'd championed him to his grandfather.

No one had ever done that before—spoken so passionately on his behalf. Not since his mother, who would implore his father to treat him as an equal to Helios only to be slapped or, if she was lucky, just ignored for her efforts.

His mother had loved all her children fiercely. He could never have disappointed her, because in her eyes her boys had been perfect and incapable of doing wrong.

Jo loved Toby just as fiercely. Like his mother, she was a good, pure person. She deserved everything that was good in life. She deserved better than him.

He might not have disappointed his mother, but at some time or another he'd let the rest of his family down. When he'd selfishly left the palace to see the world he'd left the fledging business he and his brothers had just formed in their hands.

What a monstrously selfish person he had been.

Even his years of doing his princely duty had been done with the ulterior motive of gaining his family's forgiveness. His heart had never been in it. Indeed, he'd had to shut off his heart to get through it, to be Prince Theseus.

He knew that to make it through the rest of his life he would have to keep it closed. His dreams had to be stuffed away with the memories of his travels before they crowded his head with taunts of what could never be.

'Those people watching the Gala. They have no idea of our sacrifices,' Helios had said, finishing another glass.

It was the first time Theseus had ever heard his brother say something disparaging about being a member of the Kalliakis family, and with hindsight he should have probed his brother about his comment, but his mind had immediately flown to Jo and the sacrifices *she'd* made. The sacrifices she would continue to make for the rest of her life...

She'd been so pale during lunch, and when Toby had

been introduced to his grandfather she'd hung back, her eyes fluttering from Theseus to Toby and back to his grandfather.

Toby hadn't been even slightly overawed, and had happily chattered away as if the King had been a fixture in his life from birth.

But Jo…

His heart lurched.

He knew what he must do.

CHAPTER THIRTEEN

HE FOUND HER in the pool with Toby.

Her lips widened into a huge smile when she saw him. Then a quizzical expression formed as she noticed his set face and the smile dropped. She had learned to read him very well.

Toby had no such intuition. 'Daddy!' he cried. 'Look! Mummy's helping me swim. Come in with us!'

Theseus stiffened.

Daddy?

His son had called him Daddy.

It was the one word he'd been waiting to hear. He'd been content for Toby to call him Theseus, hadn't wanted to upset the apple cart by demanding a title he'd done nothing to earn. Rather like his title of Prince, he mused darkly.

He hadn't been at Toby's birth, and neither had he been there for the first four years of his life. And it was all his own fault for not seeing what his heart had known from the start—that Joanne Brookes was the best person he'd ever met.

And for that reason he had to let her go.

For her, he would cast aside his selfishness and actually do something for the benefit of someone else. To hell with the consequences.

He stepped to the pool's edge and smiled at his son. *I love you, Toby Kalliakis. I will never abandon you. I will always be there for you. Always.*

The words went unsaid.

'Chef is making cookies,' he said to Toby. 'If you get changed, they'll be ready for you to eat.'

'Can I, Mummy?' he asked eagerly, wriggling in Jo's arms.

Her eyes were fixed on Theseus, but she nodded, wading to the edge of the pool and lifting Toby onto it.

Elektra wrapped a towel around him and scooped him up.

Jo's heart shuddered and juddered. Something was badly wrong. She could feel it in her bones.

Please, not his grandfather...

Climbing out of the pool, she reached for her own towel, her heart juddering even more when Theseus made no move to hand it to her.

She wrapped the towel around herself and followed him to the poolside table. A jug of fruit juice and two glasses had been placed on it. He poured them both a glass and pushed Jo's towards her.

'Have you packed your bags yet?' he asked heavily, looking at the jug rather than at her.

'Yes. We're ready to go. Is there a problem with the apartment? It won't be a problem staying here longer. To be honest, Toby and I both love it—'

'There won't be an apartment,' he interrupted. 'Jo, you're going home.'

His words made no sense. 'What are you talking about?'

'Our wedding is off. You and Toby are going back England.'

No. They still made no sense.

'What are you talking about?' she repeated.

He lifted his gaze to meet hers. Unlike the stunned incomprehension that must be clear in her eyes, in his there was nothing. Nothing at all.

'I was wrong to insist on marriage. You conceived a child with Theo the engineer, not Theseus the Prince. None of this was your doing. I'm the one who lied about my identity and made it impossible for you to find me. For me to ask you to give up the rest of your life after all the sacrifices you've already made... I can't do it.' He kneaded his forehead with his knuckles. 'I've caused enough damage. I won't be a party to any more. You deserve the freedom to live your life as you want, not in a way that's dictated and forced on you.'

'Where has *this* come from?' she asked hoarsely. 'I don't understand. Have I done something wrong?'

'No.' He laughed without humour. 'You've done everything right. It's me who's done everything wrong, and now I'm putting it right.'

'But what about Toby?'

'Toby needs to be with *you*. I will recognise him as my son. He can come here for holidays. I'll visit whenever I can. We can video call.'

'You wanted to be a *real* father to him. You can't have a hug with a computer. It isn't the same—it just isn't.' She knew she was gabbling but she couldn't control it. 'Toby needs *you*. Wherever you are is where he'll be happy— whether it's here or in England.

'My wealth is mine to do with as I like while I'm alive.' He dug a hand into his pocket and pulled out a folded envelope. 'Here. It's a cheque. Maintenance for the past five years...for when you had to struggle alone.'

She took it automatically, having hardly heard him. Her head was cold and reeling. She thought she might be sick.

This had to be a joke. It couldn't be anything else.

'I'll buy you a house,' he continued. 'Choose whatever you like, wherever you like. There will be further maintenance too, and I'll make investments and open accounts in Toby's name...'

On and on he went, but his words were just noise.

Panic, the like of which she'd never known—not even

during the night when he'd learned about Toby—clawed at her with talons so deep they cut through to the bone.

'But you wanted Toby to be your heir...' She was clutching at straws, her pride very much smothered in her stark shock. 'If you want to get rid of me we can marry and *then* Toby and I can move back to England. We don't have to live under the same roof unless your constitution demands it.'

He shook his head. 'What if you meet another man and want to marry him?'

'Meet another man?' Now her voice rose to a high pitch. 'How can I *ever* do that? You're the only man—don't you see that? It's only ever been you. I *love* you.'

His face paled and a pulse throbbed at his temple. 'I never asked for your love. I told you to keep your heart closed.'

'Do you think I had a *choice*?' Her whole body shook, fury and anguish and terror all circling inside her, smashing her heart. She wanted to lash out at him so badly, to inflict on him the pain he was wreaking on her.

Theseus jumped to his feet, gripping on to the edge of the table as he leaned over. 'Love does not equate to happiness. My mother loved my father and all he gave her was misery. I can't make you happy. Maybe for a few weeks or a few months—but what then? What happens when you wake one day with a hole of discontent in your stomach so wide that nothing can ever fill it? When the reality of your life hits you and you understand that this is all there is and all there will *ever* be?'

'But *why* is that all there will be?'

And as she shouted the words understanding hit her.

'Haven't you punished yourself enough?' she demanded, lowering her voice. 'You've spent years making amends for the times when you were less than dutiful—do you really have to sacrifice the rest of your life too?'

With lightning-quick reflexes Theseus grabbed the jug

of juice and hurled it. It flew through the air and landed with an enormous splash in the middle of the swimming pool.

She had never seen him so full of fury, not even when he'd learned about Toby.

'Do not speak as if you know anything. My grandparents made more sacrifices than I could make if I lived to be a thousand years old. My grandmother loved me, but I was such a selfish bastard I wasn't even there to say goodbye.'

'What...?'

'I was too late. By the time I got home she'd already died.'

Her hands flew to her cheeks, wretchedness for him—for her—raging through her. He'd been so desperate to get back to her. 'Please...you can't blame yourself for that. You tried...'

'Yes, I can—and I do. If I'd taken my phone with me when I went climbing, Helios would have reached me sooner and I would have had three extra days to get home. Dammit, she was *asking* for me.'

'It wasn't your fault.'

'Wherever the fault lies, the result is the same—I failed her when she needed me. I made a vow that as I failed to honour her in life I would honour her in death, and honour my grandfather in the manner I should have done from when I was old enough to know better. *This* is who I am. It's who I was born to be and who I will be for the rest of my life. I am a prince of Agon, and if we marry you'll be my wife—a princess. All the freedoms you take for granted will be gone. I will not do that to you. I know the cost, and I will not allow you to pay it.'

Loud silence rang out. Even the birds had stopped chirping.

On jelly-like legs, Jo rose. 'There's nothing wrong with wanting your freedom. You can have it still. It doesn't have to be all or nothing. The happiness you had when you travelled the world and the happiness we've shared here, in this villa—'

He cut her off. 'Your time here hasn't been real, you know that. I saw your reaction to the number of staff you'd need to employ, the schedule you'd have to follow. And that's only the beginning. It will swallow you up and spit you out.'

Despite the harshness of his tone, there was something in his eyes that gave her the courage to fight on.

'My feelings for you are real. I'm not a precious flower, ready to wilt at the first sign of pressure. Don't you see? You've made me strong enough to bloom. Meeting you all those years ago… Theo, you made me feel as if I was actually *worth* something. Even here, even during the days when you hated me, you still made me feel like a woman deserving of desire and affection in her own right.'

It was the wrong thing to say. His eyes turned into two black blocks of ice.

His voice was every bit as cold. 'When are you going to understand? I am not Theo. The man you love is dead.'

'No.' She shook her head desperately and gave a last roll of the dice. 'No. Theo's still there. He's a part of you.'

But she might as well have been talking to the leaves on the trees.

'Nikos will be here in a couple of hours to take you to the airport,' he said, turning away from her and heading back to the villa.

No, no, no, no, no. It *couldn't* be over.

But the stiffness in his frame told her that it was.

He stepped through the patio doors without looking back.

Was it possible to hear someone's heart breaking?

Theseus sat with Talos, discussing a new company he'd

discovered that had the potential to be a good investment, but all he could think about was Jo.

He had the impression Talos was only half paying attention too. He'd announced his engagement to his beautiful violinist and it was clear his mind was on how quickly he could get back to her. And Helios had stayed at their meeting for all of five minutes before staggering out, saying he had stuff to do.

Even in the depths of his own misery Theseus could see something was badly wrong with his elder brother. Usually it was Helios who was the sunniest of the three Kalliakis brothers, while Talos normally walked around with a demeanour akin to that of a bear with a sore head. The switch between them would have been startling if Theseus had been able to summon the energy to care.

He'd assumed Jo would be happy to leave, that once it sank in that she had her freedom back she would grab Toby and speed away to the airport, singing, 'Freedom!' at the top of her voice.

She'd been like a wounded animal.

There he'd been, giving her a way out, handing it to her on a plate, and she'd refused to take it. He'd had to force it.

She'd said she *loved* him.

How could she love him? It wasn't possible. He'd done nothing to earn it, nothing to deserve it. He'd lied to her, impregnated her... Yes, she'd lied about being on the pill, but if he'd had his wits about him he would have seen her inexperience and not used her for his own selfish needs. He'd forced her to give up the job she loved, to give up *everything*, and she said she *loved* him?

Theos, he missed her. He missed her sunny smile at breakfast. He missed resting his head on her breasts while she stroked his hair.

'What is wrong with you?' Talos demanded, breaking through his thoughts.

'Nothing.'

'Well, your "nothing" is getting on my nerves.'

'Sorry.'

Talos shook his head with incredulity. 'Get up.'

'What?'

'Get up. You're coming to my gym. You need to work your "nothing" out. You're no good for anything with your head in Oxford.'

Theseus jumped to his feet. 'What would *you* know about it?' he snarled.

Talos folded his arms and fixed him with his stare. 'More than you think.'

Her coffee had gone cold.

Oh, well, it was disgusting anyway.

The coffee Theseus's staff served had ruined her palate for anything else.

At least it was only her taste buds. It wasn't as if the coffee had ruined everything else. No, Theseus had done that all on his own.

She'd been back in England for a week. A whole week. One hundred and sixty-eight interminably long hours, spent doing little other than trying not to wallow in front of Toby.

His preschool had taken him back with open arms so she had a few hours each day in which to bawl and rant and punch pillows. He was a resilient little thing, and his resilience had been helped when her landlady had let them move straight back in as she'd not yet relet their flat.

It was as if they'd never left England in the first place.

Their whole time on Agon might as well have been a dream.

Except no dream would have had her waking with cramping in her chest and awful flu-like symptoms.

She was thankful she'd never told Toby they were moving permanently to Agon. She'd figured it was best to just take things one day at a time. Having achieved his dream of meeting the King—his great-grandfather—and with the promise that he could go back and visit his daddy soon, he'd been happy to return to England and see his friends and his aunt, uncle and cousin.

At a loss for what to do, she stood at the window and looked out over the bustling street below. All those people going somewhere in the miserable spring drizzle.

Pressing her cheek against the cold glass, she closed her eyes.

What was he doing right now? Who was he with?

Did he miss Toby?

Did he miss *her*?

Did he even think about her?

She brushed away another tear, wondering when they would dry up. So many pathetic tears…

She had battled too hard in her life to be a victim.

If Theo didn't love her, then there was nothing she could do about it. All she could do was pull herself up and carry on.

But she felt so cold.

She would give anything to feel some warmth.

Theseus sat in his grandfather's study, ostensibly studying the chessboard while waiting for his grandfather to make his move. Yet his mind was far from the intricately carved black and white pieces before him. It was thousands of miles away. In Oxford. Where it had been for well over a week now.

'Are you going to make your move?'

He blinked rapidly, snapping himself out of the trance he'd fallen into.

His grandfather was staring at him, concern on his aged face.

It was the first game of chess they'd played since the

Gala. Since he'd sent Jo away. He'd made a brief visit to his grandfather to inform him that the engagement was off and that Jo and Toby would be returning to England. He'd braced himself for a barrage of questions but none had come forth. His announcement had been met with a slow nod and the words, 'You're a grown man. You know what's best for you and your family.'

Theseus moved his Bishop, realising too late he'd left his Queen exposed.

'It will get better,' his grandfather said.

Instead of denying that there was anything to improve, Theseus shook his head. 'Will it?'

His grandfather's eyes drilled into him. 'Can it get any worse?'

'No.'

But of course it could get worse. One day Toby—who now had his own phone, on which he could have face-to-face conversations with him at any time he liked—would casually mention a new uncle.

It wouldn't happen soon. Jo wasn't the kind of woman to jump out of one man's bed and straight into another...

He closed his eyes, waiting for the lance of pain imagining her with another man would bring. It didn't come. The picture wouldn't form. His brain simply could not conjure up an image of Jo with someone else.

She'd said there had been no other. She'd been a virgin when she had met him. He remained her only lover.

It suddenly occurred to him that she'd been his last lover too.

There had been no one but her since Illya.

'Do I understand that you finally gave her the choice of whether or not to marry you and she chose the latter?' his grandfather asked, studying the board before them.

Theseus swallowed. 'No. I set her free.'

'Did she want to be set free?'

He paused before answering truthfully, 'No.'

His grandfather's finger rested on his castle. 'You took away her choice in the matter?'

'For her own good.'

The watery eyes sharpened. 'People should make their own choices.'

'Even if they're the wrong ones?'

'I thought your grandmother was the wrong choice for me,' his grandfather said lightly, after a small pause. 'She was born a princess, but I thought her too independent-minded to cope with being a queen. If I'd been given the choice I would have chosen someone else—and that would have been the wrong choice. We complemented each other, despite our differences. She gave me a fresh perspective on life.'

A twinkle came into his grandfather's eyes.

'She understood *your* struggles and helped me to understand them too. She was a queen in every way, and I thanked God every day of our life together that the choice had been taken out of my hands, because I would never have found the love we shared with anyone else.'

Theseus rubbed the nape of his neck, breathing heavily.

There was that word again. *Love*.

He'd loved his parents, but they'd died before he'd had the chance to know them properly. Losing them, especially losing his mother, had smashed his heart into pieces.

He'd loved his grandmother. Her death had smashed the pieces that had been left of his heart.

He looked at his grandfather, spears of pain lancing him at the knowledge that soon he would be gone too.

He thought of Jo—her sweet smiling face, her soft skin, her gentle touch. Her sharp tongue when it came to protecting their son.

Theos, if anything were to happen to her...

It would kill him.

And as this realisation hit him his grandfather slid his Castle to Theseus's Queen and knocked it over.

'Your Queen is the heart of your game both in chess and in life,' his grandfather said quietly. 'Without her by your side your game will be poorer. Without her by your side…' His eyes glistened with a sudden burst of ferocity as he growled, 'Checkmate.'

There was a light knock on the door and then Nikos entered.

'You said to tell you if anything significant occurred.' He handed Theseus a piece of paper and left.

Theseus read it quickly. Then he read it again.

A ray of warmth broke through the chill that had lived in his veins for these past ten days. It trickled through him, lightly at first, then expanded until every single part of him was suffused with it.

CHAPTER FOURTEEN

Jo slipped her brown leather flip-flops off and dangled them from a finger, letting her toes sink into the warm Illyan sand.

She tilted her head back and breathed in the salty scent, feeling the light breeze play on her skin.

She stood there for ages, soaking it all in. There was no rush. No need to be anywhere or do anything.

There was only one place she wanted to visit.

She walked along the shore, the cool lapping waves bouncing over her feet and sinking between her toes, the May sun bright and inviting and heating her skin, driving out the coldness that had been in her bones since she'd left Agon a fortnight ago.

Her time on this island five years ago had been the happiest of her life. On this island she had lost her inhibitions, her virginity and her heart. And, for all the heartache, she wouldn't trade a second of it.

Nothing much had changed in Illya. It was part of a cluster of rocky islands in the Adriatic, and the daily ferry was still the only means of getting to or from the mainland without a yacht, or a canoe and very strong arms. And Marin's Bar was still the only bar on the south of the island.

Really, 'bar' was a loose term for what it was—a large wooden shack with a thatched roof and a kitchen stuck on at the back, surrounded by tiny chalets. Most people who found the island were real travellers, not university graduates like Jo, Jenna and Imogen, who had been there for a cheap couple of weeks in the sunshine.

She supposed one day it would change. Developers would get their tentacles on it. Maybe it would lose its charm. Maybe it wouldn't. Change was often scary, but it didn't have to be bad. She'd gone through a lot of change recently and it had made her stronger.

Soon she was standing at the front of the shack with her heart in her mouth, taking deep, steadying breaths.

No more tears. That was what she'd promised herself. No more. Even if today *was* the day she had been supposed to marry Theseus...

What was she even doing here?

Three days ago she'd dropped Toby off at preschool, then walked back along a busy shopping street. A travel agent's window had been advertising trips to Korcula; another Croatian island.

Three days later and here she was. Back on Illya. Back in the same spot where she'd once watched Theseus play football on the beach with his Scandinavian friends.

The bar was empty, save for a blonde barmaid who greeted her with a friendly smile.

'Is Marin here?' Jo asked. She'd always liked the owner; an aging hippy with a pet Dalmatian that had a habit of falling asleep by customers' feet. She'd lost count of the number of people she'd seen trip over him.

'He's gone out, but he'll be back soon. Can I get you a drink?'

'A lemonade, please.'

While the barmaid poured her drink Jo cast her eyes around. It was pretty much as she remembered it. The walls were covered with photos of the travellers who had passed through—hundreds and hundreds of pictures, crammed in every available bit of space. And the large noticeboard where people could leave messages for friends still hung above the jukebox.

Sipping at her lemonade, she gazed at the pictures, wondering if she would see any familiar faces…

There was one image that rooted her to the spot.

It was a picture of her and Theo, the night after he'd come to her rescue. Their glasses were raised, their cheeks pressed together and they were both poking their tongues out at the camera.

When had that been put up?

She reached out a shaking finger and traced their image. Together their faces formed a heart shape.

A roll of pain gushed through her, so powerful that she had to grip a table for support.

Taking deep breaths, she waited for it to pass. The waves of pain always did, leaving nothing but a constant heavy ache that balled in her chest and pumped around her blood.

'I thought I'd find you here.'

Sending lemonade flying everywhere, Jo spun around to find Theseus standing in the doorway.

She blinked. And blinked again. And again.

He was still there, dressed in a pair of familiar cargo pants and nothing else. His hair was tousled; dark stubble covered his jaw. Wry amusement played on his face, but his eyes…his brown eyes were full of apprehension.

She opened her mouth but nothing came out.

She blinked again, totally uncomprehending.

'What are you doing here?' she croaked eventually.

'Waiting for you.'

'But how…?'

He smiled ruefully. 'You're the mother of my child. You and Toby have had bodyguards watching you since you left Agon. As soon as they told me you'd booked a holiday to Korcula I knew you'd come here.'

He came over to stand beside her.

'I put this up,' he said, putting his finger on their picture and brushing it lightly, just as she'd done minutes before.

'You did?' Her words sounded distant to her ears.

Any second now and she would wake up and still be on the ferry from Korcula, the large Adriatic island an hour's sail away, where she'd left Toby in a family hotel with her brother and sister-in-law.

'I found it last week in a box in my dressing room. When I returned from Illya I put everything to do with my travels in boxes and tried to forget about them. In one of the boxes was my old phone. I got Stieg—do you remember him?—to take that picture of us.' He finally looked at her, a crooked smile on his handsome face. 'There were a lot of pictures of you on that phone. More pictures of you than anyone else. Let me show you.'

He reached into the back pocket of his cargo shorts and pulled out his old phone. He went to his photo gallery and offered it to her. 'See?'

But her hands were shaking too much to take it.

With his warm body pressed against her, Theseus scrolled through the photos of his time on Illya—dozens and dozens and dozens of them. Most of them were of the surf on the north side of the island, or the mountains of the neighbouring islands. Only a few had people in them. Of those she was in over half. Only in two of them was she posing—in the rest he'd captured her unawares.

There was even a picture of her sitting alone on the beach in her swimsuit. She remembered that day. She'd been too embarrassed at the thought of what she'd look like in a wetsuit to surf with him and the others. She'd been scared someone would call her a hippo, and even more scared that Theo would laugh at it.

But now she knew differently. If anyone had insulted her he would have probably flushed their heads down a toilet.

How she wished she'd had the confidence to say to hell with them all and go surfing.

'There's more,' he said quietly, opening his phone's contacts box. 'There. Do you see?'

She nodded. It was all she was capable of.

There was her name. *Jo*. And beneath it was her old mobile number.

'Come,' he said, tugging at her frozen hand. 'Let's go and sit on the beach together.'

In a daze, Jo let him guide her out into the sun.

They sat on the deserted beach and Theseus leaned back on his elbows. Jo sat forward, hugging her knees and watching the sailing boats in the distance.

Had she fallen into a dream?

'Why do you think I remembered you had royal blood in your veins?' he asked quietly.

'Because you remember everything,' she whispered.

From out of the corner of her eye she saw him shake his head.

'I have a good memory, but when it comes to *you* I remember everything. I remember standing on the ferry and pressing "delete" on your number. But when I got the message asking if I wanted to carry on with the action I cancelled it. I couldn't do it. When I got home…'

He sat up and grabbed her hand, pulling it to his mouth. It wasn't a kiss. It was a brush of his lips and a warm breath of his air that sent tingles of sensation scurrying through her.

Dear God, he really was here. Theseus was *here*.

And just like that the stupor left her and her heart kick-started in thunderous jolts.

His eyes were dark and intense. 'Helios has always known he will one day be king. His destiny is carved in stone. My own destiny was to be nothing more than his shadow—his spare—but I wanted something so much more. I craved freedom. I wanted to play with other children and run free.' He pointed to the cobalt sky. 'I wanted to be up there in the stars. But I was born to be a prince. After my parents died I kept thinking, *Is this it?*, and I struggled endlessly to reconcile myself with my destiny, never realising that to my family it was like I was spitting on the Kalliakis name.

'When I was too late to say goodbye to my grandmother, and I saw the depth of my grandfather's pain, I knew I had a choice to either be a real part of my family or leave it for ever. So I put everything about my time exploring the world into boxes, taped them up and put them away. All my memories. I packed Theo into that box. I couldn't be that man *and* be the Prince I had to be.'

He swallowed.

'I wanted to make amends to my grandmother's memory and prove to my grandfather that I *am* proud to be a Kalliakis. I'd spent thirty years pursuing my own pleasure and it was time to grow up and be the man he'd raised me to be. I threw myself into palace life and the Kalliakis business with my brothers. I was determined to prove myself. But inside I was empty. And then you walked back into my life.'

He reached to brush a thumb down her cheek, a wan smile playing on his lips.

'If you'd told me a month ago that I'd fallen in love with a woman I slept with once five years ago I would have said you were mad. But that's the truth. You were there to catch me when I was at my lowest point and you caught my heart. It's been yours ever since that night. There hasn't been another, and only now do I know why—it's because I've belonged to you heart, body and soul since the night we conceived Toby. You came back into my life and the emptiness disappeared. But I didn't see it until I sent you away and the hole was ripped open again. Don't speak,' he urged when she parted her lips. 'I *know* you love me. I've always known. Just answer me this. When I sent you back to England it was so you could have your freedom. I was so high and mighty, thinking that I was doing the right thing, that I took away your freedom to make a choice.'

'My choice would be you,' she said immediately, before he could ask.

'But—'

This time Jo placed her finger to his lips. 'Your turn to keep quiet. I've never craved to see the stars. All I've ever wanted was to find a place where I belong, and I've found that with you. You make me whole. You make me proud to live in my skin. And that's the greatest gift you could ever have given me.'

She traced her fingers across his jaw, finally able to believe that this was real—that he had come to her, had met her back in the place where it had all started between them.

'Palace life doesn't frighten me the way you think it should, and as long as you're by my side I will adapt. I will be proud to be your princess and to represent the greatest family on this planet.'

He sighed and pressed a light kiss to her mouth. 'After the way I treated you I didn't dare to presume...'

'Freedom comes in many forms,' she said gently. 'You don't have to hide the essence of yourself away for ever.'

'I know that now. My grandmother was a strong, warm-hearted woman—she would have forgiven me. Now it's time to forgive myself.'

The look he gave her warmed her right down to the marrow of her bones.

'It's strange, but when I'm with you all my craving for freedom disappears. *You* make me feel free. You bring sunshine into my life and I swear I will never let you or Toby go again.'

She cupped his cheeks in her hands. His skin felt so warm. 'I will love you for ever.'

'And I will love *you* for ever.'

His hands dived into her hair and then his mouth came crashing onto hers.

It hadn't been a kiss, Jo thought a few hours later, when they were entangled in the sheets of the bed in the cabin where they'd first made love five years before. It had been more like the breath of life. It had been filled with promises for the future, something that bound them together for ever.

'Where are you going?' she asked when he slid off the bed.

He grinned and dug his hands into his shorts pocket. He pulled out the penknife he carried everywhere.

He climbed back onto the bed and placed the blade on the wooden wall. He etched the letters 'TK' and 'JB' into the wood.

'There,' he decreed in his most regal voice, snapping the blade shut and dropping it onto the floor. 'It's official. You and me—together for ever.'

EPILOGUE

'GOOD MORNING, PRINCESS.'

Jo opened a bleary eye and found her husband sitting on the edge of the bed beside her.

She smiled and yawned. 'What time is it?'

'Six o'clock.'

'It's the middle of the night.' And, considering they'd spent most of the night making love, she was shattered.

He laughed and ruffled her hair.

'The surf's up.'

That woke her up.

Theseus had insisted on giving her surfing lessons, and she'd been thrilled to discover that she wasn't completely awful at it. Now, three months after their wedding, they loved nothing more than leaving their villa early, when surf conditions were right, and spending the morning with Toby in the sea and on the beach before heading off to the palace to undertake their royal engagements. As per their instructions to their respective private secretaries, their mornings were always kept clear.

Yes, it had all worked out beautifully. With the family's blessing they had decided to make the villa their main dwelling. They used their apartment in the palace when it was convenient, but to all intents and purposes the villa was their home.

Theseus was staring at her expectantly.

'I think it might be a good idea for me to give it a miss today,' she said, her heart thumping at the thought of the news she was about to share with him; a secret she'd been hugging to herself for almost a week.

'Oh?' He cocked an eyebrow. 'Are you not feeling well?'

'I'm feeling fine. Fantastic. I just think it would be wise to get a doctor's advice before I go surfing over the next seven or eight months.'

She giggled when his mouth dropped open.

It was good few moments before comprehension spread over his features. 'You're not...?'

She couldn't stop the beam widening over her face. 'I'm over a week late...' She'd noticed her breasts growing tender, but it had been her stomach turning over at the scent of the barbecued spare ribs they'd had for dinner two nights before that had decided it for her.

'I'm going to be a father again?'

'There's only one way to find out.'

Jumping out of bed, she hurried into her dressing room and pulled a pregnancy test out of the chest of drawers. She'd got Elektra, whom she trusted implicitly, to buy it for her the day before. With Theseus hovering outside the bathroom, she did the necessary.

Three minutes later, buzzing with excitement, she poked her head out of the door.

'What do you want? A boy or a girl?'

The dazed look on his face evaporated. With a whoop, Theseus lifted her into his arms and carried her back to bed.

* * * * *

HELIOS CROWNS
HIS MISTRESS

MICHELLE SMART

This book is for Aimee—
thank you for all the support and cheerleading
over the years. You're one in a million.

This book is also dedicated to Hannah and Sarah—
the mojitos in this are for you!

xxx

CHAPTER ONE

'DO YOU REALLY have to shave it off?' Amy Green, busy admiring Helios's rear view, slipped a cajoling tone into her plea.

Helios met her eye in the reflection of the bathroom mirror and winked. 'It will grow back.'

She pouted. Carefully. The clay mask she'd applied to her face had dried, making it hard for her to move her features without cracking it. Another ten minutes and she would be able to rinse it off. 'But you're so sexy with a beard.'

'Are you saying I'm not sexy without it?'

She made a harrumphing sound. 'You're always sexy.'

Too sexy for his own good. Even without a beard. Even his voice was sexy: a rich, low-pitched tone that sang to her ears, with the Agon accent which made it dance.

Impossibly tall and rangy, and incredibly strong, with dark olive colouring and ebony hair, currently tousled after a snatched hour in bed with her, Helios had a piratical appearance. The dangerous look was exaggerated by the slight curve of his strong nose and the faint scar running over its bridge: the mark of a fight with his brother Theseus when they were teenagers. Utterly without vanity, Helios wore the scar with pride. He was the sexiest man she'd ever met.

Soon the hair would be tamed and as smooth as his face would be, yet his innate masculinity would still vibrate through him. His rugged body would be hidden by a formal black evening suit, but his strength and vitality would permeate the expensive fabric. The playful expression emanating from his liquid dark brown eyes would still offer sin.

He would turn into Prince Helios Kalliakis, heir to the throne of Agon. But he would still be a flesh and blood man.

He lifted the cut-throat blade. 'Are you sure you don't want to do it?'

Amy shook her head. 'Can you imagine if I were to cut you? I would be arrested for treason.'

He grinned, then gave the mirror a quick wipe to clear away the condensation produced from the steam of her bath.

Smothering a snigger, she stretched out her right leg until her foot reached the taps, and used her toes to pour a little more hot water in.

'I'm sure deliberately steaming up the bathroom so I can't see properly is also treasonous,' he said with a playful shake of his head, striding lithely to the extractor fan and switching it on.

As with everything in his fabulous palace apartment it worked instantly, clearing the enormous bathroom of steam.

He crouched beside the bath and placed his gorgeous face close to hers. 'Any more treasonous behaviour, *matakia mou*, and I will be forced to punish you.'

His breath, hot and laced with a faint trace of their earlier shared pot of coffee, danced against her skin.

'And what form of punishment will you be forced to give me?' she asked, the desire she'd thought spent bubbling back up inside her, her breaths shortening.

Those liquid eyes flashed and a smirk played on the bowed lips that had kissed her everywhere. It was a mouth a woman could happily kiss for ever.

'A punishment you will never forget.' He snapped his teeth together for effect and growled, before throwing her a look full of promise and striding back to the mirror. Half watching her in the reflection, Helios dipped his shaving brush into the pot and began covering his black beard with a rich, foamy lather.

Amy had to admit watching him shave as if he were the leading man in a medieval film fascinated her. It also scared her. The blade he used was sharp enough to slice through flesh. One twitch of the hand...

All the same, she couldn't drag her eyes away as he scraped the cut-throat razor down his cheek. In its own way it had an eroticism to it, transporting her to a bygone time when men had been *men*. And Helios was all man.

If he wanted he could snap his fingers and an army of courtiers would be there to do the job for him. But that wasn't his style. The Kalliakis family were direct descendants of Ares Patakis, the warrior whose uprising had freed Agon from its Venetian invaders over eight hundred years ago. Agon princes were taught how to wield weapons with the same dedication with which they were taught the art of royal protocol. To her lover, a cut-throat razor was but one of many weapons he'd mastered.

She waited until he'd wiped the blade on a towel to clean it before speaking again. 'Do I take it that despite all my little hints you haven't put a space aside for me tonight?'

Her 'little hints' had taken the form of mentioning at every available opportunity how much she would love to attend the Royal Ball that was the talk of the entire island, but she hadn't seriously expected to get an invitation. She was but a mere employee of the palace museum, and a temporary employee at that.

And it wasn't as if they would be together for ever, she thought with a strange stab of wistfulness. Their relationship had never been a secret, but it hadn't been flaunted either. She was his lover, not his girlfriend, something she had known from the very start. She had no official place in her life and never would.

He placed the blade back to his cheek and swiped, revealing another line of smooth olive skin. 'However much I adore your company, it wouldn't be appropriate for you to attend.'

She pulled a face, inadvertently cracking the mask around her mouth. 'Yes, I know. I am a commoner, and those attending your ball are the *crème de la crème* of high society.'

'Nothing would please me more than to see you there, dressed in the finest haute couture money can buy. But it would be inappropriate for my lover to attend the ball where I'm to select my future wife.'

The deliciously warm bath turned cold in the beat of a moment.

She sat up.

'Your future wife? What are you talking about?'

His reflected eyes met hers again. 'The underlying reason for this ball is so that I can choose a wife.'

She paused before asking, 'Like in *Cinderella*?'

'Exactly.' He worked on his chin, then wiped the blade on the towel again. 'You know all of this.'

'No,' she said slowly, her blood freezing to match the chills rippling over her skin. 'I was under the impression this ball was a pre-Gala do.'

In three weeks the eyes of the world would be on Agon as the island celebrated fifty years of King Astraeus's reign. Heads of state and dignitaries from all around the world would be flying in for the occasion.

'And so it is. I think the phrase is "killing two birds with one stone"?'

'Why can't you find a wife in the normal way?' And, speaking of normal, how were her vocal cords performing when the rest of her body had been subsumed in a weird kind of paralysis?

'Because, *matakia mou*, I am heir to the throne. I have to marry someone of royal blood. You know that.'

Yes, that she *did* know. Except she hadn't thought it would be now. It hadn't occurred to her. Not once. Not while they were sharing a bed every night.

'I need to choose wisely,' he continued, speaking in the same tone he might use if he were discussing what to order from the palace kitchen for dinner. 'Obviously I have a shortlist of preferred women—princesses and duchesses I have met through the years who have caught my attention.'

'Obviously…' she echoed. 'Is there any particular woman at the top of your shortlist, or are there a few of them jostling for position?'

'Princess Catalina of Monte Cleure is looking the most likely. I've known her and her family for years—they've attended our Christmas Balls since Catalina was a baby. Her sister and brother-in-law got together at the last one.' He grinned at the scandalous memory. 'Catalina and I dined together a couple of times when I was in Denmark the other week. She has all the makings of an excellent queen.'

An image of the raven-haired Princess, a famed beauty who dealt with incessant press scrutiny on account of her ethereal royal loveliness, came to Amy's mind. Waves of nausea rolled in her belly.

'You never mentioned it.'

'There was nothing to say.' He didn't look the slightest bit shamefaced.

'Did you sleep with her?'

He met her stare, censure clear in his reflection. 'What kind of a question is *that*?'

'A natural question for a woman to ask her lover.'

Until that moment it hadn't been something that had occurred to her: the idea that he might have strayed. Helios had never promised fidelity, but he hadn't needed to. Since their first night together their lust for each other had been all-consuming.

'The Princess is a virgin and will remain one until her wedding day whether she marries me or some other man. Does that answer your question?'

Not even a little bit. All it did was open up a whole heap of further questions, all of which she didn't have the right to ask and not one of which she wanted to hear the answer to.

The only question she *could* bring herself to ask was 'When are you hoping to marry the lucky lady?'

If he heard the irony in her voice he hid it well. 'It will be a state wedding, but I would hope to be married in a couple of months.'

A couple of months? He expected to choose a bride and have a state wedding in a few months? Surely it wasn't possible…?

But this was Helios. If there was one thing she knew about her lover it was that he was not a man to let the grass grow beneath his feet. If he wanted something done he wanted it done now, not tomorrow.

But a couple of months…?

Amy was contracted to stay in Agon until September, which was five whole months away. She'd imagined… Hoped…

She thought of King Astraeus, Helios's grandfather. She had never met the King, but through her work in the palace museum she felt she had come to know him. The King was dying. Helios needed to marry and produce an heir of his own to assure the family line.

She *knew* all this. Yet still she'd shared his bed night after night and allowed herself to believe that Helios would hold off his wedding until her time on Agon was up.

Gripping the sides of the free-standing bath, she got carefully to her feet and stepped out. Hands trembling, she pulled a warm, fluffy towel off the rack and held it to her chest, not wanting to waste a second, not even to wrap it around herself.

Helios pulled his top lip down and brought the blade down in careful but expert fashion. 'I'll call you when the ball is finished.'

She strode to the door, uncaring that bathwater was dripping off her and onto the expensive floor tiles. 'No, you won't.'

'Where are you going? You're soaking wet.'

From out of the corner of her eye she saw him pat his towel over his face and follow her through into his bedroom, not bothering to cover himself.

She gathered her clothes into a bundle and held them tightly. A strange burning buzzed in her brain, making coherent thought difficult.

Three months. That was how long she'd shared his bed. In that time they'd slept apart on only a dozen or so occasions, when Helios had been away on official business. Like when he'd gone to Denmark and, unbeknownst to her, dined with Princess Catalina. And now he was throwing a ball to find the woman he would share a bed with for the rest of his life.

She'd known from the start that they had no future, and

had been careful to keep her heart and emotions detached. But to hear him being so blasé about it...

She stood by the door that opened into the secret passageway connecting their apartments. There were dozens and dozens of such secret passageways throughout the palace; a fortress built on intrigue and secrets.

'I'm going to my apartment. Enjoy your evening.'

'Have I missed something?'

The fact that he looked genuinely perplexed only made matters worse.

'You say it isn't appropriate for me to come tonight, but I'll tell you what isn't appropriate—talking about the wife you're hours away from selecting with the woman who has shared your bed for three months.'

'I don't know what your problem is,' he said with a shrug, raising his hands in an open-palmed gesture. 'My marriage won't change anything between us.'

'If you believe that then you're as stupid as you are insensitive and misogynistic. You speak as if the women you are selecting from are sweets lined up in a shop rather than flesh and blood people.' She shook her head to emphasise her distaste, watching as her words seeped in and the perplexity on Helios's face darkened into something ugly.

Helios was not a man who received criticism well. On this island and in this palace he was celebrated and feted, a man whose words people hung on to. Affable and charming, his good humour was infectious. Cross him, however, and he would turn with the snap of two fingers.

If she wasn't so furious with him Amy would probably be afraid.

He strode towards her, magnificently naked. He stopped a foot away and folded his arms across his defined chest. A pulse throbbed at his temple and his jaw clenched tightly.

'Be careful in how you speak to me. I might be your lover, but you do not have a licence to insult me.'

'Why? Because you're a prince?' She hugged the towel and the bundle of clothes even tighter, as if their closeness could stop her erratically thumping heart from jumping out of her chest. 'You're about to make a commitment to another woman and I want no part of it.'

Benedict, Helios's black Labrador, sensed the atmosphere and padded over to her, his tongue lolling out as he sat on his haunches by her side and gave what looked like a disapproving stare at his master.

Helios noticed it too. He rubbed Benedict's head, the darkness disappearing as quickly as it had appeared, an indulgent smile spreading over his face as he looked at Amy. 'Don't be so dramatic. I know you're premenstrual, and that makes you more emotional than you would otherwise be, but you're being irrational.'

'Premenstrual? Did you really just say that? You really are on a different planet. God forbid that I should become "emotional" because my lover has had secret dates with other women and is about to take one of them for his wife and still expects me to warm his bed. But don't worry. Pat me on the head and tell me I'm premenstrual. Pat yourself on the back and tell yourself you've done nothing wrong.'

Too furious to look at him any more, she turned the handle of the door and pushed it open with her hip.

'Are you walking away from me?'

Was that *laughter* in his voice? Did he find this *amusing*?

Ignoring him, Amy raised her head high and walked up the narrow passageway that would take her to her own palace apartment.

A huge hand gripped her biceps, forcing her to twist around. He absolutely dwarfed her.

Regardless of the huge tug in her heart and the rising

nausea, her voice was steady as she said, 'Get your hands off me. We're over.'

'No, we're not.' He slid his hand over her shoulder to snake it around her neck. His breath was hot in her ear as he leaned down to whisper, 'While you're sulking tonight I will be thinking of you and imagining all the ways I can take you when the ball's over. Then you will come to me and we will act them all out.'

Despite her praying to all the gods she could think of, her body reacted to his words and to his closeness the way it always did. With Helios she was like a starved child, finally allowed to feast. She craved him. She had desired him from the moment she'd met him all those months ago, with a powerful need that hadn't abated with time.

But now the time had come to conquer the craving.

Pressing a hand to his solid chest, resisting the urge to run her fingers through the fine black hair that covered it, she pushed herself back and forced her eyes to meet his still playful gaze.

'Enjoy your evening. Try not to spill wine down any princess's dress.'

His mocking laughter followed her all the way to the sanctuary of her own apartment.

It wasn't until she arrived in her apartment, which was spacious compared to normal accommodation but tiny when compared to Helios's, and caught a glimpse of her reflection that she saw the clay mask was still on her face.

It had cracked all over.

Helios led his dance partner—a princess from the old Greek royal family—around the ballroom. She was a very pretty young woman, but as he danced with her and listened to her chatter he mentally struck her off his list. Whoever he married, he wanted to be able to hold a conversation with them about something other than the latest catwalk fashions.

When the waltz had finished he bowed gracefully and excused himself to join his brother Theseus at his table, ignoring all the pleading female eyes silently begging him to take their hand next.

Amy's words about him treating the women here as sweets in a shop came back to him. He was man enough to admit they held the ring of truth. But if he had to choose someone to spend the rest of his life with and to bear his children, he wanted a woman as close to being perfect on his palate as he could taste.

If Amy could see the ladies in question and their eager eyes, the way they thrust their cleavages in his direction as they passed him, hoping to garner his attention, she would understand that they *wanted* to be tasted. They wanted him to find them exactly to his taste.

Theseus's gaze was directed at their younger brother, Talos, who was dancing with the ravishing violinist who would play at their grandfather's Jubilee Gala in three weeks.

'There's something going on there,' Theseus said, swigging back his champagne. 'Look at him. The fool's smitten.'

Helios followed his brother's gaze to the dance floor and knew immediately what he meant. The other couple of hundred guests in the room might as well not have been there for all the attention Talos and his dance partner were paying them. They had eyes only for each other and the heat they were producing…it was almost a visible entity. And strangely mesmerising.

Not for the first time Helios wished Amy could be there. She would adore waltzing around the great ballroom. For a conscientious academic she had a fun side that made her a pleasure to be with.

Theseus fixed his gaze back on Helios. 'So what about you? Shouldn't you be on the dance floor?'

'I'm taking a breather.'

'You should be taking it with Princess Catalina.'

Helios and his brothers had discussed his potential brides numerous times. The consensus was that Catalina would be a perfect fit for their family.

Only a generation ago, the marriages of the heirs to the Agon throne had been arranged. His own parents' marriage had been arranged. It had been witnessing the implosion of their marriage that had led his grandfather King Astraeus to abandon protocol and allow the next generation to select their own spouses, providing they were of royal blood.

For this, Helios was grateful. He was determined that whoever he selected would have no illusions that their marriage would be anything but one of duty.

'You think…?' he asked idly, while his skin crawled at the thought of dancing another waltz with any more of the ladies in attendance, no matter how beautiful they were. Beautiful women were freely available wherever he went. Women of substance less so.

He glanced at his watch. Another couple of hours and this would be over. He would call Amy and she would come to him.

Now, *she* was a woman of substance.

A frisson of tension raced through him as he recalled their earlier exchange. He'd never seen her angry before. There'd been a possessiveness to that anger too. She'd been jealous.

Usually when a lover showed the first sign of possessiveness it meant it was time for him to move on. In Amy's case he'd found it highly alluring. Her jealousy had strangely delighted him.

Helios had long suspected that she kept parts of herself

hidden from him. She gave her body to him willingly, and revelled in their lovemaking as much as he did, but the inner workings of her clever mind remained a mystery.

She'd been different from his usual lovers from the very start. Beautiful and fiercely intelligent, she held his attention in a way no other woman ever had. Her earlier anger hadn't repelled him, as it would have done coming from anyone else; it had intrigued him, peeling away another layer of the brilliant, passionate woman he couldn't get enough of. When he was with her he could forget everything and live for the moment, for their hunger.

The seriousness of his grandfather's illness clung to him like a barnacle, but when he was with Amy it became tamed, was less of a thudding beat of pain and doom. When he was with her he could cast aside the great responsibilities being heir to the throne brought and simply be a man. A lover. *Her* lover. She was a constant thrum in his blood. He had no intention of giving her up—marriage or no marriage.

'Has anyone else caught your attention?' Theseus asked him.

'No.'

Helios had always known he would have to marry. There had never been any question about it. He had no personal feelings about it one way or another. Marriage was an institution within which to produce the next set of Kalliakis heirs, and he was fortunate to be in a position where he could choose his own bride, albeit within certain constraints. His parents hadn't been so lucky. Their marriage had been arranged before his mother had been out of nappies. It had been a disaster. His only real hope for his own marriage was that it be *nothing* like theirs.

Princess Catalina, currently dancing with a British prince, caught his eye. She really was incredibly beautiful. Refined.

Her breeding and lineage shone through. Her brother was an old school friend of his, and their meals together in Denmark had shown her to be a woman of great intelligence as well as beauty, if a little serious for his taste.

She had none of Amy's irreverence.

Still, Catalina would make an excellent queen and he'd wasted enough time as it was. He should have selected a wife months ago, when the gravity of his grandfather's condition had been spelt out to him and his brothers.

Catalina had been raised in a world of protocol, just as he had. She had no illusions or expectations of love. If he chose her he knew theirs would be a marriage of duty. Nothing more, nothing less. No emotional entanglements. Exactly as he wanted.

Making a family with her would be no hardship either. He was certain that with some will on both their parts a bond would form. Chemistry should ensue too. Not the same kind of chemistry he shared with Amy, of course. That would be impossible to replicate.

A memory of Amy heading barefoot down the dimly lit passageway, her clothes and towel huddled to her, her dark blonde hair damp and swinging across her golden back, her bare bottom swaying, flashed into his mind. She'd been as haughty as any princess in that moment, and he couldn't wait to punish her for her insolence. He would bring her to the brink of orgasm so many times she would be *begging* him for release.

But this was neither the time nor the place to imagine Amy's slender form naked in his arms.

With titanium will, he dampened down the fire spreading through his loins and fixed his attention on the women before him. For the next few hours Amy had to be locked away in his mind to free up his concentration for the job in hand.

Before he could bring himself to dance again he beckoned a footman closer, so he could take another glass of champagne and drink a large swallow.

Theseus eyed him shrewdly. 'What's the matter with you?'

'Nothing.'

'You have the face of a man at a wine-tasting event discovering all the bottles are corked.'

Helios fixed a smile on his face. 'Better?'

'Now you look like a mass murderer.'

'Your support is, as always, invaluable.' Draining his glass, he got to his feet. 'Considering the fact I'm not the only Prince expected to marry and produce heirs, I suggest you get off your backside and mingle with the beautiful ladies in attendance too.'

He smirked at Theseus's grimace. While Helios accepted his fate with the steely backbone his upbringing and English boarding school education had instilled in him, he knew his rebellious brother looked forward to matrimony with all the enthusiasm of a zebra entering a lion enclosure.

Later, as he danced with Princess Catalina, holding her at a respectable distance so their bodies didn't touch—and having no compulsion to bridge the gap—his thoughts turned to his grandfather.

The King was not in attendance tonight, as he was saving his limited energy for the Jubilee Gala itself. It was for that great man, who had raised Helios and his brothers since Helios was ten, that he was prepared to take the final leap and settle down.

For his grandfather he would do *anything*.

Soon the crown would pass to him—sooner than he had wanted or expected—and he needed a queen by his side. He wanted his grandfather to move on to the next life at peace, in the knowledge that the succession of the Kalliakis line was secure. If time was kind to them his grandfather might just live long enough to see Helios take his vows.

CHAPTER TWO

WHERE THE HELL was she?

Helios had been back in his apartment for fifteen minutes and Amy wasn't answering his calls. According to the head of security, she had left the palace. Her individual passcode showed that she'd left at seven forty-five; around the time he and his brothers had been welcoming their guests.

Trying her phone one more time, he strolled through to his bar and poured himself a large gin. The call went straight to voicemail. He tipped the neat liquid down his throat and, on a whim, carried the bottle through to his study.

Security monitors there showed pictures from the cameras that ran along the connecting passageways. Only Helios himself had access to the cameras' feeds.

He peered closely at the screen for camera three, which faced the reinforced connecting door. There was something on the floor he couldn't make out clearly...

Striding to it and unbolting the door, he stared down at a box. Crammed inside were bottles of perfume, jewellery, books and mementos. All the gifts he had given Amy during their time together as lovers. Crammed, unwanted, into a box and left on his doorstep.

A burst of fury tore through him, so sudden and so powerful it consumed him in one.

Before he had time to think what he was doing he raised his foot and brought it slamming down onto the box. Glass shattered and crunched beneath him, the sound echoing in the silence.

For an age he did nothing else but inhale deeply, trembling with fury, fighting the urge to smash what was left of the box's contents into smithereens. Violence had been his father's solution to life's problems. It was something Helios had always known resided inside him too but, unlike in his father's case, it was an aspect of himself he controlled.

The sudden fury that had just overtaken him was incomprehensible.

Acutely aware of how late she was, Amy slammed her apartment door shut and hurried down the stairs that led to the palace museum. Punching in her passcode, she waited for the green light to come on, shoved the door open and stepped into the private quarters of the museum, an area out of bounds to visitors.

Gazing longingly at the small staff kitchen as she passed it, she crossed her fingers in the hope that the daily pastries hadn't already been eaten and the coffee already drunk. The *bougatsas*, freshly made by the palace chefs and brought to them every morning, had become her favourite food in the whole world.

Her mouth filled with moisture as she imagined the delicate yet satisfying filo-based pastries. She hoped there were still some custard-filled ones left. She'd hardly eaten a thing in the past couple of days, and now, after finally managing to get a decent night's sleep, she'd woken up ravenous. She'd also slept right through her alarm clock, and the thought made her legs work even quicker as she climbed another set of stairs that led up to the boardroom.

'I'm so sorry I'm late,' she said, rushing through the door, a hand flat on her breathless chest. 'I over...' Her words tailed off as she saw Helios, sitting at the head of the large round table.

His elbows rested on the table, the tips of his fingers rubbing together. He was freshly shaven and, even casually dressed as he was, in a dark green long-sleeved crew-neck top, he exuded an undeniable power. And all the force of that power was at that very moment aimed at her.

'Nice of you to join us, Despinis Green,' he said. His tone was even, but his dark brown eyes resembled bullets waiting to be fired at her. 'Take a seat.'

Utterly shaken to see him there, she blinked rapidly and forced herself to inhale. Helios was the palace museum's director, but his involvement in the day-to-day running of it was minimal. In the four months she'd worked there, he hadn't once attended the weekly Tuesday staff meeting.

She'd known when she'd stolen back into the palace late last night that she would have to face him soon, but she'd hoped for a few more days' grace. Why did he have to appear today, of all days? The one time she'd overslept and looked awful.

Unfortunately the only chair available was directly opposite him. It made a particularly loud scraping sound over the wooden floor as she pulled it back and sat down, clasping her hands tightly on her lap so as not to betray their tremors. Greta, one of the other curators and Amy's best friend on the island, had the seat next to her. She placed a comforting hand over hers and squeezed gently. Greta knew everything.

In the centre of the table was the tray of *bougatsas* Amy had hoped for. Three remained, but she found her appetite gone and her heart thundering so hard that the ripples spread to her belly and made her nauseous.

Greta poured her a cup of coffee. Amy clutched it gratefully.

'We were discussing the artefacts we're still waiting on for my grandfather's exhibition,' Helios said, looking directly at her.

The Agon Palace Museum was world-famous, and as such attracted curators from across the world, resulting in a medley of first languages amongst the staff. To simplify matters, English was the official language spoken when on duty.

Amy cleared her throat and searched her scrambled brain for coherence. 'The marble statues are on their way from Italy as we speak and should arrive in port early tomorrow morning.'

'Do we have staff ready to welcome them?'

'Bruno will message me when they reach Agon waters,' she said, referring to one of the Italian curators accompanying the statues back to their homeland. 'As soon as I hear from him we'll be ready to go. The drivers are on call. Everything is in hand.'

'And what about the artefacts from the Greek museum?'

'They will arrive here on Friday.'

Helios *knew* all this. The exhibition was his pet project and they'd worked closely together on it.

She'd first come to Agon in November, as part of a team from the British Museum delivering artefacts on loan to the Agon Palace Museum. During those few days on the island she'd struck up a friendship with Pedro, the Head of Museum. Unbeknownst to her at the time, he'd been impressed with her knowledge of Agon, and doubly impressed with her PhD thesis on Minoan Heritage and its Influences on

Agon Culture. Pedro had been the one to suggest her for the role of curator for the Jubilee Exhibition.

The offer had been a dream come true, and a huge honour for someone with so little experience. Only twenty-seven, what Amy lacked in experience she made up for with enthusiasm.

Amy had learned at the age of ten that the happy, perfect family she'd taken for granted was not as she'd been led to believe. *She* wasn't what she'd been led to believe. Her dad was indeed her biological father, but her brothers were only half-brothers. Her mum wasn't her biological mother. The woman who'd actually given birth to her had been from the Mediterranean island of Agon.

Half of Amy's DNA was Agonite.

Since that bombshell discovery, everything about Agon had fascinated her. She'd devoured books on its Minoan history and its evolution into democracy. She'd thrilled at stories of the wars, the passion and ferocity of its people. She'd studied maps and photographs, staring so intently at the island's high green mountains, sandy beaches and clear blue seas that its geography had become as familiar as her own home town.

Agon had been an obsession.

Somewhere in its history was *her* history, and the key to understanding who she truly was. To have the opportunity to live there on a nine-month secondment had been beyond anything she could have hoped. It had been as if fate was giving her the push she needed to find her birth mother. Somewhere in this land of half a million people was the woman who had borne her.

For seventeen years Amy had thought about her, wondering what she looked like—did she look like *her*?—what her voice sounded like, what regrets she might have. Was she ashamed of what she'd done? Surely she was? How could anyone live through what Neysa Soukis had done and *not* feel shame?

She'd been easy to locate, but how to approach her…? That had always been the biggest question. Amy couldn't just turn up at her door; it would likely be slammed in her face and then she would never have her answers. She'd considered writing a letter but had failed to think of what she could say other than: *Hi, do you remember me? You carried me for nine months and then dumped me. Any chance you could tell me why?*

Greek social media, which Greta had been helping her with, had proved fruitful. Neysa didn't use it, but through it Amy had discovered a half-brother. Tentative communications had started between them. She had to hope he would act as a conduit between them.

'Have you arranged transport for Friday?' Helios asked, the dark eyes hard, the bowed, sensual mouth tight.

'Yes. Everything is in hand,' she said for a second time, as a sharp pang reached through her as she realised she would never feel those lips on hers again. 'We're ahead of schedule.'

'You're confident that come the Gala the exhibition will be ready?'

His voice was casual but there was a hardness there, a scepticism she'd never had directed at her before.

'Yes,' she answered, gritting her teeth to stop her hurt and anger leeching out.

He was punishing her. She should have answered one of his calls. She'd taken the coward's way out and escaped from the palace in the hope that a few days away from him would give her the strength she needed to resist him. The best way—the only way—of beating her craving for him would be by going cold turkey.

Because resist him she must. She couldn't be the other woman. She couldn't.

But she hadn't imagined that seeing him again would physically *hurt*.

It did. Dreadfully.

Before her job had been rubber-stamped, Helios had interviewed her himself. The Jubilee Exhibition was of enormous personal importance to him and he'd been determined that the curator with the strongest affinity to his island would get the job.

Luckily for her, he'd agreed with Pedro that she was the perfect candidate. He'd told her some months later, when they'd been lying replete in each other's arms, that it had been her passion and enthusiasm that had convinced him. He'd known she would give the job the dedication it deserved.

Meeting Helios… He'd been *nothing* as she'd imagined: as far from the stuffy, pompous, 'entitled' Prince she'd expected him to be as was possible.

Her attraction to him had been immediate, a chemical reaction over which she'd had no control. It had taken her completely off guard. Yet she hadn't thought anything of it. He was a prince, after all, both powerful and dangerously handsome. Never in her wildest dreams had she thought the attraction would be reciprocated. But it had been.

He'd been much more involved with the exhibition than she'd anticipated, and she'd often found herself working alone with him, her longing for him an ever-growing fire inside her that she didn't have a clue how to handle.

Affairs in the workplace were a fact of life, even in the studious world of antiquities, but they were not something she'd ever been tempted by. She loved her work so much it took her entire focus. Her work gave her purpose. It grounded her. And working with the ancient objects of her own people, seeing first-hand how techniques and social mores had evolved over the years, was a form of proof that the past didn't have to be the future. Her birth mother's actions didn't have to define her, even if she did feel the taint of her behaviour like an invisible stain.

Relationships of any real meaning had always been out of the question for her. How could she commit to someone if she didn't know who she truly was? So to find herself feeling such an attraction, and to the man who was effectively her boss, who just happened to be a prince... It was no wonder her emotions had been all over the place.

Helios had had no such inhibitions.

Long before he'd laid so much as a finger on her he'd undressed her with his dark liquid eyes, time and again. Until one late afternoon, when she'd been talking to him in the smaller of the exhibition rooms, she on one side, he on the other, and he'd gone from complete stillness to fluid motion in the beat of a heart. He'd walked to her with long strides and pulled her into his arms.

And that had been it. She'd been his for the taking. And he'd been hers.

Their three months together had been a dream. Theirs had been a physically intense but surprisingly easy relationship. There had been no expectations. No inhibitions. Just passion.

Walking away should have been easy.

The eyes that had undressed her a thousand times now flickered to Pedro, giving silent permission for him to move the discussion on to general museum topics. There might be a special exhibition being organised, but the museum itself still needed to be run to its usual high standards.

Clearly unnerved—Helios's mood, usually so congenial, was unsettling all the staff—Pedro raced through the rest of the agenda in double-quick time, finally mentioning the need for someone to cover for one of their tour guides that Thursday. Amy was happy to volunteer. Thursday was her only reasonably quiet day that week, and she enjoyed taking on the tours whenever the opportunity arose.

One of the things she loved so much about the museum was the collaborative way it was run, with everyone helping each other when needed. It was a philosophy that came from the very top, from Helios himself, even if today there was no sign of his usual amiability.

Only at the very end of the meeting did Pedro say, 'Before we leave, can I remind everyone that menus for next Wednesday need to be handed in by Friday?'

As a thank-you for all the museum staff's hard work in organising the exhibition, Helios had arranged a night out for everyone before the summer rush hit, all expenses paid. It was a typically generous gesture from him, and a social event Amy had been very much looking forward to. Now, though, the thought of a night out with Helios in attendance made her stomach twist.

There was a palpable air of relief when the meeting finished. Today there was none of the usual lingering. Everyone scrambled to their feet and rushed for the door.

'Amy, a word please.' Helios's rich voice rose over the clatter of hurrying feet.

She paused, inches from the door, inches from escape. Arranging her face into a neutral expression, she turned around.

'Shut the door behind you.'

She did as she was told, her heart sinking to her feet, then sat back in her original place opposite him but also the greatest distance possible away.

It wasn't far enough.

The man oozed testosterone.

He also oozed menace.

Her heart kicked against her ribs. She clamped her lips together and folded her arms across her chest.

Yet she couldn't stop her eyes moving to his, couldn't stop herself gazing at him.

His silver chain glinted against the base of his throat. That chain had often brushed against her lips when he'd made love to her.

And as she stared at him, wondering when he was going to speak, his eyes studied her with the same intensity, making her mouth run dry and her hammering pulse race into a gallop.

His fingers drummed on the table. 'Did you have a nice time at Greta's?'

'Yes, thank you,' she replied stiffly, before she realised what he'd said. 'How did you know I was there?'

'Through the GPS on your phone.'

'What? You've been *spying* on me?'

'You are the lover of the heir to the throne of Agon. Our relationship is an open secret. I do not endanger what is mine.'

'I'm not yours. Not any more,' she spat at him, running from fear to fury in seconds. 'Whatever tracking device you've put in my phone, you can take it out. Now.'

She yanked her bag onto the table, pulled out her phone and threw it at him.

His hand opened to catch it like a Venus flytrap catching its prey. He laughed. But unlike on Saturday, when he'd thought he'd been indulging her, the sound contained no humour.

He slid the phone back to her. 'There's no tracking device in it. It's all done through your number.'

'Well, you can damn well *un*track it. Take it off your system, or whatever it's on.'

He studied her contemplatively. His stillness unnerved

her. Helios was *never* still. He had enough energy to power the whole palace.

'Why did you leave?'

'To get away from you.'

'You didn't think I would be worried?'

'I thought you'd be too busy cherry-picking your bride to notice I'd gone.'

Finally a smile played on his lips. 'Ah, so you were punishing me.'

'No, I was not,' she refuted hotly. 'I was giving myself space away from you because I knew you'd still expect to sleep with me after an evening of wooing prospective brides.'

'And you didn't think you'd be able to resist me?'

Her cheeks coloured and Helios felt a flare of satisfaction that his thoughts had been correct.

His beautiful, passionate lover had been jealous.

Slender, feminine to her core, with a tumbling mane of thick dark blonde hair, Amy was possibly the most beautiful woman he'd ever met. A sculptor wouldn't hesitate to cast her as Aphrodite. She made his blood thicken just to look at her, even dressed as she was now in an A-line navy skirt and a pretty yet demure lilac top.

But today there was something unkempt about her appearance that wasn't usually there: dark hollows beneath her taupe eyes, her rosebud lips dry, her usual glowing complexion paler than was normal.

And he was the cause of it. The thought sent a thrill through him. Whatever punishment she had hoped to inflict on him by disappearing for a few days, it had backfired on her.

He would never let her know of the overwhelming fury that had rent him when he'd seen the box she'd left by his door.

Which reminded him…

He slid the thick padded envelope he'd placed on the table towards her. Smashing the box when his anger had got the better of him had caused the perfume bottles to spill and ruin the books, but the jewellery had been left undamaged.

Her eyes narrowed with caution, she extended an elegant hand to it and opened it gingerly. Her mouth tightened when she saw what was inside.

She dropped the envelope back on the table and got quickly to her feet. 'I don't want them.'

'They're yours. You insult me by returning them.'

She didn't blink. 'And you insult me by giving them back when you're about to put an engagement ring on another woman's finger.'

He got out of his chair and stalked over to her. With the chair behind her she had nowhere to retreat. He pulled her to him, enfolding her in his arms so that her head was pressed to his chest. He was too strong and she was too slender for her to wriggle out of his hold, and in any case he knew her attempts didn't mean anything.

He could feel her heat. She *wanted* to be in his arms.

Her head was tilted back, her breaths quickening. He watched as the pupils of her eyes darkened and pulsed, as the grey turned to brown, with a passionate fury there that set his veins alight.

'There is no need to be jealous,' he murmured, pressing himself closer. 'My marriage doesn't change my feelings for you.'

Her left eye twitched, an affliction he'd never seen before. Her top teeth razed across her full bottom lip.

'But it changes my feelings for you.'

'Liar. You can't deny you still want me.' He brushed his cheek against hers and whispered into her ear, 'Only a few days ago you screamed out my name. I still have your scratches on my back.'

She reared back. 'That was before I knew you were looking for an immediate wife. I will not be your mistress.'

'There is no shame in it. Generations of Agon monarchs have taken lovers after marriage.' His grandfather had been the exception to the rule, but only because he'd been fortunate enough to fall in love with his wife.

Of the thirty-one monarchs who'd ruled Agon since 1203, only a handful had found love and fidelity with their spouses. His own father, although he'd died before he could take the throne, had had dozens of lovers and mistresses. He'd revelled in waving his indiscretions right under his loving wife's nose.

'And generations ago your ancestors chopped your enemies' limbs off but you've managed to wean yourself off that.'

He laughed at her retort, running a finger over her chin. Even with her oval face free of make-up Amy was beautiful. 'We don't marry for love or companionship, as other people do. We marry for the good of our island. Think of it as a business arrangement. *You* are my lover. You are the woman I *want* to be with.'

His mother had been unfortunate in that she'd already loved his father when they had married, and it was that love which had ultimately destroyed her, long before the car crash that had taken both his parents' lives.

He would never inflict the kind of pain his father had caused, not on anyone. He had to marry, but he was upfront about what he wanted: a royal wife to produce the next generation of Kalliakis heirs. No emotions. No expectations of fidelity. A union founded on duty and nothing more.

Amy stared at him without speaking for the longest

time, searching for something. He didn't know what she hoped to find.

He brought his face down to meet her lips, which had parted, but she pulled back so only the faintest of touches passed between them.

'I mean it, Helios. We're finished. I will never be your mistress.' Her words were but a whisper.

'You think?'

'Yes.'

'Then why are you still standing here? Why is your breath still warm on my face?'

Brushing his lips across the softness of her cheek, he gripped her bottom and ground her against him, letting her feel his desire for her. The tiniest of moans escaped her throat.

'See?' He trailed kisses over her delicate ear. 'You do want me. But you're punishing me.'

'No, I...'

'Shh...' He placed a finger on her mouth. 'We both know I could take you right now and you would welcome it.'

Heat flared from her eyes but her chin jutted up mutinously.

'I am going to give you exactly five seconds of freedom. Five seconds to leave this room. If after those five seconds you are still here...' he spoke very quietly into her ear '...I will lift up your skirt and make love to you right here and now on this table.'

She quivered, a small tell but one so familiar he knew the expression that would be in her eyes when he looked into them.

He was right. The taupe had further darkened; the pupils were even more dilated. The tip of her pink tongue glistened between her parted lips. He knew that if he placed his hands over her small but beautifully formed breasts he would feel her nipples strain towards him.

He released his hold on her and folded his arms across his chest.

'One.'

She put a hand to her mouth and dragged it down over her chin.

'Two.'

She swallowed. Her eyes never left his face. He could practically smell her longing.

'Three… Four…'

She turned on her heel and fled to the door.

'One week,' he called to her retreating back. She was halfway out of the room and made no show of listening to him, but he knew she heard every word. 'One week and you, *matakia mou*, will be back in my bed. I guarantee it.'

CHAPTER THREE

AMY GAZED AT the marble statues that had arrived on Agon by ship that morning and now sat in the grand entrance hall of the museum on their plinths. Three marble statues. Three kings at the height of their glory. All named Astraeus. The fourth, specially commissioned for the exhibition, would be transported from the sculptor's studio in a week's time. It would depict the current monarch, the fourth King Astraeus, as a young man in his prime.

Helios had personally commissioned it. She didn't want to think of Helios. But she couldn't stop.

He was everywhere. In every painting, every sculpture, every fragment of framed scripture, every piece of pottery. Everything was a reminder that this was all his. His people. His ancestors. Him.

Her attention kept flickering back to the statue of the second King Astraeus, a marble titan dating from 1403. Trident in hand and unashamedly naked, he had the same arrogant look with an underlying hint of ferociousness that Helios carried so well. If she had known nothing of the Agon royal dynasty, she would have known instinctively that her lover was a descendent of this man. Agon had been at peace for decades but their warrior roots dated back millennia, were ingrained in their DNA.

Helios had warrior roots in spades.

She had to stop thinking about him.

God, this was supposed to be easy. An affair with no promises and no need for compromise.

She'd been so tempted to stay in the boardroom with him. She'd *ached* to stay. Her body had been weighted down with need for him. But in the back of her mind had been an image of him exchanging his vows with a faceless woman who would become his wife.

Amy couldn't be the other woman. Whatever kind of marriage Helios had in mind for himself, it would still be real. He needed an heir. He would make love to his wife.

She could never allow herself to be the cause of pain and humiliation in another. She'd seen first-hand the damage an affair could cause. After all, she was the result of an affair herself. She'd spent seventeen years knowing she was the result of something sordid.

She was nothing but a dirty secret.

Helios's driver brought the car to a stop at the back of the palace, beside his private entrance. Dozens and dozens of schoolchildren of all shapes and sizes were picnicking on the lawn closest to the museum entrance: some playing football, some doing cartwheels and handstands. In the far distance a group were filing out of the Agon palace's maze, which was famed as one of the biggest and tallest mazes in the world.

Helios checked the time. He was always too busy to spend as much time with the palace visitors as he would like.

He had a small window before he was due at a business meeting he'd arranged with his brothers. His brothers ran the day-to-day side of their investment business, but he was still heavily involved. Then there were his royal duties, which had increased exponentially since the onset of his grandfather's illness. He was in all but name Prince Regent, the highest ranking ambassador for his beloved island. It was his duty to do everything he could to bring investment and tourists to his island, to spread his country's influence on the world's stage and keep his islanders safe and prosperous.

As he neared the children, with his courtiers keeping a discreet distance, their small faces turned to him with curiosity. As often happened, it took only one to recognise him before his identity spread like wildfire and they all came running up. It was one of the things he so liked about children: their lack of inhibition. In a world of politeness and protocol he found it refreshing.

One thing he and Catalina were in agreement about was the wish for a minimum of two children. They agreed on many things. Most things. Which was a good omen for their forthcoming marriage. On paper, everything about their union appeared perfect. But…

Every time he tried to picture the children they would create together his mind came up blank. The picture just would not form.

Despite her ravishing beauty, his blood had yet to thicken for her. But this was only a minor issue, and one he was certain would resolve itself the more time he spent with her. Tomorrow he would fly to Monte Cleure so he could formally ask her father for Catalina's hand in marriage. It was only a formality, but one that couldn't be overlooked.

At least times had moved on from such issues as a dowry having to be found and trade alliances and so on being written into the contract of any royal betrothal. Now all he had to worry about was his bride having blue blood.

He'd always found blue so cold.

He turned his attention on the English children and

answered a host of questions from them, including, 'Is it true your toilet is made of gold?'

His personal favourite was 'Is it true you carry a sub-machine gun wherever you go?'

In answer to this he pulled from his pocket the pen-knife his grandfather had given him on his graduation from Sandhurst; an upgraded version of the one he'd been given on his tenth birthday. 'No, but I always carry *this*.'

As expected, the children were agog to see it. It was termed a penknife only in the loosest sense; on sight any-one would recognise it for the deadly fighting instrument it truly was. Children loved it when he showed it to them. Their basic human nature had not yet been knocked out of them by the insane political correctness infecting the rest of the Western world.

'Most Agonites carry knives with them,' he said to the enthralled children. 'If anyone wants to invade our island they know we will fight back with force.'

Their teacher, who had looked at the knife as if it had come personally from Eurynomos himself, looked most relieved as she glanced at her watch. Immediately she clapped her hands together. 'Everyone into their pairs—it's time for our tour.'

Today was Thursday… Amy was taking on some of the tours…

The hairs on the back of his neck lifted. He looked over at the museum entrance. A slender figure stood at the top of the steps. Even though she was too far away for him to see clearly, the increasing beat of his heart told him it was her.

He straightened, a smile playing on his lips. Only two days had passed since she'd called his bluff and walked out of the boardroom, leaving him with an ache in his groin he'd only just recovered from. He would bet anything she had suffered in the same manner. He would bet she'd spent the past two days jumping every time her phone rang, waiting for his call.

Her pride had been wounded when she'd learned he was taking a wife, but she would get over it. She couldn't punish him for ever, not when she suffered as greatly as he did. Soon she would come crawling back.

After a moment's thought, he beckoned for one of his courtiers and instructed him to pass his apologies to his brothers. They could handle the meeting without him.

The time was ripe to assist Amy in crawling back to him.

The Agon palace dungeons never failed to thrill, whatever the visitor's age. Set deep underground, and reached by steep winding staircases at each end of the gloom, only those over the age of eight were permitted to enter. Inside, dim light was provided by tiny electrical candles that flickered as if they were the real thing, casting shadows wherever one stood. Unsurprisingly, the children today were huddled closely together.

'These dungeons were originally a pit in which to throw the Venetian invaders,' Amy said, speaking clearly so all twenty-three children on the tour could hear. 'The Venetians were the only people to successfully invade Agon, and when Ares the Conqueror, cousin of the King at the time, led the uprising in AD 1205, the first thing he ordered his men to do was build these pits. King Timios, who was the reigning King and whom the Agonites blamed for letting the Venetians in, was thrown into the cell to my left.'

The children took it in turns to gawp through the iron railings at the tiny square stone pit.

'The manacle on the right-hand wall is the original manacle used to chain him,' she added.

'Did he die in here?' a young boy asked.

'No,' said a deep male voice that reverberated off the narrow walls before she could answer, making them all jump.

A long shadow cast over them and Helios appeared. In the flickering light of the damp passageway in which they stood his large frame appeared magnified, as if Orion, the famously handsome giant, had come to life.

What was he *doing* here?

She'd seen him only an hour ago, standing in the gardens talking to the school parties, as at ease with the children as he was in every other situation. That had been the moment she had forgotten how to breathe.

It will get better, she kept assuring herself. *It's still early days and still raw. Soon you'll feel better.*

'King Timios was held in these cells for six months before Ares Patakis expelled him and, with the consent of the people, took the crown for himself,' Helios said to the captivated children. 'The palace was built over these dungeons so King Ares could have personal control over the prisoners.'

'Did he kill anyone?' asked the same bloodthirsty boy.

'He killed many people,' Helios answered solemnly. 'But only in battle. Prisoners of war were released and sent back to Venice.' He paused and offered a smile. 'But only after having their hands chopped off. King Ares wanted to send a warning to other armies wishing to invade—*Step on our shores and you will never wield a weapon again.* That's if they were lucky enough to live.'

The deeper they went into the dungeons, which were large enough to hold up to three hundred prisoners, the more questions were thrown at him as the children did their best to spook each other in the candlelit dimness.

It was with relief that Helios handled everything asked

of him—his presence had made her tongue tie itself into
a knot.

'Have *you* ever killed anyone?' an undersized girl asked
with a nervous laugh.

He shook his head slowly. 'But since I could walk and
talk I've been trained to use knives, shoot arrows and
throw a spear. My brothers and I are all military trained.
Trust me, should any other nation try to invade us, Agonites are ready. We fight. We are not afraid to spill blood—
whether it's an enemy's or our own—to protect what's
ours. We will defend our island to the death.'

Utter silence followed this impassioned speech. Twenty-
three sets of wide eyes gazed up at Helios with a mixture
of awe and terror. The teacher looked shell-shocked.

It had had the opposite effect on Amy.

His words had pushed through her skin to heat her
veins. It had never so much been his looks, as gorgeous
as he was, that had attracted her. It had been his passion.
The Kalliakis family was a dynasty whose blood ran red,
not blue. And no one's blood ran redder than Helios's. On
the outside he was a true prince. Beneath his skin lay a
warrior.

'And that, children, proves that it's not only Ares the
Conqueror's blood Prince Helios has inherited from his
ancestor but his devotion to his homeland.' Amy spoke
quickly, to break the hush and to distract herself from the
ache spreading inside her. 'Now, who here would like to
be adopted by the Prince? Any takers? No? Hmm... You
surprise me. Come on, then, who wants to visit the museum gift shop?'

That brought them back to life; the thought of spending
their money on gifts for themselves.

'It's a good thing you'll never have to be a tour guide
as your day job,' Amy couldn't resist saying to Helios as

she climbed the stairs a little way behind the school party. 'They'll all have nightmares.'

He followed closely behind her. 'They're learning my family's history. I was putting it into the context of the present day for them.'

'Yes. They were learning about your *history*. There's a big difference between hearing about wars and blood-spilling from centuries ago and having it put into the here and now, especially in the dungeons, of all places. They're only ten years old.'

'The world is full of bloodshed. That's never changed in the history of mankind. The only way to stop it creeping to our shores is through fear and stability.'

Her hand tightened on the railing as she carried on climbing. 'But Agon *is* stable. You have an elected senate. You are a democracy.'

'The people still look to us, their royal family, for leadership. Our opinions matter. Our actions matter even more so.'

'Hence the reason you're marrying Princess Catalina,' she stated flatly.

'We are a prosperous, stable island nation, *matakia mou*, and it's the hard work of generations of my family that has made it so. Until the entire world is stable we are vulnerable to attack in many different forms. We lead by example, and as a people we are united as one. Stability within the royal family promotes stability for the whole island. My grandfather is dying. My marriage will bring peace to him and act as security to my people, who will be assured that the future of my family is taken care of and by extension their own families too. They know that with a descendant of Ares Patakis on the throne their country is not only ready to defend itself but able to weather any financial storm that may hit our isles.'

Somewhere during his speech they'd both stopped climbing. Amy found herself facing him from two steps above, coming to eye level with him. His eyes were liquid, the shadows dancing over his features highlighting the strength of the angles and planes that made him so darkly handsome. Her fingers tingled with the urge to reach out and touch him...

'I need to catch up with the children,' she breathed, but her rubbery legs made no attempt to move.

'They know where they're going,' he murmured, placing a hand on the damp wall to steady himself as he leaned in close.

His other hand caught her hip, jerking her to him. Delicious heat swirled through her; moisture pushed out the dryness in her mouth. Her skin danced and her lips parted as she moved her mouth to meet his...

She only just pulled away in time.

Swiping at his hand to remove it from her hip, she said, 'I haven't said goodbye to them.'

'Then say your goodbyes.' His eyes were alight with amusement. 'Keep running, *matakia mou*, but know you can't run for ever. Soon I will catch you.'

She didn't answer, turning tail and racing to the top of the steep staircase, gripping tightly onto the rail, and then out into the corridor.

At least in the corridor she could breathe.

What had just happened? She'd been a breath away from kissing him. Did she have no pride? No sense of preservation?

She wanted to cry with frustration.

Whether Helios believed it or not, they were over. He was marrying someone else. It was abhorrent that she still reacted so strongly towards him.

There was only one thing she could do.

She had to leave.

As soon as the exhibition was officially opened, to co-incide with the Gala in just over a fortnight, she would leave the palace and never come back.

After a long day spent overseeing the arrival of artefacts from the Greek museum Amy should have been dead on her feet, but the email she'd just received had acted like a shot of espresso to her brain.

After months of searching and weeks of tentative communication, Leander had agreed to see her. Tomorrow night she would meet her half-brother for the first time.

She looked at her watch. If she moved quickly she could run to Resina and buy herself a new dress to wear for their meal, before late-night shopping was over. She wouldn't have time tomorrow, with Saturday being the museum's busiest day.

After hurriedly turning her computer off and shuffling papers so her desk looked tidy, and not as if she'd abandoned it whilst in the middle of important work, she rushed out of her office and headed downstairs to see if Pedro was still about and could lock up.

She came to an abrupt halt.

There, in the museum entrance, talking to Pedro, stood Helios.

She wasn't quick enough to escape. Both of them turned their faces to her.

'Speak of the woman and she shall appear,' said Pedro, beaming at her.

'What have I done?' she asked, squashing the butterflies in her stomach and feigning nonchalance.

Pedro grinned. 'Don't look so worried. Helios and I have been discussing your future.'

Within the confines of the museum the staff addressed Helios by his first name, at his insistence.

'Oh?' Her gaze fell on Helios. 'I thought you were going to Monte Cleure,' she said before she could stop herself.

'My plane leaves in an hour.'

Her chest compressed in on itself. Stupidly, she'd looked up the distance between Agon and Monte Cleure, which came in at just over one thousand two hundred miles. Just over two and a half hours' flying time. With the time difference factored in he would be there in time to share an intimate dinner with the Princess.

She pressed her lips together to prevent the yelp of pain that wanted to escape and forced her features into an expression of neutrality. Helios had so much power over her she couldn't bear for him to know how deeply it ran.

Oblivious to any subtext going on around him, Pedro said, 'I was going to leave this until tomorrow, but seeing as you're here there's no time like the present—'

'We were saying how impressed we are with your handling of the exhibition,' Helios cut in smoothly. 'You have exceeded our expectations. We would like to offer you a permanent job at the museum when your secondment finishes.'

'What kind of job?' she asked warily. A week ago this news would have filled her with joy. But everything was different now.

'Corinna will be leaving us at the end of the summer. We would like you to have her job.'

Corinna was second only to Pedro in the museum hierarchy.

'There are far more qualified curators than me working here,' she said non-committally, wishing Pegasus might fly into the palace at that very moment and whisk her away to safety.

'Pedro is happy to train you in the areas where you lack experience,' said Helios, a smile of triumph dancing in his eyes. 'The important thing is you can do the job. Everyone here likes and respects you…curators at other museums enjoy collaborating with you. You're an asset to the Agon Palace Museum and we would be fools to let you go.'

If Pedro hadn't been there she would have cursed Helios for such a blatant act of manipulation.

'What do you think?' he asked when she remained silent. His dark eyes bored into her, a knowing, almost playful look emanating from them. 'How do you like the idea of living and working here permanently?'

She knew exactly what he was doing and exactly what he was thinking. He knew how much she loved her job, his island and its people. Helios was working tactically. He thought that if he threw enough incentives at her she would be so overcome with gratitude she would allow him back into her bed.

She'd entered their relationship without any illusions of permanency. It had suited her as much as it had suited him. Desire was what had glued them together, and it scared her to know that despite all the protective barriers she'd placed around herself he'd still slipped inside. Not fully, but enough for pain to lance her whenever she thought of him and the Princess together. When she thought of her own future without him in her life.

How could she continue to be his lover feeling as she did now, even putting aside the fact of his imminent engagement?

His engagement had hammered home as nothing else could that she was good enough to share his bed but not good enough for anything more.

She knew she was being unfair—Agon's constitution and Helios's position in life were not his fault or within his control—but for the first time she felt the reality on an emotional level and that terrified her.

In her heart of hearts she'd always longed to meet someone she could trust with the truth about her conception and not fear they would turn away in disgust or believe that the fruit never fell far from the tree. To meet someone who could love her for herself.

During their time together she had come to trust Helios. He was a man she'd thought she could confide the truth to, and she was almost certain he wouldn't turn away in disgust. But still she'd kept her secrets close. He couldn't give her the other things she'd always secretly craved but had never quite believed she deserved. Love. Fidelity. Commitment. It had been wiser to keep her heart as close as her secrets.

She considered her words carefully, although her head swam. 'I'm going to need time to think about it.'

'What is there to think about?' he asked, his dark eyes narrowing slightly.

'My life is in England,' she said evenly, although she knew there was really nothing to think about. He could offer to quadruple her salary and the answer would be the same.

She was saved from elaborating by Helios's phone ringing.

'My cue to leave,' he said, flashing her a grin. 'We can continue this discussion another time soon.'

She knew what 'soon' meant. He meant to visit her on Sunday evening, when he returned.

With Pedro there she was in no position to refuse or challenge anything. And even if she'd wanted to Helios didn't give her the chance, wishing them both a good weekend before striding off and out of the museum. On his way to Monte Cleure to spend his weekend with the Princess and her family.

And she…

As soon as she returned from her last-minute shopping trip she would write her resignation letter. She would give it to Pedro tomorrow, safe in the knowledge that Helios would be over a thousand miles away.

CHAPTER FOUR

AMY PUT THE lip gloss tube to her mouth, but before she could squeeze the gel-like substance on, a loud rap made her jerk her hand back. The banging had come from the door outside her bedroom that connected the passageway between her apartment and Helios's.

She pressed her hand to her pounding heart.

What was he doing here?

He was supposed to be spending the whole weekend in Monte Cleure, using his time there to officially ask Princess Catalina's father's blessing for their marriage. He should still be there, celebrating their forthcoming union, not here on Agon, banging on his ex-lover's door.

Breathing heavily, she closed her eyes and willed him away.

Another loud rap on the door proved the futility of her wish.

Suddenly galvanised into action, she dropped the lip gloss into her handbag and slipped out of her room, hurrying past the connecting door as another knock rang out. Snatching her jacket off the coat stand, she left her apartment through the main exit and hurried down the narrow stairs. With her heart battering against her chest she punched in the code that opened the door and stole outside into the warm spring evening air.

She felt like an escaped convict.

Security lights blazed everywhere, and she kept as close to the palace wall as she could for as long as she could until she had to dart out to cross into the courtyard used by the palace staff. The car she'd ordered earlier was already waiting for her. She jumped straight into the passenger side, making Eustachys the driver, who was busy on his phone, jump.

'You're early,' he said with a grin, before adding, 'Where do you want to go?'

She forced a smile. Whenever she needed one of the pool of cars and drivers that were on permanent standby for the palace staff she was invariably given Eustachys, who spoke excellent English. 'Resina, please.'

She gave him the name of the restaurant she was dining at and tried not to betray her impatience as he inputted it into his satnav, especially as she was perfectly aware that he knew every inch of the island and had no need for it.

A minute later they were off, starting the twenty-minute drive to Agon's capital, a cosmopolitan town rich in history and full of excellent shops and restaurants.

She didn't want to think of Helios, still standing at her door demanding entry. She didn't want to think of him at all.

All she wanted at that moment was to keep her composure as she met the man who shared her blood for the first time.

When Eustachys collected her from the restaurant later that evening Resina's streets were full of Saturday night revellers and stars were twinkling down from the black sky above them.

Amy's head throbbed too hard for her to want to be out amongst them.

Although not a complete disaster, her meeting with Leander had been much more difficult than she'd anticipated. It hadn't helped that she'd still been shaken from Helios's unexpected return to Agon and that she'd been half expecting him to turn up at the restaurant. Discovering where she'd gone would have been as easy for him as buttoning a shirt.

Leander hadn't helped either. She'd already gathered from his social media profile and his posts that he wasn't the most mature of men, but now, reflecting on their meal together—which she had paid for with no argument from him—she came to the sad conclusion that her newly found half-brother was a spoilt brat.

He'd been honest as far as he'd wanted to be. He'd told his mother—Amy's birth mother—about their meeting. He'd made it clear to Amy that it would be his judgement alone that would determine whether Neysa would meet the child she'd abandoned, and that power was a wonderful thing for him to crow about.

Scrap being a spoilt brat. Her half-brother was a monster.

Through all the crowing and the sniffing—she was almost certain he was on drugs—Amy had gleaned that his wealthy father had no idea of her existence. The Soukises had a nice, cosy life, and Amy turning up was in none of their interests. As far as Leander was concerned, Amy was a can of worms that was one twist of the can opener away from potentially destroying his comfortable life.

So, their meeting hadn't been a *complete* Greek tragedy. But not far off.

After being dropped back in the courtyard she made her way on weary legs to her apartment, removing her heels to walk up the staircase to her apartment.

She couldn't elicit the tiniest bit of surprise at finding Helios on her sofa, feet bare, in snug-fitting faded jeans and a black T-shirt, his muscular arms folded in a manner she knew meant only one thing—trouble.

'How did you get in here?' she asked pointlessly. This was his palace. He could go where he pleased.

'With a key,' he answered sardonically, straightening up and rolling his shoulders. 'Where have you been?'

'Out.'

Helios threw her a stare with narrowed eyes, taking in the pretty mint-green dress that fell to her knees, the elegantly knotted hair and the hooped earrings. It was an outfit he'd never seen her wear before. 'Have you been on a date?'

She gazed at him with tired eyes. 'It doesn't matter where I've been. Shouldn't you be with your fiancée? I assume she *is* your fiancée now?'

'Her father gave his blessing. We will make the official announcement during the Gala.'

'So why aren't you in Monte Cleure, celebrating?'

'Some unwelcome news was brought to my attention, so I came back a day early.'

A flicker of alarm flashed across her pretty features. 'Has something happened to your grandfather?'

'My grandfather's fine.' As fine as an eighty-seven-year-old man riddled with cancer could be.

He visited his grandfather every day that he was in the country, always praying that a miracle had occurred and he would see signs of improvement. All he ever saw was further deterioration. The strong, vibrant man who'd been not just the head of his family but the very heart of it was diminishing before his eyes.

Helios and his brothers' business interests had been so successful that their islanders no longer had to pay a cent of tax towards the royal family's upkeep and security. They had enough money to keep their people afloat if the worst economic storm should hit. But not even their great wealth was enough to cure the man who had given up so much to raise them, and it hadn't been enough to cure their beloved grandmother of the pneumonia that had killed her five years ago either. Her death was something their grandfather had never recovered from.

But for once, this evening, he had hardly thought of his grandfather. He'd been sitting rigidly on Amy's hard sofa, trying to keep a lid on his temper as the hours had passed and he'd waited for her to return.

And now here she was, dressed for a romantic night out *with someone else*. It was the final punch in the guts after what had been a hellish day.

The straightforward task of asking the King of Monte Cleure for his daughter's hand in marriage had turned into something infinitely more stomach-turning. The King had received him as if he were a long-lost son, his pride and happiness in his daughter's choice and her future prospects evident.

Throughout the entire private audience a bad taste had been lodged in Helios's throat. Words had formed but he'd spoken them as if they were being dragged over spikes. And throughout all the formalities his brain had been ticking over Amy's less than enthusiastic response to his offer of a permanent role at the palace museum.

To Helios it had been the perfect solution—a way to prove to Amy that she still had a role to play in his life for as long as she wanted, and that he wasn't throwing away what they had for the sake of a piece of paper tying him to another woman. And, besides, she'd earned the job offer. All his reasoning, everything he'd said to her, had been the truth.

Her response had grated on him.

And then he'd received that message from Pedro and taken his jet straight back to Agon.

'Where have you been?' he asked for a second time, noting the way she avoided his gaze at the question.

She sank onto the armchair in the corner, put a palm to her eye and rubbed it, smearing a trail of smoky-grey make-up across her cheek. 'You have no right to ask. Who I see and what I do with my time is my own business.'

'If you have taken another lover then I have every right to question you about it,' he retorted, smothering the nausea roiling in his guts. If she'd taken another lover...

'No, you *don't*,' she said hotly. 'You're the one marrying someone else, not me. That makes me a free agent. I don't owe you anything.'

Staring at her angry face, it struck him for the first time that Amy was serious about their relationship being over. Until that precise moment he'd assumed her pride and jealousy had been speaking for her. That she'd been punishing him.

'Who have you been with?' he demanded. 'Was it a man?'

She met his eyes and gave a sharp nod.

'Is it someone I know?'

'No.'

'Where did you meet him?'

'That doesn't matter.' She sucked in a breath. 'Look, Helios—please—leave me alone. What we had...it's over...'

'So you've jumped straight into bed with another man? Is this your way of punishing me for doing my duty to my family and my country?'

The distaste that flashed over her face answered for her. 'That's disgusting.'

He hid the immediate rush of relief that she hadn't been intimate with this elusive man. The relief died as quickly as it had been born.

'If you're not punishing me then why were you out with someone else? Are you so keen to prove your point that we're finished that you'd humiliate me?'

'How is me dining with someone else humiliating? And how can you dare say that when you're the one *marrying* someone else?'

'And how can *you* dare think I'll let you walk away?'

She stilled, her eyes widening, the flicker under her left eye returning.

'The reason I came back early from Monte Cleure is because Pedro called to inform me that the curator in charge of my grandfather's Jubilee Exhibition—a woman who, may I remind you, was taken on despite her lack of experience, because Pedro and I were both convinced she had the knowledge and enthusiasm to pull it off—has decided to quit five months early.'

His anger burned, enflaming him. He would never have believed Amy could be so underhand.

'Helios…' She reached out a hand, then dropped it back to her side with a sigh. 'What other choice do I have? I can't stay here now.'

'You're not the heroine of some old-fashioned melodrama,' he said scathingly. 'What did you think would happen? That I would hear you had resigned and shrug my shoulders and say that it's okay? Or that I would be so upset at the thought of you leaving my life permanently I would abandon my plans to marry Catalina, renounce my claim to the throne and marry you?'

She clutched at the knot of hair at the nape of her neck. 'I hoped you would accept it and at least try to understand where I'm coming from.'

'Well I don't understand or accept it. Your resignation has been refused. You will stay until your contracted period is up or I will sue you for breach of contract.'

Her shock was visible. 'You wouldn't…'

'Wouldn't I? Leave before September and see for yourself.'

'The exhibition is almost complete,' she said, breathing heavily, angry colour heightening her cheeks. 'Come the Gala and we'll be ready for visitors—my job will be done. Anyone else can carry on.'

'"Anyone else" will not have the breadth of knowledge you've developed about my grandfather and our ancestors. You signed that contract and you will damn well fulfil it.'

She jumped to her feet, her hands balled into fists. 'Why are you doing this? Why can't you just let me go?'

'Because we belong together,' he snarled. 'You're mine—do you understand that?'

'No, the *Princess* belongs to you. Not me. I belong only to myself. You can insist I work the rest of my contract—that's absolutely within your rights—but that doesn't change anything else. I will work out the contract if I must, but I will not share your bed. I will not be your mistress.'

Helios could feel the blood pumping in his head. His veins were aflame; needles were pushing into his skin. Deep in his gut was something he couldn't identify—but, *Theos*, whatever it was, it hurt.

He'd known from the outset that Amy was a woman of honour. Her excitement at his job offer had been so evident it had been contagious, but she'd refused to agree or to sign the contract until she'd spoken to her bosses at the British Museum face-to-face. If there had been any hesitation from them in letting her take the role she would have refused it, even though it was, by her own admission, a dream come true.

If it was such a dream then why was she prepared to walk away from it now?

And if she was so honourable how could she already be actively seeking a new lover?

He needed to get out of this apartment before he did something he would regret. So many emotions were riding through him it was impossible to distinguish them. He only knew his fists wanted nothing more than to smash things, to take every ornament and piece of furniture in this apartment and pulverise it.

For the second time in as many weeks the violence that lived in his blood threatened to boil over, and he despised himself for it almost as much as he despised Amy right now for seeking to leave him. But, unlike his violent father, Helios knew his own temper would never be directed at a woman. It was the only certainty he could take comfort from.

Striding over to her, he took her chin in his hand and forced her to look at him. *Theos*, she had such delicate features and such gorgeous skin. He didn't think there was an inch of her he hadn't stroked and kissed. He refused to believe he would never make love to her again. He *refused*.

'If you understand nothing else, understand this—you will *always* belong to me,' he said roughly, before dropping his hold and walking out of her apartment.

Amy's phone vibrated, breaking her concentration on the beautiful green sapphire ring she was supposed to be categorising but instead could only stare at with a lump in her throat.

This ring had belonged to Helios's mother. This ring would one day soon slide onto Princess Catalina's finger.

The message from Leander was simple and clear.

She doesn't want to meet you. Do not contact me again.

She read it a number of times before closing her eyes

and rubbing at the nape of her neck. A burn stung the back of her retinas.

She had never expected her birth mother to welcome her long-abandoned daughter with cheers and whistles, but she had expected *something*. Some curiosity, if nothing else. Did she not even wonder what Amy looked like? Or who she had become?

But there was too much shame. To Neysa Soukis, Amy was nothing but a scar on her memories; a scar that had to remain hidden.

If Amy were a different person she would force the issue. She would stalk Neysa at her house until she was browbeaten into seeing her. But even if she was capable of doing that what would it accomplish? Nothing more than Neysa's further contempt and probably a restraining order to boot.

All she wanted was to talk to her. Just once. But clearly she wasn't worth even that.

'Are you ready to go yet?'

Blinking rapidly, she looked up and found Greta standing in the doorway.

Amy turned her phone off. 'She doesn't want to meet me.'

At least with Greta she didn't have to pretend.

Greta came over to her and put an arm around her back. 'I'm sorry.'

Amy sniffed. 'I just thought...'

'I know,' said Greta softly. 'But learning you were here probably came as a big shock to her. She'll change her mind.'

'What if she doesn't?'

'She will,' Greta insisted. 'Now, turn your computer off. We've a night out to get ready for.'

'I'm not going.'

'You are. A night out is exactly what you need.'

'But Helios will be there.'

'So what? This will be your chance to let him see you having a great time and that you're completely unaffected by your break-up.'

Amy gave a laugh that came out as more of a snort than anything else. Thank God for Greta. Without her cheering friendship and positive attitude life on Agon would be unbearable right now.

Was it only four months ago that she'd arrived on this island full of excitement for what the future held? With a handsome prince as her boss and the opportunity to find the woman who'd given birth to her?

Now she was stuck here for another five months, and she would have to watch the handsome prince marry his princess and her birth mother wanted nothing to do with her.

She wished she'd never come to Agon.

Greta rubbed her arm in solidarity. 'Let's get your dress and go back to my flat. There's a bottle of ouzo waiting for us.'

'But…'

'Are you going to give that man so much power over you that you'd give up a free night out with all your friends and colleagues?'

Amy sighed and shook her head. Greta was right. She'd spent the past four days hiding away, mostly holing herself up in the museum's enormous basement, on the pretext of categorising artefacts, desperate to avoid bumping into Helios. And she'd been successful—other than one brief glimpse of him in the palace gardens she'd not had any dealings with him. Of course he was incredibly busy, with the Gala being only ten days away.

'Maybe he won't come,' she said with sudden hopefulness.

'Maybe…' Greta didn't look convinced.

But the thought of him not coming made her feel just as rotten as the thought of him being there.

If he did come, she had to pray he didn't bring the Princess as his guest.

To meet his future wife in the flesh would be one wound too many.

CHAPTER FIVE

THE MAIN REASON Helios had chosen Hotel Giroud for the staff night out was because his staff deserved to enjoy themselves in the most exclusive hotel on Agon. The fact its gardens led to a private beach was a plus.

Owned by Nathaniel Giroud, an old friend from his schooldays, it was the sister establishment of Club Giroud, the most exclusive and secret club on the island. The hotel was only marginally more inclusive, provided one had the funds and the connections. The quality of Helios's connections went without saying, and of course he had the funds, more than he could ever spend. He didn't begrudge spending a cent of his money on the staff who worked so hard for him.

He took his museum staff out twice a year: once at the beginning of the summer season, and once right at the end. Although the events weren't compulsory everyone attended, even those curators and conservators who would live in the museum basement if he'd let them. Most of his museum staff were a breed unto themselves, deeply dedicated to their work. He'd never imagined he would *desire* one of them.

And yet he had. He did.

During what was possibly the busiest time of his life, he couldn't flush Amy from his mind. Even after the news his brother Theseus had given him a couple of days ago he couldn't rid himself of her. Here he was, wrestling with the bombshell that Theseus had a secret child, a Kalliakis heir, and still she remained at the forefront of his mind.

It was taking everything he had to keep away from the museum. There was far too much going on for him to spend any time there, but knowing Amy was within its spacious walls meant the place acted like a magnet to him.

There were only ten days now until the Gala, and he had a mountain of work to do for it. He was determined to make it a success for his grandfather and for all his people.

On Agon, heirs traditionally took the throne at the age of forty. His father had died a few years short of that age and so his grandfather—without a word of complaint— had abandoned his retirement plans to hold the throne for Helios. His grandparents had sacrificed their dreams of travelling the world and his grandmother had put aside her thoughts of returning to her first love of performing as violin virtuoso. Those dreams had been abandoned so they could raise their orphaned grandchildren and mould them into princes the whole of Agon could be proud of. They had sacrificed everything.

There was no person on this earth Helios respected more or felt a deeper affection for than his grandfather. He would do anything for him. And, out of everything, it was marriage he knew his grandfather wanted the most for him. King Astraeus the Fourth wanted to leave this world secure in the knowledge that his lineage would live on and that the monarchy was in safe hands.

Although his engagement was now an open secret, the official announcement would bring his grandfather peace. That more than anything was Helios's overriding concern. He didn't like to think what it would bring for his own state of mind.

Catalina wouldn't return to Agon until the Gala. He'd dissuaded her from coming any earlier, using his busyness as an excuse to keep her away. A shudder ran through him as he recalled her obvious disappointment when he'd left Monte Cleure a day early. When he'd said goodbye she'd raised her chin in anticipation of his kiss. The most he'd been able to do was brush his lips against her cheek. She'd smelled fantastic, and she'd looked beautiful, but he might as well have been dead from the waist down for all she did for him.

Catalina knew what she was marrying into, he reminded himself. She had no illusions that their union would ever be about love. She'd assured him of that herself. But now he wondered if mutual respect would be enough when he couldn't even bring himself to kiss her.

He stood in the hotel lobby, personally greeting his staff and their partners. In all, over one hundred people were expected. He always enjoyed seeing their transformation, enjoyed seeing the back-room staff, who tended to live in jeans and baggy tops, and the front-line staff, who wore smart uniforms, all dressed to the nines in smart suits and cocktail dresses.

As each person entered he welcomed them with an embrace while Talia, his private secretary, handed them all an envelope.

Soon the lobby was full and waiting staff with trays of champagne were circulating. Conversation was stilted, as it always was at the beginning of such evenings, but he knew that wouldn't last long. Once everyone had had a drink or two their inhibitions would fall away and they would enjoy themselves properly. They all worked so hard they deserved to let their hair down.

Through the lobby's wide glass doors he saw two figures approach, their heads bent close together, laughing. His heart jolted, making him lose the thread of the conversation he'd struck up with one of the tour guides. Closer they came, until they reached the doors and showed their identification to the guards on duty, who inspected them closely before standing to one side to admit them.

The doors opened automatically and in they walked.

He greeted Greta first, with the same kind of embrace he'd shared with everyone else. She returned it warmly, gushing about how excited she was. And then it was time to greet Amy.

The same smile she'd entered the lobby with stayed fixed on her face, but her eyes told a different story.

His throat ran dry.

He'd seen her dressed up on a few occasions before: when he'd taken her out on dates away from the palace, and last weekend for her 'date' with someone else, but tonight...

Theos. She looked stunning.

She wore a sleeveless navy blue chiffon dress that floated just above her knees, with silver diamond-shaped beads layered along the hem and across the high round neckline. On her feet were simple high-heeled black shoes that showcased her slender legs. She'd left her dark blonde hair loose, so that it fell across her shoulders and down her back. Her large taupe eyes were ringed with dark grey eyeshadow and her delectable lips were painted nude.

He couldn't drag his eyes away.

For what had to be the first time ever he found himself at a loss for words.

Judging by the expression in her wide eyes, pain emanating from them as she gazed back at him, she was struggling to form words on her own tongue too.

It was Greta who broke the silence, with a shout of, 'Champagne!' She grinned at Helios, slipped her arm through Amy's and whisked her off to find them a glass each.

'Thanks,' Amy muttered the second they were out of

his earshot. Her heart was hammering so hard she could swear she was suffering from palpitations.

'You're welcome. Here,' said Greta, thrusting a glass into Amy's hand. 'Drink this.'

'I've had enough already.' They'd had a couple of shots of ouzo each in Greta's flat, before the car had arrived for them, and while not drunk she definitely felt a little light-headed.

Greta shook her head. 'You're going to need a lot more than this to get through the night without throwing yourself at him.'

'I'm not going to throw myself at him.'

'You could have fooled me from the way you were just staring at each other.'

'We're over,' Amy stated flatly.

'So you keep telling yourself.'

'I mean it.'

'I know you do. The problem is I don't think your heart believes it.' Greta squeezed her hand. 'Don't worry. I'll stop you from entering the big bad wolf's clutches again.'

Fighting to stop her gaze flickering back to him, Amy nodded and swallowed half of her champagne.

'Let's see what's in these envelopes,' Greta said, ripping hers open.

Amy followed suit and found inside a personalised card, thanking her for all her hard work since joining the museum, and two hundred euros to spend in the casino.

'Last year we spent a day on Helios's yacht,' Greta confided, fingering her own pile of notes lovingly. 'It was amazing—when we got back to shore Talia was so drunk Pedro had to carry her off.'

Her words did the trick, making Amy laugh at the image of Helios's prim private secretary, brought along to keep events ticking along smoothly, losing control of herself in such a manner.

Some of her angst loosened and she made a pledge to enjoy herself. At some point just about *everyone* who'd had a work-based affair had to deal with an ex being present. She didn't have to make a big deal of it. If she stuck to Greta's side and avoided even looking at Helios she would be fine.

But stopping herself from staring became harder when they were taken through to the restaurant, which had been put aside for their private use. The seating plan meant she had an excellent view of the top table, where Helios was seated. So good was her view that the moment she took her seat his eyes found her.

She cast her eyes down to her menu, ostensibly familiarising herself with her selections. When she dared to look back up he was engaged in conversation with Jessica, an American curator who had worked at the museum for two decades.

'You're staring,' Greta hissed.

Smiling tightly, Amy forced small talk from her lips, taking a small breath of relief when the starters were brought out.

Her plate was placed before her, and the waiter removed the silver lid with a flourish to release the beautiful aromas of roast sea scallops and smoked celeriac purée sitting in a shellfish broth. It tasted as wonderful as it smelled, and she wished she could appreciate it more, but as hard as she tried her awareness of Helios two tables away was all-consuming.

She was powerless to stop her eyes flickering to him, taking in the strong brown throat exposed by his unbuttoned white silk shirt—all the other men wore ties—and the way his dark blue dinner jacket emphasised the breadth of his chest. If she could only ever stare at one thing for the rest of her life it would be him.

He was laughing at something Jessica had said, his generous smile wide, his liquid eyes lively. A burst of jealousy ripped through her to see him enjoying Jessica's company so much, a totally irrational feeling, considering that Jessica was old enough to be his mother, but real nonetheless.

It was some consolation that he hadn't brought the Princess with him. If she'd had to watch him talking and laughing with her, Amy was certain she would have been sick.

And then his gaze found hers again and her stomach somersaulted. He raised his glass of wine slowly and took a long swallow.

An elbow in her ribs brought her back to earth.

'Stop it!' Greta whispered fiercely.

But she couldn't.

Even when her main course of fillet of beef and truffle mash was brought out to her she couldn't stop her eyes from constantly darting to him.

There was nothing wrong in looking, she told herself helplessly. So long as she kept away from him she could look. She just couldn't touch.

After what felt like hours the meal was over. Before she could flee into the casino, away from the magnetism of Helios's stare, he was on his feet and making a speech, which ended with him raising his glass and offering a toast to them all.

'If you'd all make your way to the private beach at midnight you'll find a last surprise for you,' he finished with a grin. 'Until then, enjoy the casino and the music and most of all have fun—you've earned it.'

Keeping herself glued to Greta's side, Amy headed into the casino, which was every bit as opulent as she'd expected and very busy. However, Helios had arranged for them to have their own private poker, blackjack and roulette tables. She had no interest in playing but it was fun to observe, especially to watch Jessica, who seemed to be cleaning up on the blackjack table, to everyone's amazement. There was soon a crowd forming around her.

The only blot on the landscape was a prickle on her neck: the weight of Helios's stare upon her. It took everything she had not to return it. Without the dining tables separating them she felt vulnerable. It was only a matter of time before he sought her out.

Except it never happened. From out of the corner of her eye she watched him make his way around the casino and the adjoining dance room, speaking to all his staff in turn, his easy smile evident.

So many free drinks were being pressed into their hands that Amy felt herself becoming more light-headed by the minute. Soon it was enough to make herself switch to coffee.

She couldn't stop her heart from jolting every time Helios moved away from one person and on to another. Irrationally, she longed for him to bestow his attentions on her. But other than with his eyes he made no such attempt. She must be the only member of staff he hadn't made an effort to speak to. Apart from Greta, who hadn't let Amy out of her sight all evening.

Maybe he'd finally accepted that they were over, despite his proclamation that she would always be his. Maybe their short time apart had convinced him she had been right to end things between them.

A dagger speared her stomach at the thought of never feeling his strong arms around her again, or the heat of his kiss.

She needed to get out of there, to go back to her apartment and lick her wounds in peace before she gave in to the howl building in her throat. She'd done her best tonight, but not even the alcohol had numbed the ache pounding beneath her ribs. If anything, it had got worse.

But what peace could she find in her apartment when Helios was only the other side of a secret passageway? How could she survive another five months of living so close to him? With her resignation rejected and his threat of legal action if she left hanging over her head, her choices were limited. Her career would be ruined. Who would trust her if she were to breach her contract and be sued by the heir to the throne of Agon?

Because she believed that if she were to leave now he *would* carry out his threat.

He wasn't a cruel man, but when provoked Helios was hot-tempered, passionate and filled to the brim with pride. Her attempted resignation had punctured his ego.

But then, if he had finally accepted they were finished maybe he'd be more understanding and amenable to her leaving if she broached the subject again, once the Gala was over.

She wished so hard that she could hate him, but she couldn't. How could anyone hate him?

'It's nearly midnight,' Greta said animatedly. 'Let's go to the beach.'

Amy nodded. The low buzzing noise of all the surrounding chatter was making her head ache. Some fresh sea air would do her good. She'd go out and watch the last of the entertainment and then she would slip away and lick her wounds in earnest.

The hotel's curved private beach brought gasps of delight from everyone. Helios was pleased by their reaction. Indeed, the whole evening had been a marked success. He was sure there would be plenty of foggy heads in the morning, but he doubted anyone would regret them.

Rows of wooden tables with benches had been set along the sand, and gas lamps had been placed on them for illumination under the moonless sky. The hotel's beach bar was open and cocktails were being made.

To get to the beach you had to cut through the hotel's garden and follow a gentle, meandering trail, then take half a dozen steep steps down to it. It wasn't until the tables were half-full that he spotted Amy, making her way down with Greta, whom she'd clung to like a shield for the entire evening.

He knew why.

Amy didn't want to be alone because she was scared he would pounce the second he had the chance. And if she was scared of him pouncing there could only be one reason— she knew she would struggle to resist.

Her eyes had followed him everywhere that evening. She might try, but she could no more deny the chemistry between them than he could. Soon she would realise resistance was futile. Did the tide resist the pull of the moon? Of course not. Nature worked in perfect harmony, just like the desire that pulled him and Amy together.

And yet... Shadows darkened her eyes. There was pain there, the same pain he'd seen when she'd arrived at the hotel. Seeing it had made him...uneasy. It disturbed him in ways he couldn't explain, not even to himself.

It had made him think twice about approaching her. Could *he* be the cause of that pain?

When she got to the bottom of the pathway she held Greta's arm while she took her shoes off, then the pair of them took themselves to a table where some of their fellow curators were seated. Within moments of her sitting down her eyes roamed until they found him.

Even with only the soft glow of the lamps to illuminate her face he could see her yearning. He could sense her resistance waning. The uneasiness that had pulled at him all evening abated. He'd been imagining it.

With all the stress in his life—from his grandfather's deteriorating health, Theseus's shocking news, the forthcoming Gala, his own engagement and everything in between—it was no wonder his mind was playing tricks on him and making him see things that weren't there.

Music from the DJ's deck began to play; a soft dance beat for everyone to tap their bare feet to, its pulse riding through his veins.

Soon Amy would be his again. And when he got her back in his bed he was never going to let her go.

CHAPTER SIX

DESPITE HER LONGING to be away from the hotel, far from the pull of Helios, Amy was enchanted by what surrounded her. The beach, under the light of the twinkling stars, was the most perfect scene imaginable. The noise of the lapping waves mingled with the dance beat playing behind them and gave her a sense of serenity that had been missing from her life since Helios had announced his intention to marry.

'I need to use the bathroom,' Greta murmured, rising from the table. 'Are you coming?'

'I don't think you need me to hold your hand, do you?' Amy said drily.

Greta laughed and set off into the hotel on decidedly unsteady feet.

Amy shook her head with a smile. Greta had been enjoying the steady stream of free cocktails even more than Amy had enjoyed the steady stream of free coffee.

No sooner had Greta gone than two men with matching goatee beards and dreadlocks pulled back into ponytails appeared. Both were dressed in black outfits that brought to mind samurai warriors crossed with pirates. These men were Agonites; Amy would bet her savings on it.

With interpreters translating from their Greek, the two men insisted that the table Amy was seated at be moved

back ten feet. As soon as that was done they drew a line
in the sand, marking a semicircle which they made clear
no one should cross.

Curiosity drove everyone to their feet. Without her
heels on Amy had trouble seeing anything, so she ducked
out of the crowd to stand at the top of the steps leading
down to the beach. The extra height and distance allowed
her to see unhindered.

As the men set themselves up, removing objects she
couldn't see from two huge crates, Greta came out of the
bathroom and made her way to the semicircle of people
crowding around them.

The sun had long gone down and standing alone, without the shared body heat of the people below, Amy felt the
slight chill in the air. Rubbing her arms for warmth, she kept
her gaze on the men, pretending to herself that she hadn't
seen Helios step out from the bar with two large cocktail
glasses in his hands...

'I thought you looked thirsty,' he said, climbing the
steps to stand with her.

Her heart and throat catching, she shook her head. Deep
down she'd known that separating herself from the group
would be perceived as an open invitation.

His smile was knowing as he handed her one of the
drinks. 'Try this. I think you'll like it.'

The glass was full of crushed ice, and the liquid within
it was pink. Fresh strawberries had been placed around the
rim, and sprigs of mint laced the cocktail. Wordlessly, she
took it from him and placed the straw between her lips.

He knew her tastes too well. 'It's delicious. What is it?'

'A strawberry mojito.'

'Did you make it?'

He laughed lightly and shook his head. 'I wouldn't know
where to begin.'

She took another sip. The combination of fresh mint and crushed strawberries played on her tongue, as did the taste of rum.

'What are you drinking?'

'A Long Island iced tea. Try some?'

She shouldn't. Really, she shouldn't.

With the moonless sky filled with twinkling stars, the scent of the sea, the background throb of music, the laughter coming from the crowd of people before them…it was a scene for romance, one she should turn and run away from.

Yet her hand disobeyed her brain, reaching out to take the glass from him, bringing the straw his own lips had wrapped around to her mouth so she could take a small sip.

Her eyes widened. 'That packs a punch!'

He grinned and took the glass back from her, brushing his fingers against hers for a second too long.

Little darts raced through her hand and up her arm. She took another sip of her mojito, fighting desperately to stop herself from leaning forward and into him. He was so close…

'I found out the other day that I'm an uncle,' Helios said, making conversation before she could remember to flee again. Besides, this was something he really needed to talk about, before his head exploded with the magnitude of it all.

'Really?'

Her shock mirrored his own initial reaction to the news. 'Theseus. He had a one-night stand with a woman he met on his sabbatical.'

'Wow. That was a few years ago, wasn't it?'

'The boy is four. His name's Toby. Theseus only found out by accident and a quirk of fate—he lied about his identity to the mother, so she was never able to tell him. And then she turned up at the palace to work on the official biography.'

'That really *is* a quirk of fate. Is he going to recognise him?'

'Yes. And he's going to marry the mother to legitimise him.'

She took another long sip of her mojito, her eyes wide as she finally met his gaze. 'Does your grandfather know?'

'Theseus is going to tell him after the Gala. We've agreed it's best to let that day be for our grandfather.'

She looked down at the ground. He wondered if she was thinking the same thing, that he was using the Gala to make the announcement of his marriage. But his announcement was different—for his grandfather it would be the pinnacle of the day, confirmation of the security that would come with knowing his heir was going to embark on matrimony.

'Theseus's relationship with my grandfather is complicated. Being a Prince of Agon is not something he's ever liked or adjusted to. It's the reason why he's been working so hard on the biography, to prove that he is ready to embrace who he is.'

'Whereas you've always embraced your destiny?' she said softly.

'I am who I am,' he answered with a shrug, not admitting that for a fleeting moment his brother's news had given him pause for thought. Theseus had a ready-made heir and a fiancée he certainly was not indifferent to...

But, no, the thought had been pushed aside before he'd allowed it to float too far into his mind. The throne would be his. It was his destiny. It was his pride. Being King was a role Theseus would hate with every fibre of his being.

Seeing Amy using her straw to fight through the ice to

the liquid left in the bottom of her glass, he signalled to a passing bartender for two more drinks.

'The news about Toby is confidential, of course,' he said, once the man had returned to the bar. 'Only you and I and Theseus's private staff know.'

'Which means half the palace knows.'

He laughed. 'The palace grapevine has a life of its own, I admit, but I hadn't heard anything before Theseus told me, so I don't think word has got out yet.'

'No one will hear anything from me.'

'That goes without saying.' In their time together he had learned to trust Amy completely. He'd never had to watch what he said to her... Apart from the time he'd failed to tell her about the real purpose behind the pre-Gala ball.

Something glistened in her eyes, a spark that flew out to touch him and cut the last of the smile from his face. Had it not been for the bartender, carrying their fresh drinks up the steps, he would have leaned in to kiss her.

Amy blinked herself out of the minor stupor she'd been in danger of falling into and took a grateful sip of her fresh mojito.

It was crazy, but Helios's news about his nephew had brought a spark of hope within her. If there was a ready-made heir in the family...

But, no. Such hopes were futile. Helios had been born to rule this great nation with a royal bride at his side. It was his destiny. And she, Amy, was a nobody.

'The entertainment's about to begin.'

'Sorry?'

That knowing smile spread once again over his handsome face. He nodded at the crowd on the beach.

Following his gaze, she saw the two piratical men standing side by side in the semicircle they'd created, their legs parted in a warrior stance. What ensued was an acrobatic display of perfect synchronicity that on its own would have been marvellous but which then switched to a whole new level.

The men ducked out of Amy's eyesight before reappearing with thick, long sticks, the ends of which were ablaze. Her mouth opened in awe as she watched them dancing and twirling and leaping and whirling whilst the fire made patterns in the darkness, bringing the very air to life.

'You look cold,' Helios murmured, stepping behind her and wrapping an arm around her waist to secure her to him.

Transfixed by what was happening on the beach, her skin dancing with something like the same flames that were playing out before her, Amy didn't resist, not even when he brought his mouth down to nuzzle into her hair. Her insides melted and despite herself she leant back into his hardness, dizzying relief rushing through her at the sensation of being back where she belonged. In Helios's arms.

She gasped as she felt his hand slide over her stomach and drift up to rest under her breasts. She knew she should throw off his hand and walk away, that allowing herself to be held like this was the height of stupidity and danger, but no matter how loudly her brain shouted at her feet to start walking her body refused to obey.

A thumb was raised up to brush against the underside of her breast and he pressed his groin into the small of her back, letting her feel his arousal. The fire-wielding acrobats became a blur in her vision as her senses all turned inwards to relish the feel of Helios against her.

She should be like a marble Minoan statue. Unresponsive. Cold. But his touch turned her molten.

Send her to hell, but she rubbed against his arousal. He hissed in her ear, dropping his hand to her hip and gripping it tightly. She could feel his racing heart beating against her back.

Only the loud sound of applause cut through the sensuous fog she'd fallen into.

The show had finished.

The crowd was dispersing.

Blinking hard, aware of Greta searching for her, Amy finally managed to make her body obey, grabbed Helios's hand and pushed it away.

She took a step to distance herself from the security of his hold and drank the last of her mojito.

'Come back with me,' he said. For once, there was no arrogance in his voice.

She kept her eyes from his, not wanting him to see the longing she knew would be written all over her face. 'I can't.'

'You can.'

Greta had spotted them and was heading for them, or rather weaving unsteadily towards them.

'Come back with me,' he repeated.

'No.' She propelled herself down the steps, desperate to be away from him before her vocal cords said the *yes* they so yearned to speak.

He followed her, grabbing her hand when she reached the bottom step and spinning her around.

She waited breathlessly for him to say something, but all he did was stare at her as if he was drinking her in, his thumb brushing little swirls over the inside of her wrist. The message he was sending didn't need words.

Tugging out of his hold, she hurried away before she could respond to his silent request.

Helios pressed a hand to his forehead and growled to his empty bedroom. He'd been back for over an hour and not even his two Long Island iced teas, which had virtually every spirit imaginable in them, had numbed his brain enough to allow him to sleep.

His body still carried remnants of the arousal that had been unleashed by holding Amy in his arms. One touch was all it had taken. One touch and he'd been fit to burst.

If he'd been one of his ancestors from four hundred years ago he would have marched down the passageway, broken down her door and demanded she give herself to him. As he was a prince of these lands she wouldn't have been allowed to refuse him. She would have had to submit to his will.

But good Queen Athena, Agon's reigning monarch from 1671, had been at the forefront of the abolition of the law which had allowed women to be little more than chattels for the royal family's pleasure.

And even if he could he wouldn't force Amy into his bed. If she came back to him he wanted it to be under her own free will.

He knew she'd returned to the palace. After the fire show she'd disappeared into the throng, and then the last he'd seen of her had been when she'd climbed into one of the waiting palace cars with some of the other live-in staff.

Why was she doing this to him? To *them*? She was as crazy for him as he was for her, and he struggled to understand why she was resisting so hard.

He knew that she wanted to punish him because he had to marry someone else—if he were in her shoes he would probably feel the same way. The mere idea of her with another man was enough to make his blood pressure rise to the point where his veins might explode.

As ashamed as he was to have done so, he'd got his security team to find out who she'd dined with on Saturday night. Leander Soukis, a twenty-two-year-old layabout from a small village on the outskirts of Resina. How Amy had met this man was a mystery. And there was something about their meeting that ground at him.

Never mind that Leander was five years younger than Amy, when Helios distinctly remembered her saying she couldn't relate to younger men, he was also a slight, skinny thing, with a bad reputation. He came from a wealthy family, but that counted for nothing—Leander had been kicked out of three schools and had never held a job for longer than a week. Indeed, he was an ideal candidate for his brother Talos's boxing gym, which he'd opened in order to help disaffected youths, teaching them to channel their anger and giving them a leg up in life.

Why had she gone on a date with him of all people? Had it been her way of proving to Helios that she was serious about their relationship being over? Maybe he should have accepted her resignation rather than let his pride and ego force her into staying. If she was gone from Agon he wouldn't be lying in his bed with a body aching from unfulfilled desire.

But he knew such thoughts were pointless. Amy didn't need to be in his sight to be on his mind. She was there constantly.

And he would bet the palace that right at that moment she was lying in her bed thinking of him.

A soft ping from the security pad on his wall broke through his thoughts.

Jumping out of bed, he pressed a button on it, which brought up the screen issuing the alert. It was from the camera and the sensors in the secret passageway.

Peering closely, he saw a figure moving stealthily along the passageway, getting closer and closer to his room. With his heart in his mouth he watched as she hesitated, and willed her to take the final step and knock on the door.

* * *

Amy stared at Helios's door, not quite certain what she was doing or how she had got to this point.

Knowing she was vulnerable to temptation, she'd accepted an invitation to go to one of the other curator's apartments for a drink: a mini-soirée she would usually have loved attending. She'd tried so hard to pull herself out of the trance she'd fallen into, but her contribution to the conversation had been minimal. She couldn't remember a word of it. It was as if she'd been floating above it all, there in body but not in spirit.

She wanted to blame the alcohol, especially the mojitos Helios had given her, but that would have been a lie. It was all down to him.

She'd gone back to her own apartment after just one drink, but before she'd even stepped into her bedroom she'd stopped and stared at the door that led to the secret passageway. Her breaths had shortened as a deep yearning had pulled at her.

Impulse had overridden common sense. She'd unlocked the connecting door and stepped into the passageway in the same dreamlike state she'd ridden back to the palace in, not consciously thinking about where she was going. But now, standing at his door, sanity had pushed its way back through into her mind.

She couldn't do this. It was all wrong.

Closing her eyes, she pressed the palm of her hand to his door, holding it there.

This was as far as she dared go. If she were to knock and he were to answer...

She heard the telltale click of the lock turning.

She snatched her hand away, her breath catching in her throat.

The door opened.

Helios stood in the doorway, naked, nonchalant, as if Amy sneaking up to his room and doing nothing but touch his door was an everyday occurrence. Except the nonchalance was only on the surface. His chest rose and fell in tight judders. His jaw was taut; his nostrils flared. His eyes bore through her as he did nothing but stare.

And then he moved, sending out a hand to wrap around the nape of her neck and pull her to him and over the threshold. As soon as they were in his room he held her firmly and pushed the door shut. He pressed her against it, trapping her.

'Why are you here?' he asked roughly, leaning close enough for his warm, faintly minty breath to touch her skin.

'I don't know,' she whispered.

She *didn't* know. The closest she could come to describing it was her subconscious overriding her resolve. Now, though, the opposite was true. The sensations darting through her had overridden her subconscious and every inch of her had sprung into life. There was not a single atom of her body that wasn't tilting into him, yearning for his kiss, his touch.

'*I* know.'

Then, with a look that suggested he wanted to eat her alive, he brought his mouth to hers and caught her in his kiss.

CHAPTER SEVEN

IF HIS KISS had been the demanding assault she'd anticipated Amy would have been able to resist and push him away. But it wasn't. His lips rested against hers but he made no movement, stilling as if he was breathing in her essence. Amy inhaled deeply in turn, letting the warmth of his breath and the scent of him creep through her pores and inhabit her.

It was as if everything that had happened in the past ten days had been blown away, and with it all the reasons why being alone with him in his apartment and in his arms was all wrong. This was everything she wanted, everything she needed. How could something so wrong feel so *right*?

And now she didn't even want to think about right and wrong. All she wanted was to be in his arms. For ever.

She was the one to part her lips, to dart her tongue into the darkness of his mouth, to wind her arms around his neck and press into him. She was the one to break the kiss and drag her lips over his stubble-roughened cheeks and jaw and down the strong length of his neck, to run her tongue over the smooth skin, tasting his musky, masculine scent. And she was the one to draw her tongue back up his throat, dig her nails into his scalp and capture his lips with her own.

A tiny sob escaped her mouth when Helios growled and drew his arms around her. He crushed her to him. His lips parted and he kissed her so deeply and so thoroughly that in the breath of an instant she was lost in him.

A large hand dived into her hair whilst his other hand roamed down her back to clutch her bottom, which he squeezed before spreading his palm over her thigh and lifting it. He ground into her and she gasped to feel him huge against her, her underwear the only barrier to stop him entering her there and then.

In a mesh of lips and tongues he pushed her back against the wall, kissing her as if she were a banquet to be feasted on, before pulling away, tugging at her bottom lip painlessly with his teeth as he did so. His chest rising and falling in rapid motion, the palm of one hand held against her chest to still her, Helios lowered himself, pinched the hem of her dress and slowly raised it up. He kissed her stomach as he lifted the dress to her abdomen, his tongue making a trail upwards, through the valley of her breasts, into her neck, until he'd pulled it over her head and thrown it onto the floor.

Amy dug her toes into the hard flooring, her head spinning. Everything inside her blazed as fiercely as the whirling fires she'd seen on the beach. Her skin was alive to his touch. *She* was alive to his touch. Her senses had sprung to life from the very first moment she'd looked at him all those months ago and since then she'd been helpless to switch them off.

He straightened to his full height and stared down at her, his throat moving as his liquid eyes took in her semi-nakedness. He clasped her cheeks in his hands and brought his nose to hers. 'Not being able to touch you or make love to you has driven me crazy,' he said hoarsely. '*You've* driven me crazy.'

She pulled at his hair, wanting to hurt him, wanting him to experience the pain she'd gone through at the separation she'd had no choice but to force upon them. 'It's hurt me every bit as much as you,' she whispered, bringing her mouth back to his.

Holding her tightly, Helios lifted Amy into his arms, staring at her as he carried her through to his bedroom, delighting in the heightened colour of her cheeks and the dilation of her pupils.

All his dreams and fantasies had come true.

She'd come to him.

He hadn't realised how badly he'd prayed for it until he'd opened the door to her.

But he could still see the last vestiges of doubt and fear ringing in her eyes and he was determined to drive them away.

How could she not know that *this*, here, being together, was exactly how it was supposed to be?

Laying her down on his bed, he kissed her rosebud mouth and inhaled the sweet scent he had come close to believing he would never delight in again. All that separated them was her pretty black underwear. He remembered how once he'd peeled it off with his teeth, in those early hedonistic days when the desire between them had been so great he'd been certain it would *have* to abate. But it had only developed into something deeper, something needier.

Whatever it took, he would keep her in his bed.

As he gazed down, seeing the pulse beating in the arch of her neck, the way she stretched out her legs before raising her pelvis, the urgency grew. *Theos*, but he needed to be inside her.

She raised a lazy hand and pressed it to his chest, then spread her fingers over him, touching him in the way that always filled him with such gratification, as if he were one of the Seven Wonders of the World.

The knowledge that she would explore him in the same manner with which he delighted in exploring her had always been indescribable. There was not a fraction of her he had not tasted and not a fraction of him she had not touched. He would *never* tire of tasting her and making her his.

He slipped a hand behind her back and unclasped her bra, then carefully pulled the straps down her arms, kissing the trail they made and throwing it onto the floor with a flick. With her delectable breasts now bare, the dusky nipples puckered in open invitation, he dipped his head to take one tip in his mouth, groaning as she immediately arched her back to allow him to take more of her in.

Her fingers tugged through his hair as she twisted and writhed beneath him, the urgency in her movements matching the urgency flowing through his veins. She skimmed a hand down over his back before slipping it across his stomach, reaching for him. His attentions now on her other breast, he raised himself a little to make it easier for her to take his erection into her hand, groaning again as she held it in the way she knew he adored, rubbing her thumb over the head and guiding him to the apex of her thighs.

Gritting his teeth and breathing heavily, he kissed her neck and moved her hand away, squeezing her fingers between his own. Immediately she raised her thighs and rubbed against his length, moaning, begging him with soft murmurs.

But there was still the final barrier of her underwear between them.

He kissed her hard on the mouth, then pulled back, drifting his lips down the creaminess of her neck and breasts until he reached her abdomen. There, he pinched the elastic of her underwear between the fingers of both hands and tugged it down, past her thighs and calves and delicate ankles, until she was fully naked before him.

'Please...' she beseeched him, raising her thighs higher and reaching out a hand to touch him. *'Please.'*

Swallowing hard at the sight of her, so full of desire and need for him it made him heady, he guided his erection into her welcoming heat.

He pushed himself in with one long drive and buried his face in her neck, biting gently into the soft skin. And as she gripped him tightly within her he knew without a shadow of a doubt that *this* was where he belonged.

Skin against skin, heartbeat to heartbeat, arms and legs entwined, he made love to her.

And she made love to him.

He could sense the tension within her building, could hear it in the shortening of her breaths, the shallowness of her moans, feel it in the way she gripped his buttocks, deepening his thrusts. And then he felt her pulses pulling at him, pulling him even deeper inside her, her slender frame stilling, her teeth biting into his shoulder.

He didn't want it to end. He wanted it to last for ever, to be locked in her tight sweetness with her legs wrapped around him and her nails digging into his back for eternity...

And then there was no more consciousness. His own climax surged through him, tipping him over a precipice he hadn't known he was on the edge of and exploding in a wash of bright colours that took him to a place he'd never been before.

Amy awoke in the comfort of Helios's embrace, her face pressed against his chest, his arm hooked across her waist, his thigh draped heavily over hers.

Remorse flooded her in an instant.

What had she done?

Everything she'd sworn she wouldn't do had been ripped away in one moment of madness.

She should go. She had to go. She couldn't stay here.

How many times had she awoken in the night in his arms and felt the stirring to make love to him all over again? How many times had she lifted her head a touch and met his kiss? Had him fully hard and inside her in an instant? Too many to count. Sometimes she would wake in the morning and wonder if she'd dreamt their lovemaking in the early hours.

But at this moment Helios's breathing was deep and even. If she was careful she might be able to sneak out without him waking. Then she could flee to her apartment, pack a suitcase and check into a hotel. That was it. That was what she had to do.

Because she couldn't stay here—not now when she knew how hopeless she was at resisting him.

She'd tried so hard to stay away.

Oh, God, what had she *done*?

She could dress it up any way she liked but she'd given in to temptation, and now the ecstasy of being back in his arms had gone, replaced with an acrid taste in her mouth and a gutful of guilt.

She had to leave. Right now.

Carefully, after stealthily slipping out of his arms, she edged her way out of the bed, holding her breath until her feet touched the floor.

Scrambling, half-blind in the dark, she found her dress thrown across an armchair. She had no idea where her underwear had got to and was in too much of a panic to escape to hunt for it for long. She shrugged her dress on and, fearful of choking on the swell rising in her chest, tiptoed to the door.

'You wouldn't be running away, would you?'

Helios watched as Amy's silhouette froze at the bedroom door. Switching on the bedside light, he propped himself up on an elbow as she slowly turned around to face him with wide, pain-filled taupe eyes. To see her mussed-up hair and her beautiful face contorted in such misery... Something sharp pierced him.

'I'm sorry,' she whimpered. 'I know it's cowardly to sneak away.'

'Then why are you?'

'I shouldn't be here. We shouldn't have...' Her voice tailed away and she looked down at the floor.

'Made love?' he supplied.

She gave a tiny nod. 'It was wrong. All wrong.'

'It felt damn right to me.'

'I know.' She gave a sudden bark of harsh laughter and her eyes flashed. 'It's what I keep thinking. How can something so wrong feel so right?'

'If it feels so right then how can it be wrong?' he countered.

'It just is. You're getting *married*.'

That little fact was something that constantly played on his mind. Only being in Amy's arms had driven it and the accompanying nausea away.

Tightness coiled in his stomach. Throwing off the covers, he climbed out of bed and strode over to her, slamming his hand on the door to prevent her from escaping.

He spoke slowly, trying to think the words through before he vocalised them, knowing that one wrong word would make her flee whether or not he barricaded the door. 'Amy, I might be getting married, but it's *you* I want.'

'We've been through this before. It doesn't matter what you want or what I want. It doesn't change the reality of the situation. Tonight was a mistake that can't be repeated.'

'Running away won't change anything either. Admit it, *matakia mou*. You and I belong together.'

Her jaw clenched in response.

'So what are you going to do?' he asked scathingly, leaning closer to her ashen face. 'Run away and start a relationship with Leander? Is that how you intend to prove we're over?'

'How do you know about Leander?' She shook her head and took a deep inhalation. 'Don't answer that. I can guess.'

He felt no guilt for seeking information about her date. Helios looked out for those he cared for. 'He's too young for you. I know you, Amy. You don't need a boy. You need—'

'He's my brother,' she snapped suddenly, angry colour flushing her cheeks.

Her declaration momentarily stunned him into silence. Stepping back to look at her properly, he dragged a hand through his hair. 'But Leander is from Agon. Your brothers are English, like you...'

'I'm only half-English.'

'Your parents are English.' *Weren't* they? Wasn't this something they had talked about...?

'My father's English. Elaine—my mum—didn't give birth to me. My birth mother's from Agon.'

How had he not known this?

Amy must have sensed the direction his mind was travelling in. 'Do you remember once asking me how I'd developed such an obsession and a love for your country?'

'You said it was... You never gave a proper answer...'
Realisation dawned on him as he thought back to that

conversation, months ago, when they had first started sleeping together. She'd brushed his question aside.

'And you never pursued it.' She shook her head in a mixture of sadness and anger.

'I didn't know there was anything to pursue. I'm not a mind reader.'

'I'm sorry.' She gave a helpless shrug. 'A huge part of me wanted to tell you, and ask for your help in finding her, but I knew that confiding in you would change the nature of our relationship.'

'What would have changed?' he asked, completely perplexed.

From the first the chemistry between them had been off the charts. Making love to Amy had always felt different from the way it had felt with his other lovers. He'd never felt the urge to ask her to leave at night—he liked sharing his space with her, this incredibly sexy woman with a brain the size of a watermelon. He loved it that she could teach him things he didn't know about his own country.

To learn now that she had *roots* in his country...

'I didn't keep any secrets from you,' he added, his head reeling.

'Apart from throwing a party to find a wife?'

He inhaled deeply. Yes, the real purpose of the ball *was* something he'd kept from her for as long as he could. But this information was on a different scale. He'd known Amy had kept a part of herself sheltered from him, but he'd had no idea it was something so fundamental.

Her eyes held his. 'I was scared.'

Another stabbing pain lanced him. 'Of me?'

'Of what you would think of me. At least I was in the beginning.' Her voice lowered to a whisper. 'And I was scared because you and I came with time constraints. We had a fixed marker for when we would end, we both knew that. We both held things back.'

'I never held anything back.'

'Didn't you?' There was no challenge in her eyes, just a simple question. 'Helios, I couldn't take the risk of what we had developing into something more—of us becoming closer. We can't be together for ever. I was trying to protect myself.'

For an age he stared at her, wishing he could see into her mind, wishing he could shake her...wishing that everything could be different.

'Do not go anywhere,' he said, turning his back to her and striding to his dressing room. 'You and I are going to talk, and this is not a conversation to have naked. We're long past the point of keeping secrets from each other.'

While Helios slipped on a pair of boxers Amy used the few moments alone to catch her thoughts before he reappeared.

It wasn't long enough.

She pressed her back tightly against the door, her vocal cords too constricted for speech.

'I mean it, Amy,' he said with a hard look in his eye. 'You're not going anywhere until we've talked this through.'

'What's the point?' she asked, her voice hoarse.

'If your history is what's stopping us from being together then I damn well deserve to know the truth.' He strolled back to the bed and sat in the middle of it, his back resting against the headboard. 'Now, come here.'

What an unholy mess. It had never been supposed to end like this. Her memories of her time with him were supposed to be filled with wonder, not sorrow and despair. Losing him wasn't supposed to *hurt*.

She perched on the end of the bed and twisted to face him. Blowing out a puff of air, she gazed at the ceiling.

'My father had an affair with the au pair. She dumped me on him when I was two weeks old and has wanted nothing to do with me since. Her husband and her parents don't know I exist.'

CHAPTER EIGHT

OTHER THAN A slight shake of his head and a tightening of his lips, Helios gave no response.

'My birth mother had me when she was nineteen. I know very little about her—she didn't work for them for long.'

'When you say *for them*…?'

'My parents. My mum—as in the woman who raised me—was pregnant and had a three-year-old son when they employed Neysa, my birth mother, as an au pair. She quit after a couple of months but then turned up at my dad's workplace seven months later and left me with the receptionist.'

Amy studied Helios's reaction carefully. She no longer really feared, as she had at the beginning of their relationship, that he would think any less of her, but nagging doubts remained. Cruel words spoken in the playground still haunted her, clouding her judgement.

'You must have been one ugly baby for your own mum to dump you.'

'Do you have 666 marked on the back of your head?'

'Your real mum's a slut.'

She'd had to force herself to rise above it and pretend the taunts didn't affect her when in reality they had burned. For years she had tortured herself, wondering if the taunts held the ring of truth. For years she'd tried to live a life as pure as the driven snow to *prove* she wasn't intrinsically bad.

For years she'd wondered how Elaine—to her mind, her mum—could even bring herself to look at her.

Helios stared at her as if she'd just told him that all the scientists and even physics itself were wrong and the world was actually flat.

'Did she leave a note?' he asked quietly. 'Give a reason?'

'Her note to my father said only that I was his and that she couldn't keep me.'

'So your father had an affair with the au pair when your mum was pregnant? And they're still together?'

She nodded. 'God knows how Mum found it in her to forgive him but she did, and she raised me as her own.'

Helios shook his head, amazement in his eyes. 'She raised you with her own children?'

'Yes. Danny was born five months before me. We were in the same school year.'

He closed his eyes with a wince. 'That must have been difficult.'

'At times it was horrendous—especially at secondary school. But we coped.'

Amy's existence could have caused major friction between her and her siblings, but both Danny and their older brother, Neil, had always been fiercely protective of her, particularly during their teenage years.

'Did you always know?'

'Not when I was a young child. My family was my family. Danny being five months older than me...it was just a fact of our lives. Neil always knew I was only his half-sister but, again, it was just a fact of our lives and something he assumed was normal. My parents never mentioned it so he didn't either. Then we got older and other kids started asking questions… Mum told me the truth when I was ten.'

She shuddered at the memory of that sudden realisation that her whole life had been a lie.

'She'd been waiting until I was old enough to understand.'

It had been the most significant moment of Amy's life. It would have been easy to feel as if her whole world had caved in, but Danny and Neil had simply shrugged it off and continued to treat her as they always had—as their sister. That, more than anything, had made it easier to cope with.

'Did you not have *any* idea you weren't hers?'

'Not in the slightest. She loved me. Any resentment was hidden.'

'What about your father? Where does he fit in with all this?'

'He left it to my mum to tell me. When it came out he carried on as normal, trying to pretend nothing had changed.'

But of course everything had changed. *She'd* changed. How could she not? Everything she'd thought she knew about herself had been a lie.

She looked back at Helios, wanting him to understand. 'When I was told the truth it became important, I guess, to pretend that nothing had changed. They still treated me the same. They still scolded me when I was naughty. My mum still tucked me up in bed and kissed me goodnight. Outwardly, nothing did change.'

'And how does she feel about you being here now, trying to find your birth mother?'

'She understands. She's adopted herself—I think that's why she was able to raise me without blaming me for the sins of my birth mother. She knows what the urge to find out who you really are is like.'

Her mum had encouraged Amy's quest to learn all there was to know about Agon. She'd been the one to take her to the library to seek out books on Agon and Minoan culture and to record any television documentary that featured the island. So encouraging had she been that a part of Amy had been scared her mum *wanted* her to go to Agon and stay there. She'd been afraid that she wanted to get rid of the living proof of her husband's infidelity, that all the love she had bestowed on Amy had only been an act.

But Amy couldn't deny that she'd seen the apprehension in her mum's eyes when she'd left for Agon. Since she'd been on the island she'd received more daily calls and messages than she had when she'd first left home for university. Was she secretly worried that Amy would abandon her for Neysa…?

Secretly worried or not, wanting to get rid of her or not, being adopted herself meant her mum had first-hand experience of knowing what it was like to feel a part of you was missing. Helios had always known exactly who he was. There hadn't been a single day of his life when he hadn't known his place in the world or his destiny.

'She sounds like a good woman.'

'She is. She's lovely.' And she was. Loving and self-less. Amy knew her fears were irrational, but she had no control over them. They were still there, taunting her, in the deepest recesses of her mind.

'So why do you want to meet your birth mother?' Helios asked, puzzled that Amy could want *anything* to do with someone who'd caused such pain and destruction. 'She abandoned you and destroyed your mum's trust.'

She looked away. 'I don't want a relationship with her.

I just… I want to know what she looks like. Do I look like her? Because the only thing I've inherited from my dad is his nose. And I want to know why she did what she did.'

'Even if the truth hurts you?' If her birth mother was anything like her layabout son, he would guess she'd abandoned Amy for purely selfish reasons.

'I've been hurt every day of my life since I learned the truth of my conception,' she said softly. 'I know there are risks to meeting her, but I can't spend the rest of my life wondering.'

'Has your father not been able to fill in any of the gaps for you?'

'Not really. He doesn't like to talk about her—he's still ashamed of his behaviour. He's a scientist, happily stuck in a laboratory all day, and what he did was completely out of character.' She gave a sad smile. 'Even if he did want to talk about it there's not much for him to say. He hardly knew her. She was hired on a recommendation from one of Dad's colleagues who left his research company before I was dumped on him. All he and my mum knew was that Neysa—my birth mother—was from Agon and had come to England for a year to improve her English.'

And so the Greens had allowed a stranger into their home, with no foreknowledge of the havoc that would be wreaked on them.

'Everything else I've learned since I came here,' she added wistfully. 'Greta has helped me.'

But she hadn't confided in *him* or approached him for help.

Helios tried to imagine the pain and angst she'd been living with during all the nights they'd shared together. She hadn't breathed a word of it, although she must have known he was in the best position to help her.

'How's your parents' marriage now?'

Amy shrugged. 'When it all happened I was still a new-born baby. They patched their marriage up as best they could for the sake of us kids. They seem happy. I don't think my dad ever cheated again, but who knows?'

'My mother was a good woman too,' he said.

He was realising that Amy was right in her assertion that they had both kept things hidden. Both of them had kept parts of their lives locked away. And now it was time to unlock them.

'And my father was also a philanderer. But, unlike your father, mine never showed any penitence. The opposite, in fact.'

Her taupe eyes widened a touch but she didn't answer, just waited for him to continue in his own time.

'My father was hugely unfaithful—to be honest, he was a complete bastard. And my mother was incredibly jealous. To shut her up when she questioned him about his infidelities he would hit her. She deserved better than him.'

This was not a subject he'd ever discussed with anyone outside of his family. His father's infidelities were well documented, but his violence...that was something they'd all closed ranks on. Being the sons of such a vicious, narcissistic man was not something any of the brothers had found it easy to reconcile themselves with.

'I'm sorry,' Amy said, shaking her head slowly as if trying to take in his words. 'Did you know it was going on? The violence, I mean?'

'Only on an instinctual level. It was only ever a feeling.'

'How was *your* relationship with your father?' she asked quietly.

He grimaced as decades-old memories flooded him. 'I was the apple of his eye. He adored me, to the point that he excluded my brothers. It felt good, being the "special" one, but I also felt much guilt about it too. He was cruel—especially to Theseus. My mother struggled to make him treat us all fairly.'

Amy didn't say anything, just stared at him with haunted eyes.

'I was a child when they died. My memories are tainted by everything I learned after he'd gone, but I remember the looks he would give my mother when she stood up for Theseus or made a pointed remark about his other women. I would feel sick with worry for her, but he was always careful to make sure I was out of sight and earshot before hitting her. It got worse once I left for boarding school,' he continued. 'With me gone, he didn't have to hide it any more.'

'You surely don't blame yourself for that?'

'Not any more. But I did when I first learned the truth.' He met her gaze. 'It took me a long time to truly believe I couldn't have stopped him even if I had known. But, like you when your life fell apart, I was a child. Talos tried to stop it—that last day, before my parents were driven to the Greek Embassy and their car crashed, Talos was there, right in the middle of it. He got hurt himself in the crossfire.'

'Oh, the poor boy. That must have been horrendous for him.'

'It screwed up his ideas of marriage. He has no intention of ever marrying.'

'Not an option for you,' she said softly.

'No.' He shook his head for emphasis. 'Nor for Theseus. The security of our family and our island rests in our hands. But I swear this now—my parents' marriage will not be mine.'

'What if it was an option?' she asked suddenly, straightening. 'What if you'd been born an ordinary person? Who would you be now?'

'I don't know.' And he didn't. 'It's not something I've ever thought about.'

'Really?'

'Theseus spent most of his life fighting his birthright and all it brought him was misery. Why rail against something you have no control over? I had no control over my conception, just as I had no control over my parents' marriage or their deaths. My destiny is what it is, and I've always known and accepted that. I am who I am and I'm comfortable with that.'

It was only in recent weeks that the destiny he'd always taken for granted had gained a more acrid tang.

During their conversation Amy had moved fully back onto the bed and was now facing him, hugging her knees. Reaching forward, he took her left foot into his hands and gently tugged at it so it rested on his lap.

A strange cathartic sensation blew through him, and with it a sense of release. His father's violence and complete disrespect to his mother were things that he'd locked away inside, not wanting to give voice to the despicable actions he and his brothers felt tainted by. But Amy was the last person who would judge a child for the sins of its parents. In that respect they shared something no other could understand.

'The main reason I selected Catalina is because she has no illusions about what our marriage will be,' he said, massaging Amy's foot. 'She has been groomed from birth to marry someone of equal stature. I will be King, but I will never be like my father. Marrying Catalina guarantees that she will never expect more than I can give.'

'But your mother was a princess before she married your father.'

His mouth twisted. 'Their marriage was arranged before she could walk. She grew up knowing she would marry my father and she built an ideal in her head of what their marriage would be like. She loved him all her life and, God help her, she was doomed to disappointment. The only person my father loved was himself. Catalina doesn't love me any more than I love her. There will be no jealousy. She has no expectations of fidelity.'

'Has she said that?' Amy asked doubtfully.

'Her only expectation is that I be respectful to her and discreet, and that is something I will always be. Whatever happens in the future, I will *never* inflict on her or on anyone the pain my father inflicted on my mother.'

'I know you wouldn't hurt her intentionally. But, Helios, what she says now…it doesn't mean she'll feel the same way once you've exchanged your vows.' Amy closed her eyes and sighed. 'And it doesn't change how I feel about it. I won't be the other woman. Marriage vows should be sacred.'

Helios placed her foot gently onto the bed before pouncing, grabbing her hands and pinning her beneath him.

Breathing heavily, she turned her face away from him.

'Look at me,' he commanded.

'No.'

'Amy, look at me.' He loosened his hold only when she reluctantly turned her face back to him. 'You are not Neysa—you are Elaine's daughter, with all *her* goodness. Catalina is not your mother. Nor is she mine. And I am *not* my father. The mistakes they all made and the pain they caused are not ours to repeat. That's something neither of us would ever allow to happen.'

He came closer so his lips were a breath away from hers.

'And I'm not married yet.'

Her eyes blazed back at him, desire and misery fighting in them. He leaned down and placed a kiss to her neck, smoothing his hand over her breasts and down to her thighs. He inched the hem of her dress up and slid between her legs.

'Neither of us are ready for this to end. Why deny ourselves when my vows are still to be made and we're not hurting anyone?'

Amy fought the familiar tingles and sensations spreading through her again as the need to touch him and hold him grew stronger than ever. How was it possible to go from wanting to wrap him in her arms, to chase away what she knew were dreadful memories for him, to sensual need in the blink of an eye?

She writhed beneath him. Her words came in short breaths. 'I can't think when you're doing this to me.'

'Then don't think. Just feel. And accept that we're not over.'

In desperation she grabbed at his hair, forcing *him* to look at *her*. 'But you've made a commitment.'

'A commitment that won't be fulfilled for two months.' He slid inside her, penetrating as deep as he could go.

She gasped as pleasure filled her.

'Until then,' he continued, his voice becoming heavy as he began to move, 'you are mine and I am yours.'

Amy tightened her hold around Helios, wishing she didn't feel so complete with his weight upon her and his steadying breaths softly tickling the skin of her neck. She was a fool for him. More so than she could have imagined.

They'd laid their pasts bare to each other and the effect had been the very thing she'd been scared of. She felt closer to him, as if an invisible emotional bond had wrapped itself around them.

He finally shifted his weight off her and she rolled over and burrowed into his arms.

'Don't even think about trying to sneak out,' he said sleepily.

'I won't.' She gave a soft, bittersweet laugh. Her resolve had deserted her. Those bonds had cocooned her so tightly to him she could no longer envisage cutting them. Not yet. Not until she really had to. 'You and I...'

'What?' he asked, after her words had tailed off.

'No one can know. Please. Everyone who knew we were together knows we split up. I couldn't bear for them to think we're having an affair behind the Princess's back.'

When they'd been together originally Helios had made no secret of her place in his life. She might not have accompanied him to official functions, or been recognised as his official girlfriend, but she had been his almost constant companion within the palace.

She'd spent far more time in his apartment than she had in her own, and whenever he had come into the museum he would seek her out. He would touch her—not sexually... he at least had a sense of propriety when it came to *that* in public...but he would rest his hand in the small of her back, lean close to her, all the little tells of a possessive man staking his claim on the woman in his life. And if work or duty took him away from the palace she would be the one to look after Benedict.

It had only been on the inside, emotionally, that they had been separated. But not any more. At this moment she didn't think she had ever felt as close to anyone in her life.

'Discretion will be my new name,' he acquiesced.

'And when you marry you will let me go.'

He stilled.

Watching for his reaction, she saw his eyes open. 'That gives you two months to find my replacement,' she whispered. 'I want to know that you'll release me from the palace and from your life. I appreciate it means bringing my contract to an early end, but I don't think I'll be able to cope with living and working here knowing it's the Princess you're sleeping with.'

When he married their bonds would be destroyed.

He breathed deeply, then nodded. 'I can agree to that. But until then…'

'Until then I am yours.'

CHAPTER NINE

HELIOS CLICKED ON Leander Soukis's profile and stared hard at it. There was something about the young man's chin and the colouring of his hair that reminded him of Amy, but that was the only resemblance he could see. How could Amy share half her DNA with this layabout? Amy was one of the hardest workers he'd ever met, which, in a palace and museum full of overachievers was saying something.

And how she could be from the loins of Neysa Soukis was beyond his comprehension. Helios had done his homework on Amy's birth mother and what he had learned had not given him hope of a happy ending.

Neysa was a social climber. Approaching fifty, she still had a refined beauty. She had a rich older husband, who doted on her, and a comfortable lifestyle. Helios vaguely recalled meeting her husband at a palace function a few years back. Neysa had married him when she was twenty-one, less than two years after having Amy. Why she hadn't confessed to having had a child he could only speculate upon, but his guess was that it had nothing to do with shame and everything to do with fear. No doubt she'd been scared of losing the wealth that came with her marriage.

Neysa had put money before her own flesh and blood. If Helios had his way Amy wouldn't be allowed within a mile's radius of the woman. But he understood how deep blood could go. That morning he'd met his nephew for the first time. He'd felt an instant thump in his heart.

This little boy, this walking, talking dark-haired creation was a part of *him*. His family. His bloodline. He was a Kalliakis, and Helios had felt the connection on an emotional level.

It might break her heart in the process, but Amy deserved to know her bloodline too.

Whether the Soukis family deserved *her* was another matter...

If they did break her heart he would be there to pick up the pieces and help her through it, just as Amy had been there with a comforting embrace whenever the pain of his grandfather's illness had caught him in its grip.

Thinking quickly, Helios drafted a private message. If having a decree from the heir to the throne didn't motivate Leander to bring his mother and half-sister together, nothing would.

'Amy, you're late for your meeting.'

'What meeting?' she asked Pedro in surprise, looking down at him from her position on a stepladder, from where she was adjusting the portraits lining the first exhibition room. She wanted them to be hung perfectly, not so much as a millimetre out of alignment.

The museum and the palace tours had been closed to visitors all week in order to prepare for the Gala. As a result the palace and its grounds were in a state of absolute frenzy, with helicopters landing on the palace helipad on a seemingly constant basis. And the Gala was still a day away!

She'd never known the palace to be such a hive of activity. There was a buzz about the place, and information and gossip were being dripped in from so many sources, including the more serious museum curators, whose heads were usually stuck in historical tomes, that it seemed like a spreading infection.

The Orchestre National de Paris had arrived to great fanfare, a world-famous circus troupe had been spotted lurking in the grounds, the gardens had been closed off to allow even more blooms to be planted... Everywhere Amy went something magical was occurring.

The exhibition was to all intents and purposes ready for the *very* exclusive private tour that would be conducted after the pre-Gala lunch. Another, less exclusive tour would take place on Sunday, and the museum and exhibition would open to the public on Monday. From then on it really would be all systems go. Ticket demand had exceeded expectations.

She wanted it to be perfect—not just because of her professional pride, but also for Helios, his grandfather and his brothers.

'Your meeting with Helios,' Pedro said. 'He's waiting for you in his private offices.'

'Oh.' She rubbed at her lips, avoiding Greta's curious stare, willing them both not to notice the flames licking at her face.

Helios had been as good as his word. No one knew they were sharing a bed again, not even Greta. It wasn't just guilt preventing Amy from confiding in her friend, but the feeling that what she and Helios had now was just too intimate to share.

'Yes. Yes, I remember.'

Excusing herself politely, still not meeting their eyes, Amy hurried away. When she'd kissed Helios goodbye that morning, before coming to work, she'd assumed that he would be flat-out busy all day. His itinerary had given her a headache just looking at it. A frisson ran up her spine as she

imagined what he might be wanting from her. She doubted
very much that it had anything to do with the museum.

Helios's private offices were attached to his private
apartment. Getting there was a trek in itself. She could cut
through her own apartment and use their secret passageway, but during daylight hours it wasn't feasible, not when
this was an 'official' meeting, even if it would shave ten
minutes off her walk.

The usual courtiers guarded his quarters. They were
expecting her and opened the door without any questions.
She stepped inside, into a large reception area. The door
to the left led to his apartment. She turned the handle of
the door to the right.

Talia, Helios's private secretary, rose to greet her, a pas-
try in her hand. 'Hello, Amy,' she said with a welcoming
smile. Usually immaculately presented, today Talia had a
wild-eyed, frazzled look about her. 'He's expecting you.'

Did Talia suspect Amy and Helios had resumed their
relationship? Did *anyone* suspect?

Amy smiled back politely. 'How are things?'

Talia crossed her eyes and pulled a face. 'Busy. This is
the first time we've stopped all day.' She pressed a key on
one of her desk phones. 'Despinis Green is here,' she said.

'Send her in,' came the response.

Amy found Helios sitting behind his sprawling desk
with Benedict, his black Labrador, snoozing beside him.
Benedict cocked an ear and opened his eyes when she
walked into the office, then promptly went back to sleep.

'Take a seat,' Helios said politely, his eyes following her
every movement with a certain knowingness.

As soon as the door was closed and they had some privacy he rose from his chair and stepped round the desk to
take her in his arms.

'Was there a reason you made up a non-existent meeting

other than to make out with me in your office?' she asked
with bemusement when they came up for air.

His hands forked through her hair and he kissed her
again. 'The French Ambassador's flight was slightly delayed, giving me an unexpected half-hour window.'

'It took me that long to get here,' she said teasingly.

'I know.' He gave a mock sigh. 'I suppose a few kisses
are better than nothing.'

She laughed and rested her head against his chest.
'Should I go now?'

He looked at his watch. 'Five minutes.'

'That's hardly any time.'

Not that she could do anything more than share a few
kisses with him in his office, with Talia on the other side
of the door and the palace full of Very Important People
who all demanded his time. How he kept his good humour
was a mystery...

'There's always time for kissing,' he said, tilting her chin
up so he could nuzzle into her cheek. 'Especially as I won't
get the chance to touch you again for at least another ten
hours...' Before she could get too comfortable, however,
he stepped away. 'To answer your original question—yes,
I did have an ulterior motive for seeing you other than the
insatiable need to kiss you.'

She rolled her eyes.

'Before I tell you... I don't want you to think I've been
interfering.'

'What have you interfered with?'

'I told you, I'm not interfering. I'm helping,' he added,
with a deliberate display of faux innocence.

'What have you done?'

His features became serious. 'I've been in contact with
your birth mother.'

Her heart almost stopped. 'And?' she asked breathlessly.

'She has agreed to meet you in a neutral place on Monday.'

She shook her head, trying to clear the sudden buzzing that had started in her brain at this unexpected development.

'Are you angry with me?'

'No. Of course not.' She wrapped her arms around him and breathed him in. His scent was so very reassuring. 'It's in your nature to take charge and boss people around.'

He laughed and rubbed his hands down her back. 'I wrote to her in my capacity as your boss. And in my capacity as her Prince.'

'It's amazing how people are able to do an about-turn on the basis of a simple word from you.'

'It certainly is,' he agreed cheerfully.

'If I were a princess I would throw my weight around everywhere.'

He pulled back and tapped her on the nose. 'No, you wouldn't... And I don't throw my weight around,' he continued, feigning injury.

She grinned. 'You don't need to.' Stepping onto her toes, she pressed a kiss to his lips. 'Thank you.'

'Don't thank me yet—there are no guarantees the meeting will go well.'

She shrugged. 'Having met Leander, I have no expectations. I don't want to be part of her family or cause trouble for her. I just want to meet her.'

'Just...be careful. Don't build your hopes up.'

'I won't,' she promised, knowing his warning came from a place of caring, just as his interference had. If their roles had been reversed she would be warning him too.

'Good. I'll email you the details.'

'Thank you.'

One of the landlines on his desk buzzed. Sighing, Helios disentangled his arms from around her and pressed a button. 'Yes?'

'The French contingent have landed and are expected in twenty minutes.'

'Thank you. I'll leave in a moment to greet them.' Disconnecting the call, he shook his head and grimaced. 'One more kiss before duty calls?'

Obliging him, Amy leaned closer, raised herself onto the tips of her toes and brought her mouth to his, giving him one last, lingering kiss before he broke away with a rueful smile.

'I'll see you later and we'll do a *lot* more than kissing,' he said, then strode to the office door and opened it.

'The Koreans will be arriving within the hour,' Talia called as he walked past her.

He shook his head. 'Whose idea was it to have so many guests arrive a day early?'

'Yours,' Talia said, her expression deadpan.

'The next time I come up with such an idea you're welcome to chop my hands off.'

Hoping her demeanour was as nonchalant as his, Amy said goodbye to Talia. When she stepped out into the corridor Helios had already gone.

Gala day had arrived.

If Helios had been busy the day before, it was nothing compared to today. His whole morning had been spent meeting and greeting guests and making sure everything was running perfectly.

This was a day he'd looked forward to. No one could organise an occasion better than the Agon palace staff and he always enjoyed celebrating the events they hosted. He was immensely proud of his family and his island, and never turned down an opportunity to discuss its virtues with interesting people.

With his grandfather's situation as it was, he'd expected

the day to feel bittersweet, with the joy of celebrating the great man's life certain to be shadowed by the knowledge that it would soon be ending.

What Helios hadn't expected was to feel flat.

There was a strange lethargy within him which he was fighting against. Merely shaking hands and making eye contact felt like an effort. His mouth didn't want to smile. He hadn't even found the energy to be disappointed by the news that the solo violinist Talos had been working so closely with would not be able to perform due to severe stage fright.

One bright spot had been the unveiling of his grandfather's biography, which he and his brothers had looked through with their grandfather privately before the pre-Gala lunch. To see the man who'd raised them make his peace with Theseus had warmed him. And King Astraeus had surprised them all by revealing that he knew about Theseus's son and his plans to marry the boy's mother, and had given his blessing.

These were all things that should have had Helios slapping his brothers' backs and calling for a glass of champagne.

They'd gone through to the lunch together. Again, he should have revelled in the occasion, but the food had tasted like cardboard, the champagne flat on his tongue.

His fiancée, who'd arrived with her father and her brother, Helios's old school friend, had sat next to him throughout the lunch. He'd had to force the pleasantries expected of him. When Catalina's father, the King of Monte Cleure, had commented about the announcement of their engagement it had taken all his willpower not to slam his knife into the table and shout, *To hell with the announcement!*

And now, with the lunch over, the clock was ticking

furiously fast towards the time when he would make his engagement official to the world.

First, though, it was time for his grandfather to have a very exclusive viewing of his exhibition. It would include just the King and his three grandsons. Above everything else occurring that day, taking his grandfather to the exhibition created in his honour was the part Helios had most been looking forward to. The biography was the culmination of Theseus's hard work—a tangible acknowledgement of his love and pride—and this exhibition was the pinnacle of his own.

With his brothers by his side, Helios and a couple of courtiers now led his grandfather out into the palace grounds and along the footpath that led to the museum.

The joy and pride he'd anticipated feeling in this moment had been squashed by a very real sense of dread. And when they arrived at the museum doors he understood where the dread had come from.

Amy, Pedro and four other staff members closely involved in the exhibition were there to greet them at the museum's entrance. All were wearing their official uniforms and not a single hair was out of place. This was their big moment as much as his.

Talos wheeled their grandfather up to the line of waiting staff so they could be spoken to in turn. When they reached Amy the thuds in Helios's heart became a painful racket.

This was the first time she would meet his family. It would also be the last.

Bracing himself, he said, 'This is the exhibition curator, Amy Green. She's on secondment from England to organise it all.'

Not looking at Helios, Amy curtsied. 'It is an honour to meet you, Your Majesty.'

'The honour is mine,' his grandfather replied with that

wheeze in his voice Helios didn't think he would ever get used to. 'I've been looking forward to seeing this exhibition. Are you my tour guide?'

Her eyes darted to Pedro, who, as Head of Museum, was supposed to take the role of the King's guide.

Sensing her dilemma, Helios stepped in. 'Despinis Green would be delighted to be your guide. Let's get you inside and we can make a start.'

Inside the main exhibition room the four King Astraeus statues were lined up on their plinths. The sculptor of the fourth, which was covered and ready for unveiling, awaited his introduction to the King. When that was done, and the official photographers were in position, in a hushed silence the cover was removed and the King was able to see his own youthful image portrayed in marble for the first time.

For the longest, stillest moment the King simply stared at it, drinking in the vibrant, enigmatic quality of his statue. There was a collective exhalation of breath when he finally spoke of his delight and reached out a wizened hand to touch his own marble foot.

It was a moment Amy knew would be shown in all the world's press.

From there, the group progressed through to the rest of the exhibition.

The thought of being the King's personal tour guide should have had Amy in fits of terror, but it was a welcome relief. She had to concentrate so hard to keep up with etiquette and protocol that she could almost act as if Helios meant nothing to her other than as her boss.

But only almost.

After the King had examined and admired all of the military exhibits, they moved through to the room dedicated to his marriage to Queen Rhea, who had died five years previously. It was heartbreaking and yet uplifting to see the King's reaction first-hand.

Their wedding outfits had been carefully placed on mannequins and secured inside a glass cabinet. Queen Rhea's wedding dress was one of the most beautiful creations Amy had ever been privileged to handle, covered as it was with over ten thousand tiny diamonds and crystals.

King Astraeus gazed at it with moist eyes before saying to her, 'My Queen looked beautiful that day.'

Amy murmured her agreement. On the opposite wall hung the official wedding portrait. Queen Rhea had been a beauty by anyone's standards, but on that particular day there had been a glow about her that shone through the portrait and every photo that had been taken.

What would it be like to have a marriage such as theirs? Her own parents' marriage had seemed mostly happy, but once Amy had learned of her true parentage her memories had become slanted.

Her father's infidelity, although mostly never spoken of, remained a scar. Danny knew their father had cheated on his mother whilst she'd carried him. Neil knew their father had cheated on his mother back when he'd still been talking in broken sentences. They might love Amy as a true sister, and have nothing to do with anyone who saw things differently, but their relationship with their father bordered on uncomfortable. They didn't trust him and neither did Amy. She loved him very much, but the nagging doubts remained. When they'd still been living at home, and he'd been kept late at work, although they'd never said anything they'd all wondered if his excuses were true. And as for her mum…

To anyone looking in, their marriage would seem complete. They laughed together and enjoyed each other's company. But then Amy thought of the times she'd caught her mum going through her father's phone when she'd thought no one was looking and knew the pain she'd gone through had never fully mended. Once trust had been broken it was incredibly hard to repair.

King Astraeus and Queen Rhea's marriage had bloomed into that rarest of things: enduring, faithful love. The kind of love Amy longed to have. The kind of love she could never have when the man she loved was going to marry someone else...

The truth hit her like a bolt of lightning.

She *did* love him.

And as the revelation hit her so did another truth of equal magnitude.

She was going to lose him.

But he'd never been hers to lose, so she already had.

There was nothing for her to hold on to for support. All she could do was keep a grip on herself and wait for the wave of anguish to pass.

The only man she could ever be happy with, the only man she could ever find enduring love with, the only man she had trusted with the truth of her conception... He was marrying someone else. The happy ending she'd always hoped she would one day have would never be hers.

When she dared to look at Helios she found his gaze on her, a question resonating from his liquid eyes. He was as sensitive to her changes of mood as she was to his.

She forced a smile and straightened her posture, doing her best to resume her professional demeanour. Whatever personal torment she might have churning inside her, she still had a job to do.

This was King Astraeus's big day, one he'd spent eighty-seven years of duty and sacrifice working towards. This was his moment. It was also Helios's and his brothers' moment too. The three Princes loved their grandfather, and this day was as much for them to show their appreciation of him as to allow their great nation to celebrate. She wouldn't do anything to detract from the culmination of all their hard work.

Amy kept her head up throughout the rest of the tour, but as soon as it was over she fled, using the pretext of needing to change her outfit for the Gala. Thankfully all the other staff wanted to change too, so saw nothing strange in her behaviour.

Finally alone in her apartment, she sank onto the edge of her bed and cradled her head in her hands. The tears that had threatened to pour throughout the exhibition tour had now become blocked. The emotions raging inside her had compacted so tightly and painfully that the release she needed wouldn't come.

The truth of her feelings and the hopelessness of her love had hit her so hard she had shut down inside.

CHAPTER TEN

Five thousand people were settled in the amphitheatre, watching the Gala, enjoying the multitude of performances taking turns on the stage, the glorious sunshine, the food and the drink.

Amy, sitting with the rest of the museum staff, tried to enjoy what was a truly spectacular occasion. A world-famous operatic duo from the US had just completed a medley of songs from *The Phantom of the Opera*, and now a Russian ballet troupe had taken to the stage, holding everyone spellbound.

When they were done, the compère came bounding back on. 'Ladies and gentlemen, boys and girls, in a small addition to our official programme, I am proud to welcome to the stage His Royal Highness, Prince Helios.'

Huge cheers broke out around the amphitheatre as the crowd rose to their feet to applaud the popular Prince.

Amy's stone-filled feet moved of their own accord and she stood too. The coldness rippling through her was such that it felt as if someone had injected ice into her veins. All the hairs on her arms had sprung upright. Nausea didn't churn—no, it turned and twisted, as if her stomach had been locked in a superfast waltzer. And yet the tightness in her chest remained, coiling even tighter if that were possible.

Helios started his address by thanking everyone for attending, then launched into a witty monologue about his grandfather, which led him neatly into entreating the audience and the hundreds of millions of worldwide viewers to visit the exhibition of the King's life now being held in the palace museum.

And then he cleared his throat.

Amy's own throat closed.

'I would also like to take this opportunity to confirm the speculation about my private life that has been documented in the world's press for these past few weeks. I am honoured to announce that Princess Catalina Fernandez of Monte Cleure has consented to be my wife.'

Such raucous cheers broke out at the news that they drowned out the rest of his speech. The crowd was still whooping when Helios bowed to them all and left the stage, with a grin on his handsome face that looked to Amy's eyes more like a grimace.

Looking around the crowd, blinking to clear the cold fog enveloping her mind, Amy saw that the happiest faces were those of the Agonites who'd been lucky enough to get tickets for this event.

So now it was official.

Helios and the Princess were betrothed. There could be no backing out of the marriage now; not when the pride of two nations was at stake.

And the tiny spark of hope she hadn't even realised she carried in her extinguished into nothing.

Helios shook the hand of yet another post-Gala party guest and silently cursed Talos for disappearing with the violinist, who'd overcome her stage fright and wowed everyone that evening. His grandfather had retired to bed, exhausted after such a full day, leaving Helios and

Theseus to welcome all the people on the three-hundred-strong guest list.

Thank goodness protocol dictated that his fiancée acted in no official capacity until their nuptials had been exchanged. He still couldn't imagine her by his side. Or in his bed.

For the first time he accepted that Amy leaving Agon when he married would be a good thing. The best thing. For all of them.

All he knew was that he wouldn't be able to commit himself to Catalina as a husband if Amy resided under the palace roof and worked in the palace museum.

He'd thought when she had come back to him that everything would be all right and they could return to the way they'd been. But everything was not all right. Everything was worse.

His feelings for her...

There was a trapdoor looming in front of him and every step he made took him closer to falling through it. But he couldn't see in which direction the trapdoor lay. He just knew it was there, readying itself to swallow him whole.

As was normal at a Kalliakis party, none of the guests was in a hurry to leave. But, as was not normal, Helios was in no mood to party with them.

He did his duty and danced with the Princess. Again he felt nothing. His body didn't produce the slightest twinge. Nothing.

When Catalina finally left to catch her flight back to Monte Cleure with her father and brother Helios sought out Theseus, who was still going through the motions with the last of the straggling guests, and bore him away to his apartment.

From the look on his brother's face he needed a drink as much as Helios did.

For someone with a newly discovered son he adored, and a wedding to the boy's mother on the horizon, Theseus was acting like someone who'd been told he was to spend the rest of his life locked in the palace dungeons.

Much as Helios himself felt.

He'd never thought of alcohol as a tool for making problems better—on the contrary, he knew it tended to make matters worse. But he wasn't trying to make himself feel better. That wouldn't be possible. All he wanted was a healthy dose of numbness, even if only for a short time.

Was Amy waiting up for him?

They hadn't made their usual arrangement. It had been on the tip of his tongue to say his customary 'I'll come to you when I'm done' that morning, but this time something had stopped him. A sense of impropriety. Indecency. To parade the news of his fiancée to the world, then expect to slip between the covers with his mistress...

An image flashed into his mind of Amy standing in the cathedral in a wedding dress, of his mother's sapphire ring sliding onto her finger... It was an image he'd been fighting not to see for weeks.

He closed his eyes and breathed deeply.

This was madness.

He took another swig of neat gin and said without thinking, 'Those people watching the Gala. They have no idea of our sacrifices.'

'What?' Theseus slurred, staring at him with bloodshot eyes Helios knew mirrored his own.

'Nothing.'

Even if he'd wanted to confide in his brother, Theseus was clearly in no state to listen. He knew he should ask him what was wrong, but the truth was he was in no state of mind to listen either.

Moody silence followed, both brothers locked in their

own thoughts. The anticipated numbness failed to materialise. All the gin had brought on was the monster of all headaches.

Helios slammed his glass on the table. 'It's time for you to crawl to your own apartment—I'm going to bed.'

Theseus downed his drink without a murmur of protest and got to his unsteady feet. At least his brother was drunk enough to pass out without any problems, he mused darkly.

As Theseus staggered out Helios promised himself that he would leave Amy to sleep. It was long past midnight. Soon the sun would rise. To wake her would be cruel. To go to her at all, tonight of all nights, would be the height of crassness.

Dammit. He'd just become officially engaged. Couldn't he show some decorum for *one* night?

But the memory of Amy's ashen face during the exhibition tour refused to leave him and he knew he had to go to her. He had to see for himself that she was all right.

He walked down the passageway, promising himself that he would leave if there was no answer. When he reached her bedroom door, he rapped on it lightly.

Within seconds he heard the telltale turning of the lock.

When she'd opened the door Amy gazed up at him with an expression he couldn't distinguish. One that combined anguish, desire and need in one big melting pot.

And as he stepped into her welcoming arms he realised that, for all his talk of sacrifice, he didn't yet know how great his biggest sacrifice would be.

With the early-morning sunlight peeking through the curtains, Amy gazed at Helios's sleeping form.

Hours after the post-Gala party had finished he'd come to her. And for the first time since they'd started their relationship all those months ago, nothing physical had happened between them.

Until he'd quietly knocked on her door she'd been trying to sleep, without any luck. She hadn't wanted to stay awake for him. She'd been scared that he wouldn't come to her and equally scared that he would.

Images had tortured her: thoughts of Helios and the Princess dancing together, becoming an official couple, discussing their wedding plans, showing the world how perfect they were for each other. Her stomach had ached so much it had been as if she'd swallowed a jug of battery acid.

With the hours ticking down until morning, she'd assumed the worst. She'd seen the helicopters and limousines taking their honoured guests away from the palace and had been unable to stop herself from wondering which of them carried the Princess.

Then, just as any hope that he would appear had gone, Helios had arrived at her door with bloodshot eyes, exhaustion etched on his face. He'd stripped off his clothes, climbed into her bed, pulled her into his arms and promptly fallen asleep.

How many more nights would he do this? How many more nights would they have together?

The official announcement had set off an alarm clock in her battery-acid-filled stomach and its persistent tick was excruciating.

Careful not to wake him, she sat up, doing nothing but drink him in.

How many more nights could she do this? Simply look at him?

Later that day he would be flying to the US for the start of an official state visit.

In her heart she knew that now, this moment, truly was the beginning of the end for them.

She reached out a hand and gently palmed his cheek. He nuzzled sleepily into her hand and kissed it. Lightly, she began to trace her fingers over the handsome face she loved so much, from his forehead—over which locks of hair had fallen—to his cheekbones, then over the bump on his nose, the bow of his lips, the jawline where thick stubble had broken out, and down his neck. She took his silver chain between her fingers and then touched the mandarin garnet necklace around her own neck.

It had been a birthday present from him, one he'd given her shortly after they'd started sleeping together. Of all the gifts he'd bestowed upon her, it was the one to which she felt the closest. The meaning behind it, the fact Helios had gone out of his way to find an item of jewellery made with her birthstone, meant that she'd swallowed her guilt and taken it out of the padded envelope where the rest of the jewellery he'd given her remained.

Whatever lay in the future, she knew she would never take it off again.

Slowly she explored his naked body, trailing her fingers over his collarbone and shoulder, down his right arm, lacing them through the fine black hair covering his forearm. When she reached his hand and took each finger in turn, gently pressing into them, he gave a light squeeze in response but otherwise remained still.

After repeating her exploration down his left arm, she moved to his chest. Helios's breathing had changed. It no longer had the deep, rhythmic sound of sleep. A heavier, more ragged sound was coming from him.

Over his pecs she traced her hands, encircling his dark brown nipples, catching the dark hair that was spread finely across his chest, pressing her palm down where the beat of his heart was strongest, then moving them across his ribcage and down to his abdomen…

His erection stopped her in her tracks.

Sucking in a breath, she ignored it, outlining the smooth skin on either side and drawing her fingers over his narrow hips. Gently spreading his muscular thighs, she knelt between them and carried her exploration down his left leg, tracing the silvery scar on his calf—the result of being thrown from a horse at the age of nine—and down to his feet. Then she moved to his right leg, this time starting from his toes and making her way up…all the way to the line where his thigh met his groin.

Helios's hand dug into her hair, spearing it, his breaths now erratic. Still only using her fingers, she traced the long stretch of his erection, cupping him, delighting in his tortured groans, before she put him out of his misery and ran her tongue along its length, then took him into her mouth.

For an age she moved him with her hand whilst licking and sucking. His hand cradled her scalp, massaging it, but he let her set the pace. Heat bubbled deep inside her, burning her from her core outwards, enflaming her skin. Giving him pleasure gave her as much joy as when he pleasured her.

When she sensed him getting close to breaking point she pulled away, unable to give him the playful smile she would normally give. She had never felt less playful when making love to him.

Moving up to straddle him, she gazed into his eyes, thrilling to see the heady desire ringing in them. He cupped her neck and pulled her down to meet his mouth. His tongue swept into hers, his kiss full of all the dark, potent neediness flowing through her own veins.

Slowly, with their lips and tongues still entwined, she sank onto him until he was fully sheathed inside her.

Breaking the kiss, she pulled back to sit atop him, needing to look at him.

As his groans became louder he placed one hand flat on her breast, whilst his other hand held tightly to her hip, steadying and supporting her. Then, with her hands resting lightly on his shoulders, she began to move. The feel of him deep inside her, the friction of their movements, it all built on the sensations already whirling inside her.

She could make love to this man every day for the rest of her life and it still wouldn't be enough. She would always want—need—more. Even if they had all the time in the world it wouldn't be enough time for her to look at his face, to touch him, to hear his voice, to witness his smile.

But there was only now, this moment in time when it was just them. There was no palace, no duty…

Just them. One man. One woman.

She wished she could hold on to it for ever.

She tried to hold back the climax growing within her, tried to blunt her responses, but it was all too intoxicating. With a cry that was as much dismay as it was delight, the pulsations swept through her, starting deep in the very heart of her and rippling out to embrace her every atom.

She threw herself down to bury her face in his neck and his arms immediately wrapped around her. A strangled groan escaped his mouth and he gave one last thrust upwards as his own climax tore through him with the same strength as her own. Both of them rode it for as long as they could until there was nothing left but their breaths, burning heavily into each other's necks.

The hotel, arranged by Talia under Helios's instructions, had a charming air to it, an ambience that carried through inside, through the cosy lobby and into the even cosier restaurant.

It was Agon's oldest hotel and a favourite on the tourist trail. It was guaranteed to be busy, whatever the time of year. Thus, two women could meet and dine together during the lunchtime rush without attracting any attention. It was safe for Amy's birth mother here. No one would know who she was. No one would report back to her husband. Ignorance would continue to be bliss for him.

As strange as she knew it to be, Amy would have recognised Neysa even if she hadn't known who she was. Her heart stuttered as she was caught in the gaze of eyes that were identical to her own.

This was the woman who had carried her in her womb for nine months.

This was the woman who had abandoned her.

Neysa Soukis hesitated before asking, 'Amy…?'

'Neysa?' Calling her Mum or Mother was *not* an option.

Grasping the outstretched hand, Amy marvelled at how it was an identical size to her own. It was like seeing a model of herself twenty years from now, although she doubted she would ever be as well groomed. Neysa was expensively dressed and immaculately coiffured.

After ordering drinks and some mezzes Neysa gave a brittle smile, opened her mouth and then closed it again.

Amy filled the silence. 'Why didn't you want to meet me?'

Fingers similar to her own but older, and with buffed nails, drummed on the table. 'You are a stranger to me.' Her English accent was heavy and unpractised.

'You carried me. You gave birth to me.' *You abandoned me.* 'Weren't you curious?'

'I have a life now. Husband. A son.'

Yes… Her son. Leander. The man-child Neysa doted on. 'What made you change your mind?'

She gave a harsh bark of laughter. 'The threat that my husband would learn of you.'

That would be Helios's doing. He was not a man one could say no to. Neysa was here because Helios had effectively blackmailed her, not because she wanted to meet the child she'd given up.

'Leander could tell your husband.'

'Leander would never tell.'

Neysa's confidence in this statement didn't surprise her. Helios had done some more digging into the mother-son relationship and discovered that Leander's father had all but given up on him. Neysa was the one to lavish him with love and the all-important money. He was dependent on her. If she withdrew her funds he would, heaven forbid, have to get a job and keep it.

If her husband was to learn that Neysa had been keeping such a monumental secret from him throughout their twenty-five-year marriage who knew how he would react? Both Neysa and Leander might be thrown off the gravy train they worshipped so much.

A waiter appeared with a tray of drinks.

'Did you ever think of me?' Amy asked when they were alone again.

A flicker of something she couldn't decipher crossed Neysa's face. 'Many times.'

She was lying. Amy didn't know how she could be certain of this, but certain she was. Neysa had forged a new life for herself, with a rich husband two decades her senior. Amy was a dirty little secret she couldn't afford to let anyone find out about. She had no interest in her child. Her only interest was in protecting her secret.

'I knew your father would take good care of you,' Neysa explained earnestly. Too earnestly.

She had known nothing of the sort, and neither had she tried to find out. For all she knew Amy might have been dumped in an orphanage. She'd had no way of knowing that Elaine—the woman who had taken Neysa into her home and trusted her with her young son, the woman Neysa had betrayed in such a heinous way without one word of remorse—had raised Amy as her own.

Amy had spent seventeen years hoping that it had been shame which had kept Neysa away. That she'd acknowledged that what she'd done to the Green family had been so great a sin that she couldn't bring herself to face Elaine and say sorry.

She couldn't have been more wrong.

At least her father had been genuinely remorseful. Her mum had promised her that. *He'd* acknowledged the terrible deed he'd done and had spent twenty-seven years trying to make amends for it. One mad weekend alone, without his wife and with a hot young woman parading herself around the house before him... He'd been too weak not to take advantage and he'd paid the price every day of his life since.

Looking at her birth mother now, Amy couldn't believe her mum had been able to love her the way she did. Amy was the image of Neysa. Every time her mum had looked at Amy's face she must have seen the image of the woman who had betrayed her and the living proof of her husband's infidelity.

How could Amy even be in the same room as this woman? Neysa hadn't cared that she'd almost destroyed Amy's mum—her *real* mum...the woman who had loved her every day of her life from the age of two weeks.

And she'd been scared that her mum secretly wanted to get rid of her? Never. Not her loving, generous mum.

The waiter returned to the table with their food.

Amy waited until he'd laid everything out before getting to her feet and hooking the strap of her handbag over her shoulder.

'You have nothing to fear from me,' she said slowly. 'I want no part of your life. I wanted to see you. And now I have.'

'You are going?'

'I shouldn't have come. Goodbye, Neysa.'

Leaving her birth mother open-mouthed in shock, Amy made her way out of the hotel and into the warm spring street brimming with tourists.

She stood for a moment, breathing in the sweet scent. She hadn't found a single place in Agon where the air didn't smell good. And yet an acrid odour lingered around her from her encounter.

Breathing heavily, Amy raised her eyes to the sky and thanked whatever benevolent being that was up there for allowing Neysa to abandon her.

Who would she be if she'd been raised on Agon under Neysa's narcissistic hand? If she'd grown up with Leander? If she'd lived without Danny and Neil's fierce protection, her mum's loving guidance and her dad's silent but constant presence?

And she thanked Helios too. His interference had allowed her to put to bed one of the biggest questions in her life: who had made her?

That *'who'* was someone she had no wish to see again. But at least she knew that now. Thanks to Helios she could move on and stop wondering *what if...?*

As she thought his name her phone buzzed. It was a brief message from him, checking that everything was okay. Her darling Helios was on a state visit to America and had still found the time to think of her and send her a message.

But how could she be okay? she thought as she replied, saying that she was fine and that she would explain everything to him later, when he called. Which he would. He called her every night when he travelled abroad.

How could everything be okay when very soon she would have to say goodbye to the one person who *did* make everything okay?

CHAPTER ELEVEN

AMY CARRIED ON as best she could over the next few days, never letting her smile drop or her shoulders slouch. She was determined that no one looking at her would have reason to suspect that she was suffering in any way.

The entire island was aflame with gossip following the confirmation of Helios's engagement to the Princess. Naturally this enthusiasm was tripled in the palace itself. Everywhere she went she heard excited chatter. It had got to the stage where, even if she didn't understand what was being said, she imagined it was all about the forthcoming wedding.

The date had been set. In six weeks and one day Helios would marry. It was going to happen sooner than she had thought. She had forgotten about all the work for the wedding that had been going on behind the scenes. Helios had wisely never mentioned it in any of their calls.

Other than in the privacy of her apartment, the only place she found any crumb of solace was amongst the staff in the museum. Whereas the visitors—whose numbers were daily in the thousands—kept up a non-stop commentary about the wedding, the staff took a different approach. They knew Amy had been Helios's lover. *Everyone* had known. So when she was in the same room conversation was kept as far away from matrimony as it was possible to get. But she caught the pitying, often worried glances that were thrown her way.

Her colleagues were a good, kindly, close-knit bunch who supported and looked out for each other. It was in this vein that Claudia, one of the tour guides, approached her in the staff room during Amy's break on the Friday after the Gala.

'I'm sorry to disturb your lunch, but Princess Catalina is here.'

Amy immediately froze, as if a skewer of ice had been thrust into her central nervous system. Somehow she managed to swallow her mouthful of tomato and feta salad, the food clawing its way down her numbed throat.

The tour guide bit her lip. 'She is asking for you.'

'For *me*?' she choked out.

Claudia nodded. 'She wants a tour of the King's exhibition and has asked for you personally.'

It was on the tip of her tongue to ask if Helios was with her, but she stopped herself in time. If Helios was with the Princess they wouldn't need Amy. Helios could do the tour himself.

She didn't even know if he was back from his trip to America. She'd thought he was due back sometime that afternoon.

She'd spent five nights without him.

It had been much harder than any of their other separations. She'd missed him desperately, as a small child missed home.

It was a pain she would have to get used to.

Her main source of comfort had come from Benedict, who had stayed in her apartment during Helios's absence. The lovable black Labrador had seemed to sense Amy's despondency and had kept close to her. Their evenings

together had been spent on the sofa, watching films,
Benedict's head on her lap.

When she returned to England she would get her own
Labrador for company.

Blowing out a long breath of air, Amy closed the lid of
her salad box and forced herself to her feet. She couldn't
manage another bite.

'Where is she?'

'In the entrance hall.'

'Okay. Give me two minutes to use the bathroom.'

Concentrating on her breathing, Amy took her handbag
and locked herself in the staff bathroom. She took stock of
her reflection in the mirror and pulled a face. Hastily she
loosened her hair from its ponytail, brushed it and then
tied it back again. From her handbag she pulled her compressed face powder and a make-up brush and applied a
light covering. She would have added eyeliner and lip gloss
but her hands were shaking too much.

As a means of buying time for herself, her trip to the
bathroom was wasted. The hopes she'd had of making it
through the next few months without having to meet the
Princess had been blown to pieces.

Why *her*? Why had the Princess asked for her by name?
How did she even know who she was?

Terror gripped her, but she forced herself to straighten
up and pushed air into her cramped lungs.

The Princess was an honoured guest, she reminded herself. It was natural she would ask for the exhibition's curator to be her guide. *Just be professional,* she told herself
as she left her sanctuary.

The Princess awaited her in the entrance hall, flanked
by two huge bodyguards.

She was the epitome of glamour, wearing skintight
white jeans, an off-the-shoulder rose-pink top, an elegant

pale blue silk scarf and blue high heels. Her ebony hair was loose around her shoulders, and an expensive pair of sunglasses sat atop her head.

But there was more to her than mere glamour; a beautiful, almost ethereal aura she carried effortlessly. She was a princess in every sense of the word. If she slept on a hundred mattresses no doubt she would still feel the pea at the bottom.

Swallowing down the dread lodged like bile in her throat, Amy strode towards her with a welcoming smile. 'Your Highness, I am Amy Green,' she said, dropping into a curtsy. 'It is an honour to meet you.'

The Princess smiled graciously. 'Forgive me for disturbing your break, but I wanted a tour of the exhibition. I've been told you're the curator and that you have a wealth of knowledge about my fiancé's family. I couldn't think of a better person to show me around.' All of this was delivered in almost faultless English.

'I am honoured.' And it *was* an honour. A true honour.

They went slowly around the exhibition rooms, with Amy politely discussing the various artefacts and their context in the Kalliakis family's history. She answered the Princess's questions as best she could whilst all too aware of her constantly clammy hands.

Princess Catalina might look as if she would feel the pea through a hundred mattresses, but she was so much more than a princess from the realms of fairy tales.

She was a flesh and blood human.

It wasn't until they entered The Wedding Room, with the bodyguards keeping a close but respectable distance, that the Princess showed any real animation. She was immediately drawn to Queen Rhea's wedding dress, staring at it adoringly for long, excruciating seconds before she turned to Amy.

'Isn't this the most beautiful dress?' she said with her gaze fixed on her, her eyes searching.

Amy nodded, the bile in her throat burning.

'The dressmaker who made this has agreed to come out of retirement to make mine. I'm having my first fitting tomorrow—did Helios tell you I will be staying at the palace for the weekend?'

'I've heard it mentioned,' she whispered. She'd overheard a couple of the tour guides discussing the visit. They'd been wondering whether the Princess would bring her fabulous Vuitton bag with her. She had.

The Princess smiled. Despite her amiability, sadness lurked behind her eyes. It filled Amy with horror.

'There isn't much that happens within the palace that's kept secret, is there?'

Flames licked her cheeks. It took all her willpower for her not to cover them with her hands.

The Princess seemed not to want a response of the verbal kind. Her sad, probing eyes never left Amy's face, but she smiled. 'I thank you for your time.'

'Do you not want to see the other exhibition rooms?' Caught off guard, Amy took the Princess's hand; a major breach of protocol. She had the softest skin imaginable.

The Princess's squeeze of her hand was gentle and... forgiving? The smile thrown at her was enigmatic. 'I have seen what I came to see.'

Nodding at her bodyguards, she glided away, tall, lithe and poised.

Amy stared at the retreating figure and rubbed the nape of her neck, feeling as if all the wind had been knocked out of her.

The Princess knew.

Dear God, the Princess *knew*.

* * *

Her concentration lost, Amy wandered around the exhibition rooms, praying no one would ask her anything that required any thought to answer. Feeling nauseous to the bone, she eventually settled in the entrance hall, trying her hardest to keep herself together.

But all too soon the influx of guests had reduced and reality was given space to taunt her.

The marble sculptures of the four Kings kept drawing her attention, and as much as she knew she shouldn't she went and stood before them.

King Astraeus the Third had been famed for his wisdom. She wished he could transmute some of it to herself. But it was King Astraeus the Second she couldn't tear her eyes away from. His resemblance to Helios was so strong she could fool herself into thinking it *was* him.

One day, decades from now, a statue much like this would be made of him. If she closed her eyes she could see it, could envisage every inch of the ten-foot marble figure. If the sculptor were to show her the block of stone she would be able to tell him where every line and sinew should go.

It came to her then what she'd been doing that night after the Gala—or early morning—when she'd touched every part of him. She'd been committing him to memory. She hadn't been able to face the truth at the time, but it hit her now. She'd imprinted him on her mind because her subconscious had known that it would be their last time.

Their time together was truly over.

The walls of the great exhibition room suddenly loomed large over her, swallowing her. The statues and the other exhibits blurred. She needed air. But to flee outside would mean risking seeing the Princess or, worse, Helios. She couldn't face him with an audience watching. The next time she saw him she had to be alone with him.

Pulling her identity card from around her neck and stuffing it in her pocket, she walked into the main museum, hurrying through the crowds of visitors until she found Claudia.

'I've got a migraine coming,' she said. 'I need to rest—can you give my apologies to Pedro?'

'Sure.' Claudia looked at her with concern Amy knew she didn't deserve. 'Can I get you anything?'

'No, thank you. Please, I just need to get some sleep in a darkened room.'

Not waiting for a response, Amy wove her way through the remaining people to the private staff entrance to the palace, then hurried up the stairs to her apartment, kicked off her shoes and threw herself onto the bed.

She might not really have a migraine, but her head pounded as if a dozen church bells were ringing inside it. Let it pound. Let the bells clang as loudly as they could and the decibels increase.

She deserved nothing less.

Helios stood in the green stateroom, holding discussions with a group of German business people who wanted to invest considerable sums in Agon's infrastructure and, naturally, recoup their investment with considerable profit. With them was Agon's Transport Minister.

Agon had its own senate, and committees which decided on issues such as outside investors, but an endorsement from one of the royal Princes meant this would be as good as a done deal. Helios knew his opinions carried a great deal of weight and did his utmost to use his influence wisely.

When his phone rang he was tempted to ignore it, but

it was his personal phone and only the most important people in his life had been given the number. He frowned when he saw Amy's name on the screen.

He hadn't had a chance to call her and let her know he was back from his trip to the US. In any case he'd assumed she would be busy at the museum... She hardly ever called him and *never* out of the blue.

'Excuse me,' he murmured to the delegation, stepping away from the group with an apologetic smile. He swiped the screen to answer. 'Amy?'

'I'm sorry to disturb you,' she said, her usual soft tones sounding strangely muffled. 'I know you're busy, but I wondered if you're coming to me tonight.'

Not only did she never call him, she never questioned his movements either. A dark sense of foreboding snaked up his spine. 'Is something the matter?'

He heard her hesitation.

'I just need to see you.'

He looked at his watch. 'Where are you?'

'In my apartment.'

'Are you ill?'

'No. Not really. Not ill, ill.'

He wanted to pump her for information but, aware of the delegation, Talia and all the courtiers eyeing him with curiosity, he resisted.

'I'll be with you as soon as I can,' he said, before hanging up.

He'd be with her as soon as he could politely extricate himself. Something was wrong. The cold dread wedged in the marrow of his bones told him that.

It was half an hour before he was able to extract himself from the group, saying he had some personal business to catch up with and that he would see them at the dinner being held in their honour. He then told Talia that she

could leave early. Talia didn't argue the matter—in fact
he would swear she left so quickly she left a trail of dust
in her wake. He didn't blame her. It had been a long few
weeks and she must be exhausted.

When he reached his office he cut through to his apartment and slipped through the passageway into Amy's
apartment. She answered his knock quickly, with a startled expression on her face.

'I didn't think I would see you until much later,' she
said wanly. 'I hope I haven't put you out.'

'You could never put me out.' He studied her carefully.
Her face was grey, her eyes were bloodshot and her hair
looked unkempt. 'Have you been crying?'

She bit her lip and took a shuddery breath. Closing
the door, she rested her hand on the handle. 'The Princess knows.'

'Catalina? What does she know?'

'About us.' She met his gaze. 'She came to the museum.
She wanted me, personally, to give her a tour of the exhibition.'

'You're the exhibition's curator,' he pointed out.

She shook her head. 'It was more than that. She knows,
Helios. I think… I think she's heard rumours about us.
Maybe someone saw me walking Benedict… I think she
was looking for confirmation. Whatever I did, I don't
know, but I'm sure something confirmed her suspicions.'

He ran a hand through his hair. 'Even assuming you're
right, there is nothing for you to worry about. Catalina isn't
stupid. She knows there will be other women.'

It was the wrong thing to say. Amy looked as if he'd
slapped her.

'I didn't mean it like that,' he added hastily. 'All I meant
was that Catalina has no illusions of fidelity. You know
there is no love between us.'

There was nothing between them. Not the smallest twinge.

Shaking her head again, Amy sidestepped past him and went through to her kitchen. 'You're a fool if you believe that. She *wants* it to be a love match.'

'No…'

'Yes,' she said through gritted teeth. 'She does. Whatever you think you know about her, you've got it wrong.'

'She does not love me.'

'Not yet.'

Her eyes bored into his as her words hung in the air between them, then she turned sharply and pulled a bottle of white wine out of the fridge.

'Glass?' she asked.

'You're drinking already?' A trace of his bemusement cut through the darkening atmosphere.

'Right now I need it.'

She leant against the work surface and closed her eyes briefly, then poured them both some wine. When she passed his glass to him she snatched her hand away before there was any chance of their fingers brushing.

She went to take a sip from her own, but as she brought it to her mouth her face crumpled.

Stepping quickly to her, Helios took the glass from her shaking hand and placed it with his own on the counter, then wrapped his arms around her.

At first she resisted, but then she gave in to it, almost burying her head in his chest. Within seconds his shirt was wet with her tears.

'Don't cry, *matakia mou,*' he whispered, stroking her hair. 'It will all work out. I promise.'

'How?' she asked between sobs. 'How can it ever work out? We're breaking her heart.'

'No, we're not.'

'We *are*. Maybe she doesn't love you yet, but she wants to. She wants your marriage to work. Have you even seen her since you got back from America?'

'I've been busy.'

Disentangling herself from his hold, Amy grabbed a handful of tissues from a box. The tears kept falling.

'Helios, the Princess is your fiancée. She's come all this way to see you. You should be with her. This time before your marriage should be spent getting to know each other...'

'We do know each other.'

'Do you?' She raised her shoulders. 'Then tell me this— what are her dreams? What are her fears? Can you answer any of that? You're going to be spending the rest of your life with her.'

'Yes,' he agreed tightly. 'The rest of my life. But the rest of my life hasn't started yet.'

'It started the minute you put an engagement ring on her finger.'

The engagement ring. He'd told Catalina to choose her own, with the excuse that she would be the one wearing it and so she should have something that was to her own taste. He hadn't been able to bring himself to do the deed himself.

He knew she coveted his mother's sapphire ring. Growing up, he'd always known that ring would be given to the woman he made his wife. He'd had the ready-made excuse that it was a feature of the exhibition to stop him sliding it onto Catalina's finger yet, but he'd promised that when the exhibition was over it would be hers.

'I can't do this any more,' Amy said, her voice choking on the words. 'What we're doing to the Princess is abhorrent. She's a princess but she's *real*, not a fairy-tale creation. She's human, and the guilt is eating me alive.'

He moved to take her back into his arms but she held up a hand to him and shook her head.

'We can't. *I* can't. I won't be the cause of someone else's misery. How can I when I've seen first-hand the damage it causes?' Wiping away a fresh batch of tears, she swallowed before saying, 'When I came to Agon and I wanted to find my birth mother, it wasn't because I wanted to form a relationship with her. I wanted to know my other family and my roots, yes, and I was *desperate* to see what she looked like. But what I really wanted from her was to know why.'

'Why she abandoned you?' She had told him on the phone about the meeting. How she had left within minutes, abandoning the mother who'd abandoned her.

'Partly. What I really wanted to know was how she could have done what she did to my mum. She was her au pair— Mum had trusted her with her child and welcomed her into her home. My mum is the most loving woman in the world. There is no way she would have treated Neysa with anything but kindness. How could she sneak around behind her back with her husband? What kind of evil selfishness makes a person act like that?'

'Did you ask her that?'

'No. I was so desperate to get away from her that I didn't ask her any of the questions I'd been storing up for seventeen years.' She gave a half-hearted shrug. 'And now I don't want to know. I don't want to hear her excuses because that's all they'll be. I don't think she feels any remorse.'

'Amy, our situation is very different. How Neysa and your father behaved…it's not like for like.'

'You might not be married yet, but the intention and commitment are still there. The agony my mum must have gone through… She never got over it. She forgave my father but she's never forgotten, and she's not been able to trust him properly since.'

More tears fell, harder now, turning her face into a torrent of salt water.

'I can't live with the guilt. I've spent my entire life, through no fault of my own, being a person people point at and whisper about. I've had to work so hard to make myself believe that I didn't deserve it and that I was innocent. But how can I be innocent when *I'm* the one now causing someone's misery? I don't want to be the selfish woman Neysa is. I don't want to hurt anyone. The Princess is a good and lovely person and she doesn't deserve this—no one does. Whatever she's been raised to be, she's still human.'

The depth of Amy's guilt and misery stabbed at him, right in his guts, evoking a wave of shame that came rushing through him, a wave so powerful that he reeled and held on to the small kitchen table for support.

'Listen to me,' he said urgently. 'The very fact you feel such guilt proves you are *nothing* like Neysa, so put such thoughts from your mind. You would never hurt anyone, not on purpose.'

'But that is what I've been doing!' she cried. 'I'm *exactly* like her.'

'No! All you inherited from Neysa was her looks. Everything else came from Elaine and the rest of your English family and the goodness that is *you*. You are a good person—the best I know.'

She didn't look the slightest bit convinced by anything he'd said. Helios's mind worked frantically as he tried to think of a solution whereby Amy's guilt could be obliterated. But nothing came to him. He *had* to marry someone of royal blood to secure the Kalliakis line.

He was hurting her, the last thing he'd ever wanted to do. Not Amy. Not her. Not ever.

His father had done more than hurt his mother physically; the destruction had been emotional too. Helios had always known he would never follow his footsteps on the physical side, but to discover he was guilty of an emotional destruction every bit as great...

Something that felt suspiciously like panic clawed at him, biting and contracting through every part of him, converging in his stomach into a pain so acute he wanted to shout out with the agony of it all.

His relationship with Amy was long past being the light, playful interlude it had begun as. Along the way it had developed into something so deep he feared he would no longer be able to see the light if they went any further.

If he had the slightest ounce of decency he would let Amy go before he destroyed her completely.

CHAPTER TWELVE

FOLDING HIS ARMS across his chest, Helios stared at Amy, wondering how he was going to cope without seeing her beautiful face every day and making love to her every night. She was so much more to him than just his lover. She was his best friend, the first true friend he'd ever had. She'd been brought into his life not through her own wealth or social standing but simply by being Amy.

Amy gazed back at him with the same intensity and attempted a brave smile. 'Do you think there's a parallel world out there, where we can be free to be together and love each other?'

Love?

She must have registered the shock in his eyes at her use of the *L* word for she laughed wanly. 'Oh, I do love you. Very much. More than I ever knew was possible.'

He stepped out of her reach, backing himself against the kitchen door. He didn't know how to answer. He couldn't think.

His private phone buzzed in his pocket. He pulled it out and rejected the call without looking at it.

'Love is not something I have ever required,' he finally said, his brain reeling as much as his body.

'I know that.' Her chin wobbled and she took deep breaths, raising her eyes to the ceiling.

'*Theos*, Amy, you...' He blew out a long breath as his brain scrambled to unravel itself. 'I've always known I must marry for duty. Love isn't something I've ever expected or thought about. It has no place in my life, you must see that?'

'Yes, I do.'

Of course she did. Amy knew his full ancestral history better than she could ever know her own.

'If you love me then how can you leave me?' he asked, still shell-shocked at her declaration but grasping at straws.

'Because I want to be able to look at my reflection every day and not throw darts at it,' she answered with a choked laugh. 'And my leaving isn't just to do with Catalina.'

There. She'd finally uttered the Princess's name aloud.

'I might have been made from a dirty secret but I don't want to live my life as one. You're right that I'm not Neysa, and I will not allow myself to be like her. Even if you wanted it—even if you loved me—you're not in a position to give me the commitment and fidelity I need. I want to be yours. Just yours. Openly yours. With the whole world knowing we belong together. I can't make love with you while you're sleeping in the bed of another, and I can't make love knowing I'm good enough for sex but not good enough for for ever.'

What she didn't say was that Helios had lodged himself so deeply into her heart she doubted there was room left in there for any other man to find an opening. Her heart belonged to him now.

She should have left weeks ago. The physical pain she'd experienced when he'd told her of his intention to marry as soon as possible should have acted as a warning. If she'd gone then she would have left with her pride intact and her heart would still have enough room for someone else.

His face contorted. 'Don't you *ever* say you're not good enough.'

'But that's how I feel,' she said, shrugging her shoulders helplessly. 'I know that's not your intention, and that you don't think or believe that—I *know*—but I've spent most of my life feeling like a dirty secret. For us to carry on, even if it's only until you marry, will *make* me one.'

He didn't say anything, just stared at her as if he were seeing her for the first time.

'Helios, when you marry the Princess be faithful to her. Give your marriage a chance. She deserves that and so do you.'

'You sound like you're planning to leave now...' A strange look flashed in his eyes and suddenly he sprang to life like *Galatea*, the statue created with such love by Pygmalion.

He strode out of the kitchen and into her bedroom, taking in the suitcases on the bed, half-filled with clothing.

His face contorted and he shook his head. 'No.'

'Helios...'

'No.' His hands clenched into fists.

She could see him fighting the urge to throw her cases out of the window.

His phone buzzed again, the third time it had rung in as many minutes.

'Answer it,' she insisted. 'It might be important.'

'This is important.' After a moment's pause he swore and pulled the phone to his ear. 'Yes?'

After a few moments his demeanour changed. As he listened he straightened his neck and rolled his shoulders, breathing deeply. His only contribution to the conversation was a few short words of Greek.

'I need to go,' he said when he'd finished the call. 'My

grandfather's suffering from a mild infection and is fighting with the doctors over his treatment.'

'I hope it's nothing too serious,' she said, immediately concerned.

'Just my grandfather being a stubborn old man.' He rubbed his chin and glared at her with his jaw clenched. 'I'll be back later. Don't even *think* of going anywhere.'

She didn't answer.

'I need to hear it, Amy. Tell me you won't go anywhere or do anything until I get back. Promise me.'

Knowing even as she spoke them that her words were a lie, she said, 'I'll be here.'

His shoulders loosened a little. Pacing over to her, he took her face in his hands and crushed her lips with his mouth, kissing her as if he'd been starved of her kisses for ever. And then he dropped his hold on her and walked out of her bedroom.

She heard the slam of the interconnecting door as he left.

Theos, his grandfather had to be the most stubborn man alive. He was refusing the intravenous drugs his doctors wanted to give him.

What could he do? He couldn't force him. The King wasn't a baby to be coaxed into doing his elders' bidding.

That hadn't stopped Helios from trying to make him see reason. Now he wanted to tear his hair out, to claw at his scalp and draw blood.

'At least he's not in pain,' Talos said quietly.

Their grandfather hadn't resisted painkillers for the pain racking his body. The cancer, kept at bay by months of chemotherapy, was making another, deadlier assault on his body. No one would say it, but time was slipping away from them.

One good thing to come out of the mess this day had turned into was the news from Theseus, who had gone tearing after Jo, the mother of his child, a couple of days ago. The fool had realised when it was almost too late that he truly did love her, and luckily it seemed Jo loved him too and had agreed to marry him.

No coercion, no thoughts of duty. They were marrying for love. Helios had never heard his brother sound so happy.

Both his brothers were marrying.

As Talos—who was marrying his violinist—had chosen someone not of royal blood, any child he had would not be in the line of succession to the throne, but Toby, Theseus's beautiful son, had already secured the throne for the next generation. Until Helios's own children were born.

Helios sighed and got to his feet. 'I need to change for dinner.'

He wished he could pull out of it, but it was a matter of honour amongst his family that personal matters never got in the way of duty. And this dinner was duty.

Nausea fermented in him as he remembered that Catalina would be attending. She was already there in the palace. He still couldn't bring himself to call her.

As much as he wanted to, there wasn't time to make a diversion to Amy's apartment and check that she was okay. Instead he fired off a quick message to her before showering and changing into his dinner jacket. He put his cufflinks on during his walk to the designated dining room for the evening, his courtiers struggling to keep up with his long strides.

Forcing bonhomie, Helios plastered a smile on his face and entered the dining room, where the delegation was waiting for him. Catalina was already there, holding court like a professional. When she saw him she excused herself to join him.

If she really did suspect him and his relationship with Amy, she covered it well.

'I understand your grandfather is unwell?' she said quietly.

'He's been better.' It was all he could bring himself to answer with.

Why couldn't he feel anything for her? Here was a beautiful, compassionate woman of royal blood and all he felt when she touched him was cold.

He tried again, using a milder tone of voice. 'He has an infection.'

She smiled sympathetically. 'I hope he recovers quickly.'

'So do I.'

But he didn't hold out much hope. These past five months had been a battle to keep him alive long enough for him to see the Gala. That was all his grandfather had been focusing on. Now, with the Gala over, his grandsons all paired off and the succession to the throne secured, King Astraeus was preparing to die.

His duty was done. His grandfather wanted to be with the woman he'd loved for his entire adult life.

And Amy had said she loved *him*.

Helios wished he could unhear those words.

What kind of selfish monster was he to tie her to him when he knew doing so was destroying her?

It was possibly the longest meal of his life. For once, the power of speech had deserted him. He couldn't think of a single witty remark or any of the tales that usually had guests enthralled.

Throughout the meal disquiet grew within him, a foreboding which came upon him from an unseen direction.

As soon as the coffee had been cleared away he cleared

his throat. 'My apologies, ladies and gentlemen, but I need to retire for the evening. I know I haven't been very good company this evening—I think exhaustion has crept up on me—but be assured that I am very impressed with everything you've told me and will give my recommendation to the committee early next week.'

When he'd finished speaking he glanced at Catalina. She was staring at him with a cool, thoughtful expression.

It took fifteen minutes, time spent saying goodnight to everyone individually, before he was finally able to leave the dining room.

Catalina made no effort to follow him.

The disquiet in his chest grew with every step he took towards his apartment. By the time he reached his door and was able to shake off the courtiers, perspiration had broken out on his brow and his pulse had surged.

He headed straight down the passageway and rapped on Amy's connecting door.

No answer.

He banged again, louder.

No answer.

'Amy?' he shouted, pounding on the door with his fist.

On impulse he tried the handle, even though Amy always kept the door locked…

The door opened.

His heart thundering painfully beneath his ribs, he stepped into her apartment.

'Amy?' he called into the silence.

His heart knew before his head could comprehend it.

On legs weighted down with lead, he stepped into her bedroom.

The room was spotless. And empty.

All that lay on the dressing table, which was usually heaped with cosmetics and bottles of perfume, was a large padded envelope he recognised as the one he'd given to her all those weeks ago, containing the jewellery he'd bought her. Next to it lay a scrap of paper. Written on it were two words.

Forgive me.

'You look troubled, Helios,' his grandfather said, in the wheezing voice Helios hated so much.

They were playing chess, his grandfather's favourite game. The King was in his wheelchair, an oxygen tank to his right, a nurse set back a little to his left.

'I'm just tired.' Helios moved a pawn two spaces forward, unable to stop his stomach curdling with the fear that this might be the last game they played together.

'How are the wedding preparations going?'

'Well.'

Not that he was having anything to do with them. The palace staff were more than capable of handling it without his input. And without Catalina, who seemingly had as much interest in the preparations as he had. None at all.

His grandfather placed the oxygen mask on his face for a minute, before indicating for the nurse to take it off.

'I remember my own wedding day well.' The misty eyes grew mistier. 'Your grandmother looked like an angel sent from heaven.' Then the old eyes sharpened. 'Your mother looked beautiful on her wedding day too. It is my eternal sorrow that your father couldn't see her beauty. Your mother was beautiful, inside and out.'

Helios's spine stiffened. His parents' marriage was a subject they rarely touched upon other than in the most generic terms.

'The biggest regret of my life—and your grandmother's, rest her soul—was that your father couldn't choose his own wife. Would it have made a difference if he'd been able to choose?' He raised a weak, bony shoulder. 'We will never know. Despite our best efforts he was a vain and cruel man. He thrived on power. Your mother didn't stand a chance.'

He moved his castle forward with a quivering, gnarled finger.

'We pushed through the changes in law that would allow you and your heirs to select your own spouses in the hope that your parents' marriage would never be repeated.' His voice weakening with each word he said, the King turned his gaze to Helios again. 'However important duty is, marriage to someone you feel no affection for can only bring misery. And for ever is a long time to be miserable.'

The nurse, attuned to his weakening, placed the oxygen mask back over his face.

Helios waited for him to inhale as much as he needed, all the time his mind was reeling over what it was, exactly, that his grandfather was trying to tell him. Was it a reproach that he wasn't spending enough time with Catalina and that his indifference to her was showing?

But how could he feel anything *but* indifference when his head was still consumed with thoughts of Amy? She'd left the palace a week ago but she was still *everywhere*.

He moved his knight, then opened his mouth to pose the question, only to find his grandfather's head had lolled to one side and he'd dozed off mid-game and mid-conversation.

He looked at the nurse, who raised her shoulders sympathetically. Helios exhaled and gazed at his sleeping grandfather, a huge wave of love washing through him.

Whatever his grandfather had tried to tell him, it could wait.

'I'll put him to bed tonight,' he told the nurse, whose eyes immediately widened in fright.

'It's okay,' he assured her with a wry smile. 'I know what I'm doing. You can supervise if you want.'

Half an hour later the King was in his bed, his medication having been given and the oxygen mask attached to his face. His gentle snores were strangely calming.

Helios placed a kiss to his grandfather's forehead. 'I love you,' he said, before leaving him to sleep.

Movement beside her woke Amy from the light doze she'd fallen into. Since returning to England a week ago she'd slept a lot. She liked sleeping. It was the perfect route to forgetting. It was waking that was the problem.

Her mum handed her a cup of tea and sat in the deck-chair next to her.

When she'd returned to England she'd given the taxi driver directions to her childhood home rather than the flat she shared in central London. Sometimes a girl just needed her mum. Her *real* mum. The woman who'd loved and raised her since she'd barely been able to open her eyes.

And her mum had been overjoyed to see her.

Amy's last lingering doubts had been well and truly banished.

A late-night confession between them had culminated with the admission that her mum had been terrified that Amy would forge a relationship with Neysa.

'Never,' Amy had said with a firm shake of her head. 'You're my mum. Not her.'

'Good.' Ferocity had suddenly flashed in her mum's usually calm eyes. 'Because you're *my* daughter. Not hers.'

'Then why did you encourage me to learn about my roots?' she'd asked, bewildered.

'We all need to know where we come from. And I was scared that if I discouraged it you would do it in secret and one day you'd be gone and I would lose you.'

'You will never lose me.'

The tears had flowed easily that night.

Now they sat in companionable silence in the English sun, the only sound the chirruping of fledgling birds in the garden's thick hedges. It was a quintessentially British beautiful late-spring day.

'Are you ready to talk now?' her mum asked.

A lump forming in her throat, Amy shook her head. For all their late-night talks, she hadn't been able to bring up the subject of Helios.

To even think of him was too painful.

She'd had only one piece of correspondence from him since she'd left—a text message that said: I do.

He forgave her for running away.

Judging by his silence since, he'd accepted it too. She had no right to feel hurt that he'd made no further attempt to contact her.

'What's that you keep fingering around your neck?'

Wordlessly, Amy leaned forward to show her the garnet necklace.

Her mum took it between her fingers and smiled. 'It's lovely.'

Amy couldn't find the words to answer. When her mum let the necklace go Amy clasped it in her own hand and held it close.

'Broken hearts do mend,' her mum said softly.

Amy gave a ragged nod and swallowed, terrified of crying again. 'It hurts,' she choked out.

Her mum took her hand and squeezed it. 'Do you know what to do when life gives you lemons?'

'Make lemonade?'

'No. You throw them back and get yourself an orange.'

Amy spluttered, laughing. 'I haven't the faintest idea what that means.'

'Neither do I! It was something my mother used to say when I was a child.'

Still holding on tightly to each other's hands, they settled back in their deckchairs, sunglasses on, and basked in the sun.

After a while, her mum spoke again. 'I think what my mother was trying to say is that, whatever life throws at you, there are always choices and options other than the obvious ones. When your father first brought you home the obvious solution for me would have been to throw him out, and you with him. That would have been me making lemonade. But when I looked at you all I saw was an innocent, helpless newborn baby—a sister to the child I already had and a sister to the child I carried in my belly. So I chose to get myself an orange instead. I kept you— *you* were my orange. And I have never regretted it. My only regret is that I never carried you in my womb like I did your brothers.'

She took her sunglasses off and smiled the warm, motherly smile Amy loved so much.

'This man who's broken your heart…is he a good man?'

'He's the best,' she whispered.

'Is he worth the pain?'

She jerked a nod.

'Then you have to decide whether you're going to make lemonade or find an orange. Are you going to wallow in your pain or turn it into something constructive?'

'I wouldn't know where to start.'

'You start by accepting the pain for what it is but refusing to let it define you.'

Amy closed her eyes. If anyone knew how to cope with pain it was her mum. She'd handled a mountain of it and had never let it define her.

Compared to her mum she had nothing to complain about. Her mum had been innocent. She, Amy, had brought her misery upon herself.

Helios stood at the door to his grandfather's apartments and braced himself for the medicinal odour that would attack his senses when he stepped over the threshold.

Inside, all was quiet.

Stepping through to what had once been the King's bedroom and now resembled a hospital ward, he found his grandfather sleeping in his adjustable medical bed, with an oxygen mask over his nose and mouth.

At his side sat Helios's brothers. A nurse read unobtrusively in the corner.

'Any change?' he asked quietly. He'd only left the room for an hour, but the speed of his grandfather's deterioration over the past couple of days had been frightening. They all knew it wouldn't be long now.

Talos shook his head.

Taking his place on the other side of the bed from his brothers, Helios rolled his shoulders. Every part of his body felt stiff.

Theseus was holding their grandfather's right hand. Leaning forward, Helios took the left one, assuming the same position his grandfather had taken when his Queen had lain in an identical bed in the adjoining room, the life leaching out of her.

After a few long, long minutes their grandfather's eyes fluttered open. 'Water...' he croaked.

With Helios and Theseus working together from separate sides of the bed to raise him, Talos brought a glass to his mouth and placed the straw between his lips.

When he'd settled back the King looked at his three

grandsons, his stare lingering on each of them in turn, emotion ringing the rapidly dulling eyes.

The pauses between each of his inhalations grew. Then the corners of his lips twitched as if in a smile and his eyes closed for the last time.

CHAPTER THIRTEEN

AMY SAW THE announcement on the morning news.

'A statement from the palace said, "His Majesty King Astraeus the Fourth of Agon passed away peacefully in his sleep last night. His three grandsons were at his side."'

There then followed some speculation by the presenters and royal correspondents about what this meant for the island nation.

Without warning a picture of Helios and Catalina flashed onto the screen. It was an unofficial shot taken at the Gala. And then there was an off-screen voice saying, 'It is believed the heir to the throne will marry the Princess before taking the crown.'

Amy switched off the television, grabbed a pillow and cuddled into it, her head pounding.

Helios's grandfather, the King, had *died*.

She'd known it was coming, but still it hit her like a blow. She'd created his exhibition. During those happy months of curating that tribute to his life and the ancestors closest to him she'd felt as if she'd got to know him. Somehow she'd fooled herself into believing he was immortal. He had been a proud, dutiful man and she'd been privileged to meet him.

And then she thought of his eldest grandson, who had revered him.

Her phone lay on the floor beside her and she stared at it, wishing with all her heart that she could call Helios.

Would he even want to hear her condolences? The condolences of the woman who had sneaked out of the palace while he was dining with potential investors, supporting the island he loved?

She'd told him she would stay.

He'd forgiven her lie, but he had Catalina now. Without Amy's presence there, distracting him, he would turn to the Princess for comfort. Just as he should. Maybe grief would bring them together properly.

And as she prayed for a happy ending for her Prince and his Princess, hot tears spilled out of her eyes. She brought her knees to her chest and cried her broken heart out for the happy ending that would never be hers.

The funeral, a full state affair, was a sombre occasion.

People lined the streets in tens of thousands, all there to bow their heads in silence and pay their respects to the man who had served them with such dedication for fifty years.

The wake was an entirely different matter.

Out on the streets the atmosphere changed markedly. Television coverage showed military re-enactments from throughout the ages, even children dressed in loincloths and armed with plastic tridents. Barbecues lit up Agon's famous beaches, music played on every corner and there was food, drink and dancing everywhere in abundance.

Agon was putting on a show in the only way it knew how.

In the blue stateroom of the palace solemnity had given way to merriness too. The King was with his Queen. His suffering was over. His country and his family had laid him to rest and now they could celebrate his life.

For Helios, the occasion brought no joy. He accepted

that his grandfather had moved on to a better place, but the hole in his heart felt so great he didn't know how it would ever heal.

To know he would never talk to him again, dine with him, play chess… All the things he'd taken for granted were all gone. The man he'd worshipped, a man ten times the man his own father had been, was gone.

Helios watched his brothers, stuck like glue to the sides of their respective fiancées, and smiled for them. Their parents' marriage had been the worst template a child could have asked for. That his brothers were heading into marriages that would be more like their grandparents' gave him much hope. They would be happy.

He was under no illusions that he would follow suit.

Although he had seen little of her since his grandfather's death, Catalina had been at his side throughout the funeral service, a calm presence who had known exactly what to say in all the right moments.

But, however perfect she might be, he knew that fifty years of marriage wouldn't bring them the bond Talos and Theseus shared with their fiancées.

That last smile his grandfather had given them was a white shadow in Helios's mind. It gave him comfort. His grandfather had welcomed death. He'd left the world knowing his grandsons—all of them—would take care of his beloved island, freeing him to move on to his beloved Rhea.

His *three* grandsons.

Three boys raised to be princes.

Catalina came to stand by him. He stared down at her and met her thoughtful gaze.

'Marriage to someone you feel no affection for can only bring misery.'

Those were the words his grandfather had said the last time they'd spoken lucidly together. And in that moment he knew those words hadn't been a reproach. They'd been a warning from a man who knew how powerful love could be and had witnessed the destructive nature of his son's contempt for the wife he didn't love.

And in that instant everything became clear.

He couldn't marry Catalina.

If he'd never met Amy everything would be different. *He* would be different.

If he'd never met Amy he would be marrying Catalina with no expectations or knowledge of how things might be. He would be King. She would be Queen. Their only bond would be of duty. He wouldn't know what it felt like to love or be loved.

Love.

The one word he'd never expected to apply to himself other than in an abstract form. Familial love he'd felt and believed in, but romantic love…? That was not something he'd ever been able to hope for, so not something he had ever allowed himself to think about. And, if he was being honest with himself, it was something he'd hidden away from. The scars of his parents' marriage ran so deep that what he'd convinced himself was rational acceptance of his future union was in fact a mask to hide the real truth—that love in all its forms was the most terrifying emotion of all.

But also the most wonderful.

Because, *Theos*, he loved Amy. With everything he had.

Try as he might, he couldn't get used to walking into the museum and not seeing her there. He couldn't get used to being in his apartment and seeing the connecting door, knowing she wasn't at the end of the passageway.

Not a second of his waking day was spent without him wondering where she was and what she was doing.

After his grandfather's death had been announced he'd

kept staring at his phone, willing it to ring. Knowing it wouldn't. Knowing she was right not to call him.

But his intellectual acceptance that she was gone and that it was all for the best wasn't something his heart had any intention of agreeing with.

He'd long trusted Amy with his confidences. Now he understood that he'd also trusted her with his heart, and that a relationship with any other woman was doomed to failure because he belonged to Amy. All of him.

When the day of his own death came the last thing his conscious mind would see would be her face.

Three weeks without her.

The time had dragged like a decade.

How could he think straight without her?

How could he breathe without her when she was as necessary to him as air?

He loved her.

He cast his eyes around the room until he found Theseus, deep in conversation with his fiancée, Jo, and a Swedish politician the three Princes had been at school with. Theseus was settled. He had a child. His marriage would be taking place in a week.

Helios took a deep breath. Before he spoke to his brother there was someone else who needed to be spoken to first.

He looked at her, still by his side, the silence between them stark.

'Catalina…'

'We need to talk, don't we?' she said quietly.

'Yes.'

Weaving their way through the crowd, they walked through a corridor, and then another, and then stepped out into the palace gardens.

'Catalina, I'm sorry but I can't marry you.'

She closed her eyes and breathed deeply.

'I've been grossly unfair to you. I'm not...' It was his turn to take a breath. 'I'm in love with someone else.'

She bowed her head and eventually met his gaze. 'Thank you for finally being honest with me—and with yourself.'

'I never meant to hurt you.'

Her smile was stoical. 'All you have hurt is my pride.'

He opened his mouth to speak further but she raised a hand to stop him.

'It would never have worked between us. I've known it for a while now, but I didn't want to add to the burden you've carried with your grandfather's illness.' She sighed. 'I will get my people to issue a press release in a couple of days, saying I have called the engagement off due to an incompatibility between us.'

It was the least he could let her do. 'Catalina, I am sorry. I never wanted...'

'No. Do not say anything else.' She lifted her chin. 'Let me leave here with *some* dignity.'

For a moment Helios did nothing but stare at the woman he had intended to spend the rest of his life with. Then, taking her shoulders, he pulled her into his embrace. It warmed his heart to feel her arms wrap around his waist.

'You will find a better man than me,' he whispered.

'I doubt that,' she answered drily. 'But perhaps I will find a man whose heart is free to love me.'

'I hope that for you too.'

Pulling apart, they kissed each other on both cheeks and smiled.

The weight he carried on his shoulders lifted a fraction.

'I expect an invitation,' she said as she walked away.

'An invitation to what?'

'To your wedding to your English curator. Your mother's ring will look wonderful on her finger.'

With one final wink she sashayed into the palace, not looking back.

Alone in the gardens Helios did a slow turn, taking in the verdant lawns, the sweet-scented flowers in bloom, the distant maze. It was a paradise of nature and life. Whether he became custodian of it all, as he'd spent his entire life believing he would, or not, the flowers would continue to bloom. That he knew with absolute certainty.

His heart beating loudly, echoing through every chamber of his body, he took his phone out of his pocket and dialled the number he had spent the past three weeks fighting not to call.

It went straight to voicemail.

He tried again.

The same thing happened.

Back in the palace, he entered the stateroom and found the person he was looking for.

'I need to borrow you,' he said to Pedro, interrupting his Head of Museum's conversation with a person he did not recognise.

'Where are we going?' Pedro asked.

'To the museum. I need to get something.'

The museum was closed out of respect for his grandfather and to allow all the staff to pay their respects too.

With long strides they followed the corridors into the museum's private entrance and cut through the large exhibition rooms until they reached the rooms that mattered to Helios at that moment. The Kalliakis Family exhibition rooms.

After he'd explained to Pedro what he wanted, a thought struck him.

'Do you know where Amy's working now?'

'She's back at the British Museum.'

No wonder she'd turned her phone off. She would be working. 'Do you have the number?'

Pedro scrolled through his phone until he found the relevant number and thrust the phone at him.

Helios put it to his ear whilst indicating that Pedro could start on the task he'd set for him. It rang a couple of times, a passage of time that to Helios's ears was longer than for ever, before it was answered.

'Put me through to Amy Green,' he said.

'One moment, please.'

There followed a merry little game in which he was routed to varying offices until a voice said, 'Ancient Greece Department.'

'I wish to speak to Amy Green.'

'I'm sorry, sir, but Amy is on leave. She'll be back on Monday.'

'Do you know where she's gone?'

'As far as I'm aware she's attending a funeral.'

'Thank you.'

Disconnecting the call, his brain reeling, Helios rubbed the nape of his neck.

Now what?

And as he wondered what the hell his next step should be his heart went out to her. To think she too had lost someone important... She would be in need of comfort just as he—

And in the space of a heartbeat he knew whose funeral she'd attended.

Hope filled him, spreading from his toes right to the roots of his hair.

He put a call through to his private secretary. 'Talia,' he said as soon as she answered, 'I need you to find Amy Green for me. She's in the country. Go through to Immigration and take it from there.'

To her credit, Talia took his instructions in her stride. 'The Immigration Minister is here.'

'Good. Speak to him. Now.'

While all this was going on Pedro had completed the task he'd been set and so the pair of them reset the alarms, closed the museum and went back to the wake.

Helios found Talia in a quiet corridor, with her phone pressed to her ear by her shoulder, writing information on her hand. She gave him a thumbs-up and carried on her conversation.

'She's at the airport,' she said without preamble a few minutes later. 'Her flight back to England leaves in forty-five minutes. The passengers for her flight will be boarding any minute.'

'I need to get to the airport.'

A tremor of fear flashed over Talia's face. 'All the roads are blocked. You'll never make it in time.'

'Watch me.'

With that, he headed back into the stateroom and, ignoring everyone who tried to speak to him, found the butler of Theseus's private villa, Philippe, a man who looked as if he should be catching the surf, not running a Prince's household.

He pulled him aside to speak to him privately.

'You have a motorbike, don't you?'

'Yes, Your Highness.'

'Is it here at the palace?'

'It's in the staff courtyard.'

'I need to borrow it.'

'Now?'

'Now.'

'Do you know how to ride?'

'You have the time it takes us to walk there to teach me. Let's go.'

* * *

Amy stared out of the oval window with a heavy heart.

She was glad she'd come.

It had been a snap decision, driven by a sense of certainty that she had to go, to pay her respects to the man for whom she'd devoted almost six months of her life to creating an exhibition of *his* life.

Watching Helios and his brothers walking with military precision in front of the coffin, their gazes aimed forward, knowing how they must be bleeding inside…

The crowds had been so thick there had been no chance of Helios catching sight of her, but even so she hadn't taken any chances, keeping a good distance from the barrier.

What good would it have done for him to see her? The Princess had been there for him, just as Amy had known she would be, travelling in an official car with Theseus's and Talos's fiancées.

A steward made his sweep down the aisle, checking everyone's seat belts were fastened. The plane began to move. Over the speakers came the sombre voice of the captain, welcoming them all to this flight to London.

The ache in her chest told her she'd been wise to get a return flight home straight after the funeral. Any longer and the temptation to call Helios and seek him out would have become too great to resist. One night on Agon was as much as she'd been prepared to risk.

She'd taken her mother's advice to heart, and God knew she was trying to get herself an orange.

She'd taken up her old job at the museum and enrolled in a postgraduate course on the Ancient Romans, which she would start in September. She figured she might as well expand her knowledge so that her life wasn't all about Agon and its people, whether from history or the present. There was a big world out there to explore and learn about.

She'd kept herself busy, working by day and socialising by evening. It was the nights that were unbearable. Despite the mild heatwave sweeping through the UK, her nights were always cold.

Somehow she would find a way to forget him.

The plane had reached the place where it would turn around and face the runway.

The woman sitting beside her gripped the armrests, her knuckles turning white in anticipation of take-off.

But no sooner had the plane started its journey down the runway than it was brought to a stop.

It took a while before the passengers realised something was wrong, and then low murmurs began spreading throughout the plane.

The voice of a stewardesses came over the speaker. 'Could passenger Miss Amy Green please make herself known to a member of the cabin crew?'

Amy barely heard, her attention caught by a motorcyclist, speeding over the tarmac, heading towards them. Behind him was a buggy, with two men in orange high-visibility jackets towing metal steps. There was something about the figure riding the motorbike...

'Amy Green? Miss Amy Green—please make yourself known to a member of the cabin crew.'

With a jolt she realised it was *her* they were asking for. Tearing her gaze away from the window, she raised a hesitant hand.

A stewardess bustled over to her, looking harassed. 'Amy Green?'

Amy nodded, bemused and not a little scared.

'I need you to come with me.'

'Why?'

'We've been asked to escort you off this flight.'

'But *why*? Have I done something wrong?'

The stewardess shook her head. 'I don't know why.'

The couple she was sitting next to had to get out of their seats to let her pass, but it wasn't long before she was trailing the stewardess to the exit, her face burning with mortification, her brain burning with confusion.

What the hell was going on...?

At the rear exit of the plane the crew were all staring at her unabashedly, no doubt wondering if she was some kind of fugitive.

Was she a fugitive? Had she unwittingly committed a crime that necessitated her being escorted off a plane and arrested?

And then the door opened, the metal stairs were hastily bolted on and she stood at the threshold, looking to see if a dozen police officers were waiting at the bottom to take her into custody.

The only person waiting for her was the motorcyclist she'd spotted. He sat astride the bike, his helmet resting under an arm...

CHAPTER FOURTEEN

AMY'S HEART LEAPT so hard it almost jumped out of her mouth.

Behind her came a collective sigh from the crew. One of them squeezed her shoulder. 'Go to him.'

But she couldn't. Her legs had turned to jelly.

She covered her mouth, unable to believe her eyes.

What was he doing here?

His handsome face immobile, he got off his bike, placed the helmet on the seat and climbed the stairs with heavy treads.

It was only when he was at eye level with her and she was able to gaze into the liquid dark brown eyes she loved so much that Amy dared to breathe.

'Helios,' she whispered, raising a hand to brush it against his cheek, to feel for herself that he truly was there and that this wasn't some dream she'd fallen into.

But no. No dream.

His cheek was warm and smooth, his jawline rough, at the stage where stubble was just starting to poke through the skin. His warm, familiar scent played under her nose.

'Sneaking away again?' he asked, in a voice that was meant to be humorous but that cracked on the last syllable.

'What...? What are you doing here?'

His eyes bored into her, emotion seeping out of them.

'I'm taking you home.' Then he took the final step up and lifted her into his arms. 'I'm taking you home,' he repeated.

Another collective 'Ooh…' sounded from behind her, and as Helios carried her down the steps a round of applause broke out. One of the men in high-visibility jackets, who was waiting by the buggy, wolf-whistled.

Amy heard it all, but none of it penetrated. All her senses were focused so intensely on her lover that everything else had become a blur.

At the bottom of the steps Helios placed her carefully on her feet.

Suddenly the biggest, widest grin spread over his face. 'Would Despinis Green like a ride on my bike?'

Laughter bubbled up in her throat and broke through her daze. She flung her arms around him. 'Yes. Please. Take me anywhere.'

Amy kept a tight hold on Helios as he drove them through the streets of Resina. She didn't *have* to hold him tightly—the dense throng of partying people meant he had to ride at a snail's pace—but she needed to. Keeping her cheek pressed into the solidity of his back and her arms around his waist grounded her, helped her accept the reality of what had just happened.

Soon they had passed through the capital and were out in the verdant countryside, with Agon's mountains looming before them. Helios found a road that took them up Mount Ares, the rockiest of Agon's mountains, past goats casually chewing grass by sheer drops, taking them higher and higher until they arrived at a clearing.

He turned the engine off and clicked the stand down to keep the bike upright before helping her off.

She looked at him, laughing as she properly noticed for the first time that he'd ridden with her up a mountain in a pair of handmade black trousers, black brogues, now covered in dust, and a white shirt with the sleeves rolled up that had probably been as crisp as freshly baked pie earlier but was now crumpled and stained.

'Your clothes are ruined.'

He shrugged, his eyes sparkling. 'I couldn't care less.'

Taking her hand, he led her to a flat grassy area and sat down, enfolding her in his arms so her back rested against his chest and her head was tucked beneath his chin.

'When I was a child my brothers and I would race to the top of this mountain. When we'd all reached the summit we would come down to this clearing and eat our picnic. This spot has the best view of the sunset on the whole of Agon.'

The sun was already making its descent, causing a darkly colourful hue to settle over the island.

'How did you know I was here?' she asked eventually.

'Your museum told me you'd gone to a funeral. I guessed.'

'But how did you know what plane I was on?'

'Do you really need me to answer that?' he said with bemusement.

She smiled to herself, tightening her hold on his hands, which were still wrapped around her waist. And then she remembered *why* she had come to Agon today.

'I'm so sorry about your grandfather,' she said softly.

He kissed her head. 'He was ready to go.'

'I wanted to call you.'

'I know you did. And you were right not to.'

She sighed. Now that she had come to her senses, reality was poking at her painfully.

'How did you manage to sneak out without your body-guards?'

'Simple. I didn't tell them what I was doing. The palace was so busy with the wake it was easy. Talia will have told them by now.'

'She knows you came for me?'

'Yes. So does Pedro.'

'How long do we have? Here, I mean?'

'As long as we want.'

'But you'll be missed,' she said with another sigh, thinking that, however wonderful it was to be sat in his arms again, she would be dragged away from him again soon.

She was here now, though. A short interlude. Two lovers snatching a few minutes together to watch the sunset. One final sweet goodbye.

'I have done my duty by my grandfather today. And, *matakia mou*, he would want me to be here with you.'

'He would?'

'My grandfather was a great believer in two things— duty and love.'

Her heart gave a little skip at his words, a skip she tried frantically to dampen.

'Please, Helios, don't say things like that. It isn't fair.'

He caught her chin and turned her face to look at him. 'How can the truth not be fair? You are my whole world. I love you.'

'Please, stop,' she beseeched, clutching at his shirt. 'Don't speak of love to me when you will be marrying Catalina—'

'I'm not marrying Catalina,' Helios interrupted, castigating himself for being foolish enough to believe Amy was a mind reader who would have known the truth from the minute she'd seen him from her plane window. 'The wedding is off.'

Her eyes widened into huge round orbs. 'It is? Since when?'

'Since about three hours ago, when I realised I couldn't live another day without you. Catalina and I had a talk.' Knowing Amy would be concerned for the Princess, he took pains to reassure her. 'She will be fine. She's as good a woman as you always told me, and I promise you we have her blessing.'

'But…' Nothing else came. Her mouth was opening and closing as if her tongue had forgotten how to form words.

He pressed his lips to hers, inhaling the warm, sweet breath he had believed he would never taste again.

'I love you,' he repeated, looking at her shocked face. 'It's you I want to marry. Just you. Only you.'

'I want that too. More than anything in the world.'

'Then why do you look so sad?'

'Because I know it can never be. You aren't allowed to marry a commoner.'

He took hold of her hand and pressed it to his chest. 'Listen to my heart,' he said quietly. 'I knew I had to find a wife when my grandfather was given his diagnosis, but I put it off and put it off because deep down I knew it would mean losing you. My heart has been beating for you from the very start.'

Her breath gave a tiny hitch.

'You asked me what I would have been if I hadn't been born heir to the throne and I had no good answer for you, because it wasn't something I had ever allowed myself to think about. The throne, my country…they were my life. I didn't expect love. My only hope for marriage was that it would be better than what my parents had. However it panned out I would do my duty and I would respect my wife. That was the most I hoped for. I didn't *want* love. I saw the way my father abused the power of my mother's love and I never wanted to have the power to inflict such hurt on a woman. That's why Catalina seemed so perfect— I thought she was emotionally cold.'

Amy shivered.

Helios tightened his hold and gently kissed her. 'I know

I have the power to hurt you, *matakia mou*, and I swear on everything holy that I will never abuse it. But you need to understand one thing.'

'What's that?' she whispered.

'You have equal power to hurt me.'

'I do?'

'Living without you… It's been like living in an emotional dungeon. Cold and dark and without hope.' He brushed his thumb over her soft cheek. 'If spending the rest of my life with you means I have to relinquish the throne, then that's the price I'll pay and I'll pay it gladly.'

Her hold on his shirt tightening, her eyes wide and fearful, she said, 'But what about the throne? What will happen to it?'

'I don't know.' He laughed ruefully. 'Theseus is next in line. That's one of the things that struck me earlier—my grandparents raised *three* princes. It doesn't have to be me. We're all capable and worthy of taking the throne. Except Talos,' he added as an afterthought. 'Never mind that he's marrying a commoner too. He can be particularly fierce. He'll probably scare more people away from our country than attract them.'

She managed a painful chortle at his attempt at humour. 'But what if Theseus doesn't want it?'

'He probably *won't* want it,' he answered honestly. 'But he understands what it's like to be without the one you love. His fiancée has royal blood in her. It should be enough.'

'And if it isn't?'

'Then we will work something out. Whatever happens, I swear to you that we will be together until we take our dying breaths and that the Agon monarchy will remain intact. Have faith, *matakia mou*. And to prove it…'

Disentangling himself from her arms, he dug into his

pocket and pulled out the object Pedro had set about re-
trieving a few short hours ago.

Dumbstruck, she simply stared at it as he displayed it
to her.

'This, my love, belongs to you.' He took her trembling left
hand, slid the ring onto her engagement finger, then kissed
it. 'One day the eldest of our children will inherit it, and in
turn they will pass it to the eldest of their children—either to
wear themselves upon marriage or for their wives to wear.'

'Our *children*?'

'You do want them, don't you?' he asked, suddenly anx-
ious that he might have made one assumption too many.
'If you don't we can pass the ring to Theseus...'

'No, no—I *do* want your children,' she said. And then,
like a cloud moving away from the sun, the fear left her
eyes and a smile as wide as the sunset before them spread
across her cheeks, lighting up her whole face. 'We're really going to be together?'

'Until death us do part.'

Such was the weight of her joy that when she threw
herself into him he fell back onto the grass, taking her
with him, and her overjoyed kisses as she straddled him
filled him with more happiness than he had ever thought
possible.

She was *his*. He was hers.

And as they lay on the grass, watching the orange sun
make its final descent through the pink sky, he knew in
his heart that the rest of his life would be filled with the
glorious colours of this most beautiful of sunsets.

EPILOGUE

Six months later

THE RED DOME of the Aghia Sophia, the cathedral located in the exact central point between the Agon palace and the capital, Resina, gleamed as if it were burnt liquid gold under the autumn sky.

As Amy was taken through the cheering crowds on a horse-drawn carriage she turned her face upwards, letting the sun's rays warm her face, and sighed with contentment. Unlike many brides on their big day, she had no fear or apprehension whatsoever.

Beside her sat her father, who would be walking her down the aisle, and little Toby, proud as Punch to have been given the important role of ring bearer. In the carriage ahead of them sat her three bridesmaids: her soon-to-be sisters-in-law, Amalie and Jo, and Greta. Ahead of them were seven mounted military guards, in all their ceremonial attire, with the front rider holding the Kalliakis Royal Standard. More guards rode alongside the carriages, and there were a dozen at the rear.

It was pure pageantry at its finest. Triple the number of military guards were scheduled for a fortnight's time, when she and Helios would return to the cathedral to be crowned King and Queen of Agon.

In the sky were dozens of helicopters, sent from news outlets across the world to film the event.

Unbelievably she, Amy Green—a woman abandoned as a two-week-old baby by her birth mother, a woman who had never been quite sure of her place in the world—was going to be Queen of Agon.

Helios would be King. And it was the woman who'd abandoned her who'd made it all possible.

According to Helios, Theseus had turned the colour of puce when he'd sat his two brothers down and explained the situation to them. As Helios had suspected, Theseus had reluctantly agreed he would take the throne but only if all other avenues had first been explored.

Constitutional experts had been put on the case, to no avail, until Talos had come up with the bright idea of changing the constitution, rightly pointing out it had been changed numerous times before.

A meeting with the Agon senate had been arranged, and there the president, who, like all the members of the senate, was sympathetic to the Crown Prince's plight, had murmured about how much easier it would be to bring about the constitutional change if the bride were of Agon blood…

A referendum had taken place. Of the ninety per cent turnout, ninety-three per cent had voted for changing the constitution to allow a person of non-royal blood to marry into the royal family, provided that she was of Agon blood.

And now, as the carriage pulled up at the front of the cathedral, where the cheers from the crowd were deafening, Amy was helped down. She stepped carefully, so as not to trip over the fifteen-foot train of her ivory silk dress, handmade by Queen Rhea's personal designer, Natalia.

How she loved her dress, with its spaghetti straps and the rounded neck that skimmed her cleavage, the flared skirt that was as far from the traditional meringue shape as could be. Simpler in form and design than both Queen Rhea's dress and Helios's mother's dress, it was utterly perfect for her. And it was lucky she had insisted on something simpler considering they'd had to expand the waistline at the last fitting, to take into account the swelling of her stomach...

She and Helios had taken the decision a couple of months ago for Amy to come off the contraceptive pill, both of them figuring that it would take a good few months for the hormones to get out of her system. The hope had been that she would conceive after their coronation.

Whoops.

A month after taking her last pill Amy's breasts had suddenly grown in size. Their baby—the new heir to the throne—was due in six months, something they had decided not to make public until after their coronation. Naturally half the palace knew about it.

Greta had been given Corinna's job at the museum and was thoroughly enjoying bossing Amy about. Amy had gone back to curating King Astraeus's exhibition and then, when the exhibition had closed, she'd taken on the role of museum tour guide. It was a job she would be able to fit around the royal duties she would have to take on when she was crowned Queen.

Helios still thought it appropriate to give bloodthirsty Agon history lessons to children in the dungeons.

In all, everything had worked out perfectly, as if the stars had aligned for them.

Jo stepped forward to adjust Amy's veil, having to stretch to accommodate her own swollen stomach, which was fast resembling a beach ball, and then it was time.

When her arm was held tightly in her father's, the doors of the cathedral were thrown open, the music started and Amy took the first step towards the rest of her life.

The congregation rose as one, every head turning to stare. The first face she saw was that of Princess Catalina, who, as gracious as ever, smiled at Amy with both her lips and her eyes. When the press had bombarded her with questions about Helios and Amy's marriage her statement of support for them had been heartfelt and touching.

Surely somewhere in this packed cathedral stood a prince in need of a beautiful, elegant princess to make his own?

In the back row was the woman who had made all this happen—Neysa Soukis, there with her husband, and their son, Leander. It was amazing how the thought of being Queen Mother had spurred Neysa to recognise Amy as her child with enthusiasm and thus proclaim her a child of Agon blood. No doubt Neysa had imagined this moment many times, had thought she would be sitting in the front row of the congregation.

Alas, Neysa had soon learned that the only place she had in Amy's life was as a name on a piece of paper. Elaine—her mum, the woman who had raised and loved her—would be the officially recognised Queen Mother.

And, thinking of her mum, there she stood in the front row, beautiful in a pea-green skirt suit and an enormous hat, beaming with pride. Next to her stood Amy's *real* brothers, Neil and Danny, with identical grins on their faces. Both of them had been fit to burst with pride when Helios had appointed them as his ushers. Their wives had a dazed, 'someone pinch me to prove this is really happening' look about them.

And best of all, standing at the front, beside the altar, his brothers by his side, stood Helios; her lover and her best friend all rolled into one.

The three Princes were dressed in their military uniforms: the Kalliakis livery complete with sashes. They all looked magnificent, like three benevolent giants.

Helios might not be able to see her face through her veil, but she could see his, and see the full beard he'd grown especially for her. The expression in his eyes made every step she took closer to him feel as if she were bouncing on the moon.

When she reached him Helios took her hand, and together they knelt at the altar to pledge their lives, fidelity and love to each other for ever.

They were pledges neither of them would ever break.

* * * * *

COMING SOON!

We really hope you enjoyed reading this book. If you're looking for more romance, be sure to head to the shops when new books are available on

Thursday
6th September

LET'S TALK
Romance

For exclusive extracts, competitions
and special offers, find us online: